The One Who Fell   Carolyn Vaden

I am sincerely grateful for my family and friends, who encouraged and supported me even when they weren't sure what I was doing.

Special thanks to Dr. Jacki who read my drafts and rewrites and provided constructive comments and advice. Thank you for keeping me on track and not letting me give up. I really appreciate all your help and insights.

3773

Numbers mean so much to me

3773

Numbers help me to see

Nekita, Oracle of Milendor

CHAPTER 1

Sitting cross-legged on the white flowered quilt draped over her mother's four post bed, Elize pressed her fingernails against the lid of the old wooden cigar box. The bed creaked, as old beds do, as she slipped off and tiptoed into the kitchen to fetch a butter knife. Even though she barely made a sound, it was enough to stir Olive Oyle. The slim tortoise shell cat wrapped herself around Elize's legs and purred loudly. Knowing Olive Oyle would give her no peace until she was fed, Elize opened the fridge and dumped what was left in the small can of cat food into the fish shaped bowl with me-ow written in cursive in the center. Leaving Olive Oyle happily munching away, Elize took the knife back to her mother's room. Her eldest stepbrother, Paddy had given her the old cigar box the night before. Of course, Elize had wanted to open it then, but Paddy had insisted she wait until her mother's memorial service was over and all the guests had left the boarding house Elize had been helping her mother run for the last few years. After seeing the last two guests off just after dawn, Elize had slipped into her mother's room to retrieve the box. To her dismay the lid was shoved down under the lip of the box and was stuck tight.

Not one to be easily foiled, Elize carefully slipped the flat edge of the knife between the lid and the front of the box and slowly pried it up. Paddy discovered the box while searching for old photos in the attic of the old family home in Cumberland to use for the memorial. Paddy believed the box might hold some of the answers to questions Elize had been asking over the years. Questions her mother had either refused to answer or insisted she'd forgotten.

Wrinkling her nose at the musty old paper smell, Elize peered inside and extracted a folded piece of yellowed paper. Elize reached over and lifted the window shade to let the light in. It was a note written in a curly, cursive style that made the words difficult to make out, especially since the ink was so faded.

"Elll-leeze!" Ellen, Elize's best friend and the only boarder currently living in the large house screamed from the top of the stairs. "You're bleeping alarms going off!"

"Sorry!" Elize dropped the note back into the box and stuffing it under the lumpy goose down pillow.

"You're going to be late," Ellen grumbled, stomping into Elize's room, and yanking the power cord free from the wall. The loud bleeping stopped immediately.

"No meetings with the Professor this morning," Elize teased as she rushed up the steps.

"He went to visit the queen mother," Ellen mumbled sleepily before disappearing back into her room. "I wasn't invited."

"Well come down to the diner later I want to run something by you." Elize yelled through Ellen's now shut door.

Elize stood in front of the bathroom mirror staring at her image in the glass. She wondered for the hundredth time that week whether to cut her hair short or not. It's so hot, she told herself, and unmanageable she added picking up her brush and dragging it through the tangles. At first it was rough going, but after fifty-two strokes she had most of the tangles smoothed out and by a hundred the brush gilded easily through the long wavy strands. Putting down the brush she twisted her hair in several different positions inspecting each carefully in the mirror in a vain attempt to see what she would look like with her hair short. I'll decide tomorrow she promised the image in the mirror grabbing a black hair tie and pulling her hair into a tight ponytail. She washed her face but didn't waste time applying makeup. She didn't really need it now that her face had tanned nicely. Besides, she didn't want to cover up the cute freckles dotting her nose and cheeks.

Glancing over at the unplugged alarm clock Elize groaned and grabbed her pink uniform from the closet. Before pulling it on she looked disdainfully at the label. It was a large, she was not a large, but it was the only one she could find that didn't look like a mini dress on her long frame. Pulling the white belt as tight as it would go, Elize slipped on her new tennis shoes and jotted down the steps. As she dashed out the door, she grabbed her white glove off the end table.

Elize pulled the fingerless glove over her right hand to hide the odd blue blotch covering the center of her right palm. The blotch had been there as long as Elize could remember. Her mother had told her teachers she had been burnt badly as a baby, but Elize had no memory of being burnt. She had worn a glove over her hand since grammar school. It kept the other kids from asking too many questions about the blotch. Questions she still didn't have the answers to. Even though her mother had never wanted to talk about it, Elize knew there was more to the strange blotch than her mother let on. She had hoped to find some link to her past in the box. There was so much she didn't know about who she was and why she was so different from other people. Normal people.

Elize's mind was still on the old box when she rounded the corner and plowed into an odd, floppy haired guy wearing a long purple coat that you'd expect to see on a circus clown.

"Oh God, I'm so sorry." Elize apologized as she helped the stranger to his feet. Looking into his face Elize had the distinct sensation she knew him, but the feeling disappeared as quickly as it came. Noticing the bank clock, Elize left the stranger staring after her, as she rushed through the chrome rimmed glass door of Dan's Diner.

Hearing the bells at the top of the door, Dan poked his ruddy face through the window that separated the kitchen from the counter area and jabbed his stubby cigarette-stained finger at his wristwatch. She was seven and a half minutes late.

"Well look what the cat drug in." Dan scoffed. Elize started to make an excuse but stopped when she realized Dan wasn't talking about her.

"That's something you don't see every day." Mary laughed, grabbing a menu.

Elize glanced over her shoulder. The strange guy she had just run over on the sidewalk had followed her into the diner and was grinning at her like a fox in a chicken coop.

"I'll let you take this one." Mary told Elize when she joined her behind the counter. "He gives me the creeps. Reminds me of a stray dog that used to hang about my uncle's house when I was a kid. He'd wag his tail and act like he wanted to be petted, but when you put out your hand, he'd nip you."

"Gee thanks." Elize teased filling a glass with ice and water and taking it over to the table.

Elize studied her customer's face as she stood by the booth, pencil ready to take his order. It wasn't a great looking face, but it had a uniqueness about it. His wide forehead and sharp cheekbones gave his face a boxy look, but it was his fantastic eyes, large and golden like a harvest moon that really struck her.

"Have we met?" Elize asked awkwardly certain she had seen him before.

"Perhaps." The man said with a heavy accent. Looking up and smiling at Elize he added. "But not in this place. Not in this time." When Elize didn't respond he stuck out his hand. "I am Ori."

"I'm Elize." Elize replied, tapping the tip of her pencil against the pad. "Are you ready to order?"

Ori stared at Elize a few seconds before lowering his hand. Elize didn't mean to come off rude, but she didn't like to touch people. She wasn't a germaphobe or anything like that, but often when she touched someone she could hear what they were thinking and Elize had learned early on that most of the time it was better not to know what other people were thinking. Finally, Ori looked down at the menu and began to point at the faded images of eggs, bacon, ham and sausage."

"You have money for all this right?" Elize asked, frowning. Again, she didn't mean to be rude, but she had learned the hard way that the customers who over ordered were more likely to skip out without paying the tab.

Ori flashed Elize a wounded look and pulled a wrinkled dollar from his deep coat pocket. "You take American money, yes?"

"Yes," Elize replied warily, glancing down at the pad, "about seven more of those should cover it." He nodded and licked at the top of his water glass like a dog.

"What a weird guy." Elize thought looking down at the order pad. "How do you want your eggs?"

"Raw." Ori answered without looking up. Elize shook her head and walked away.

Dan took one look at the order and grumbled.

"He said he had enough money to cover it." Elize assured him.

"You'd better hope so," Dan huffed and slapped sausage on to the grill, "or you know whose treat it'll be."

Yeah, Elize knew. She'd worked for Dan long enough to know she'd be covering the bill if Ori skipped out.

While Ori waited for his food, he sat in the booth and patiently ripped his napkin into seven rectangular strips. Although she thought it was a bit odd, Elize didn't think much about it until he paid his tab.

Walking to the cash register Elize noticed something strange about one of the dollar bills. Holding it up to the sunlight she examined it carefully. It was fake. Holding up the other dollars Elize discovered only one of the bills was real, the other seven were napkins.

"Hilarious," Elize snapped, slapping the napkin dollars down on the table. "Now pay with real money." A look of genuine surprise crossed Ori's face, but he quickly blinked it away.

"I no understand," Ori exclaimed loudly. His accent was much thicker than it had been a moment ago. "Is this not American dollars?" He waved the napkin strips over his head.

"Not cool!" Elize hissed and tried to grab his hand. Ori laughed keeping his hand just out of reach. The smell of grease and stale cigarettes alerted Elize that Dan was standing behind her.

"What the ferk is going on?" Dan demanded. Elize had never heard Dan actually curse, but he took great pride in coming up with new substitutes for curse words. He rarely repeated the same one.

"He tried to rip me off!" Elize yelped pointing at Ori who sat in the booth looking innocent as a lamb.

Dan grabbed the napkins and held them close to his nose. "They look real to me!" He snarled stomping over to the cash register and slamming them into the till.

Elize started to say something but caught herself. If Dan wanted to believe a stranger off the street instead of a loyal worker, well screw him. Ori stopped by the door and whistled. When Elize turned he tossed a shiny brass button at her.

"Your tip!" He jested dancing out the door. Elize was not amused. She fumed about it all night and was not at all happy to find Ori sitting in her kitchen the next morning drinking coffee with Ellen.

"Hello Elize," Ori greeted Elize cheerfully, tipping an imaginary hat at her.

"What are you doing here?" Elize demanded.

"Oh!" Ellen exclaimed looking up at Elize through big, rimmed glasses. "He said he was your friend."

"Hardly." Elize scoffed glaring at Ori as she poured herself a cup of hot coffee.

"Oh crap!" Ellen exclaimed, glancing at her watch. "I told Prof I'd be there by eight!" She downed what remained of her coffee and grabbed the basket off the table.

"But it's Saturday," Elize shouted after her.

"I know," Ellen replied, winking her big brown eye. "We're going for a drive and a picnic!"

"Oooh la la," Elize joked as Ellen ran out the door.

"So, what are you doing here?" Elize asked, taking the seat just vacated by Ellen. "And how did you know where I lived?"

Ori sipped his hot coffee and petted Olive Oyle who had heard Elize get up and was expecting her breakfast now rather than later. The cat could wait, Elize decided.

"I came to say I was sorry." Ori said, setting his empty cup on the table and looking at Elize sincerely. Elize didn't buy it for a second. "I also want to know how you knew."

"What happened to your accent?" Elize asked coldly, ignoring the mournful meows from Olive Oyle.

"I pick up accents easily." Ori replied with a smile. "Now your turn. How did you know?"

"I have a knack for seeing through illusions." Elize answered simply without going into any detailed explanations. Why should she, she hardly knew Ori and what little she did know wasn't favorable.

Ori seemed to accept her explanation and asked her how long she'd lived in her house. When Elize told him about three and a half years he looked disappointed. Elize went on to explain that her mother had bought the boarding house in Cumberland after Elize's stepfather Patrick died. Her mother had been running the boarding house for several years before Elize moved in with her.

"Where did you and your mother live before Cumberland?" Ori asked, watching Elize's face carefully.

"I really don't remember." Elize admitted. "I was very young, and my mother suffered a severe head injury which affected her memory. Perhaps if she had regained her memory our lives would have made more sense, but...well she didn't and to this day there are large gaps in my past that I'll probably never have the answers for. Look, I need to get ready for work." Elize lied, well not exactly lied, but she stretched the truth. She had several hours before she had to go to the diner, but Ori was making her feel strange and she wanted him to go.

"Thanks for the coffee." Ori said, getting up from the table and handing Elize several crinkled dollar bills. "This is for yesterday."

Elize took the money, resisting the urge to hold it up to the light until Ori had left. Either he'd gotten better at the illusion, or these dollars were real.

It was almost a week before Elize saw Ori again. She was sitting on the wrap-around porch drinking pale ale with Ellen and Prof. Prof's real name was Ebenezer, but after years of being called Scrooge, after he got his PhD he started going by Prof. It was Prof that first spotted something moving along the tree line separating Elize's lot from her neighbors.

"It's a fox!" Ellen shouted excitedly, noticing the way the animal moved.

"Rather large for a fox." Prof pointed out as they watched the animal stealthy moving along the tree line. "Probably a coyote."

"No, it's legs aren't long enough for a coyote. Look at his nose. It's definitely foxlike."

"Could be a stray." Elize interjected. Neither Ellen nor Prof thought it was a dog. They were still arguing over the species when Mr. Miller charged out from his shed with a shovel. A few seconds later there was a loud shout and a yip, and the fox darted across the yard and under Elize's porch.

"I'm sure he's still under here." Elize whispered, shining her flashlight under the porch.

"Careful it could be rabid." Prof warned from the porch while Elize and Ellen searched for the injured fox.

Ignoring Prof's warning Elize got down on all fours and crawled under the porch. Using the flashlight to knock the humongous spiderwebs out of her way, Elize continued forward.

"Hey fella," Elize cooed softly at the two golden orbs flickering in the flashlights beam. "I'm not going to hurt you." She promised as she edged closer to the corner the animal had backed himself into. Elize set the light down and slowly approached the injured fox. "Don't be afraid little fella, I just want to help you."

"Oh shit!" Elize shouted backing away so fast she fell on her rear.

"What's wrong? Did it bite you?" Ellen yelled, shining her light under the porch until it hit Ori's startled face.

"How did he get under there and where's the fox?" Prof demanded as the three of them lifted Ori up the porch steps and carried him inside.

"He is the fox." Elize said pointing at the shovel shaped gash above Ori's left ear.

"You realize how crazy that sounds." Ellen said as she sopped up the blood streaming down Ori's head with a damp towel. "It doesn't look too deep, but he should probably go to the hospital and get a stitch or three."

"No... no..." Ori mumbled and grabbed Elize's hand. "You do it. You mend me."

"Well...I did go to nursing school for a while." Elize said looking up at Ellen and Prof.

"I went to med school for four years, but that doesn't make me a doctor." Prof complained wondering why Ori was so against going to the hospital.

"Well..." Ellen told Prof sensing his concern, "he probably doesn't want to go to a hospital because, well obviously, he's not from around here. Besides it's only a couple stitches."

"Make sure he stays awake for a couple hours in case he's concussed." Prof told Elize after he had finished stitching Ori's wound shut.

"While we're waiting," Ellen chirped, coming in from the kitchen with a bottle of red wine in one hand and three glasses in the other, "Prof has a proposition for you."

"Oh?" Elize said, raising an eyebrow at the now blushing Prof. Even though Prof was pushing thirty, Elize was pretty sure he was still a virgin. She was pretty sure Ellen was too, but Ellen wasn't nearly as old.

"Not that!" Ellen laughed and playfully punched Elize in the arm. "He wants to ask you about renting the third floor. I know you don't want to have to keep working at the diner to make ends meet." Ellen continued not letting either Elize or Prof to get a word in edgewise. "I told him about Linda and Pam's moms canceling their rooms for the next semester and Prof's property owner sold the building and the new owner is doubling his rent. So, I was thinking..."

"You would solve both our problems." Elize completed Ellen's sentence. "It's a great idea. You can have the third floor for what you are paying for your apartment now. If that's okay with you."

"That's great!" Prof exclaimed, raising his glass for a toast. "When can I move in?"

They spent the next couple of hours drinking wine and discussing what needed to be done to clear out the third floor and get it ready for Prof to relocate. Finally, just after midnight Prof checked Ori over one more time.

"He doesn't appear to have a concussion," Prof said as he headed out the door, "but you should let him stay here tonight just to be on the safe side."

Elize agreed to let Ori sleep on the couch. She left her door ajar so she could hear Ori if he called out or moaned in his sleep. Elize never heard him and when she woke the next morning Ori was gone. Elize wasn't surprised that Ori had left without saying goodbye. Having the ability to turn himself into a fox, now that was a different story.

The events of the night before were still vivid in Elize's mind as she began to move her things from the third floor bedroom to her mother's room. The second she stepped into her mother's room, Elize had the distinct impression that someone had been rummaging through her mother's belongings. Elize knew it hadn't been Ellen. She was familiar with Ellen's signature. Even though nothing appeared to be missing, Elize was sure someone had been in there and she was pretty sure that someone was Ori.

"I should have never let him in the house." She told Ellen over coffee later.

"What in the world could he be looking for?" Ellen asked, not convinced Ori had gone into Euna's room.

"This!" Elize said, dropping the old cigar box on the table.

Ellen looked at the old cigar box curiously.

"Paddy found it when he was looking for old photos for my mother's memorial." Elize explained opening the lid so Ellen could see inside. "Do you remember just before Mom died she told us about her lost son?"

"Yeah."

"What did you think she meant?" Elize asked, looking at Ellen's face. Ellen looked a little uncomfortable.

"Well, I guess I thought she was talking about a son that died."

"Exactly, that's what I thought too!" Elize said as she shuffled through the papers in the box and pulled out the scribbled note. "We were wrong!" Elize handed the note to Ellen.

"Oh." Ellen exclaimed as she read the note. "Your mother literally lost her son, and someone found him. I wonder if she tried to contact him."

"I don't know," Elize answered slowly, "but I don't think so. I think it has something to do with why we left wherever we lived before we slid down the mountainside."

"Don't you remember anything?"

"Not much. I was pretty young, and my mom's memory got all scrambled when she smashed her head in the fall."

"I thought that happened from a car accident?" Ellen said. She was sure Euna said she had injured her head in a car accident.

"No, that's just what she told everyone." Elize admitted with a half-smile. "Paddy told me the real story. Paddy and his father found mom and I among the debris left by a huge mudslide. My mom had hit her head on a rock when we tumbled down the mountainside and her skull was crushed. Paddy said it was a miracle she survived."

"And she never remembered how you two got there?"

"Not that I know of." Elize said sadly. "Sometimes she would start to remember something, but her thoughts would become jumbled, and the memory would be gone as fast as it came."

"So, why would Ori be looking for the box? You don't think he's your long-lost brother, do you?" Ellen said excitedly.

Elize considered the idea of Ori being her brother for exactly three seconds before shaking her head. "No, I'm sure he's not. My brother was much taller, and his eyes were gray."

"I thought you didn't remember your brother."

"I didn't, but now I do." Elize shrugged.

"So why would Ori want the box?" Ellen insisted taking the box from Elize.

"Maybe he knows where I came from and has come to take me home." Elize suggested. "Mom used to say she was an Empress or something like that, but I never believed her. I mean what are the chances of that?"

"This death certificate has your name on it." Ellen gasped, handing Elize the document she was holding.

"Yeah, that was for Patrick's daughter." Elize explained not sounding surprised at all. "She died a few months after she was born. Paddy told me about it."

"So, why do you have the same name? That's kind of creepy. Don't you think?"

"I guess." Elize had never really given it much thought until now. "Paddy said that when they found us, we didn't speak English and we didn't have any identification on us. Patrick had recently been widowed and decided to give us the names of his late wife and daughter. I legally changed my name from Elizabeth to Elize when I turned twenty-one, but mom didn't see any sense in changing her name from Anna to Euna."

"When I met her, she told me her name was Euna. I just figured it was a nick name of something." Ellen said, scrunching her eyebrows together as she continued to look through the papers in the box.

"That was her real name. It was one of the few things I remember."

"So, are you going to try to track your big brother down?" Ellen asked excitedly. Elize looked at the note lying on the bed between them and smiled.

"Yeah." She said picking up the note and reading it again. "Maybe Paddy knows where mom got this."

"I think I know." Ori said, hopping off the window ledge where he'd been listening from behind the long blue curtains. Elize bounded across the room and grabbed Ori before he could slip away.

"Enough games." Elize snarled as she pinned Ori's shoulders to the floor. A trick she learned from being raised with five older step-brothers.

"Mind the head." Ellen called from behind Elize. Elize ignored her and pressed down harder on Ori's shoulders.

"Who are you and why are you here?" Elize demanded. Ori blinked at her but didn't answer. Elize pressed harder. "What were you doing going through my mother's things?"

"I needed proof." Ori told her.

"Proof? Proof of what?"

"Proof that you are who I think you are."

"And just who do you think I am?" Elize said cautiously.

"Monetelizadora, daughter of Euna..." Ori began to reply before his eyes rolled back into his skull and his body went limp.

"I think you killed him." Ellen whispered as she lifted Ori's arm and checked for a pulse.

"He's not dead." Elize assured Ellen.

"Are you sure?" Ellen asked not finding a pulse. Elize was sure. She could feel Ori's heart beating and his blood circulating through his veins.

CHAPTER 2

If you asked her today, Elize still couldn't give a good reason for letting Ori into her life. Let alone trusting him. He'd done little to win her trust since the day she ran into him in front of the diner. But truth be told she did trust him, well mostly and she liked him. Not just because he was cute. Which he was. Puppy dog cute with fluffy hair and autumn eyes. But because Ori knew things about her, about her past, and he claimed he could help her find her long lost brother Alzo.

Ellen wasn't keen on Elize running off on a wild goose chase with Ori and insisted Elize talk to her eldest stepbrother first. After all, Paddy or Patrick O'Sullivan, as he was now known, had been there the night his father had found Elize and her mother maybe he knew where Elize's mother had gotten the mysterious note in the cigar box.

Paddy sat behind his desk and ran his sausage-like fingers through what was left of his salt and pepper hair. Even at home Paddy looked like a lawyer. As she sat waiting for him to reply, Elize wondered if he ever let his guard down.

"I don't recall seeing this," Paddy said as he carefully folded the paper in two, "but I think it might have been in a bottle Mother found on one of our day trips. As you know Mother never learned to drive. When I was a teenager I would take Mother out for a drive. Of course, Father was not aware of these adventures. He was afraid Mother's memory would return and she would leave us. I believe that was the main reason he sent you away to school. Anyway, on warm summer days Mother liked to go for drives out in the country. She often asked me to take her to the spot where Father and I had found her. Other times we would drive around the mountain into West Virginia. On one of these trips around the mountain, Mother became quite agitated and insisted on pulling off the road and hiking up a rocky path. That's where Mother found the blue bottle. You know the one she always kept on the window shelf by her bed. She never told me what was inside the bottle, but if I'm not mistaken, she found this note. See here on the corner." Paddy held the note so Elize could see. "There's a smudge of blue paint just there."

"Do you remember where it was?" Elize asked, taking the note back. "It's the best clue I have for finding Alzo. I mean who else could it be talking about? 'If you lost your boy, I found him. He is safe and happy.' Did Mother ever try to find him?"

"Not that I know of." Paddy answered, rubbing the faint stubble on his chin. "That was the last time I took her to the mountain. I left for college shortly after that."

"Do you remember how to get there?" Elize asked more determined than ever to find Alzo.

Paddy wasn't exactly sure where he had pulled off all those years ago, but he had a general idea. A few days later Elize and Ori set off with a wrinkled map of West Virginia and the rough directions Paddy had jotted down on his office memo pad. After taking a couple wrong turns Elize stopped at a gray, clapboard farmhouse propped on a rocky hillside to ask for directions. The old man who answered the door looked surprised to see Elize and asked her if she was related to his neighbor Al who lived up the mountain.

The road up the mountain was more of a dry creek bed than a road. When the car's muffler scraped bottom, Elize parked it and got out to walk the rest of the way. She could see the odd brown house built between two large elms from where they parked the car.

"You folks lost?" A man's voice boomed from behind a row of corn stalks. Elize stopped walking and waited as the tall man with hair like a tumbleweed made his way down to the road.

"I'm looking for a guy named Alzo." Elize said her eyes fixed on the man's sparkling silvery gray eyes.

"What the Hell are you doing here?" The man growled. Elize started to repeat herself but stopped when she realized the man was talking to Ori. Ori yelped and shifted into a fox. Elize gasped and tripped over her own feet. It was the first time she'd actually seen Ori shift into a fox and it had startled her. Alzo stopped chasing Ori to catch Elize.

"Al!" A woman yelled from the farmhouse. "You didn't tell me you were expecting visitors." Alzo let out a long sigh.

"You should choose your friends more wisely." He hissed at Elize through tightly gritted teeth before releasing her and walking towards the farmhouse. Elize glanced around for Ori before jogging after him.

"I thought there were two of you." The woman said looking behind Elize, her dazzling blue eyes glimmering in the sunlight. Alzo and Elize exchanged glances.

"He went back to the car." Elize explained awkwardly.

"And you are?"

"I am Elize. I think I'm Alz...Al's little sister." Elize curled her top lip over her bottom lip and lifted her shoulders in a funny shrug.

"I thought your sister was dead." The woman said looking skeptically from Elize to Alzo.

"That's what I thought too Susan." Alzo said smiling widely as he waved his large hand towards Elize. "That is, until this little lady walked up the road looking for me."

"I thought you were dead too." Elize told him and pulled the note she'd found out of the small backpack she used as a purse. "Until I found this." Elize handed Alzo the note.

Alzo read the note and handed it to Susan. "Where'd you get that?"

Elize quickly explained how she had found the note and what Paddy had told her about the blue bottle. To her relief, Alzo laughed.

"Emma and her blue jars." He laughed and tugged at the tip of his beard. "So, why didn't my mother come and find me?"

"She died a few months ago." Elize explained sadly.

"But she must have found this note a long time before that." Alzo exclaimed, no longer laughing. "Emma's been dead for over ten years."

Elize wasn't surprised that Alzo was less than thrilled about her showing up after all these years. She had expected him to be skeptical at first, but she hadn't expected him to be angry.

"I can't believe Mayme knew I was alive all these years and never looked for me!" Alzo shouted and slammed through the front door.

"Maybe I should go." Elize told Susan, her voice shaking slightly. "I... I didn't mean to..."

"Nonsense!" Susan said with forced cheerfulness wrapping her arm around Elize's shoulder. "It's just the shock of learning all this at once. Come in and have a cup of tea at least. I'm sure once Al calms down he'll want to hear your story."

Elize wasn't sure either of them believed her, but once she removed her glove and showed Alzo her right palm she knew he believed her. That night after Susan went to bed, Elize and Alzo sat outside by the firepit drinking Alzo's home brewed ale.

"You're lucky you caught me here." Alzo told Elize as he tossed her another bottle. "Susan and I just arrived last week. I haven't been back here for years, but Susan insisted on seeing where I'd grown up and of course she fell in love with the place. So, what in God's name are you doing hanging out with a Vanji?"

"A what?" Elize asked, not familiar with the term.

"A Vanji. Ori. Ori is a Vanji. A trickster who can change his shape from a man to a fox."

"Like a werewolf?" Elize asked furrowing her brows as she tried to make sense of what Alzo was saying.

"No, not really." Alzo said, reaching over to pull another ale out of the cooler. "Vanji's don't need a full moon to shift. They can shift whenever they feel like it and they are fully aware of what they are doing in both forms. Not like a werewolf who goes berserk and rips people apart willy-nilly."

Elize cracked a smile. She never would have imagined that she'd be sitting on a mountain in West Virginia talking to her brother about the difference between Vanji's and werewolves.

"So, what's Ori doing here?" Alzo asked seriously.

"I don't know. He just showed up." Elize said before licking a drop of ale off her lip.

"I wonder how he got to Earth?"

"What?!" Elize sputtered spilling ale on her pants. "You think Ori's not from Earth? That's crazy!"

"Have you ever seen a human turn into a fox before?"

"No," Elize admitted slowly. "But I hadn't made the alien connection. I thought maybe he was a warlock or wizard or something like that."

"Oh, I see. Ori being an alien is crazy, but being a warlock is normal?" Alzo teased, shaking his head. "So where is he now?" Alzo asked, looking straight into Elize's eyes. Elize felt the sides of her mouth twitch.

"He's hiding behind the third fir tree to our right." Elize said. Alzo blinked, jumped to his feet, ran over to the tree, and grabbed Ori by the scruff of the neck. When he returned to the fire with Ori kicking and cursing, Elize tilted her head to one side and asked.

"So, no more doubts that I'm your sister?"

"Never had any," Alzo smirked as he sat back down keeping one arm wrapped firmly around Ori's shoulders. "I knew it was you the second I spotted you on the road."

"You did?"

"Yeah, you look a lot like Mayme." Alzo said before he turned his attention to Ori. Giving Ori's shoulder a tight squeeze, Alzo smiled at him menacingly. "Now Ori, my old friend, it's time you told Elize and I just how you got here and who sent you."

Ori squirmed under Alzo's grip. Elize would have bet her last dollar that Ori was going to shift back into a fox, but to her surprise he didn't. Which was probably smart. Elize doubted Alzo would let him get away with it twice.

"Let me go!" Ori whined pushing at Alzo's hand. Alzo considered this a second.

"Tell you what," Alzo said, squeezing Ori's shoulder even tighter. "You answer my questions and maybe I'll let go."

"You know why I'm here." Ori sulked letting his body go loose. "The time has come."

"Time for what?" Elize asked as she exchanged her empty bottle for a full one.

"Time to return." Ori replied, his orange eyes locked on Alzo's gray ones. "You were too young to remember much, but Alzo is older. He remembers who he is and why he must return."

"Why now?" Alzo asked coldly, glancing towards the farmhouse where Susan stood at the open door looking out.

"Your father is sick."

"That's not new. He's always been sick."

"This time is different. This time he's dying for real." Ori replied, his eyes glittered in the firelight giving him a feral look. Despite the warmth of the fire, Elize shivered as she sensed just how wild and dangerous her new friend could be if provoked.

"Why now?" Alzo repeated and gave Ori's shoulder another squeeze.

"On the night of the full moons, your father had a vision. He claimed your mother appeared to him and told him that the realms were about to align as they had on the day she had disappeared with you guys. She also told him you were both still alive and living in the fourth realm on a planet known as Earth. Your father always insisted that you were all still alive. Even when everyone else gave up, even after all these years, he held on to the hope that one day you would return."

"How did you find us? How did you cross the realms?" Alzo asked, still skeptical. "Surely not the same way we did?"

"In the vision, your mother showed your father how to find you, but no I did not travel the way you did." Ori explained. "I traveled in my fox body. Animals are not held to the same laws as the human genus. Of course, Mal, you remember Mal the Mage don't you?" Alzo nodded. "Mal took me on as his apprentice some years back, but I'm afraid I've been somewhat of a disappointment to the old mule, but he should have known better. Anyway, the map your father drew from the vision looked a lot like the maps you and I saw in that old book we found. You remember the book."

"I do." Alzo said, raising his hand up and rubbing the jagged scar on his left cheek that he kept hidden underneath his beard. If only he and Ori hadn't found that stupid book.

"Your mother figured out how to read the map which showed the locations of the hidden pathways. In the vision she told your father that she had misread the map and instead of coming out on the other side of Toboria near her childhood home in the islands of Palenina she ended up traveling to the fourth realm where she landed on the planet Earth. Unfortunately, she didn't realize her mistake until she came out of the cave and found herself on the top of a mountain during a horrible storm. Before she could return to the cave, you" Ori nodded at Alzo, "vanished. She was searching for you when the ground broke apart and a mudslide swept your mother and Elize down the mountain."

"So, she did remember," Elize sniffed and reached out for Alzo's hand.

"Maybe, remember this was a vision your father had, not an actual conversation." Ori said shifting uncomfortably under Alzo's grip. "Using the map your father scratched out, Mal and I searched for the hidden entrance to the pathway, but it was sealed shut."

"So how did you get here?"

"Well, although Mal may appear absentminded, there are times when his mind is quite sharp. Mal assumed that since birds of the air and fish of the sea can slip between the realms unhindered, I should be able to do the same in my fox form. It took some trial and error, but I finally managed to find Earth. Of course, I had no idea how large Earth was, but once I got to the right continent I was able to make my way to the right state and find the address your father had written down for me. Unfortunately, it took more time than I ever expected and now we have little time to be in the right place at the right time to return to Toboria."

"And just what is the right place and time?" Alzo asked.

"I'm not sure of the place, in the vision your mother wasn't exactly clear on where it was exactly, but Mal says we must be at that place at daybreak on the 21st of June. I was hoping you remembered the spot. Do you?"

Elize shook her head. What little she remembered from that night came back in nightmarish thunder and lightning, Alzo vanishing in the streams of torrential rain, her mother's terrifying screams. the ground melting under their feet, a river of mud and rocks, and finally, blood, so much blood gushing out of her mother's head.

"I know where it is." Alzo mumbled as he lifted his hand off Ori's shoulder. "Emma and I went there every year on the first day of summer to lay flowers on the spot. Like Payape, I believed that Elize and Mayme were still alive and would find me there one day. I didn't know Emma had left a message for Mayme. She must have gone by herself without telling me. I stopped going there after Emma passed away. It seemed like a waste of time. By then I realized it was just a silly dream. No one was coming to find me."

"And now I'm here." Elize said, squeezing Alzo's hand and smiling at him.

"And now you're here." Alzo said sadly, slipping his hand free from Elize's and getting up. "And now Susan is wondering why I'm not in bed." He added and motioned towards the light flowing out of the open door of the farmhouse. "Come Elize you can sleep on the sofa."

"What about Ori?" Elize asked, getting to her feet and brushing the dirt off her jeans.

"He can sleep in the barn." Alzo shouted over his shoulder. Elize looked over at Ori.

"It's okay." Ori assured her. "I prefer sleeping outdoors."

The next morning Elize joined Alzo out in the garden where he was pinching leaves off the lettuce plants.

"Susan says you are expecting a crowd for a summer equinox festival."

"Yes, actually Stan should be arriving this afternoon. He'll be taking the spare bedroom upstairs. The other's will be sleeping in tents."

"Oh, I hope we aren't imposing." Elize said, taking the pile of lettuce leaves from Alzo.

"Not really." Alzo said reaching over to nip a yellowing leaf off a young tomato plant. "If you want to invite a friend or two, that would be cool. The more the merrier. Just make sure they know they'll need a tent if they plan to spend the night."

"Ori says we need to be at the place we arrived at sunrise on the 21st." Elize said wondering how Ellen and Prof would feel about camping out in the rough. She decided to invite them. Knowing their fascination with plants and dirt they would probably love it.

"If you and Ori help me, we can go there tomorrow before it gets dark." Alzo said as they walked back towards the farmhouse. "Stan and some others will be here to help Susan with the final setting up. If nothing happens I don't see why we won't be back here for breakfast. I'm sure Susan will understand."

Of course, Alzo was wrong, Susan didn't understand at all and stood on the porch pouting as Alzo kissed her on the forehead and ran his hands down her silky blond hair.

"We'll be back before breakfast," he promised again as he turned to leave.

"If my friend Ellen gets here before I get back, tell her to go ahead and set up her tent." Elize told Alzo's friend Stan, a self-proclaimed guru who would be leading the weekend long festival. "If for some reason we don't get back," Elize pressed a note into Stan's palm. "Make sure Ellen gets this. Tell her to take it to Paddy. Paddy will know what to do." Stan nodded and without commenting stuffed the paper in his pocket.

An hour later Alzo pulled his rusty jeep behind a long abandoned gas station and turned the engine off.

"Are you sure this is the right spot?" Elize asked as she climbed out of the jeep and surveyed the jagged mountain in front of them.

"Yeah, I'm sure," Alzo replied standing nonchalantly with his hands planted on his hips. "Emma brought me here every year until I turned 18. Come on I'll show you where we camped."

"Where are we exactly?" Elize asked, rubbing her bare arms and wishing she had remembered to bring a jacket.

"Folks around here call the mountain Gray Beard. Part of the Allegheny mountains I reckon." Alzo looked down at Elize's flimsy tennis shoes and frowned. "You should have hiking boots."

"I'll be alright." Elize said, grabbing her small knapsack and heading after Ori who had jogged ahead to pee.

"What was she doing here?" Elize said still not convinced by the story Ori had told them. She waved her hand at the loose and fallen shale scattered about their feet. "It just doesn't make sense. Was her mind already scattered before the fall?"

"No, like Ori told you, Mayme didn't mean to come here," Alzo explained as he reached out to help Elize up the slippery slope. "She told me she was taking us to see her family in Palenina, the islands where she grew up. She didn't mean to end up here."

"That I can believe, but how did we get up here? Fly?" Elize asked. Being in a small plane that crashed made more sense than coming through a portal. Alzo shook his head.

"We didn't fly. We walked. Look, I don't know how we got up here," Alzo admitted, "but I know it had something to do with this." Alzo poked the hard, purply-blue blotch hidden under the dirty glove on Elize's right palm. Elize felt the stone embedded in her skin flicker in response.

"And the book," Ori interjected, poking his fluffy head around Elize. "Don't forget the book."

"How could I?" Alzo grumbled rubbing the long, ragged scar hidden beneath his thick rusty beard. "This is it." He said, stopping at the base of a thick slab of rock jutting upward. "We'll camp here and wait for the crack of dawn."

"I...I think I remember this." Elize stammered, pulling the glove off her right hand.

"I doubt it." Alzo said. "The night we walked out of Gray Beard's mouth this wasn't here."

Ignoring Alzo's last comment, Elize knelt and pressed her palm against the rock. Almost at once an image appeared. "This stone is ancient," Elize muttered, running her palm across the rough surface. "It was placed here as a safeguard." Elize's eyes blinked erratically as images flashed across her mind. "Somethings wrong." Elize exclaimed loudly. "This isn't right." Elize reached out her left hand and clasped Alzo's hand tightly in hers.

"What is it?" Alzo asked, almost afraid of what his sister might say. Elize lifted her hand from the stone and blinked several times until her vision cleared and her eyes returned to their normal emerald-green color.

"What? What did you see?" Alzo asked again, taking a step back and causing a small avalanche of rocks to tumble over the ledge.

"I saw the three of us coming out of the mouth. It was very dark and pouring rain. The moment we stepped out there was a flash of lightning followed almost immediately by a clap of thunder so loud it shook the whole mountain."

"I remember." Alzo said, his voice tight. "That's when I slipped."

"But Mayme didn't know that. She was blinded by the light and when your hand slipped out of hers she thought you had run back inside. She believed you were trapped in there by this." Elize pounded her fist against the rock. "That's why I remember it. She thought you were trapped inside. That's why we were on the other side of the mountain. Don't you see she was trying to find another way in to rescue you."

"So, the answers we're seeking are on the other side of the rock." Alzo said, pacing back and forth in front of the rock. "Let's see if we can push it out of the way." Using all his strength Alzo shoved at the large rock from one end and then the other. The slab didn't budge.

"Let me try," Elize said brushing past him. Alzo laughed and backed away. If he couldn't move the stone, there was no way Elize was going to have any luck. Instead of trying to push the massive rock, Elize squatted down and wrapped her fingers around one of the long flat stones wedged underneath it. After wiggling the wedged stone back and forth several times it came free.

"Try now," Elize told Alzo, stepping aside so he could give the slab another shove. The slab rocked forward and back. With Elize and Ori's help Alzo continued rocking the large slab of granite until they had 'walked' it far enough sideways to reveal the gap behind it. Ori shifted into his fox shape and slipped inside.

"You guys really need to get in here." Ori shouted from the other side of the slab. Elize and Alzo continued rocking the slab until there was enough room for them both to squeeze through.

"Look at this." Ori shouted waving excitedly at the spiral markings on the wall.

"We'll camp in here." Alzo said and went back out to retrieve their bags.

Elize woke as the first rays of the longest day of the year began to lighten walls of the cave.

"Wow," Elize gasped as she joined Alzo who was standing in front of a T-shape indention carved into the solid rock wall.

"This is it." Alzo whispered, a crease forming on his forehead as he examined the indentation in the stone.

"What's wrong?" Elize asked.

"Déjà vu." Alzo replied, watching in awe as sunlight hit the center of the T-shape and began filling it with light.

"Oh my God!" Elize squealed and jerked her hand away. "I remember…" she stammered her emerald eyes glowing like cat's eyes in the sunlight flowing into the gap between the slab and the cave entrance.

"This is it!" Alzo shouted excitedly. "This is the way back!"

Ori pulled a ragged, leather bound book from his back pocket and opened it to the page marked by a thin piece of brown twine.

"Hey," Alzo snapped when he saw what Ori was holding, "where did you get that?"

"It doesn't matter!" Ori replied and jumped backward to keep the book out of Alzo's reach. "We need to act now before the sun gets any higher!"

"Where did you get that?" Alzo growled. The last time he had seen that damn book his mother had been holding it. He could almost hear her singing.

"I found it in the barn." Ori squeaked as he leapt to one side to avoid Alzo. "It was hidden in a blue jar under the floor."

Before Alzo could lunge at him again, Ori started to sing. Alzo froze, it was the same strange song his mother had sang the night she brought him and Elize through the light.

As Ori continued to sing, the light illuminating the T-shaped carving started to pulse. Without missing a note, Ori winked and leapt into the light.

"Oh no you don't!" Alzo shouted and leapt after him. Elize took a deep breath and followed her brother into the light.

"Watch out!" Alzo shouted at Elize as she tripped over his arm. Elize felt Alzo's fingers rip across her ankle, as she tumbled into the thick misty clouds.

"Noooo!" Alzo screamed and reached helplessly out with one arm while the other clutched the thick toe of a stone giant. The only remains of the gigantic figure and the massive stone bridge it had once guarded.

Elize didn't realized how dire her situation was until she looked down. Fighting back panic she twisted her head from side to side searching the towering black pillars jutting up out of the ground like two massive skyscrapers for something to grab hold of. Both pillars were too far away for her to reach and even if she could find something to grab hold of the momentum of her fall would surely yank her arms off. Not a pleasant thought.

As she continued to fall Elize heard shouting. She supposed it was Ori, even though it didn't sound like him. With all the wind rushing past her ears she was only able to make out one word.

"Milendor."

"Milendor," she repeated to herself. She had no idea what milendor meant and no time to waste thinking about it as she plummeted to her death. The very thought of plummeting to her death should have filled Elize with paralyzing fear. Instead, it really pissed her off.

"Son of a bitch!" Elize screamed and kicked at the air. Her body twisted erratically in response. Spinning in a lopsided circle, Elize fumed cursing the day Ori walked into her life. She should have told him to get lost when she had the chance. This was all Ori's fault, except it wasn't really. Elize stopped kicking knowing that no amount of cursing was going to help her.

"I refuse to be smashed to smithereens!" She screamed at her right hand. The power had come to her rescue in the past and she needed it now more than ever before. Elize extended her fingers out, flattening her palm and willing the power to come. Nothing happened.

"Great!" Elize screamed as the wind battered her face. "What good is power when it won't come when you need it." Elize squinted her eyes and forced herself to look down at the wide expanse beneath her. Water, there was water beneath her. Perhaps today was not her day to die after all.

With the space between her and the water rapidly decreasing Elize realized that in her current position, she would belly flop. That would not only hurt like hell but surely kill her. With mere seconds to spare Elize pulled her knees to her chest, wrapped her arms tightly around them and shouted "cannonball!"

She hit the water hard and sunk down, down, down.

CHAPTER 3

Ori watched in horror as Elize fell past him. Elize was falling too fast to notice Ori sprawled out on the minuscule ledge a few feet below Alzo's dangling feet. Ori realized at once that something had gone wrong. Unfortunately, before he could shout out a warning, Alzo tumbled out and knocked him onto the ledge. Ori barely had time to shift into his fox body before he landed hard onto the bit of rock where he now lay. Gingerly getting to his feet, Ori realized he had a decision to make and decided it would make more sense to go after Elize than try to climb back up to Alzo. Ori knew it would take a miracle for Elize to survive the fall, but he was sure she would. In fact, he refused to believe any other option. Ori was making his way down the pillar when he heard someone yell 'Milendor.'

Alzo felt his heart break into a thousand pieces as his fingers slipped off Elize's ankle. Seconds after his little sister disappeared into the clouds Alzo thought he heard her call out. Sobbing he clung to the stone toe and struggled to find a foothold. Using all the upper body strength he could muster Alzo forced his torso up. Still grasping onto the toe, he looked up. A honey-colored face surrounded by long, silky black hair looked down at him.

The girl was as surprised to see Alzo as he was to see her. Seeing his dilemma, she lowered her body onto what was left of the stone giant's foot and grabbed Alzo by his shoulders. It wasn't easy, with her help Alzo was able to pull himself to safety.

"Hohi said you'd be here," the girl gasped, staring at Alzo with brown tiger eyes. Ilee had never seen a man like Alzo before. None of the men on the islands were over five and a half feet tall or as muscular as Alzo and none had hair on their faces. Ilee was astonished that the Ancient had sent her to find such a wild man.

Alzo stared at Ilee. She spoke a language he hadn't heard since he was a boy. It was his mother's native language.

"Who is Hohi," Alzo asked, getting to his feet and brushing the dust off his jeans.

Ilee jumped back so suddenly she almost slipped off the side. Alzo reached out and caught her by the arm. Ilee's cheeks blushed red. She stared in wonder at this strange, wild man. Surely he knew who Hohi was? Why had he asked such a strange question? Maybe the Ancients were testing her.

"Hohi is the Ancient who speaks out of the fire," Ilee answered, pulling her hand free. "I am Ilee, Keeper of the Flame, servant of the most-wise Hohi."

"Oh," Alzo said, trying not to smile. "It is an honor to meet you Ilee, Keeper of the Flame. I am Alzo. Thank you for coming to my rescue and thanks to Hohi for sending you."

Ilee's cheeks burned again. She was not used to being thanked.

"This is a sacred place," Ilee told Alzo nervously, "a forbidden place. You should not be here. Who are you and why have you come?"

"I am Alzo." Alzo repeated, holding out his hand. "My sister came here to find our father."

"I see no sister." Ilee said, looking around them.

"My sister fell." Alzo said sadly. "I tried to catch her, but I wasn't able to."

"Your sister fell from the sky?!" Ilee exclaimed, peering over the stone foot. Alzo nodded. "I see nothing but clouds."

"She fell through the clouds."

"If your sister fell from the sky," Ilee said excitedly, "then you must be the great change!"

"What?" Alzo shouted as Ilee crawled off the foot. Pressing her back against the flat pillar Ilee began to inch sideways.

"The prophecy!" Ilee replied, emphasizing 'the.' The one the Oracle of Milendor foretold. You know, 'the one who falls from the sky brings great change'."

"Milendor?" Alzo mumbled pulling at his beard, "I swear I heard someone yell that when my sister fell."

"Hohi will know what to do!" Ilee squealed excitedly. "We must consult her at once!"

"But I need to get down there and see if my sister survived." Alzo protested.

"Hohi will know." Ilee insisted grabbing Alzo's hand and pulling him after her.

"But Elize…" Alzo protested again unable to shake the feeling that Elize was in trouble.

Alzo was right, Elize was in trouble. The force of impact when she hit the water had caused Elize's arms and legs to go numb. As she sank deeper and deeper into the water Elize fought to move her arms, but her legs remained frozen. Elize struggled to swim to the surface, but without the help of her legs it was proving impossible. Finally, the lack of oxygen started to shut down her brain. As blackness closed in on her, Elize had the odd sensation of being lifted upward.

"I'm going to heaven." Elize thought blissfully as a wave of pure joy flowed over her. The wave of joy soon dissipated when a pair of webbed paws dragged her out of the water and slapped her hard across the back. Sputtering out a stream of dirty water Elize coughed and opened her eyes.

A furry brown face with thick bristly whiskers and beady black eyes stared down at her. Not convinced Elize had ejected all the water from her lungs, the otter slapped Elize sharply across the back a second time. Elize gurgled out another stream of water.

"I'm okay." Elize gurgled trying to wiggle free. Wrapping her oily, brown arms around Elize, the otter clucked softly like a mother trying to calm a fussy baby.

"I'm okay," Elize protested. The otter wrinkled her nose at Elize and smiled. At least Elize thought it was a smile. She'd never actually seen an otter smile before. A smaller otter bobbed out of the river and handed a lump of muddy goop to the big otter. Before Elize realized what was happening, the big otter shoved the lump of goop in Elize's mouth and clamped her large, webbed paw over Elize's nose and lips. Thrashing wildly, Elize frantically tried to spit out the goop, but it was no use. Elize felt her lips and tongue go numb and then she felt no more. The last thing Elize remembered was the otter family floating her downstream like a log.

Elize woke up with that wooly, throbbing feeling one gets after too many shots of tequila.

"Damn alarm," she mumbled grumpily. Reaching out to hit the snooze button. The alarm kept buzzing. Annoyed Elize pried open her eyes. A dragonfly the size of her bulldog Popeye hovered inches from her nose.

"Holy shit!" Elize shrieked as she swatted the bug across the room where it splashed down into a bowl of warm sudsy water.

Dragging her thin, soggy body out of the water, the dragonfly buzzed angrily at Elize and stood on the longer two of her six limbs. Flashing Elize a look that could freeze fire, the dragonfly opened and closed her soaked translucent wings, tossed her tiny nose in the air, and sloshed out of the room.

"What did those otters give me?" Elize wondered aloud gingerly touching her forehead.

"Milty weed." A woman wearing a long, brown cloak and white apron answered as she entered the room. Elize watched the woman approach. She was different from any woman Elize had ever seen before. She looked like a normal woman, except her head and neck were covered with light, coarse tan fur, she had the face and ears of a white tailed deer, and instead of feet she had hoofs.

"Roz said you were awake." The woman continued unaware that Elize was staring at her. "I'm afraid you didn't make a very good first impression."

"No, I guess not." Elize agreed. "Where am I?

"The Healing Center at Qym." The woman answered and held up a flat stick. "Follow the stick please."

"Qym? Where on Earth is that?"

"Earth? Qym is not on Earth." The woman answered, looking concerned. Elize moaned and spit up a large, gray glop.

"My goodness!" The woman exclaimed, poking at the glop with her stick. "The otters gave you enough milty weed to sedate a horse."

"So, the otters were real..."

"Of course, the otters were real. The otter's rescued you and brought you here to the healing center. They claimed you fell from the sky."

"I did," Elize told her. "Well kind of. What's your name?"

"Taa. I am the healer assigned to your care." Taa replied and leaned over to examine Elize's right ear before moving to the left. "Roz is my assistant."

"The one I knocked into the water?"

"Exactly."

"Are you human?" Elize asked without considering how rude it sounded.

"Heaven's no!" Taa replied coolly. "I am a Deerling. My herd left me at the Healing Center shortly after I was born."

"What a cruel thing to do."

"It wasn't cruel. I would have put the entire herd into danger." Taa sputtered, obviously flustered by Elize's reaction. Taa was relieved when Roz sulked into the room, still flicking her long, translucent wings open and closed. Roz glared at Elize with bubbly orange eyes that covered most of her face and buzzed at Taa.

"I'm sure she didn't strike you intentionally," Taa told Roz patiently glancing over at Elize. "Did you?"

"Kind of," Elize shrugged. Taa frowned.

"Then I advise you to apologize. It is not wise to have an Isopteria on your bad side. But first what is your name and where did you originate from."

"Roz," Elize addressed the dragonfly whose face was eerily like her fourth grade teacher. "I'm sorry I hit you, but I've never seen a bug..."

"Zzzzzt!" Roz buzzed, launching herself off the floor and flying straight at Elize's head.

"Duck!" Taa warned. Elize ducked.

"What the hell?" Elize exclaimed peeking out from under the thin blanket.

"You called Roz a bug," Taa scolded, shaking her apron. "Referring to an Isopteria as a bug is a terrible insult to their noble race."

"I didn't know that." Elize told Roz sincerely. "I'm truly sorry, I didn't mean to insult you."

Taa cleared her throat and gave Roz a hard stare.

"Zzzzzalright," Roz finally buzzed. Elize knew Roz didn't really mean it.

"Now you know our names," Taa said, trying to sound calm, but not feeling at all calm. "What is your name and where do you come from?"

"Elize," Elize replied, lifting herself up on one elbow. "I come from Maryland."

"Merry Land," Taa repeated flicking her ear nervously. "I've never heard of Merry Land?" Taa smiled at Elize. "Is Merry Land above the sky?"

"What? No." Elize mumbled pressing her finger against her temple trying to think of the best way to answer Taa's question without sounding nuts. "Maryland. It's in the United States of America." Taa twitched her left ear. "Oh, for God's sake. I came from Earth!"

"Earth!" Taa shouted. Surely this strange woman was out of her mind. What she claimed was ridiculous.

"Earth," Elize replied. Roz let out a series of sarcastic buzzes.

"I find that very doubtful." Taa said, keeping her eyes on Elize's face. Earth doesn't exist. It is a mythical world."

"Earth is no more mythical than here," Elize replied curtly. "I'm telling the truth. Why don't you ask my friends?"

"Friends?" Taa said, tilting her head to one side. "What friends?"

"The otters didn't bring anyone else?"

"No, just you." Taa insisted. A wave of sadness swept over Elize. She had lost her brother once already and the thought of losing him again was devastating.

"I need to get back to the pillars!" Elize exclaimed and tried to lift herself off the bed as images of Alzo dangling from the stone toe flashed before her eyes.

"No," Taa said and firmly pushed Elize back on the straw mattress. "You're in no condition to travel and even if you were, how do you propose to get back up in the sky?"

"I have no idea! But I have to get back there!" Elize cried. "My brother must still be on top of that black pillar."

"I understand you're distraught," Taa said trying to keep her voice calm, "and I would very much like to be of assistance, but first I need to understand. If you were on Earth, how did you get to Toboria?"

"Well, Ori…"

"Ori!" Taa scowled and threw her hands up. Elize nodded slowly surprised at Taa's reaction. "If this is another one of Ori's silly Vanji tricks I'll…I'll…well I'll skin him and make a coat from his damn hide. That's what I'll do."

"And I'll help you," Elize cried, tears welling up in her eyelids and spilling down her cheeks. "If this is all a trick..." Elize buried her head in her hands. It had been a rough morning and she was still feeling woozy from the goop the otters had force fed her.

Taa awkwardly patted Elize on the back. Comforting had never been one of her strong points. Still, she felt obligated to do something.

"It was just a supposition," Taa said awkwardly, "I have no reason to believe Ori is playing a trick on us. However, he does have a reputation, like all Vanji, for having...well a rather warped sense of humor. If you know what I mean?"

Unfortunately, Elize knew exactly what Taa meant. More determined than ever to get back to the pillars, Elize sat up and pushed the blanket off.

"Where are my clothes," she demanded when she looked down and found she was naked.

"On the line drying," Taa replied, crossing her arms across her chest. "Roz washed them. They were soaking wet and reeked of otter."

"I need them back now!" Elize demanded angrily clutching the blanket. "I need to find my brother."

"No!" Taa replied sternly and stomped her hoof firmly against the dirt floor. "As the healer assigned to your care, I will not allow you to tromp off on a wild goose hunt. If your brother has not figured a way out of his predicament by now, I doubt there's much left of him to help!"

"But..." Elize protested, her eyes filling with tears again.

"No buts about it," Taa cut her off. "The best thing for you to do is rest. We can check with the birds in the morning and see if there's any news of your brother or Ori.

"The birds?"

"Yes. Birds are terrible gossips, especially starlings. If anyone saw your brother hanging from the Twin Pillars, it would be big news in the treetops.

"Can't you ask them now?" Elize asked, running her fingers through her tangled hair.

"No, the birds are roosting now. I will ask them in the morning."

When Roz returned wheeling a small tray with tea and biscuits on it, Taa hurried out and retreated to her room. It was late and she was exhausted, but sleep eluded her. She couldn't stop thinking about Elize. It all seemed so odd. First the otters arrived carrying Elize in their leathery paws claiming she had fallen from the sky. Taa knew that otters were simple folk and not prone to stretching the truth. Could it be possible that Elize was also telling the truth? Could the Oracle's prediction be real? No, that was silly talk, Taa scolded herself for being foolish and forced her eyes shut. After what felt like hours she finally drifted off into a restless sleep.

Taa was awaken by an odd scratching noise above her head. At first she ignored the noise, figuring it was just a mouse. However, it soon occurred to Taa that whatever was making the noise was bigger than a mouse. Taa picked up the tiny blue rock she kept on the little table by her bed and shook it several times until it emitted just enough light for her to see. Taa had barely slipped her cloak over her head when bits of grass and dried mud showered down, and a yellowed beak appeared in the ceiling directly over her head.

"Who," asked the beak.

"Taa," Taa answered, looking up at the hole and frowning. The beak disappeared. More scratching and scuffling followed. Taa stomped her hoof. She prided herself on a tidy room. She would need to sweep up before settling back down.

A round, brown head popped out of the hole and studied Taa with large, stern, caramel eyes.

"Who?" The small owl asked again.

"Taa, Healer at Qym," Taa replied curtly, as she brushed a mound of debris off her shoulder. The owl blinked several times and disappeared back into the hole. Taa stared up at the hole and shook her head. The messenger had obviously gotten the wrong room. All messages went directly to the head healer. Taa was about to go back to bed when the owl dropped out from the hole talons first and landed with a thump by her hoofs.

The owl emitted an ear shattering squawk and held his leg up revealing the bright yellow ribbon wrapped around it. Taa knew she should tell the owl he'd made a mistake, but curiosity got the better of her. She carefully untied the ribbon and pulled it free. Once the ribbon was off the owl wobbled to the door and began pecking at it. Afraid the odd bird would peck a hole in the door, Taa quickly opened it and let the owl out.

Taa shut the door and leaned against it holding the blue cube over the ribbon. A row of fine brown lettering scrolled down the front of the ribbon and back up the other side.

"in danger, girl, of Milendor," the ribbon read on one side," You are, bring the, to Oracle, at once," read the other side. Taa wasn't quite sure what to make of it. Then it dawned on her that she should have read the message while it was still on the owl's leg. It took her several tries, but she finally managed to wrap the ribbon around a stick in the right sequence. "You are in danger, bring the girl to the Oracle of Milendor at once."

Taa stared down at the message and shook her head. It had all the markings of one of Ori's jokes. With a huff Taa pulled the ribbon off the stick. The letters jumped about and got larger.

"DON'T IGNORE ME!" The ribbon shouted in bold letters, "GET THE GIRL AND GO! NOW!"

Stuffing the ribbon into her pocket, Taa ran out of the room. When Taa told Roz what had happened, Roz was skeptical especially when Taa pulled out the ribbon and the message was no longer visible. Insisting what she had seen was real and not a weird dream, Taa was more determined than ever and told Roz she'd be a fool not to take the message seriously. Roz did not agree and threatened to go to the head healer. Taa refused to listen to her friend. She was going to take Elize to the Oracle at Milendor whether Roz joined her or not. Furious that Taa wouldn't listen to her, Roz stormed out into the night. Concerned that Roz might actually arouse the head healer, Taa rushed over to Elize and gave her a good shake.

"Wake up!" She whispered urgently, shaking Elize's shoulders. Elize moaned and her head drooped to one side.

"What did Roz give you?" Taa wondered, shaking Elize harder. Elize yawned and opened her eyes. "Get up!" Taa shouted, "we need to go."

"What," Elize mumbled groggily, rubbing her eyes, "you said I should rest."

"Circumstances have changed and now I'm telling you it's time to leave." Taa snapped and pushed Elize's tee shirt over her head.

"Why? What's going on?" Elize asked as she shoved her arms through the arm holes.

"It has come to my attention that we're in danger and it's imperative that we must leave immediately."

"Oh," Elize yawned, barely catching the cloak when Taa tossed it at her.

"Put that over your clothes." Taa instructed as she started tossing random things into a bag. Elize pulled on the cloak which fell just above her knees. Taa frowned at Elize's blue jeans and tennis shoes, but there was little she could do about it now. Time was of the essence.

"Keep your head down and don't talk," Taa warned as they stepped out into the darkness. Taa listened for any sounds. To her relief the center was still wrapped in a blanket of sleep. Roz must have been bluffing. Still Taa wasn't about to let her guard down.

Elize barely remembered stumbling down the rough path to the stream and had no idea how she managed to get into the canoe. When Elize woke later she was lying on the bottom of the canoe gazing up at a large moon. To the left of the large moon, another much smaller moon hung lower in the sky. The smaller moon had the shape and color of a ripe plum. Elize had hoped when she woke up, she'd be at home in her nice, warm bed, but sadly that was not the case.

Elize sat up and watched Taa struggle with the long pole she was trying to steer the boat with. Taa couldn't get a good grip on the pole since her thick brown nails covered her fingertips from the second digit up. Taa cursed as the long pole slipped and smacked her cheek.

"Here let me give it a go," Elize offered. She must have sat up too fast. A wave of dizziness swept over her, but she fought it off.

"I don't understand it," Taa said handing Elize the pole. "The water shouldn't be so low."

Elize dipped her right palm over the side of the canoe and let the cold water run over it. She could feel the long, needle shaped fish weaving through the water to her left. Grabbing the pole with both hands, Elize shoved the stick into the mud and pushed hard to the left.

"What are you doing?" Taa exclaimed, grabbing at the pole, "we want to keep to the right!"

"The waters deeper to the left," Elize replied as the current caught the canoe and pulled it free from the mud.

Taa was starting to have second thoughts about taking off like she had. She had never traveled as far as the Forest of Milendor and was both exhilarated and terrified. Exhilaration won out in the end, but Taa wished Roz had come. They had always dreamed of leaving the center together. It felt wrong to be going without her.

Elize watched Taa's face. She could feel the anxiety throbbing under Taa's carefully controlled aura. "Do you want to go back for your friend?" Elize asked.

"No," Taa told her. "I just wish she had come with us. Roz and I have been friends, best friends since the first day I arrived at the Healing Center at Qym."

Taa peered at the water ahead as the current suddenly picked up. Even with the moonlight it was difficult to make out the large boulders until they were almost on top of them. Taa grabbed an oar and pushed hard to the right. The canoe lurched to one side almost capsizing.

"I need you up front!" Taa screamed at Elize as she leaned hard to the left.

"Stay right!" Elize said, spotting a dark lump in the water ahead of them.

"I could really use Roz!" Taa fussed. As if by magic, Roz dropped down and landed on the bow of the canoe. Happy to be relieved of her duties, Elize laid back down. All this rocking was making her nauseous.

"Where are we headed?" Elize asked once they were clear of the rocks.

"The Forest of Milendor," Taa replied, not taking her eyes off the water.

"Milendor," Elize repeated slowly, rubbing the side of her head. "I heard someone yell that when I was falling."

"What!" Taa yelped as the canoe tipped sharply to the right.

"I heard someone yell Milendor when I was falling," Elize repeated releasing her breath as Taa regained control of the canoe. "At first, I thought it was Ori, but it didn't sound like him. Where is Milendor?"

Even though she had never actually been to Milendor, Taa did her best to describe to Elize what little she had read about the Forest and the strange beings that lived in it. Elize felt her eyes grow heavy as Taa droned on about the strange tree which grew in the center of Milendor which was home to the Neognathae. The Oracle of Milendor was a Neognathae. An ancient race of human sized, extremely wise owls who, if you believed the legends, were once the scribes of the gods. The gods blessed the oversized owls with tiny arms to enable them to write and take care of the books in hidden libraries. It was said that the owl ladies, as they were often referred to, had escaped from Earth through the dimensional pathways that ran between the nine realms before the first drops of rain began to fall upon Earth during the great flood.

"Roz!" Taa barked softly once she was sure Elize had drifted off. "I'm so glad you're here! I never would have been able to handle those rocks without you." Roz put her top two legs on her hips and buzzed at Taa. "Well, I told you I was going with or without you." Taa snapped irritably. "The message said to bring her to the Oracle at once and that's what I plan to do.

Roz buzzed a reply. Taa set the oars on her lap and gnawed at her thick nails.

"Yes, I know I'm acting erratically, but I'm sure Elize is the one who fell," Taa explained, flicking her ear back and forth nervously. "You know the one in the Oracle's prophecy."

"Prophecy?" Elize asked, lifting her head and looking at Taa. "What prophecy?"

"Fsst! I thought you were asleep," Taa fussed and tapped Elize's shoe with her oar.

"Well?"

"There is a prophecy," Taa said, pushing the canoe forward through the water.

"and?"

"And the prophecy says that the one who falls from the sky will bring a great change."

"That's it?" Elize asked, disappointed. "That's pretty vague. Did this Oracle give any hint about what kind of change?"

"No," Taa answered, "Oracle's are rarely clear. Some believe it will be a change for the good, others a change for the worse."

Elize turned her head sharply to the left. "Someone's out there," she whispered. "They're pacing us from the shore."

"There's no way you can see the shore from here," Taa whispered back, straining her eyes towards the shore.

"I can't, but I feel a presence," Elize closed her eyes and focused. "It's not human, at least I don't think so and I don't think it means us any harm. Mostly curious."

Even though Taa didn't see anyone, she sent Roz over to investigate. Roz returned a few minutes later and reported that the only life forms she found were three water birds, several frogs, various bugs, and an old brown mule.

"I guess it was the mule," Elize said with a shrug, but she wasn't convinced. She had felt something pacing them, she was certain of it. "So, what do you think the change will be?" Elize asked Taa changing the subject

Taa rubbed her chin and thought for a minute.

"Maybe a change in the weather, or a change of scenery," Elize pondered.

"Perhaps a change of attitude," Taa suggested, flashing Elize a mischievous look, "or a change of clothes."

"A change of pace, change for a dollar, or a change of hair style," Elize joked and twisted her hair on top of her head. "It's a shame the Oracle wasn't clearer."

"They rarely are," Taa replied. "I think Oracles are vague because it makes them appear more mysterious."

"And harder to prove wrong."

"True," Taa agreed. "I never thought of it that way.

Elize shifted her body slightly and wondered silently if the change could be Alzo?

"I wonder if Alzo and Ori heard the voice?" Elize said aloud. "Maybe they're headed for Milendor too."

"Perhaps," Taa said, but she doubted it. It depended on which pillar they had landed on. Ori had a better chance of survival. After all, he had the ability to shapeshift into a fox. It would be much more difficult for a human. Both Ars on the east and Spk on the west had their hazards. If Elize's brother was on Ars, he may have survived. If he was clever and agile enough to find a way down the sheer rock. But if he was on Spk he'd already be dead. Everything Taa had read about Spk described it as a dangerous environment inhabited by vicious and carnivorous flora and fauna.

Elize must have finally drifted back to sleep because she was jolted awake when the canoe rammed into a mudbank. The sun hadn't risen, but the sky was getting lighter. Taa had jumped out of the canoe and was sloshing about in the mud.

"Somethings definitely wrong," Taa fussed as she sloshed about the reddish-brown plants clogging any hope of traveling any further in the canoe. Elize climbed out and sank to her knees in the cold, brackish mud.

"Yuck!" Elize complained as she sloshed over to Taa.

"The shoreline should be up there." Taa told Elize pointing towards the round heaps of wood ahead of them. "Those lodges are usually covered with water. This is not good. I had no idea the river had receded so much."

Elize followed after Taa. Dragging one foot at a time out of the mud that sucked at her shoes like a hungry mud monster.

"Did you hear anything I said?" Taa asked Elize when they reached what had once been the shoreline. Elize shook her head she'd been too focused on her feet to pay attention to Taa. Taa shook her head and handed Elize a skin of water. Elize swished the water around her mouth trying to get the moldy taste out.

"I said that we are about to enter a small fishing village." Taa said, keeping her voice low. "The fishermen will be up by now so keep your head down and keep walking."

"Is it dangerous?"

"It wasn't the last time I passed this way, but that was years ago. Times have changed. We don't get too many of your kind passing through nowadays."

"My kind?"

"Furless," Roz buzzed in Elize's ear. Elize had the urge to smack the irritating Roz again but didn't. Roz continued to buzz around them until Taa sent her ahead to see if the way was clear.

"She does have a valid point." Taa told Elize once she was sure Roz was out of ear shot.

"About what?" Elize asked, looking over at Taa.

"About your ability to understand us. If you come from Earth as you claim, how is it that you understand us?"

"I don't know." Elize admitted. Taa snuffed. "No, I mean it. I really don't know how I do it. The words come out of your mouth in…in your language, but when they get inside my head they unravel into words I understand. Once that happens I can understand and speak in that language. Well, for the most part. There will always be slang and words that don't translate or if they do, they don't mean the same thing at all. You are easy to understand. You say what you think. Most people don't. They say something like 'I'm glad to see you.' While they are wishing you hadn't shown up at all. Or like Roz, I can catch a word or two, but most of what she says is just a lot of buzzing."

"Yes, well it took me a while to keep up with Roz when we first met." Taa admitted with a smile fascinated by Elize's explanation. She had read about Aligist, those with the ability to understand and communicate in a multitude of languages, but she had never actually met anyone with this ability.

"It's funny," Elize said more to herself than Taa. "I suddenly remember a game Payape, my father, used to play with Alzo and I. He used to sing a song, whistle, sometimes even growl or bark and Alzo and I would try to be the first to figure out the words. Alzo was better at it then I was, but he was much older. I couldn't have been more than a toddler at the time." Taa nodded politely at Elize, her mind was focused more on the present than Elize's past.

"I wonder what's keeping Roz." Taa said, scanning the air ahead of them. "She should have been back by now."

On the outskirts of the village Roz noticed a bit of paper posted on the side of one of the huts and flew down to check it out. Unaware that Roz was no longer in front of them, Taa and Elize continued into the town. They had almost reached the other side of town when two drunken goaters, half-goat, half-men trotted out in front of them. Elize kept her head low and held onto the back of Taa's cloak.

"Well, well, well," the scrawnier of the two goaters bleated shaking his long black and white goatee in Taa's face, "what sweet treat do we have here?"

"I hears deerlings buck up a storm," the other man snorted loudly, gyrating his wide, curly fur covered hips.

Taa tried to step around them. The black and white goater leapt in front of her and grabbed at her chest. Taa trod heavily on his foot and shoved him out of her way. The man yelped and hopped after her.

The curly goater yanked off Elize's hood. "Lookie what we have here!" Curly cooed, raking his grubby fingers through Elize's knotty hair. Spotting a bucket of fish bait outside a nearby hut, Elize lurched forward, grabbed the bucket, and smashed it into the goater's face. The other goater limped towards Elize, but Taa stopped him by kicking at his good leg. The goater stumbled backward, slipped on the gooey bait, and slammed into the side of the hut.

"Hey!" An old beaver tooth fisher woman yelped as she charged out of the hut to grab Curly by the scruff of his neck.

Taa and Elize took off running and didn't stop running until the town was far behind them. Once she was sure no one was coming after them, Taa stopped to let Elize catch her breath. Roz appeared above them a few minutes later.

"Where in Zot's name have you been!" Taa snapped. Roz buzzed a half-hearted apology and she handed Taa the notice she had ripped off the side of the hut.

Taa read the notice and frowned. The notice offered a reward for any information on the one who had fallen out of the sky. Word had traveled faster and further then she had expected.

"This does not excuse you abandoning your duties," Taa said curtly, tearing the notice into tiny bits and tossing them into the wind. "As a healer's assistant you have a responsibility not only to the healer, but to the patient. It is your duty to ensure your patient is well cared for and kept safe. We could have been raped by those over stimulated goaters or butchered and made into stew!"

Roz was shocked. Taa had never spoken to her so harshly. Roz thought Taa was her friend. Her best friend. They had worked side-by-side for years. Taa had no right to speak to her like an underling!

"If that's how you feel then return to the Healing Center!" Taa huffed when Roz complained. Perhaps if she hadn't been so shaken by the ordeal with the goaters Taa wouldn't have spoken to her friend so harshly. Unfortunately, by the time Taa calmed down Roz had buzzed off in a titter gathering bits of torn paper as she made her way back towards the village.

Without Roz to help her navigate, Taa was somewhat at a loss. She knew Milendor was north of the fishing village, but also to the west or to the east. Keeping the sun to her right, Taa continued to head in what she hoped was the right direction. When the trees and bushes gave way to a sea of waving grass Taa stopped.

"What's wrong?" Elize asked, noticing the look of shock on Taa's face.

"Nothing," Taa lied, pacing back and forth in front of the tall grass biting at her nails. "I just wish Roz hadn't taken off like that. She is much better at navigating than I am." Taa kicked at the grass and scoffed. "I was trying to avoid the grasslands."

"Should we go back?"

"No, I don't want to run into the goaters again. We might as well rest." Taa said, handing Elize the water skin. Taa was not happy about the situation. The last time she visited the grasslands it had not gone well.

"Is there something I should know?" Elize asked, watching Taa's face carefully.

"We should be fine." Taa said, trying to hide her anxiety. "Afterall healers are protected. It is against the law to attack a healer." Elize raised her eyebrows. "Goaters have little regard for the laws," Taa scoffed, "especially when their meager brains are agitated by excessive quantities of paca juice. Now when we enter the grasslands keep close. Tread where I tread, keep your head down and whatever you do, don't run." Taa pressed her lips together. "Oh yeah, keep your mouth shut, silence is critical."

"Who are we trying to avoid?" Elize asked not at all fooled by Taa's acting. It was clear Taa was terrified of whatever roamed the grass.

"The Bast."

"Bass? Like a fish?"

"No, like a feline." Taa replied, giving Elize a funny look. "This is bast territory and bast are extremely territorial. Like I said before, we should be fine. Healers are protected by the laws of the land so we should be able to pass unchallenged. Still, you never know. Times are hard and when times are hard laws are easily forgotten. We must be on our guard. Now remember to stay close, keep quiet, and no matter what happens don't run!"

At first, Elize had little trouble keeping up with Taa. Although stepping where Taa stepped wasn't easy. Elize's foot was almost double the size of Taa's. As they wove their way along the tight rows of grass, Elize's uneasiness grew taller than the grass that was now well over their heads.

"I don't understand it," Taa whispered, breaking her own rule. "The grass shouldn't be so brown this early in the season."

"And it smells," Elize whispered back, "like burnt hair."

"Hush," Taa shushed and sniffed the air. Elize was right the grass did smell like burnt hair.

Soon they were surrounded by thousands of tall grainy heads waving back and forth in the breeze. Scenes from horror movies drifted into Elize's mind. Elize told herself the shadows slipping through the rows of grass on either side of her was just the light playing tricks on her, but she wasn't convinced. Overcome by a sense of dread, Elize tried to catch up with Taa who was plunging ahead at a steady pace unaware that Elize had fallen behind. Quickening her pace to a poolside jog, Elize moved as fast as she could without breaking into a run. She felt something hit her shin and stumbled on to her knees. A pair of amber eyes stared at her through the dense grass. Elize slammed her fist into the grass in front of her, but the eyes and Taa were both gone. Getting to her feet Elize rushed forward and was soon lost in a sea of waving stalks.

When a black tail brushed her chin, Elize forgot everything Taa had told her and took off running. She hadn't gotten twenty steps when an orange striped paw reached out and caught her ankle.

"Taa!" Elize screamed.

CHAPTER 4

If Ilee hadn't been there to guide him, Alzo knew he would have plummeted to his death trying to get down the sheer pillar. Unlike Ilee who skittered about like a mountain goat, Alzo had more difficulty locating the barely discernible nooks and notches. More than once Ilee had to double back to help him. Each time she looked more nervous than before. She had been gone too long. Surely her absence had been noticed by now.

"This way," Ilee told Alzo when he landed on the minuscule ledge next to her. "I'm afraid it'll be a tight squeeze for you." Ilee called over her shoulder before she slipped through a gap where two slabs of identical stone crossed over each other. Alzo would have never seen it, if Ilee hadn't been there and she wasn't kidding about the tight squeeze. Alzo had to suck in his gut and force his large frame sideways between the two slabs, but once he was through, thankfully, the space opened and there was a spiraling stairway cut down the center of the tower. Each step had been hand-hewed and were of varying heights. More than once, they had to lower their bodies down one step and drop to the next. When they finally reached the bottom, Ilee poked her head out of a crack and studied the waves lapping against the rocks. It was high tide.

"We have to wait." Ilee told Alzo slapping her hand against the rocks in frustration. Another delay. She had already wasted too much time.

Alzo nodded as he studied Ilee's face. When he first saw her, he thought she was a young teen, but after spending some time with her he believed Ilee was older than she looked. He was wrong.

"I know another way," Ilee stated and rushed past Alzo.

"Where are we?" Alzo's voice boomed in the hollow alcove which acted like an amplifier. Ilee made a face and put a slender finger in front of her lips.

"We are under the main island of Palenina," she whispered.

"Palenina?" Alzo whispered back. "My Mayme was from Palenina."

Ilee turned to look at him. "That's not possible." She hissed, keeping her voice low. "No one ever leaves the islands. Not since before I was born."

"My Mayme did." Alzo said stubbornly. "She came to Astaria from the Islands of Palenina to marry the Emperor."

"The last person to leave the islands was the Priestess Euna," Ilee replied coolly, her eyes darting from side to side. "She was my mother's cousin. No one ever speaks of her. I only know of her because Hohi told me."

"Euna was my mother." Alzo told her, smiling at the shocked look she gave him. "If Hohi knew my mother, maybe she can tell me more about her."

"Perhaps," Ilee said as she stepped into a pool of blue-green water seeping through an opening in the rocks. "Follow me."

Ilee dove under the water and swam towards the bottom of the pool. Alzo dove in after her following close behind as Ilee dipped and glided through the underwater caverns running under the large island. They swam mostly underwater, only surfacing for air. The last thing Ilee wanted was to be seen. The penalty for bringing strangers to the islands was exile. Still, Ilee was confident she was doing what Hohi wished.

When they finally emerged, they were near the hidden entrance to the Hall of the Ancients. Ilee was relieved to find the hallway empty. Ilee had been sure her sister would have noticed she was gone by now. Grabbing a handful of dried driftwood she kept by the door to the altar room, Ilee pulled open the door. Her sister, Shi was waiting inside. Ilee tried to push Alzo back, but it was too late. Shi had seen him. Before Ilee could stop her, Shi shot past them and up the steps.

"Quick get inside!" Ilee shouted, dragging Alzo into the altar room and bolting the door behind her. Ilee knew she had to act fast. Carefully arranging the driftwood onto the fire Ilee gently blew on the coals. As coals burst into flames and licked at the driftwood, the faded voice of an elderly woman flowed into Alzo's head.

"Grab Ilee and jump into the flames!" Hohi shouted inside Alzo's head.

The sound of many feet erupted outside the door followed by angry shouts and fists pounding on the bolted door. Alzo looked over at Ilee who stood frozen beside him. As the door splintered, the voice shouted inside his head again.

Without hesitation, Alzo grabbed Ilee and jumped into the flame splitting the altar stone in two. When Shi and the other Priestesses of Hohi broke through the door they found the altar room empty and the eternal fire extinguished.

"What have you done!" Ilee screamed as she and Alzo slid down the volcanic flume chased by the horrified screams of the priestesses above them.

* * * * * * *

Even though Ori's fox senses were keener than his human ones, after wasting most of the afternoon running up and down the shoreline he still hadn't found Elize's body or any evidence of her coming ashore. Discouraged and downhearted, Ori plopped under a large maple tree to sulk. Above him several birds chirped excitedly. Knowing wrens loved to gossip, Ori craned his ears and listened. The male wren was telling his mate about a family of otters floating something large downstream. The wren didn't know what it was, but he was sure it was alive.

His hope renewed, Ori left the tree and headed for the Crossroads Inn. The Inn was several miles to the west, but if the otters had rescued Elize, they would take her to the closest Healing Center, which was located at the Crossroads Inn.

Energized by the hope that Elize was still alive, Ori made good time, but it was after sunset when he reached the road. Taking advantage of the dark, Ori risked running along the side of the cobbled road. He had almost reached the inn when he heard boots on the road ahead and barely had time to jump into a patch of thorn bushes before two heavy set men stumbled into view.

"What the hell are bulimon doing here?" Ori mumbled watching the two men weaving back and forth across the cobbles. Bulimon were paid mercenaries hired by the Empire of Astaria to do their dirty work. Although bulimon claimed to be descendants of the minotaur, there was no proof to that claim. Unlike the mighty minotaur of Greek Mythology, the bulimon's massive skulls had no horns and they did not feast on the flesh of virgins.

"I heard she had the wings of an angel," the stouter of the two bulimon slurred loudly as he lifted his muscular arms and flapped them in the air, "just like an angel."

"How come she fell then?" The other bulimon challenged. "If she had wings, why didn't she use them?"

"Maybe she was hurt," the stout man stammered, rubbing his bristly chin.

"Who told ya such shat anyhow?"

"Ren, he says he heard it from a raven."

"You dumb jork! You know you can't believe nothing the ravens say!"

"Ren said she had the wings of an angel." The stout bulimon mumbled dreamily, flapping his arms again.

"There you go with that angel crap again." The other man groaned, glancing over his shoulder. "Speaking of Ren. Where's that bastard got to now?"

"I's here," a garbled voice grumbled a few inches behind Ori's left ear.

Ori winced silently as the barbs poked through his thick sandy fur and slipped further into the briars to avoid being pissed on. When Ren finished relieving himself, he stumbled over to the others. It was clear from the racket they were making, the three bulimon had been drinking heavily for some time. When Ren stubbed his toe on the cobbles and tumbled face first onto the road, Ori pulled himself from the briars and snuck behind a large rubbish heap.

"Strange," Ori thought as the stench from the heap made his eyes water. "I don't remember this being here."

"Git up!" the big bulimon snapped at the fallen Ren. Ren groaned but didn't move. The big bulimon grabbed the downed Ren with his hairy knuckled fist and lifted him off the ground. "If we're not back to camp soon there'll be blood to pay. Yours!" He yelled, tossing Ren roughly over his shoulder and stomping off. Neither he nor Ren noticed the coins slip out of Ren's pocket and bounce into the nooks between the cobbles. Ori waited until the bulimon was well down the road before jumping out from behind the heap.

Shifting into his human form Ori plucked up the coins and held them in the moonlight. They didn't amount to much, but that didn't bother him. Ori placed the coins between the fingers on his right hand and began to sing. The coins danced from one finger to the next. With his left hand he scooped up a handful of pebbles about the same size as the coins. Singing in a voice softer than the breeze, Ori moved the pebbles and the coins from one hand to the next. The pebbles soon took on the shape and color of the coins. Satisfied with his work, Ori stuffed the lot into his pocket and headed for the inn, totally unaware that the rubbish heap had been watching with wide curious eyes.

"I'm closed," the innkeeper growled when Ori pushed open the door.

"I know it's late," Ori moaned wearily hugging the doorframe and trying to look as wretched as possible, "I would have come in sooner, but I saw the bulimon and I was afraid."

The innkeeper continued to rub the bar with a musty brown rag as he studied the stranger's face. "What brings you to this shat hole anyway?" He growled.

"I need a healer." Ori mumbled, still hugging the door frame.

"Ain't been a healer around these parts for ages," the innkeeper snarled as he gave Ori the once over. "Like I told that lot, the closest Healing Center is Qym, but you're in no shape to be heading there so you might as well take a seat."

The innkeeper motioned at the stool in front of him. As Ori limped towards the stool he almost ran into the small boy who slipped past him to throw the latch on the door.

The innkeeper filled a small clay mug with mead and thrust it in Ori's direction. Ori wrapped his fingers around the mug and took a tentative sip. It was thick and brown and delicious.

"Why were the bulimon looking for a healer?" Ori asked, setting the mug on the bar.

"They wasn't," the boy piped, jumping onto the stool next to Ori. "They was looking fer the one who fell from the sky. You know the one the owl ladies foretold."

Ori took another swig. So that's what those guys were going on about. They were talking about Elize. The thought of Elize fulfilling the prophecy almost made him laugh, but it also worried him. Ori tossed a few coins on the counter, ordered another mug of mead and a bowl of brown stew. He noticed that the innkeeper poured his new mug from a jug hidden under the counter and not from the jug he kept on the bar.

"We don't get many paying guests," the innkeeper commented over his shoulder as he filled a wooden bowl with brown slop. The truth was there hadn't been a paying guest for quite a long while. The few coins he'd had in the bin had been taken by the bulimon when they forced their way into the inn that afternoon. The innkeeper was glad to have a few of the coins back and wondered how many more this little fellow had in his pockets.

"What brings you to this forsaken place?" The innkeeper asked casually while Ori ate his stew. Ori chewed at the huge lump of tough turnip longer than he needed so he could think up a plausible answer.

"I'm looking for my ass," he replied glibly and gave the boy a wink before continuing. "He wandered off a few days ago and I followed him to the road before losing his trail. You haven't perhaps seen him? He's a brown mule, about so tall with white splotches and a swayed back."

"I've seen him," the boy chimed in before his father could stop him. "We tried to catch him, but he was too darn smart. Weren't he Da?"

The innkeeper shrugged. He doubted the mule's wits had anything to do with it. He hadn't told his son, but he was sure the mule had changed itself into a raven and flown away. Which would mean the mule knew magic and if that were the case…

"What'd you say your name was?" The innkeeper asked refilling Ori's mug from the jug underneath the bar.

"I didn't," Ori replied, keeping a wary eye on the older man.

"My boy here says he saw a fox hiding behind the trash heap." The innkeeper sneered leaning forward on his meaty forearms. "He says he saw the fox shift into a man."

The hair rose on the back of Ori's neck as he continued to eat his stew. The innkeeper leaned closer.

"The bulimon weren't just looking for a woman," the innkeeper told Ori menacingly. "They were looking for a vanji too. Seems he pissed off the Emperor's bastard brother."

Ori lifted his mug up to his lips and began to sing softly to the ale.

"We'll have none of your mumbo jumbo!" The innkeeper shouted, snatching the jug off the bar and swinging it at Ori's head. Ori flung the dark mead into the innkeeper's face at the exact instant the innkeeper swung the heavy brown jug at Ori's head. Rolling off his stool, Ori kicked out the stool next to him sending the boy tumbling across the grimy floor. Ori knew he couldn't get to the door and unbolt it before the innkeeper and his son caught up with him. So, instead of running, Ori slumped to the ground and laid perfectly still. Believing he had knocked Ori out cold with the jug, the innkeeper walked over and kicked him sharply in the side.

"Not that! Get the rope boy!" The innkeeper shouted at his son who had ducked behind the bar to fetch a small cage. "That ain't going to hold him." Disappointed that Ori hadn't shifted into a fox, the boy dropped the cage and grabbed some rope.

"Should I go fetch the bulimon Da?" The boy asked eagerly. The innkeeper shook his head and spat.

"Hah! Those bastards would beat us to a pulp and rob us of the prize."

"Then what're we going to do Da? Take him to the Emperor ourselves?"

"Don't be daft boy," his father snapped as he wrapped the rough rope around Ori's wrist and ankles. "Here take his feet," he ordered his son as he lifted Ori's head and shoulders from the floor. The boy grabbed Ori's feet and together they hauled Ori outside, dumping him in the old shed behind the inn and locking him inside.

"He should sleep like the dead until the traders arrive." Ori heard the innkeeper tell the boy as they walked away. The innkeeper knew he was taking a risk keeping Ori alive, but also knew that he would get a better price for him alive than dead. He just hoped the trader barge would arrive on schedule. He didn't want to risk keeping the vanji any longer than a day or two. If Ori had been seen heading towards the inn, the bulimon would surely return and tear the place apart.

As soon as the shed door slammed shut Ori shifted into his fox body and began to gnaw through the thick, nasty tasting rope. He could hardly believe his little trick had worked. He was sure the innkeeper would have noticed he hadn't actually drunk the last two mugs of ale. Ori had barely finished freeing himself from the ropes when his sharp ears picked up the soft sound of footsteps. Sniffing along the thick wooden walls, it wasn't long before Ori found the boy's scent. The damn boy must have snuck back to keep watch. Ori shifted back into a human and leaning against the wall, began to sing, ever so softly of warm beds and pretty maidens and mounds of sugary treats. Soon the boy was snoring, Ori shifted back into a fox and scratched a hole underneath the back of the shed just big enough for him to crawl through.

"Hah!" the boy shouted, grabbing at Ori's bushy tail. "Tricked ya!"

Startled Ori swung around and sunk his needle-sharp teeth into the boy's thumb. The boy yelped and let go of Ori's tail. Ori raced towards the rubbish heap with the boy hot on his heels. Having no other choice, but to fight. Ori shifted back into a man and faced the wretched boy. The boy skidded to a stop, his eyes wide with fear.

"Da! Da!" The boy screeched and turned tail as a huge, rubbery, gray hand swung out of the rubbish heap and walloped Ori upside the head.

Later, the innkeeper's son would take great pride in telling the story of how the vanji had cast a spell on the rubbish heap and turned it into a monster. The monster grew larger and more furious each time he told it.

Truth was Ori didn't have anything to do with the rubbish heap coming alive. Changing stones into coins and making ale evaporate was small magic. Animating a rubbish heap was way out of Ori's league. As it turned out the rubbish heap wasn't a rubbish heap at all, but a downhearted swamp troll named Mukrot.

After being chased out of the swamp by his older brothers, Mukrot had wandered about doing his best to avoid the strange creatures he encountered out in the dry lands. Lost and hungry Mukrot had literally stumbled onto the large trash heap behind the inn. He had been hiding in the rubbish, sulking and binge eating rotting food for days. Whenever he saw the boy coming out of the inn with more trash, Mukrot squatted and tucked his head between his legs. The boy never expected that an eight-foot, four hundred-pound swamp troll was living in his garbage heap.

Born the seventh son of a seventh son, Mukrot's birth should have been a blessed event. It wasn't. Mukrot was a runt compared to his brothers, coddled by his mum, and prone to whining. The only reason his father hadn't killed him was because killing the seventh son of a seventh son would bring a curse on the entire clan. His father wasn't the only one that hated Mukrot, his older brothers despised him too, especially his eldest brother Zut. As the eldest son of the Grand Oup, Zut would have succeeded his father as ruler of the swamp. Then Mukrot was born. As the seventh son, Mukrot would succeed his father as ruler. It infuriated Zut to no end that his wimpy brother outranked him. From the moment Mukrot was born, his brother Zut's main mission in life was to make every second of Mukrot's life a living hell. If it wasn't for his mum, Mukrot would have surely died from despair. Just when it seemed things couldn't possibly get any worse the rains stopped. At first it wasn't a big deal, but after three seasons with hardly a spattering of rain the swamp began to dry up.

Mukrot knew something bad was going to happen when his father called an emergency assembly. With a whole lot of pomp and ceremony, the Grand Oup informed the assembly that the food supplies were almost depleted. Their only hope was for their future leader, Mukrot, to leave the swamp and bring back food. Poor Mukrot had never put a toe out of the swamp and had no desire to, but Zut and his other brothers left him no choice. They chased Mukrot out of the swamp and told him not to dare come back without food.

Mukrot had pretty much given up any hope of returning to the swamp when the fox ran out from behind the briars and hid behind his left thigh. When the fox shifted into a man Mukrot had been so surprised he almost jumped out of his skin. He had watched in wonder as Ori sang to the pebbles turning them into coins. Mukrot had never seen such magic before. If only he could do that! He'd be able to make many coins and buy wagons full of food for the swamp trolls. Mukrot could almost hear them cheering and calling him a hero! Unfortunately, Mukrot's daydream was smashed to pieces when the innkeeper and his son carried Ori out of the inn and locked him in the shed.

Mukrot had been watching the boy since he had arrived at the rubbish heap and had seen the way the innkeeper's son treated the poor dogs who lingered by the heap searching for scraps of food. The boy seemed to enjoy hurting those smaller than himself. Even though Mukrot was over four times as big as the boy, he decided it'd be best to stay where he was and see what happened. Surely the little magic man would be able to get the better of the boy.

Mukrot had almost dozed off when the boy yelped. He barely had time to think before the fox ran in front of him. Frightened by the sudden movement Mukrot rose to his feet. When the boy yelled and ran to get his da, Mukrot panicked. Fearing the boy and his father would come out of the inn any second, Mukrot grabbed Ori and stuffed him in a large sack. Unfortunately, Mukrot grabbed Ori a bit too hard and knocked him out cold. Poor Ori had no idea what hit him.

Elize on the other hand, knew exactly what hit her. It was a four and a half foot orange striped cat.

"Get off," Elize shouted at the cat who sat on her belly with his striped paws pressed firmly down on her shoulders. The orange cat wrinkled his nose and sniffed Elize. "I said get off!" Elize shoved the cat's fluffy chest with the flat of her hands. He didn't budge. Frustrated Elize swung her legs around the cat's middle and put him into a scissor hold. Just as she hoped the move caught the cat by surprise and she was able to flip him on his back.

46

"Yowl!" The cat grunted and grinned up at Elize who was now sitting on his chest pushing down on his shoulders. The cat arched his torso and tried to toss her off.

"Ha!" Elize shouted triumphantly forcing him back down. The marmalade cat hissed at her playfully. Elize pressed down harder on his shoulders and stuck her tongue at him. The orange cat smiled and winked at her.

Four very sharp claws pressed into the center of Elize's throat. Slowly backing off the orange striped cat, Elize got a sideways glance at the sleek black cat whose paw was now attached to her neck. The cat growled menacingly at Elize warning her not to try to escape.

"Mia!" Taa shouted charging through the tall reeds, "let her go!"

Mia growled deep in her throat, swishing her tail so violently that a wave of dust plumed up behind her. Instead of letting her go, Mia pressed her claws deeper into Elize's throat. Taa pawed the ground in front of her and flared her nostrils.

"I said let her go," Taa repeated, emphasizing each syllable as she stared down at the smaller animal. Mia didn't move. Taa stepped closer. "Release her at once. You know the penalty for attacking a healer." Elize had no idea what the penalty was for attacking a healer, but she hoped to God it was severe.

"What's going on?" Elize demanded.

"You ran," Taa replied, not taking her eyes off Mia. "I warned you not to run!"

"Yeah, but you failed to mention the grass was full of killer cat people."

"Well...bast are not actually cats, although they are from the feline genus, they are..." Taa stopped when Mia let out a series of growls that sounded like someone killing a bagpipe. "You'll do nothing of the kind." Taa snapped and took a step towards them.

Mia growled again and ran her claws across Elize's flesh. Elize had dealt with feral cats before, but none as fierce as Mia. Every muscle in Mia's well-toned body was tensed for action. Elize sensed a history between Mia and Taa and had the feeling that she was just a pawn in a very dangerous game she didn't understand. It wasn't the first or the last time Elize would feel like this.

"Let her go!" Taa huffed, stamping her hoof so close to Mia's hind paw that Mia flinched. Mia's luminous yellow-green eyes flashed dangerously.

Taa refused to be intimidated. "Now!"

"No!" Mia hissed, baring her fangs.

"You know the penalty for harming a healer."

Mia reached out and yanked the hood off Elize's head. "Not healer!" Mia growled, "furless!"

"Elize is under my care," Taa countered, bowing her shoulders defensively, "I will not allow any harm to come to her. I demand to speak to Scat." Taa stomped her hoof again this time making contact. When Mia jumped back, Elize pulled free and scurried behind Taa.

"Who's Scat?" Elize whispered, rubbing her neck and checking her fingers for blood, "and why is Mia so mad?"

"Scat is the Leader of the Grassland Bast. The Bast are extremely territorial. This is their territory, and you are a trespasser. The penalty for trespassing is usually death."

"What? But you said healers were protected."

"Healers are but..."

"Not Furless." Mia hissed reaching for Elize's arm. Elize swatted Mia's paw away. Mia hissed again and flatten her ears against her head.

"I think it might be best if you didn't antagonize her." Taa warned Elize.

Mia pulled a piece of rope from the mouse leather belt looped over her shoulder and fastened around her waist. The belt was well equipped with small throwing knives, razor sharp stars and bee size darts coated in a sap strong enough to paralyze an elephant.

"We go." Mia snarled eyes flickering like hot ambers waiting for Taa to challenge her.

"We go where?" Elize asked, not liking the look in Mia's eyes.

"Mia has agreed to take you to see her father, but she insists on binding your hands."

"Gerawld," Mia shouted, tossing the rope at the orange striped cat. Elize was glad Gerawld was going to tie her hands instead of Mia. She liked Gerawld. He reminded her of the stray cat she had snuck into the dorms at the Catholic school she lived in as a kid. Looking back, Elize was pretty sure Sister Mary Agnes knew about the cat, but never let on. That cat had been the first real friend Elize had made at the school. She had cried and cried the morning they found him in the parking lot with his legs sticking up in the air. It had broken Elize's heart.

Gerawld gave Elize an exaggerated wink. Elize winked back and held her hands out. Gerawld leaned forward to loop the rope around Elize's wrists. Elize took a small step back. Gerawld growled deep in his throat. Elize stepped forward. Gerawld whipped his striped tail around and tapped her on the shoulder. Elize moved one step to the right. Gerawld growled again. Elize hopped back. They continued this little game several more times until Mia hissed.

The One Who Fell

"Grrrrawld!"

Gerawld looked innocently at his sister as he wrapped the rope snuggly around Elize's wrists. Mia rolled her eyes.

"Did you say this guy Scat is Mia's father?" Elize asked Taa.

"Yes." Taa huffed, clearly unhappy about the situation. "As I said before, Scat is the Leader of the Grassland Bast. He will hear our case and decide your fate."

"Should I be worried?"

"Yes," Mia snapped, taking hold of the bit of rope Gerawld had looped between the middle of her wrists and giving it a good tug.

"You've got to be joking." Elize scoffed. Although she probably could have easily broken the rope and made a run for it, Elize knew it'd be senseless. Who knew how many more bast cats were lurking out in the grass? So, for now Elize allowed Mia to lead her around like a rogue dog. At least Mia hadn't strung her between two poles and carried her into the village like they did in old Tarzan movies.

CHAPTER 5

Alzo and Ilee splashed butt first into the warm waters of the Ishad. The Ishad is the only ocean on Toboria although it is divided into two distinct bodies of water. The East Ishad's waters are bright aqua blue while the West Ishad's waters turn a deep purple when the algae blooms in the summer. The waters of the East and West Ishad meet between Palenina's two major islands which separate the male population from the female. When the waters of the West Ishad turn deep purple all the islanders of mating age gather for a fertility ceremony. Fertility ceremonies are grand celebrations, with days and nights filled with drinking, dancing, and sex. In the past Ilee had watched the ceremonies with the other girls from palm covered rooftops. This year Ilee was old enough to participate. Unlike her older sister Shi, Ilee dreaded the upcoming ceremony, especially after she learned who had been selected to be her mate.

Ilee glanced over at Alzo swimming alongside her. If he had been selected to be her mate she would have felt much differently about the ceremony. Alzo was muscular and a strong swimmer. He had been on the swim team in high school and later in college and he had excelled in that sport almost as well as he had in football and baseball.

As before they swam under water, surfacing only to take fresh air. The purple water was warm and reminded Alzo of Susan's lavender baths. He was wondering if he would ever see Susan again when his knees scraped against the pebbly shore.

"Why did you do that? Ilee sputtered as they stumbled onto the shore of an almost non-existent island.

"What?"

"You destroyed Hohi's altar!" Ilee sobbed, stomping ahead with her hands balled into fists. "You extinguish the eternal fire! Do you have any idea what you've done?"

"I rescued you," Alzo replied not understanding why Ilee was so upset. "Hohi spoke to me. She told me to grab you and jump into the fire. That's what I did."

"Hohi spoke to you?" Ilee gasped, not sure what to think. The ground trembled slightly under their feet. "See what you've done!" Ilee sobbed.

"What was I supposed to do? Let them capture us?"

"No." Ilee said freeing a small boat from a pile of driftwood and making sure it would float. "That would not have been good." Ilee glanced back towards the big island expecting to see long boats. She didn't see any, but she was sure they were out there. After looking through the bits of driftwood for oars and not finding any, Ilee and Alzo boarded the small boat and began to row using their hands.

After hours of taking turns rowing the boat across the ocean, Ilee finally steered the boat into an inlet. Exhausted they laid on their backs and rested while the strong current carried them down the inlet. When they woke, the small boat was stuck in a tangle of twisted roots.

"They look like Mangrove trees." Alzo told Ilee, slapping his hand against the roots of the low dense bushes. He smiled as the memory of passing miles of mangrove trees on the way to Key West one very cold winter day years ago. He had just met Susan and during winter break they decided to go in search of the sun. They found it in all its shining glory dipping down into the Gulf of Mexico one evening while drinking Margaritas at Mallory Square.

"Ditch the boat," Alzo told Ilee, who was trying to force the canoe through the roots. Ilee grunted and let the boat go.

"Which way to Milendor?" He asked, slapping at hundreds of tiny gnats encircling his head like a dirty halo. Ilee shrugged. She had never ventured this far from the island before.

"Perhaps the bilee will know." Ilee suggested. Lifting her head Ilee began to warble. When she didn't get a reply she warbled again in a different pitch. A bright orange bird with a long yellow bill poked her head out from the mangroves and warbled back.

"This way," Ilee smiled, slipping through the maze of roots with the grace and ease of a ballet dancer. Alzo followed stomping behind her like a rhino putting out a fire.

Although she tried not to show it, Alzo knew Ilee was upset. "You don't have to come with me if you don't want to." Alzo said, reaching out to put his hand on her shoulder. "If you want to return to your people, I totally understand."

"No, no you don't," Ilee said without looking at him. "If you understood, you'd know that I can never return to my people. Not after what I've done."

"What? You helped a stranger? What's the crime in that?"

Ilee faced Alzo with watery eyes. How could he not know? "I have betrayed...I...I... have angered the Ancients...I left the eternal fire unattended. I brought a stranger into the sacred room...a male stranger...the altar is destroyed...Elenomnu will awake, and it is my fault. I have brought great trouble to the islands."

"Nah," Alzo said, shaking his head. "I don't believe that for a moment. Do you still believe that Hohi sent you to find me?" Ilee nodded. "I'm pretty sure it was Hohi who told me to grab you and jump into the flames. So, it seems to me that you are doing what these ancients want you to do. Have you ever thought maybe you're not the one they're angry at?"

Ilee had never even considered the ancients could be angry at anyone but her. Dumbfounded she continued making her way forward without answering.

They walked most of the night and well into the next day. Alzo found it curious and disturbing that they didn't see a soul along the way. Thirsty, hungry, and barely able to put one foot in front of the other they finally stumbled into an abandoned village.

"Something terrible happened here?" Ilee whispered, stepping over a charred beam.

"Definitely," Alzo agreed, cringing as he passed an animal pen filled with burnt carcasses.

"I don't like this place," Ilee shivered at his elbow.

"I don't like it either," Alzo said as they walked silently, hand-in-hand past the burnt-out homes and shops. In the center of the village was a stone well. Alzo motioned for Ilee to stay put while he went over to check it out. He was disappointed to find the well full of rocks.

"Help me get these out." Alzo called over to Ilee. Ilee came over and together they began to remove the rocks. They had cleared about a foot of rocks when the hit a board. After clearing off the remaining rocks, Alzo lifted the board off and peered into the well.

"I think there's water down there, but I don't see a bucket," Alzo told Ilee, sticking his head so far into the well that Ilee grabbed his shoulders to keep him from tumbling in. A pinched brown face poked out of the well wall below Alzo.

"Hey!" Alzo shouted, jerking his head out of the well.

"What was it?" Ilee exclaimed, peering cautiously into the well, but not seeing anything.

"A brownie. I think."

"A brownie!" Ilee exclaimed gleefully, clapping her hands. "Here, take this," she said, slipping the bracelet from her wrist and handing it to Alzo. "Little folk can't resist shiny things."

"Are you sure?" Alzo asked as he held the delicate silver thread with a single natural pearl in the center between his thumb and forefinger. Ilee nodded firmly. The bracelet meant nothing to her. She was glad to be rid of it. Alzo carefully swung the bracelet back and forth along the inside of the well. After several passes a small hairy hand jotted out of the stone.

"Not so fast!" Alzo snapped quickly jerking the bracelet out of the brownie's reach. "Give us a bucket first." The hand retreated and Alzo heard muffled voices behind the wall. A few minutes later the hand reappeared holding a wooden bucket with a rope tied to the handle. Alzo reached for it, but before he could take the rope, the bucket disappeared and was replaced by the hairy hand. After several tries the exchange finally took place and Alzo hauled up a bucket filled with clear, cool water.

"Any chance of some food?" Alzo yelled into the well after refilling the tiny bucket several times.

The hand reappeared snapping. Alzo glanced back at Ilee, but she had already sacrificed one of her few belongings. Searching his pockets, Alzo found a few coins but doubted they would get them much. Slipping off his watch, Alzo held it over the top of the well. The hand retreated and the pinched brown face appeared peering up at the ticking watch with lustful eyes.

"You would break your betrothal for food?" Ilee whispered, placing her hand on Alzo's arm and looking longingly into his eyes. Alzo flinched. He started to tell Ilee he wasn't betrothed to anyone, but as he looked into Ilee's eyes he realized that the truth would only confuse her. Besides in a way the watch had been kind of a betrothal gift. Susan had given it to him when they moved in together. At the time he hadn't considered the watch as a commitment of any kind but later he realized just what the watch meant. The day he left he had promised Susan he'd be back for breakfast. Susan had set the alarm on his watch so he wouldn't forget. The alarm had never gone off and the promise had not been kept.

"Getting food is more important," Alzo told her as he exchanged the watch for a bucket of bread, nuts and berries. Ilee blushed and fluttered her eyes, but Alzo was too busy eating to notice.

"You never told me what you were doing up on the pillar," Ilee stated as she helped herself to a handful of orange berries.

"I was showing my sister where our mother brought us through a passageway, but something went wrong, and we didn't come out where I thought we would."

"I saw no sister," Ilee commented, "only you."

"Elize came out after I did." Alzo explained fighting down the lump forming in his throat. "I tried to warn her, but she tripped over me and fell. There was nothing I could do to help her. She disappeared into the clouds and was gone in the blink of an eye."

"Your sister's the one who fell?!" The brownie exclaimed as he crawled out of his hiding place and climbed up on the well wall to get a better look at Alzo.

"Yeah," Alzo replied. From the looks on Ilee and the brownie's faces he was sure he was missing something.

"Alzo your sister must be the one the Oracle spoke of!" Ilee whispered in awe. "And she brought you with her!"

"He is BIG." The brownie scoffed eyeing Alzo suspiciously. "But that don't mean the prophecy is about him."

"What prophecy?" Alzo demanded.

"THE PROPHECY!" The brownie spat, tilting his head back as far as it would go so he could look Alzo in the eye. "Don't tell me you never heard of the Prophecy!"

Alzo shrugged and shook his head.

Ilee took a deep breath and recited. "The one who falls from the sky will bring great change."

"That's it?" Alzo scoffed. The only thing keeping him from bursting out laughing was the dead serious looks on their faces. "Look...uh."

"Knot."

"Look Knot," Alzo addressed the brownie. "I seriously doubt this prophecy concerns Elize and I. We're hardly the savior types."

Knot glanced over his shoulder as a brown lark landed in the tree behind them. "We'd better finish our talk down below." He whispered and jumped into the well. "Follow me and bring the bucket."

Ilee easily lowered her lithe frame into the well. Alzo's frame was almost double hers, and he had more difficulty. Luckily there was slimy mold covering the inside of the well which acted like lubricant and with Knot and Ilee pulling on his ankles Alzo was able to slip into the well without getting stuck. Of course, they had to remove a large patch in the well wall to get Alzo inside, but many hands make a large job doable.

"Welcome to Kuyu," Knot announced when Alzo had made it inside. Knot led Alzo forward while a team of brownies quickly repaired the large hole in the well wall and replaced the board and rock covering. "Mind your head, we just washed the ceilings."

Alzo had to swat and wobbled like a stout duck behind Knot and Ilee until they reached the end of the passageway and entered a vast cavern.

"Wow!" Alzo whistled relieved to finally be able to stand upright. He stared about him in amazement as they entered the subterranean metropolis carved out of the pockmarked volcanic rock running for miles underneath the hills above.

"Mind your step." Knot yelled up at Alzo as they walked down a highway lined with rows of multi-tiered dwellings. Each dwelling was illuminated by an array of multicolored glow worms which the brownies lured into intricate designs by painting the walls with paint made from dyed sweet sap. While the translucent glow worms fed on the sap the designs shone with neon-like brilliance. As they continued down the main street, Alzo noticed startled faces peeking out of round windows and doorways. Knot ignored them, keeping a brisk pace until they entered a wide, open room with rows of long, low tables.

"We don't have a chair big enough to hold him," a plump woman dressed in brown scowled at Alzo disapprovingly.

"That's okay," Alzo said, and sat on the floor at the end of the nearest table. Ilee and Knot took a seat on either side of him. A young, human girl with matted hair wearing a dress two sizes too small approached with a tray.

"Hello," Ilee greeted the girl. The girl blinked and clutched the tray tighter.

"Don't take it to heart, girlie." Knot explained after the girl had put the tray on the table and rushed off. "The last time Avie saw folks like you they were burning her village down."

"Is that why she's down here?" Alzo asked watching two boys shoving each other trying to get a better look at the strangers.

"Ya, it ain't safe up above." Knot said taking a hard biscuit and dunking it into a bowl.

"Why?" Ilee asked, wrinkling her nose at the strange glop in her bowl. It looked and smelled very different from the food she was used to eating on the island.

"Cause of the bulimon," Knot spat sourly. "If the children lived above the bulimon would snatch them up before you could say sabersabersot."

"Bulimon?" Alzo asked, unfamiliar with the term. Knot gave Alzo a hard look.

"Yeah Bulimon!" Knot barked using his sleeve to wipe a gray blob off his chin. "The heartless bastards the Emperor sends to fetch his tariffs."

"The Emperor? The Emperor of Astaria? My fa…" Alzo bit his tongue, better to keep some things to himself. "I find it hard to believe Emperor Taz would send thugs to extort taxes from the villages. The farms of the Freedlands generate more than enough money to run the Empire."

"I don't know what planet you fell off of," Knot fumed, squinting a sharp black eye at Alzo. "but Emperor Taz hasn't been in charge of the Empire since Empress Euna disappeared with their little ones."

"What?"

"Emperor Taz is batshit crazy!" Knot shouted slamming his spoon handle on the table. "After the damn giants blocked the river, the water to irrigate the fields died up as well. The lack of water devastated the lush farms of the Freedlands. When the proud Freedlander's got fed up with giving what little they could grow to the empire while their little ones went hungry, they left. It's no wonder. Better to start over then starve so those inside the palace walls could feast and dance. The Emperor tried to stop them by having the third wall built and when that didn't stop the exodus, he built the fourth wall. When that didn't work, the bulimon were sent to go fetch the Freelanders back."

"I can't believe Emperor Taz would…"

"Emperor Taz wouldn't but his bastard brother Behr would and did." Knot shot back wondering just who he had let into the underground. "What'd you say your name was?"

"I didn't," Alzo replied, plucking a bit of porridge off his beard. "I don't understand how the bastard became Emperor. Bastards have no rights…"

"Well…" Knot said, pulling at his chin, "I guess Taz is technically still the Emperor, but before he lost all his marbles, he named Behr his regent."

"What about Gran…Grumbul, surely the rule would have reverted back to the Emperor's father before it went to a bastard."

"True," Knot agreed, "but after Emperor Taz had his father and mother expelled from the palace, I doubt Grumbul would come back even if Emperor Taz begged him."

"What? Why?"

"How in blats name do I know!" Knot sputtered glaring up at Alzo. "All I know is what I hear, and I hear he kicked them all out! Sent them to the Elderwyld. Well…not the Mage. Mal managed to escape before they could toss him out."

Ilee poked at the lumpy grayish glop. She was hungry, and didn't want to appear ungrateful, but she found little satisfaction in the tasteless porridge. Setting her spoon down, she looked over at Knot.

"I don't understand why the bulimon attacked this village? Isn't this village well outside of the walls of the Empire?"

"Like I said, the bulimon are heartless bastards. They don't give a rat's ass about boundary lines. If they come upon a village, they pillage it. That's what happened here. The bulimon thundered in demanding food and coins. The village had none of either to spare. When they refused to pay, the coldhearted bastards slaughtered the men and raped the women. The women who survived were hauled off with any children strong enough to work. The babies were left to starve." Knot sniffed and wiped his eyes on his sleeve. "The villagers were always kind to us, leaving bowls of milk on their windowsills at night. We returned their kindness by bringing the babies down here. The bulimon won't come underground. They are a superstitious lot. Afraid of ghosties and demons."

Ilee got up from the table and went over to a group of small girls who had been staring at her. Taking a seat in the middle of them, Ilee started to sing of ocean breezes and sunshine.

"How many villages have been attacked like this?" Alzo asked disturbed by this news. He had been twelve when he left Astaria, but he still remembered the vast farms encircling the shops inside the inner walls. It seemed impossible that the farms had all been abandoned. It seemed impossible that the Emperor he remembered would hire thugs to extort his people.

"The bulimon have terrorized more towns and villages than I have fingers and toes to count." Knot answered, wiggling his hairy fingers and toes at Alzo.

"Why don't the villagers band together and fight? Surely the land that is rightfully theirs is worth fighting for!"

"True, true." Knot sniffed, pulling Ilee's bowl over and dipping his spoon in it. "The folk have the heart. What they need is someone to lead them." Knot looked over at Alzo and raised his spoon. "What'd you say your name was?"

"Alzo," Alzo replied. Knot licked his spoon and nodded.

"I thought that might be it," Knot said leaning back in his chair, his black eyes glinting mischievously.

* * * * * * * *

"You idiot! You ran the wrong way!" A gravelly voice shouted waking Ori from the bad dream he was having.

"It's not my fault," a second voice whined, "I didn't know. I just ran."

Ori groaned and rolled over, clamping his hands over his ears. His head felt like it had been smacked with a two-by-four. Forcing his eyes open, Ori groggily looked around. Everything was brown. Ori blinked his eyes several times. Everything was still brown.

"Zut's right," a third, gruffy voice boomed from outside the brownness, "seventh son or not Mukrot is not fit to be Grand Oup! How can Mukrot rule the swamp trolls when Mukrot can't even feed them?"

Covering his ears did little to block out the loud arguing coming from the next room. Ori banged his fists against the brown wall, his fists sunk into the wall. Ori pushed at the brown material several times before he realized that he was inside a sack. Scratching the large bump on his forehead Ori racked his aching brain and tried to recall the events of the previous evening.

He vaguely remembered going into a tavern and a rubbish heap coming alive, but his brain was too foggy to make any sense of it. Eager to get a better idea of his situation, Ori slipped his pocketknife out and cut a slit down the side of the bag. Cautiously poking his head out of the bag, Ori was surprised to find the rubbish heap sitting a few feet away from him on top of a fallen tree trunk. In the daylight, it was clear that the rubbish heap wasn't a rubbish heap at all. Keeping his head hidden in the folds of the sack, Ori studied the very large, rubbery, gray skinned swamp troll.

"Mukrot not want to be Grand Oup," the swamp troll wailed, "I just want to be left alone. Let Zut be the Grand Oup!"

"Zut can't be Grand Oup!" Growled the gruffy voice. "Not while you are still alive. Mukrot knows that!"

Ori poked his head further out of the sack and searched for the second voice, but as far as he could tell there was no one else around.

"Tell the others I'm dead." Mukrot replied defiantly. "The little magic man will make coins so I can buy a new swamp and disappear!"

"Hah!" The first voice, which Ori guessed was Zut, boomed. "You goofball! Why would the little magic man help you! You smashed him upside the head!"

Intrigued Ori eased out of the bag.

"Mukrot did not mean to hurt little man," Mukrot sobbed burying his head into his knees. "Mukrot sorry."

"Sorry ain't gonna bring him back is it!" Mukrot yelled at himself.

"Stop being mean to me," Mukrot pleaded, sinking his head deeper between his knees.

"Yeah, stop being mean to Mukrot," Ori yelled and stomped over to Mukrot with his hands on his hips. "He said he was sorry. Give the big guy a break!"

Mukrot lifted his head and stared at Ori with huge muddy eyes. "You know my name?"

"Of course, I do! I'm the magic man, aren't I?" Ori piped merrily trying not to laugh. Mukrot's eyes grew big as saucers. Ori paced back and forth in front of the swamp troll who was over twice his size and considered his next move. He could try to make a run for it, but he doubted he'd get very far and there was a good chance Mukrot would step on him trying to catch him. It was obvious that Mukrot was lost, but what was he doing out of his swamp in the first place? If Ori remembered correctly (which was doubtful at best), what his mentor Mal the Mage had told him, swamp trolls rarely if ever left their swamps. Ori glanced over at Mukrot who was sitting with his lumpy arms wrapped around his knees. Suddenly he felt sorry for him. Without giving it too much thought Ori decided to help the poor guy out.

"So, tell me Mukrot," Ori said, pacing first one way and then the other, "who are these two guys giving you such a bad time."

"Zut and Pa," Mukrot mumbled into his knees. "Zut and Pa hate me."

"I gathered that," Ori said, jumping up onto the trunk and taking a seat next to Mukrot. A move he immediately regretted. Mukrot smelled like rotten cabbage, sweaty socks, and moldy onions. "What I don't understand," Ori said, slipping back off the trunk and moving down wind, "is why? Why do Pa and Zut hate you?"

"Mukrot was born seventh. Pa was born seventh." Mukrot groaned.

"Oh," Ori raked his aching skull for Mal's lesson on seventh sons. There was something special about seventh sons, but damned if he could remember what it was. "So Zut hates you because you are the seventh son of a seventh son?" Ori fished.

"Yah," Mukrot nodded enthusiastically. "Zut hates me because I robbed his rite as heir."

"The seventh son trumps the first born," Ori exclaimed, slapping his knee. Mukrot unraveled himself and bobbed his rubbery head up and down in agreement. The golf ball sized boils dotting Mukrot's neck and chin bounced up and down. Ori's stomach lurched forcing him to duck into the bushes and barf.

Mukrot hoped Ori wouldn't make a run for it. Mukrot liked Ori and he hoped Ori would help him. Mukrot had been terrified when his brothers chased him out of the swamp, but now that he'd been out in the world a few days, he discovered he wanted to see more of it. Maybe Ori would let Mukrot travel with him. Maybe he would teach Mukrot how to sing to the stones. Mukrot was beside himself with maybes when Ori rejoined him.

"What I don't get," Ori said taking a seat across from Mukrot, "is why you insist on carrying Zut and your Pa around with you?"

Mukrot crinkled his forehead and looked over his shoulder as if he expected Zut and Pa to be on his back. "Pa and Zut not..."

"Exactly," Ori interrupted sharply, "Zut and Pa are not here!" Ori waved his hand dramatically in front of him to emphasize his point. "So why drag them around with you in here?" Ori pointed to his head. Mukrot looked totally confused. Exhaling deeply Ori tried again, "Zut and Pa didn't leave the swamp, Mukrot did," Ori pointed to his head again, "but you still carry them around in your head and let Zut and Pa bully you. Why? So, what if you ran the wrong way? It's hardly your fault. It's your first time out of the swamp. How the hell are you supposed to know which way to run?"

Mukrot rolled his lower lip as he pondered what Ori was saying. The little man's words did make sense, but it was clear from the look on Mukrot's face that it was going to take more than words to get Pa and Zut out of the swamp troll's rubbery head.

"Mukrot you look tired," Ori announced with authority and patted the ground in front of him. "Why don't you rest?"

Mukrot glared at Ori. "Mukrot not rest," he huffed. "Little man is trying to trick me."

"No, I'm not," Ori said innocently. "Ori, that's me, is not trying to trick Mukrot." Ori scooped up a handful of loose dirt and rocks. "Well, if you're not going to rest, why don't I teach you how to sing to the stones."

"Oh, oh, oh!" Mukrot exclaimed, clapping his hands. Ori had to jump back to avoid getting slapped.

"Settle down big fellow," Ori urged, pulling back the hand that held the pebbles. "You don't want to frighten the stones." Looking confused, Mukrot stopped clapping and plopped heavily onto the ground in front of Ori.

"That's better," Ori said softly, cradling the pebbles in his hands. "Rock them softly, like a baby." He poured the stones into Mukrot's cupped hands. "Keep rocking," Ori urged as he searched his pockets for a coin. Mukrot hummed softly and carefully shifted the stones from hand to hand.

His pockets empty, Ori picked up the sack and gave it a good shake. One copper coin rolled out. It was only a half penny, but it would do.

"Here take this," Ori dropped the half penny into Mukrot's hand and sat down in front of him. "Gently...GENTLY... Good, good, not so fast! That's better. Now sing what I sing."

Ori started to sing an easy tune with only a few words. Mukrot did his best to mimic Ori word for word. Soon his eyes grew heavy, and he found it hard to keep up. Ori changed the pitch and added a few new words. Mukrot yawned widely and let his eyes fall shut. Jerking awake, Mukrot looked at his hands and frowned.

"It takes a little patience," Ori explained as he continued to sing. Unable to fight off slumber any longer, Mukrot dropped off to sleep. Ori sang a tale of the brave Mukrot and his faithful friend Ori, the magic man, who fought off the evil Zut and saved the swamp.

When Ori was sure Mukrot was fast asleep, he carefully removed the coin and stones from Mukrot's rubbery hand and began to sing to them properly. A few minutes later he dropped a dozen half pennies into Mukrot's outstretched palm and tiptoed off into the woods.

When he reached the road, Ori shifted into his fox body and headed for an outcropping of boulders where he could get a better look at where he was. Scanning the landscape, Ori couldn't believe his luck. He was closer to Milendor than he ever could have hoped.

Leaping from the rocks, Ori headed back to the dirt road that would take him to the Forest. He was making good time when he spotted three boys running towards him.

"Berries!" The boys shouted racing over to the bushes to pluck the berries off them. Ori slipped as far as he could under the branches as he watched the boys hungrily stuffing the red berries into their mouths. He wondered what they were doing out on the road in broad daylight. Surely, they knew it wasn't safe traveling out in the open.

"We heard it from the ravens, so it must be true," a stout woman with dusty bare feet was saying to another woman who had come to fetch the boys. Ori bit his tongue remembering the drunkard's comments about ravens from the night before. "The ravens say the Change is coming to Milendor to meet with the Oracle. The ravens say the Change has come to lead us in the fight against the Empire and take back our lands."

"Yes, yes. I heard that too," the taller woman nodded, "that's why Stev and I ran out when we spotted you and your boys. Come on Stev!" The woman snapped, yanking the younger boy by the collar.

"You too," the stouter woman ordered, pulling the older boys by their ears, leading them towards the road.

Ori was waiting for the group to disappear around a bend when a shabby man riding a sway backed horse stopped in front of a tree and nailed a notice to it. Once the man had rode off Ori shifted into a human and read the notice.

"By the Order of The Emperor of Astaria," he read aloud, "ten pieces of silver will be awarded to anyone with information about the trespasser who was seen falling from the Pillars of the Twins. Fifty pieces will be awarded for the trespasser alive. Twenty pieces if dead."

"Son of a bitch," Ori cursed, ripping the notice from the tree. He was now more determined than ever to find Elize.

CHAPTER 6

Taa knew why Mia was being so cruel. It was revenge for what had happened with Mia's mother. Mia blamed Taa for her mother's death. Mia had been too young to understand what had happened. Taa thought by now someone would have told her the truth about what had happened to her mother. Apparently that was not the case.

When Mia's mother Merrell gave birth to Mia and Gerawld. Mia was the spitting image of her father and Gerawld was the spitting image of his. When Scat laid eyes on the orange striped kit he was sure he had not sired him. Outraged Scat attacked Gerawld and would have killed him if Merrell hadn't gotten in the way. Severely injured, Merrell took her kits and fled to her sister's hut.

Word was sent to the healing center at Qym for a healer, but by the time Taa arrived the slash across Merrell's shoulders had become infected. Taa was young and had little experience in the field. By the time she arrived, there was little she could do for Merrell except give her something to take the pain away.

Taa was shaken from her memories by half a dozen furry faces that poked out of the stalks eager to see the strange creature Mia and Gerawld had captured. A few brave kits reached out to brush the back of Elize's legs as she passed by. Mia hissed at them and shooed them back.

Elize was not expecting the Bast community to be so large. It was amazing that a village this large could be completely camouflaged inside a field of grass. The village was laid out like a wagon wheel with grass huts making up the outer ring, as well as the spokes of the wheel. The only structure not made of grass was the large, circus tent sized yurt in the village center, which was the domain of Scat, Leader of the Grassland Bast.

Scat was sitting inside the yurt flanked by his twin sons when he heard the racket outside. On the grass mat to his left, Pfft, the current queen sat licking what remained of her breakfast off her paws. The community's elders sat in a semi-circle behind Scat and Pfft.

"What is that noise?" Scat growled at the black and white cat standing to his left.

Outside the crowd had grown so thick that Mia had to force her way forward. A mangy white cat leapt out in front of Mia. The crazed cross-eyed cat yowled and shook a rattle made from rat skulls in Elize's face. His breath reeked of rotting fish. Elize backed away jerking Mia with her.

"Askar," Mia hissed, digging her hind claws into the dry ground. Askar shook the rattle in Mia's face. Mia swiped at the old cat. It was clear from his torn ears it wasn't the first time he'd been swiped at. Dodging Mia, Askar continued shaking the rattle as he danced around in a lopsided circle yowling loudly. Several other bast cats joined in the erratic dance including a tiny silver cat who held onto Askar's rat-like tail stumbling behind him like a ragdoll.

Mia shoved her way past Askar. She did not have time for his foolishness. The curtain of the yurt parted, and a tall black and white cat slipped out. The tall cat reminded Elize of a bouncer that had tossed her out of a club when she was a teenager. The tall cat nodded at Mia, but his eyes were locked on Elize.

"Who is that?" Elize whispered to Taa.

"Tux, Scat's son."

"Mia and Gerawld's brother?"

"No, Mia and Gerawld share a mother. Mia and the twins share a father."

"Oh...why is he staring at me like that?"

"Tux," Mia growled in garbled common tongue, "thinks he is superior to all but himself, even his twin."

A second cat came out of the yurt and signaled for them to approach. The second cat was the same height and build as Tux, but instead of being black and white, he was gray with long white 'socks.' Elize sensed that like Jacob and Esau, the twins had been in a struggle over their birth rite since the day they were conceived.

"Our arrival has been noticed." Mia growled keeping her voice low. "Scat, Leader of the Grassland Bast will give you an audience."

"Who's the cat with the white socks?" Elize whispered.

"Sox." Mia answered.

"Is that their real names?"

"No," Taa answered for Mia, "Their real names don't translate to common tongue, so Tux and Sox will do."

"What about Mia and Gerawld?"

"Mia's name is pronounced Mee-ahhh in bast and Gerawld's is more like a strangled growl."

"Speaking of Gerawld," Elize said, glancing from side to side, "where'd he go?"

"Gerawld is not allowed in the village." Mia replied coldly.

"Why?" Elize asked, but before Mia could answer Tux sauntered over and snatched the rope out of Mia's paws.

Fighting off the urge to snatch the rope back, Mia went to talk to Sox. She did not like Tux and made it a point to avoid him whenever possible.

Tux led Elize through the ever thickening crowd. Before they reached the entrance to the yurt Askar leapt in front of Tux howling frantically and shaking the rat heads at him. Exhibiting no emotion Tux pushed past the annoying shaman. Askar's eyes gleamed manically as he leapt in front of Elize snarling and baring his broken, yellowed teeth. Tux shot out his paw, razor-sharp claws extended. A flash of silver darted in front of Tux knocking his paw away. Placing her tiny paw on Askar's head, the silver cat pressed down. Like a toy whose battery had run out Askar sank to the ground. With Taa following on their heels, Tux pulled Elize into the yurt.

A sea of eyes glittered from inside the yurt, but only one pair stuck out. A pair of stunning blue-green eyes belonging to the regal black cat with a white diamond on his forehead sitting on a stack of finely woven mats in the center of the yurt. Scat, Leader of the Grassland Bast, waited impatiently as Tux approached with Elize in tow.

"Bow!" Tux demanded forcing Elize to her knees. Scat studied Elize intently as he stretched his long forearms out in front of him kneading the top mat with well-manicured claws.

"Are you a healer?" He asked Elize casually as he continued kneading the mat.

"No," Elize answered politely.

"Yet you wear the robes of a healer. Why?"

"I told her to." Taa answered for Elize. "I received orders to bring Elize to the Oracle of Milendor and I thought she would draw less attention dressed as a healer."

"Hmmm," Scat murmured. "Take off the robe."

Not sure what to do, Elize looked over at Taa. Tux pulled out his knife and was about to cut Elize's robe off when Askar burst into the yurt yowling.

Elize glanced over at Taa.

"He says you are a witch and that you brought sickness to the village. He demands you be sacrificed to the mists to save the village."

"What…"

"Silence!" Tux snarled, slapping Elize across the jaw.

"It's superstitious nonsense," Taa huffed.

"Oh?" Scat said, twitching his whiskers to mask the smile. "Convince me."

Taa chewed nervously at the tip of her nail. "Well… many of your community have weepy eyes so obviously the mists were already here before Elize arrived."

"What do you think?" Scat asked, turning to Elize. "Do you agree with Taa? Do you think what Askar says is superstitious nonsense?" Elize hesitated, she didn't want to tick Scat off, but she knew she was expected to say something.

"I'm not a witch," Elize said slowly, scratching her right palm which felt hot and itchy. "And I didn't bring the mists. Taa and I didn't enter your territory on purpose, but perhaps we were sent here for a reason."

"Why?" Scat demanded. "What reason would bring you here? Hmmm?"

Elize shrugged. How was she supposed to know? She just felt what she felt. Taking her shrug as insubordination Tux yanked the rope so hard Elize fell flat on her face. Scat growled low in his throat. Tux pulled Elize back on her knees without apologizing.

"You must excuse my son. Sometimes he gets a bit overzealous." Scat said, sitting up on his mat. Scat wished Tux would show more self-control. He feared his son's impulsiveness would one day cause him to make a fatal mistake. "What is your name?"

"Elize," Elize said, frantically trying to calm the power pulsating through her veins as her anxiety increased.

"What's in your hand?" Tux demanded. Afraid of what would happen if Tux touched her again, Elize jerked her hand away. Tux grabbed her right wrist, his sharp claws slicing through the grass rope. A frayed wire flash of static electricity flashed out from the center of Elize's palm. Tux hissed and batted Elize upside the head.

A bright zigzag light flashed across Elize's octave nerve sending a series of images across her brain like someone clicking the remote on a television. Elize's eyes rolled back in her head and a strange, distorted voice erupted from her lips.

"The grasslands are no longer safe. Hurry! Gather your kits and flee! Quickly! Go! The three sisters are eagerly waiting to gather you in their loving arms. Scat, Leader of the Grassland Bast, leave this place before all that is precious to you is destroyed! There is no time for doubt! Go now!"

Elize opened her eyes to find Scat standing over her and boy did he look mad.

"How dare you trespass upon my lands and speak of doom!" He snarled, his long tail whipping wildly behind him. "Who are you to upset the family with your dire predictions! "Give me one reason why I shouldn't slit your throat?" Unable to speak, Elize trembled on the ground at Scat's feet. "What's wrong with her?" Scat demanded.

The demons have taken her!" Askar shrieked, rushing up to Elize and shaking the rattle in her face.

"They have not," Taa snapped, reaching out and knocking the rat skeletons away. "She appears to be in shock."

"It is not the demons," a timid voice called out. Askar spun glaring at the tiny silver cat clinging to his tail. "Elize has fallen from the sky to safe us."

"Is this true?" Scat demanded. "Is Elize the one who fell from the sky?" Taa nodded. Scat's tail switched across Elize's feet. "I see," he pondered twitching his whiskers, "and where did she fall from? A star? Perhaps she is a fallen star?"

"I'm not a fallen star." Elize replied weakly. "I fell from Earth. Well, not exactly. I was on Earth, and I went into a cave. When I came out I tripped and fell."

"Earth?" Scat exploded. "Earth!" Scat motioned at the images painted on the yurt's walls. "A long, long time ago our ancestors lived on Earth." Scat pointed at a painting depicting basts dressed like the pharaohs lounging on temple steps. "The young humans worshipped us and treated the bast like gods. Our ancestors trusted the humans and shared their vast wisdom with them. Over time the humans grew jealous of the bast, and they turned on our ancestors slaughtering many innocents. Angered our ancestors left the Earth. They migrated to this little planet in a realm where they could live in peace. Our family has spent the warm seasons in these grasslands for many generations. If you come from Earth as you claim, you not only trespass on bast territory but on our planet as well. Why would I put my family at risk for a trespasser?"

"I'm not asking you to put your family at risk," Elize replied, trying to force down the panic welling up inside her. "I don't blame you for not trusting human's after the way they treated your ancestors. I'm not even sure I'm a human. I came from Earth, but I wasn't born there, I was born here on this planet."

"Is this true?" Scat asked, glancing over at Taa.

"I do not know where Elize was born." Taa answered, pawing at the dirt under her hoofs nervously. "The otters brought Elize to the healing center at Qym a few days ago after pulling her out of the water. The otters told me that Elize fell out of the sky by the Pillars of the Twins. That is all I know." Scat gave Taa a hard look. Taa gulped and kept talking. "I received a message from an owl that instructed me to bring Elize to the Oracle who resides in the Forest of Milendor. We were on our way to Milendor when Elize got lost in the grass and was apprehended by Mia.

"So, you claim to be the one foretold?" Scat asked Elize, his blue-green eyes flickering dangerously.

"No. I claim to be Elize," Elize answered bravely, looking Scat in the eye. "I didn't know anything about the prophecy until Taa told me."

"She's telling the truth." Taa said. "Elize had no knowledge of the prophecy."

"Hmmm," Scat tugged at his whiskers. "Askar!" Sox set the old shaman in front of his father. Askar hissed and swiped at Sox.

"Askar be still," Scat snapped. Askar went limp. "Behold the one who fell from the sky." Scat waved a paw towards Elize. "You heard her speak. Is she the one foretold or a demon? You are our shaman. What do you think?"

Askar looked scornfully at Elize and then noticing Silver still holding his tail he swatted the tiny cat away. Silver let out a pitiful mew and stared up at Elize with blank, silver eyes. She's blind Elize thought. Sox gently lifted the tiny cat off the ground and gently set her by Scat's feet. Scat patted Silver on the head before turning his attention back to Askar.

"Show Askar your hand!" Scat demanded. Elize clutched her fist. She did not want to show this crazy old cat her hand. Taa nudged her, but Elize didn't move.

Scat tilted his head to the left. Careful not to touch Elize's hand, Tux took Elize's right wrist and squeezed until Elize opened her fingers.

Askar leaned towards Elize, his blue eye staring straight ahead while his green eye focused on Elize's palm. A bit of drool dripped from Askar's lower lip. Askar's face was so close Elize could feel his clammy breath on her skin. Askar jerked his head up, switched eyes, stuck out his prickly tongue and licked Elize's palm. Elize shuddered and tried to pull her hand away, but Tux was holding it too tight.

Without warning, Askar yowled and sunk his jagged fangs into Elize's palm. When the tip of his fang struck the blue stone hidden under Elize's skin bright light flashed out from Askar's mouth and the old cat was tossed across the yurt where he landed in a heap besides the door flap. Stunned Askar lie whimpering where he landed with his mouth wide open and his white fur sticking out like a puffer fish.

Silver stumbled over to Elize and crawled into her arms. Elize cradled the tiny cat in her arms and rocked back and forth. Silver purred softly and gently as she pressed her soft pink nose against Elize's bloody palm.

"You're hurt." Silver said without speaking. Elize looked at her bloody palm.

"I'm okay." She assured Silver. Silver rubbed her head against Elize's arm.

"And what do you say little one?" Scat asked Silver fearful that his daughter had brought danger into the village.

"Elize speaks the truth." Silver said with confidence. "The grasslands are no longer safe. You would be wise to listen to her."

"Why am I hearing this from an outsider?" Scat demanded looking over at the fallen Askar. Askar whined and curled up into a dusty ball.

"Please," Silver cried when Tux kicked Askar in the ribs. "It's not my father's fault. He's just a frightened old man who can no longer see the truth and refuses to listen to it."

"You jeopardized the family to save your own ego!" Scat spat angrily. "Toss Askar into the mists!"

Silver put her paw on Scat's leg. "Please do not throw my father into the mist. Let us return to our hut. His days are short."

"Askar doesn't deserve such a dutiful daughter," Scat whispered, patting Silver's head.

"Take Askar to his hut!" Scat ordered, "and make sure he stays there." Tux dragged Askar off the ground. Askar spat and flailed as Tux carried him out of the yurt with Silver stumbling after them clutching Tux's tail.

Scat pressed his forepaws together and flexed his claws in and out as he considered what to do next. He was angry at his daughter for bringing Elize into the village, but now that Elize was here it was up to him to decide what was best for the family. If Elize was the one prophesied about it would be unwise to kill her. Still, after seeing her power he did not think it was wise to release her. At least not until he had discussed the matter with his council.

"Take Elize to an empty hut." Scat ordered Mia. "Feed her and give her a mat to sleep on. She is not to leave the hut or interact with the family. Since you brought Elize into the community she is your responsibility. You are to keep watch over her at all times. Once I have decided her fate I will send for her."

Mia nodded and took Elize by the arm. Taa started to follow, but Scat stopped her.

"Not you healer."

"But I need to make sure Elize is safe." Taa said watching anxiously as Mia and Elize left.

"You have my word. No harm will come to your charge." Scat assured Taa, motioning her forward. "My responsibility is the welfare of the family. I do not need my shaman to tell me the mists are making my family sick. I see it with my own eyes. I would consider it a great favor if you could assist in any way possible."

"Of course," Taa answered. What choice did she have? It was her duty as a healer. "I will start immediately."

Mia put Elize in one of the empty huts in the outer rim of the village. Exhausted from the energy surge, Elize plopped down on the tattered grass mat and stared at the walls. After a while the door was pushed open. A young tortoise shell cat set a bowl of warm milk and several small mice in a stick cage on the floor before silently closing the door behind her. As soon as the door closed, Elize set the mice free and watched them scurry across the dirt floor before disappearing into the grass wall. Lifting the bowl with both hands she tried to drink, but her right hand was throbbing so badly she ended up spilling most of the milk down her shirt.

"Stupid cat," Elize groused and tossed the bowl across the hut. Glancing down at her palm Elize examined the bite marks left by Askar's jagged fangs and noticed a teensy bit of blue poking out from under her torn skin. Even with just a pin prick exposed, Elize felt the energy seeping out. She hadn't felt so much power since the day she almost killed Matty, the youngest of her four stepbrothers. She hadn't meant to hurt Matty, but he was trying to drown her in Miller's pond and the power just erupted out of her. Elize would have liked to say it shocked the hell out of Matty, but that wasn't the case. After the pond incident Elize's stepfather insisted she be sent away to a Catholic boarding school. Elize had been seven and a half. Before she left her mother made her promise to keep her powers a secret and never use them again. Until today Elize had kept that promise. Well for the most part.

Elize heard something moving on the roof over her head. A soft shifting of the thatch. Thinking it was probably the mice Elize didn't pay it much attention. Feeling totally wiped out she curled up on the mat and fell to sleep.

She dreamt of a woman living in the head of a statue which looked like it was carved out of a humongous opal. It was not the first time Elize had dreamt of this woman, but it was the first time the woman had spoken to her.

"Wake up!" The woman whispered urgently.

Startled Elize opened her eyes. It was pitch dark in the hut, so it took a minute for Elize to remember where she was. Her senses now on high alert, she picked up the faint sound of paws padding across the dirt. A second later the door was flung opened, and two green eyes flickered through the darkness.

"Like a demon," Elize whispered as she inched further back into the hut. The eyes locked on her.

"Come," Tux said, stepping into the hut. "My father awaits."

"Where's Mia?" Elize demanded her back pressed against the wall of the hut. "Your father said he'd send word to Mia."

"He changed his mind." Tux sneered, reaching out in the darkness he snatched Elize's arm. "Come, it isn't wise to keep my father waiting."

Tux twisted Elize's arm behind her and forced her out of the hut. Even though she couldn't see very well in the dark, Elize was sure Tux was taking her out of the village, not into it. She tried to call out, but Tux smacked her across the head and told her to shut up.

Gerawld laid under the thatch roof. Gerawld often snuck into the village. His orange striped fur gave him the perfect camouflage for traveling across the rooftops. After spending most of the day hiding on top of the hut where Mia had put Elize, Gerawld was starting to get bored. Bored and hungry. Inching to the edge of the hut, Gerawld glanced over the edge to see if Mia was still there. Mia was slumped over, an empty bowl of milk laying on the dirt by her foot. Gerawld swished his tail. Something was wrong. Mia never fell asleep on guard duty. Never! Hearing the soft padding of someone approaching, Gerawld backed further into the thatch and flattened himself against the roof.

Tux cautiously approached the hut. When he reached Mia, Tux nudged her with his foot to make sure she was out cold and then smiling, pushed open the door to the hut. He was surprised when he saw Elize moving towards the back of the hut. He was expecting her to be knocked out like Mia. Tux was even more surprised when Gerawld leapt off the hut and landed on his back.

Not sure what was going on, Elize stumbled out of Tux's grip and ran into the grass. She hadn't gone very far when she heard voices whispering in the stalks somewhere ahead of her. At first it sounded like a couple of cats fighting, but when she focused on the noise she was able to pick up enough to be concerned.

"I have to get word to Scat." Elize thought, keeping perfectly still. There was no way she could make it to the yurt by herself in the dark. She doubted she could make it in full daylight. Still, there had to be a way to get word to him.

"Elize?" A shrill voice exploded inside her head. It was Silver, Askar's daughter.

"Silver!" Elize thought back trying to remain calm.

"Oh Elize! Something terrible is going to happen."

"I know! You must warn Scat!"

"I can't!" Silver cried as the grass parted in front of Elize and Askar's manic face appeared. Elize yelped and ran away. Several bast appeared out of the dark and grabbed her. Elize tried to fight them off, but there were too many. They lifted her off the ground and carried her deeper into the thick grass, Elize felt the power bubbling under her palm. Not wanting to start a fire, she clutched her fist and fought the power down.

"They're carrying me into the mist," Elize thought urgently, hoping Silver could still hear her. "It's up to you! You must face your fears! You must warn Scat!"

Howling Askar led the others to a tall pyre rising out of the grass like a giant scarecrow. Askar's followers carried Elize to the top and tied her tightly to the pyre. When they were done, they jumped to the ground to join Askar dancing erratically around the base of the pyre.

Tux and Gerawld rolled over top of each other several times until they broke apart. Hissing and arching their backs, they circled each other with ears pressed flat against their skulls. Tux rushed at Gerawld and tried to knock him off balance, but Gerawld sidestepped him, swiping his paw across Tux's chest. Tux leapt backward and darted away. Gerawld started to go after him but stopped when he heard Askar and his followers howling.

Even though Silver's eyes did not see the way others saw, she was not entirely blind. Images and shapes formed in her mind that the others were unable to see. Tux underestimated Silver thinking she was a harmless idiot. Silver had walked in silence behind her father and Tux when he escorted them back to their hut. Silver pretended not to hear what Tux was telling her father, but she remembered every syllable of the plan Tux laid out. That's how she knew what her father was planning to do when he slipped out of the hut that evening. Silver had followed her father from their hut to the yurt many times before, but never alone. Using her hands to guide her, Silver made her way out of the hut and into the center of the village.

After escaping Gerawld, Tux rushed into the yurt. In his panic, Tux didn't notice that his mother was not sitting on her mat. If he had, he would have been more cautious approaching his father.

Certain the sedative his mother had slipped into his father's food had worked. Tux boldly approached his father.   He had almost reached the mat when he noticed Silver sitting next to a bowl of milk.

"It appears you were right little one," Scat growled, opening his eyes, "my son is a traitor!"

Tux lunged forward and stabbed his father with the dagger he was holding. Sox grabbed his brother's arm and wrestled Tux to the ground. Tux kicked his way free, but before he could escape Scat slashed out and sliced the tip off Tux's left ear marking him as a traitor. Tux scurried out of the yurt with Sox close behind him. Silver arched her back and started screaming.

Determined to rescue Elize, Gerawld crept past the frenzied Askar and his followers and climbed up the inside of the pyre. He had almost reached the top when Askar let out a god-awful shriek. Fearing he had been discovered, Gerawld peeked out from between the stalks. Askar stood in front of the pyre with the mists swirling around him like angry ghosts. In one paw Askar held a small stone hatchet and in the other a piece of flint. Askar's followers chanted wildly as Askar struck the flint with his axe. The spark ignited the gas inside the mist causing a massive explosion which launched the pyre into the air like a rocket.

Gerawld was thrown into the sky and landed hard on all four paws several feet from Askar and his followers charred remains. Fire licked at the dry grass all around him and Gerawld knew he needed to act fast before the flames got out of control. Slicing through the stalks of grass, Gerawld gathered them into a broom and peed on it. Using the wet broom, he swatted at the flames like a madman. Other bast who had heard the blast, ran out to help him. Working together they distinguish the fire before the flames reached the village. Once the fire was under control Gerawld left to find Elize.

Taa had just finished treating the last of the sick basts kittens when the explosion shook her to her knees. Racing towards the hut where Elize was being kept, Taa found the door ripped open, and Mia slumped outside in a drug induced slumber. After checking to make sure Mia was all right, Taa ran after the pyre she had seen crossing the night sky.

The pyre lodged itself in a tangle of thick vines that had overtaken a long-abandoned orchard. Stunned from her unexpected flight, Elize laid on top of what was left of the pyre for several minutes before daring to move. She was busy trying to pull her arms free when Gerawld's big head popped out of the vines.

"Yowlalright?" Gerawld asked giving Elize a not so gentle head butt.

"Yeah." Elize fussed and held her arms out so Gerawld could sliced through the rough fibrous rope. Gerawld had just freed her legs when they heard someone approaching.

Taa stopped under the trees and frowned. She was sure the pyre had come this way, but it was nowhere to be seen. Looking up into the trees, Taa didn't notice the two orange paws drop down behind her until they grabbed her by the shoulders and yanked her off the ground.

"Gerawld!" Taa exclaimed throwing her arms around the tree's knobby trunk so fast she almost knocked him out of the tree. Gerawld placed his large paw over her nose and pointed ahead at the interlocking tree limbs. Taa tried to follow him, but her muscles would not obey. Being up so high made her giddy.

"I think she's frozen." Elize whispered crawling out of her hiding place. After several tries Gerawld finally got Taa's arms off the trunk and around his neck and slowly started to crawl forward. Elize followed keeping far enough back to avoid getting slapped by his tail. Scratched and tired they finally reached the far side of the orchard and dropped to the ground.

"Oh Elize! I'm so glad you're alive!" Taa exclaimed once she had recovered enough to talk. "What happened back there?"

"Askar tried to sacrifice me." Elize told her pulling the twigs and leaves out of Taa's fur. "When his ax hit the flint the gas in the mist went BOOM and sent the pyre off into the sky."

"Where's Askar now?"

"Dead." Mia answered dropping out of the tree and landing lightly on the ground in front of Taa. Taa jumped back, stumbled over Gerawld's tail, and knocked Elize to the ground. Rolling her eyes, Mia went over to her brother.

"I'm glad you're alive," Mia purred butting him with the flat of her head. She had taken care of Gerawld since he was a kit and even though she was hard on him Mia loved her brother dearly.

Elize quickly filled them in on what had happened inside the hut. "Where's Tux now?"

"I don't know." Elize said looking over at Gerawld. "Once Gerawld jumped on his back, I ran and didn't look back."

"Tux tried to murder Scat." Mia spat her tongue still thick from the sedative used to drug her milk. "Luckily Silver got to Scat before he could drink the milk."

"Is Scat alright?" Taa and Elize asked in unison.

"Thanks to Silver he is alive, but he was severely wounded. He has lost a lot of blood. Sox is with him, and he will coordinate the move back to the Valley of the Three Sisters."

"I should go to him." Taa said brushing the dust off her cloak.

"No, you must not return to the village." Mia told Taa firmly, flicking her tail. Glancing over at Gerawld who was busy cleaning the soot off his fur, Mia added. "Sox has ordered Gerawld and I to escort you and Elize safely to the Forest of Milendor."

"Me-rowl!" Gerawld gurgled happily swishing his tail over his head like a lasso.

CHAPTER 7

Alzo rolled over and pressed his cheek against Susan's soft blond hair, but instead of breathing in the familiar sent of lavender and sweet mint, he got spices and coconut oil. Opening his eyes, Alzo brushed the silky black hair away from Ilee's face. Again, he wondered how old she was. Surely no more than fifteen, sixteen tops. Leaving Ilee sleeping peacefully upon a pile of small pillows, Alzo crawled out into the main area and stretched.

Alzo moved quietly through the sleeping village, keeping his head low to avoid smashing it against the uneven ceiling. He had never been fond of caves. Even though this village was bright and cheerful and nothing like the caves he had explored in his younger days, he still felt like he was suffocating. Alzo glanced into one of the brightly painted dwellings with windowsills overflowing with pots of odd looking flowers. Skillfully made furniture was set in a semi-circle in front of an open hearth. Next to the hearth, stacked in neat rows were finely painted ceramic cookware and dishes.

Alzo remembered Emma placing saucers of milk on the windowsill every night for the brownies. Alzo had scoffed at her, saying it was the barn cats who drank the milk. Emma paid him no mind. She told Alzo she'd rather have him laugh at her than piss off a brownie.

"If you're good to the wee ones they'll be good to you." Emma had scolded him kindly. "If you're mean to one, expect to have a mess on your hands the next morning."

Alzo smiled and shook his head. All those bowls of milk were finally paying off. He had imagined brownies as loners. He never expected to meet one, let alone find an entire village of them.

"No rest for the weary?" Knot asked poking his head out of one of the windows.

"Nah," Alzo shrugged stifling a yawn. "I thought maybe some fresh air would help. Do you know where I can get some?"

"Yelp," Knot hopped out the window and on to Alzo's shoulder. "Take a left at the fork."

Knot navigated Alzo up a passageway that got smaller the further they went. Finally, crawling on hands and knees, Alzo felt the cool night air on his face. Climbing out onto the rocks, Alzo was surprised at how far they had traveled.

Alzo sat on the rocks next to Knot and looked at the two moons high in the night sky. His mind drifted back to a night shortly after he had arrived on Earth. He was standing in the field outside Emma's farmhouse staring up at the night sky. When he asked Emma where the little plum moon was. Emma told him the big golden moon had eaten it. Alzo didn't believe her and for years he searched the night sky for the little plum moon hoping to catch a glimpse of it. He was glad to find it back in the sky just like he remembered it.

Knot took a long clay pipe from his top pocket and lit it. Taking a couple long draws from his pipe, Knot blew a trail of smoke rings and studied Alzo's face.

"You're someone special, aren't you?" Knot asked nodding his chin firmly. He already had a notion about who his large visitor was.

"I used to be," Alzo replied and leaned back to rest his elbows against the rocks, "but that was a long time ago. I haven't been special for a long, long time. Not since I left Astaria."

"Never been to Astaria," Knot interjected yanking a silver flask from his pocket, "and I have no wish to go now that the Cobrateen is calling the shots."

"The Cobrateen? You mean Ceen," Alzo spat and took the tiny flask Knot offered him.

"Empress Ceen," Knot corrected.

"Empress?" Alzo coughed out most of his drink. Knot nodded sharply. Alzo took another swig off the flask and handed it back. "How the hell did that snake become Empress?"

Knot shrugged and emptied the flask. "All I know is what I hears." Knot said wiping his mouth with his sleeve.

"And?"

"And, what I hears is that the Cobrateen is now calling herself Empress."

"I can't believe the Emperor would allow that...unless..."

"Unless he had no choice. Well from what I hears he doesn't."

"What do you mean?"

"Well...I told you, his brother..."

"Half-brother." Alzo corrected, continuing to pace. "I still find it hard to believe that the bastard Behr is calling the shots! How is that possible?"

"How in tarnation should I know?" Knot snapped flustered. "All I know is what I hears, and I hears that it was Behr who raised the tariffs and Behr who hired the bulimon to make sure folks paid them. The bastard has bled the land dry with his tariffs. Folks have to keep drifting further and further into the outlands to escape him."

"Why don't they fight back?" Alzo demanded.

"I already told you they don't have a leader." Knot replied glancing sideways at Alzo.

"Screw that! Even without a leader, the Freelanders should have fought back and not allowed their lands to be taken from them!" Alzo stormed kicking at the loose rocks. "I think it's about time they got a leader and fought for what's rightfully theirs!"

Knot took a long puff and considered Alzo's words before deciding it was time to put his cards on the table.

"You're him, aren't you?"

"That depends on who him is." Alzo replied without looking at Knot.

"The lost prince. You're him, aren't you?"

Alzo looked out over the shadowy landscape and scratched his chin. "How far is it to Milendor?" He asked without answering Knot's question. Brownies were renown tricksters, and he had no way of knowing if he could trust him.

"Milendor? Shouldn't you be headed for Astaria?" Knot asked slyly.

"Yeah," Alzo answered gingerly twisting his head from side to side to loosen up his stiff neck, "but first I need to go to Milendor."

"I can get you there," Knot said as he tapped his pipe against the bottom of his boot, "but it'll cost you. How quick do you need to get there?"

"Yesterday," Alzo replied glibly.

"Can't do that," Knot replied curling his lips into a thin smile, "but if you hurry I may be able to get you there by mid-morning."

"What's going on?" Ilee asked Alzo when he woke her up a short while later.

Still rubbing the sleep out of her eyes Ilee followed Alzo out of the brownie village and onto a rocky crag. With the wind whipping around them, Alzo filled Ilee in on the plan while Knot negotiated their passage to Milendor. Ilee eyed the air barge moored to the ledge by several thick ropes. She was not pleased. The barge, if you could call it that, look like it was made from several large tree trunks lashed together. A hot air balloon was tied to each corner. Running across the width of the barge was a long pole. At each end of the pole a dark blue roc, ostrich sized birds that could fly, sat gripping the pole with thick, dagger-like talons patiently waiting for their Captain's signal.

The captain, a large, sketchy looking character with yellow teeth and a face like a badger was busy bartering back and forth with Knot. Finally, Knot threw up his hands and stomped over.

"The Captain says he'll take you for a price." Knot grumbled shooting a disgusted look at the captain. Alzo was pretty sure he was being played, but he reached into his pockets anyway and pulled out a handful of coins and his car keys.

Knot's eyes gleamed when he spied the shiny coins. "That will do," he squealed scooping the coins off Alzo's palm. Knot reach into his pocket and exchanged the coins for the watch Alzo had given him the day before. Alzo was amazed that Knot would give up the watch for four quarters, three dimes, two nickels and three pennies.

"I've got a bad feeling about this," Ilee whispered as they stepped aboard the air barge. Alzo started to tell her there was nothing to worry about but glancing over at the crew he figured Ilee had every right to worry.

"We'll be alright." Alzo whispered taking her hand and giving it a squeeze. "We'll take care of each other. Okay?" Ilee nodded and smiled weakly. He squeezed her hand again and led her to a spot among the wooden crates where they would be buffered from the wind, but still be able to see and hear what was going on. The captain approached just as they were getting settled in.

"Find a rope and hang on tight," Captain Bok yelled over the wind, "the barge will jerk a bit when Ming and Louy take off. Ilee grabbed onto the ropes securing the crate she was leaning against and hung on for dear life.

"Is it safe?" Alzo asked tapping the worn wooden logs that made up the floor.

"Safe enough," Captain Bok replied with a gruff laugh. "It used to be a river barge, but after the waters dried up I took to the skies."

"What kind of birds are those?" Alzo asked looking at the two blue birds who were staring intently at the captain.

"Ming and Louy are the finest Rocs you'll ever come across. Aren't you, my loves?" Ming and Louy chirped and squawked in response opening and closing their massive beaks. Captain Bok lifted the lid off the bucket he was carrying and pulled out two very dead rodents. "I found my beauties one misty morning barely hatched and squawking their heads off. Raised them as my own. Now hold on tight!" He yelled as he tossed the rodents high into the air. The two Roc's unfurled their massive blue wings and grasping the pole firmly in their talons they flew after the tasty morsels. Alzo wrapped his arm around Ilee as the raft jerked wildly into the air.

Once they were airborne the captain carefully adjusted the blue flame under each of the balloons to account for the extra weight. After a while Alzo and Ilee got used to the rhythmic motion of the barge which bobbed each time Louy and Ming flapped their wings.

"Shouldn't we be higher?" Alzo asked when the tops of the trees brushed the barge bottom.

Captain Bok winked at him. "If we fly any higher the bastards on the ground will spot us. At night if we stay just above the treetops the raft looks like a cloud passing in the night."

"So, what's in the crates?" Alzo wondered.

Captain Bok pursed his lips and gave Alzo a hard look. "Various goods," he answered waving a gnarled hand in front of him. "My boys and I provide a service. When the greedy bastards hiding behind their shiny walls hiked the tariffs so high honest merchants could no longer afford to trade...well the boys and I took up the slack. It's a crying

77

shame, I tell you." The captain spat off the side of the barge in disgust. "Folks got to eat. They need clothes and pots and pans and other stuff. Knot and his network collect the goods and the boys and I distribute them to those willing to pay. Knot tells me you are headed for Milendor. Something about a lost sister. Mind if I ask how you lost her?" The captain lowered his head and locked his beady, bird-like eyes on Alzo.

"We got separated," Alzo replied not trusting Captain Bok enough to give him too much information.

"Outside of Palenina," Ilee added before Alzo could stop her. The thin, mangey looking man who had been standing nearby shuffled to the other side of the barge. Alzo noticed him whispering to the other crew members.

"Careful what you say around my crew," Captain Bok warned in a low voice. "They're a bit too greedy for my liking. Not that I trust anyone these days."

"How far is it to Milendor?" Alzo asked glancing over at the crew who were huddled together speaking in low voices. Alzo rarely judged folks on their looks, but this lot looked especially slimy. The sooner they reached Milendor the better.

Captain Bok looked up at the fading stars, licked his fingers and held them up in the wind. "Not far now." He replied pointing to the west where the sky was much lighter.

Ilee shivered and leaned against Alzo. Another second was too long for her liking. She was all too aware of how the crew looked at her. She had heard tales about the bargemen. They were renown for stealing girls from the islands and selling them to the slavers in the Dimly. She recalled a tale her grandmother told about three girls who were stolen from their canoe and taken to the Dimly. The slavers forced the girls to dive for pearls until their skin turned rubbery and their fingernails fell off, but that wasn't the worst of it. The slavers forced the girls to have sex. In desperation, two of the girls tied the chains binding their ankles around stones and tossed them in the deep water and drowned. The third girl escaped using a broken shell to sever off her own foot. Ilee swore she would die before being sold to the slavers and she meant it.

Ilee's thoughts were interrupted by Captain Bok's shout. Alzo poked his head out from behind the crates just in time to see the crew members toss Captain Bok overboard. Outraged Ming squawked letting go the pole to dive after her beloved Captain. The barge wobbled so violently that several crates broke loose and tumbled off the side. Louy let go of the other end of the pole and flew after Ming. The barge dropped into the treetops tossing Alzo forward as several more crates tumbled passed him. When one of the crew rushed towards him, Alzo grabbed his attacker and slammed his head into a passing crate.

Looking around for Ilee, he no longer saw her on the barge, but to his great relief, he spotted her a moment later waving from a tree limb a few feet below him.

"Jump you fool!" Captain Bok shouted as he flew by on the back of Ming. Two more crew members rushed towards him. Alzo closed his eyes and jumped.

Alzo arrived in Milendor shortly after Ori had.

Ori was a few miles from Milendor when he came upon the first rough camp. Keeping well north of it, he circled around only to find his path blocked by another camp and then another. The closer he got to Milendor the harder it was to avoid the camps. Finally, giving up Ori shifted into his human form and walked over to a couple of boys who were sitting at the side of the road eating acorns.

"What's going on?" Ori asked the boys.

"We've come to join the Change." One of the boys told him.

"Yah," the other boy boasted, "we've come to fight for the Freedlands."

"The Change is here?" Ori asked hoping they were talking about Alzo. It made sense, if he heard the voice yelling Milendor, Alzo would have heard it too.

"Not yet, but the brownies sent the sparrows to let folks know the Change was coming to Milendor." The first boy thrust out his chest and said." He's looking for fighters to take back the Freedlands. We came here to join him."

"And you're sure he's coming here?" Ori asked wondering what had happened to get Alzo to start a revolt?

"Yah, yah," both boys said at once vigorously nodding their heads. "But the rangers closed the road and won't let no one in."

Ori left the boys and headed for the entrance. Sure enough it was blocked by hundreds of stick men dressed in green and brown uniforms. The Rangers of Milendor had formed a living gate across the road leading through Milendor. It would have been easy enough to slip through the tall, long needled firs encircling the forest. However, travel off the road was strictly prohibited and not at all wise. The Forest of Milendor was enchanted and it was said that anyone foolish enough to wander off the road was never heard from again.

This wasn't Ori's first time to Milendor. He had traveled through the forest several times before with Mal the Mage. Ori had never been invited into the Neognathae's tree where the Oracle of Milendor lived and that had suited him fine. He was more than happy to stay on the road and wait until Mal returned. Like every child on the planet Ori had been frightened by the tales of the Neognathae, the strange owl women with the creepy baby sized arms who could steal the memories right out of your head with one touch of their tiny fingers. He was always relieved when Mal returned with his brains intact or as intact as they had been before he went up the tree. Mal had always been a little strange. It was something he was quite proud of.

"Why's the road closed?" Ori asked one of the thin, brown skinned rangers who looked more like a tree branch than a human. Raising up on his toes to get a look at the road Ori was disappointed. All he saw was row upon row of rangers.

"The road is closed." The ranger replied crisply without looking at Ori.

"Why?" Ori asked half-heartedly not really expecting an answer. He knew the ranger was just following orders and wasn't given a reason. When the ranger refused to say anything more, Ori shrugged and headed back through the crowd.

"Hello stranger!" A ruby lipped vixen in a tight-fitting dress asked stepping in front of him and blocking his way. "Remember me?"

Ori did not, but instead of saying so he smiled widely and gave her a wink. The woman licked her juicy, red, red lips. A tell-tale sign that she had been chewing tarry root. A beet-like root that when soaked became as intoxicating as Tennessee moonshine.

"You're the farmer's daughter," Ori teased giving her another wink. The woman giggled and nodded enthusiastically. "What brings you out so far from home?"

"We ain't had a home for a long time now." The woman said sadly. "Not since the bulimon killed Pa and hauled our brothers off to work in the Neli mines."

"Why'd they do that?"

"Pa failed to make his limit." Her cheerful face now an ugly scowl. "It wasn't Pa's fault. There was a drought. But the bulimon didn't care. When they tried to take my brothers, Pa fought back, and they slit his throat. When we heard the Change was looking for fighters, May and I came to fight the bulimon for what they did to Pa!"

"I'm surprised the bulimon didn't take you and your sister too."

"They would have, but we hid underground. The bulimon won't go underground, ya know. Scared the demons will drag them back to hell."

"I've heard that but didn't know it was true." Ori said. The woman stumbled forward.

"It's true," she gushed putting her hands on Ori's chest. "May and I stayed down in that dirty cellar for days before we dared to come out. That's when we saw what they'd done to Pa. Damn bulimon! Now it is time to fight back!"

"Bee," a voice called from behind them. The young woman with the ruby lips jerked her head around.

"Got to go." Bee said leaning forward and giving Ori a juicy kiss. If Ori hadn't been so distracted he may have heard Taa shout.

"I thought I saw Roz!" Taa shouted to Elize as they made their way through the crowd loitering outside Milendor. Elize looked where Taa was pointing and soon she spotted the tattered wings of the isopteria bobbing erratically over the heads of the crowd not too far from where they were standing.

"Roz!" Taa shouted waving her arms over her head, but instead of flying towards them Roz flew the other way. Taa started to go after Roz, but Elize stopped her.

"Somethings not right." Elize said watching Roz's jerky flight. Elize felt more than saw the spiderweb thin chain attached to Roz's ankle. Following the chain down Elize was overwhelmed by a feeling of evil.

"She's hurt." Taa exclaimed dashing off into the crowd.

"No!" Elize yelled after her. "It's a trap!" Taa ignored Elize determined to find her friend. Elize turned to Gerawld. "Gerawld, get Taa and bring her back here!"

Gerawld slipped through the masses like he was covered in grease easily catching up with Taa before she reached Roz.

"Let me go you overgrown furball!" Taa fussed slapping Gerawld's back as he carried her to where Elize and Mia were waiting.

Ori heard the shouting and recognizing the voice turned to see where it was coming from.

"Gerald! Taa!" Ori called shocked to see the pair together and so far away from their homes. "What are you doing here?"

"Ori!" Elize exclaimed stepping out of the crowd and throwing her arms around his neck.

"Elize! Damn, it's good to see you!" Ori wrapped his arms around Elize's waist and lifted her off the ground.

"I'm glad to see you too!" Elize exclaimed happily. "Where's Alzo?" She asked looking around. "Is that him?"

Ori turned his head and looked behind him. "Oh shit! Get down!" Ori dragged Elize behind a sweaty man carrying a large boar across his shoulders.

"What's wrong?" Elize asked prying herself out of Ori's arms.

"I just saw someone we definitely don't want to see us." Ori explained dodging Gerawld's tail. Gerawld was clearly not happy about the way Ori had grabbed Elize and was letting Ori know not to try it again.

"You mean the guy who has Roz on a leash?" Elize whispered hoping Taa didn't hear her.

"What?" Taa shouted trying to push Gerawld out of the way. "If Roz is in trouble I've got to help her!"

"That's exactly what he wants you to do," Ori said looking Taa straight in the eye, "and the very reason you can't."

"What?" Taa and Elize asked in unison.

"I think Roz is bonded to Behr." Ori explained making sure he and Elize stayed hidden behind the boar toting man. "When's the last time you spoke to her?"

"After we left the fishing village." Taa said. "We had an argument. She had left her duties to rip a notice off a wall."

"What notice?" Ori asked keeping a tight grip on Taa's arm.

"It was offering an award for information?" Taa explained trying to pull her arm free.

"Information on what?" Ori asked refusing to let go.

"Me." Elize answered.

"It was asking for information on the person who fell from the sky." Taa corrected searching the sky for any signs of Roz.

"That's not good." Ori mumbled looking worried. Roz must of tried to collect the reward and ended up getting captured. If his suspicions were right, Behr was using Roz as bait.

"You think Roz is being used as bait?" Elize asked guessing what Ori was thinking by the look on his face. Ori nodded. "To catch me?" Ori nodded again. "Why? Why is this guy after me? As far as I know I've never met him before in my life."

"I don't know why he's after you exactly. I think it has to do with the bump in your palm."

"Oh," Elize said closing her fingers tightly over her right palm, "so why is he after you?"

"He thinks I doubled crossed him." Ori replied pulling Elize closer to the forest edge where the crowd was thicker. "He paid me to slip through the crack in the dimensions and find the book Alzo and I stole from him."

"The one you sang from?"

"Yes. It contains maps and spells from a time long forgotten."

"Is that why Alzo was attacked by a bear."

"Yes." Ori rubbed his chin nervously scanning the faces in the crowd for any sign of Behr. "But it wasn't actually a bear. It was Behr. He's a shape shifter."

"Like you?"

"No. I can only shift into a fox. Behr can change into a variety of different animals."

"Why did he attack Alzo?" Elize asked. She remembered when Alzo was attacked. It was one of the few memories she had from her childhood, but she never knew why he was attacked.

"Look, I'll explain later. Right now, we need to get out of here."

"So, the bear was Behr." Elize thought aloud recalling the jagged gash running down Alzo's face like it was yesterday.

"I see Roz!" Taa shouted. Gerawld grabbed her before she could run after Roz. "Let me go!" Taa fumed slamming her hands firmly against Gerald's broad chest. "She's in trouble! I have to help her!"

Mia put her hand on Taa's shoulder, then pulled a dime sized disc from a pocket on her belt which she flicked into the air. Taa watched the coin spin out of Mia's claws, circle under Roz and return. Less than a second later Roz zipped into the sky and disappeared in the dense treetops of Milendor.

An outraged, heart stopping, roar scattered the crowd as the thin chain fell to the ground.

"Let me go!" Taa gasped kicking Gerawld in the shin.

"No," Mia growled her yellow-green eyes flashing. "Your friend is trying to save you. Do not make her efforts be for nothing."

"Go!" Ori gasped pushing Elize behind a passing herd of rowdy goaters.

"We can't leave!" Elize protested standing her ground. "Taa received a message from the Oracle. She is waiting for us! She said it was urgent."

"I don't give a damn about the Oracle!" Ori shouted his face red with frustration. "It's not safe here. The Rangers have shut down the road anyway so there's no way in. Now trust me you need to get out of here. If Behr finds you it will be very bad."

"Why?" Elize asked coldly. She wished she could read Ori's thoughts. Clearly he was holding something back from her.

"Behr isn't working alone."

"Who else wants to get their hands on me?"

"The Cobrateen."

"Cobrateen? The snake...snake woman?"

"You remember her?" Ori said surprised. He knew from talking to her that Elize remembered next to nothing about her life before landing on Earth.

"Yeah! She was the star of my nightmares for years." Elize bit her lip. "I thought she was a figment of my imagination."

"I wish." Ori told her shaking his head. "She's calling herself Empress Ceen now and doesn't bother to hide the fact that she is running the Empire and not your father."

"How did she find out where we were?"

Ori ran his hand over the back of his head and made a face. "Well, like I told you before, your father always insisted you were alive, but he didn't know where you were. When your father told Mal about your mother appearing to him in a vision, Ceen must have been listening and passed the information to Behr. Behr knew I was the Mage's tutor and he offered me a lot of money to track you down and bring you back alive. I tried to refuse, but..."

"But you took the money," Mia hissed her eyes flashing menacingly. "You betrayed Elize." Ori tugged at his shirt collar and licked his lips.

"He would have killed me if I didn't agree." Ori said to his feet, "but I didn't betray Elize. How could I? I hadn't seen her since she was a toddler. And I never imagined Mal's crazy plan would work. If I'd known at the time…"

"Nothing would have changed!" Elize snapped shoving him in the chest and walking away.

"That's not true!" Ori insisted. "Everything's changed!" Elize kept walking she didn't want to give him the satisfaction of seeing the hot tears running down her cheeks.

"Ori!" A gruff voice screamed from the crowd. Ori jerked his head up.

"Run!" He hissed shoving Elize to the left before taking off to the right.

There has to be another way in, Elize thought as she wove through the masses keeping the perimeter of the Forest of Milendor well in sight.

"Ori!" The voice roared again.

"Oh sh..." Ori gasped. Spotting Behr above him, Ori dove behind a tent and shifted into a fox. "When did he learn to do that?"

Elize shivered as she stared after the winged man circling over the tents. She had never seen a demon before, but she had no doubt that the creature chasing Ori was one.

"We need to get into the forest," Elize told Taa who was running next to her.

"But the road is blocked!" Taa replied looking towards the entrance and shaking her head. Elize looked through a gap in the trees and noticed a path leading straight to the road that was well past the spot where it was blocked.

"This way!" Elize yelled at the others and darted into the forest.

"Elize no!" Taa screamed trying to grab her and pull her back. "It's enchanted!"

Elize felt the air change the instant her foot touched the path, and she became aware of the green clad, stick men swinging through the trees above her, long bows slung across their backs like Robin Hood and his merry men. Faces appeared from the barks of trees with hungry eyes and lips full of false promises.

"It's okay," Elize assured Taa when she stepped up next to her, "I can see the road."

"No, you can't!" Taa panted frantically, "it's a trick. We need to get out now!"

"It's okay," Elize assured her calmly. "Take my hand Taa. Walk where I walk."

"Gerawld," Mia growled dashing into the forest after him. Gerawld ignored her intent on following Taa. Mia pulled her belt tight and ran after him.

"Quick! Grab Gerawld's tail!" Elize screamed at Taa. Taa barely managed to grab his tail before his paw left the path. "Hold on to him." Elize urged grabbing Gerawld's arm and helping Taa pin him to the ground.

"He's enchanted." Taa gasped when Mia joined them. Mia looked at the goofy look on Gerawld's face and slapped him hard several times, but Gerawld didn't snap out of it.

"Grab his tail." Elize told Mia holding out her hand. "Now take my hand and don't let go of it or Gerawld's tail. Taa take my other hand. The enchantment doesn't seem to affect me so I will take the lead and get us out of here. Don't let go of my hands or step off the path."

"What path." Taa fussed keeping her feet as close to Elize's without stepping on them.

"Walk with me." Elize told her calmly. "It's not far now. The road is just ahead of us." Taa scanned the trees in front of them and saw nothing but bark and leaves.

"How can you see the path when we can't?" Taa asked nervously glancing from side to side sure she was being watched.

"I don't know." Elize admitted shaking her head to get the hair out of her face. "I've always been able to see through illusions."

"Do you see the stag standing to our right?" Taa asked her gaze fixed at a spot between two large trees?

"No, but I do see the road."

"Are you sure?"

"Yes," Elize assured her stepping out onto it. The air shifted around them again and the glassy look in Gerawld's eyes faded.

Taa blinked several times clearly not expecting to be standing on the road leading through Milendor several hundred yards behind the living gate of Rangers.

"If it hadn't been for you, we would have never gotten out of there alive." Taa gasped scanning the woods behind them. Even now she felt the eyes of the stag watching her.

"Magic." Mia hissed shaking out her fur like it was wet. She still clutched Gerawld's tail tightly in her paw afraid he might try to run back into the forest. Mia had heard the voices singing to them and wasn't about to let the dryads steal her brother.

Ori darted under a nearby tent and scanned the sky. He had been playing cat and mouse with Behr off and on for years and he had never seen Behr sprout wings like that. It was as if he were possessed.

Ori barely had time to catch his breath before the shadow appeared over him once again. His only chance was to get into the Forest where he hoped the Rangers of Milendor would distract the winged Behr until he could get away. Ori knew that the Rangers of Milendor were renown archers. Their ability to shoot while running was seconded only by the Bast Warriors. Knowing he needed to act fast, Ori plotted out his plan while he waited for Behr to circle past him. Still in his fox body Ori kept close to the ground and dashed out of his hiding place and straight for the road. Leaping on the back of a tall woman, Ori flung himself off a sapling and somersaulted over the rows of Rangers. Just before landing, he shifted into a man and took off running the instant his feet hit the ground.

"Ori!" A voice Ori didn't recognize as Behr's shrieked in outrage.

"Ori?" The rubbish heap laying behind a big tent whispered and opened his eyes scaring the daylights out of the two boys using it as a latrine. When Mukrot woke up and found Ori gone, he had been devastated. Then he saw the half pennies Ori left him scattered about the ground and convinced himself that Ori had been taken by the Innkeeper and his son. The very thought filled him with a surge of bravo. Mukrot had tracked Ori's scent to the camps outside Milendor where it became too mingled with the scents of the other travelers. Frighten by the crowds Mukrot had dropped to the ground where he had stayed until he heard someone shouting Ori's name.

"Orrrreeee!" Mukrot bellowed lifting his massive, gray-green body off the ground and running down the road after his friend smashing through the unsuspecting Rangers like a ten foot bowling ball.

Spotting Elize and the others on the road ahead of him, Ori raced towards them.

"Run!" he shouted taking Elize by the wrist and dragging him behind her. Elize stumbled forward and almost landed on top of Taa. Taa was frozen staring up at the man with leathery wings crashing through the canopy of leaves above them.

"Grab Taa!" Ori shouted at Gerawld and Mia. Gerawld nodded and grabbed the comatose Taa around the torso. Mia took her legs, and the pair ran after Ori. Above them the trees came alive with Rangers swinging through the branches filling the air with foot long arrows that rained down on their heads.

Ori was running so fast that he barely managed to stop when the path ended abruptly at the edge of the briar filled moat encircling the island where the Oracle lived. Teetering on the edge of the moat, Ori just managed to stop the others from tumbling over.

"What the hell is that?" Elize screamed as Mukrot lumbered towards them. Elize had never seen a swamp troll, or any troll, before in her life and Mukrot looked quite horrific thrashing towards them taking out the trees on either side of the road with his large limbs.

"Duck!" Screamed Ori his eyes fixated on the dark shadow rising over Mukrot's head.

"Take cover!" He yelled at Gerawld and Mia who had joined them by the moat.

Unaware of the demon over his head, Mukrot lumbered forward. Elize screamed and raised her right hand out in front of her. Unable to control the energy surging from her veins any longer Elize felt the stream of white light flash out of her. The bolt struck the swamp troll's arm, ricocheted off his rubbery skin and slammed into Behr's chest ripping him in two.

The force of the energy exploding out of her caused Elize to trip over the edge of the moat. Before her friends could react, two sets of thick, ivory colored talons wrapped around her arms and lifted her skyward.

CHAPTER 8

The raven cackled as he watched the commotion unfolding beneath his lofty perch. It seemed like everything was finally coming together. Not at all how he'd planned but coming together none-the-less. Ori had somehow managed to get both children, not that you could call them children any longer, through the gateway and to Toboria in one piece. Still, it had taken a good deal of cunning and effort on his part to get them to Milendor. Not that he could blame Ori for landing in the wrong place. Mal had spent years studying the secrets of the nine realms and he still didn't understand how those blasted gateways worked.

At least Ori had managed to get the siblings back to the right realm and with the help of his feathered network Mal had been able to track Elize to the Healing Center at Qym without much effort. He was surprised the healer had accompanied Elize to Milendor, not that it mattered much. Still, it was unusual for a healer to travel so far away from their healing center. Alzo was more of a challenge. Mal had completely lost track of him until he landed on Knot's doorstep.

The raven watched until Elize was carried up into the silvery boughs of the Taro Bora tree, home of Su Lei, Oracle of Milendor. Confident the siblings would be safe under the careful watch of the Oracle and her parliament he spread his long black wings and took to the skies. He wasn't used to so much exertion, but he couldn't rest just yet.

"Now where did he get to?" Mal cawed circling above the Forest of Milendor, his sharp eyes scanning the land below for anything out of the ordinary. Unfortunately, at present everything was out of the ordinary. It was impossible to get a clear view of anything. The mob camped outside the entrance of Milendor had swarmed down the forest road. Above their heads, hundreds of frantic rangers swung through the trees trying to gain control of the situation.

After circling the treetops several more times, the old Mage gave up and flew to an abandon barn a few miles away. As soon as his feet hit the ground he shifted into an old brown mule. 'It feels good to be in a larger body,' Mal thought as he stamped down a pile of old straw. Mal laid down and closed his eyes, but he couldn't sleep. His mind replayed what he had seen back in the forest. Several things had him worried. What had brought Behr to Milendor? What caused the flash of light? And most of all where had that damn demon gone? Mal knew he'd get no rest until he found the answers.

Far above the turmoil, high up in the Taro Bora tree was the sacred home of the Oracle of Milendor. The Oracle along with her descendants were Neognathae a race of human sized owls believed to be keepers of the vast knowledge accumulated by the ancients from the beginning of time. Like the Tara Bora tree, there were only a precious few Neognathae remaining.

The Oracle of Milendor sat perched inside her peach-colored egg which had been carved from a single, chunk of peach colored obsidian eons ago. How the egg had gotten there and who had carved it was long forgotten. It was said the egg had been given to the seventh Oracle by the Ancient Hohi and her sisters when they arrived on the tiny planet of Toboria.

Su Lei, the seventy-seventh Oracle hooted happily to herself overcome with joy that her prophecy had actually come to pass. She was beginning to doubt herself, but now she felt powerful, all knowing.

"Grand Aunt," a voice hooted softly from the other end of the elaborate garden encircling the Oracle's nesting area. "The one you've been waiting for has arrived!"

"I know, I know," the old owl chortled flapping her snow white wings and clapping her tiny hands. "I saw it! I saw it!"

"Should I bring her to you?" The younger owl asked tilting her head to one side as she entered the garden.

"It's late," Su Lei hooted fluffing her wings and hopping first on one foot and then the other. The thin shell wobbled in response. "Too late," she blinked her stunning blue eyes in the morning light. "Must get out of the light."

"Of course," Nekita, the grandniece and future Oracle nodded politely. Su Lei slipped out of the back of the shell and wobbled down a hidden ramp towards her nest.

"Put her in with the others and have Kara fix some refreshments. She'll like that," Su Lei said drowsily from deep inside her nest.

Seconds after landing on the silver limbed tree, Alzo and Ilee were greeted by a ruffled, horned owl, who reminded Alzo of his former English Lit professor, and escorted to a large, oval nest. Without as much as a howdy do the owl deposited the pair in the nest and shut them in. They had been sitting there for what seemed like hours when they heard someone approaching.

"Don't let them touch you," Ilee warned slipping behind Alzo as the flap was pulled open. Alzo shushed her. Ilee had been going on about the owls stealing their brains ever since they arrived, and it was beginning to get a bit monotonous. A blue jeaned leg stepped into the nest followed by another.

"Elize!" Alzo shouted rushing forward to catch her as she stumbled forward.

"Alzo?" Elize gasped before collapsing in his arms.

"Elize! Elize! What's wrong?"

Elize flickered her eyes but couldn't muster the strength to answer him.

"Who is she?" Ilee asked eyeing Elize suspiciously.

"She's my sister, Elize. The one I told you about. The one I was searching for." Alzo replied not taking his eyes off Elize's haggard face.

"How did she get here?" Ilee demanded. "You said she fell? How did she survive such a fall and why does she reek of smoke and," Ilee sniffed disapprovingly, "cat?"

Alzo gave Ilee a hard look. He did not appreciate her tone. They had been stuck inside the nest all afternoon. How was he supposed to know how Elize got there?

"I bet it's a trick! My Gram warned me about the Neognathae!" Ilee shuddered holding onto Alzo's bicep and trying to pry his arm off Elize. "I bet the Neognathae captured your sister and took her brains!"

"My brains are fine," Elize murmured flickering her eyes to see who had made such a ridiculous comment. "Who are you?" She asked the snip of a girl staring down at her.

"This is Ilee," Alzo answered Elize. "She rescued me."

"Why does she look like Mayme?" Elize asked opening and closing her hand which was throbbing like an over stimulated heart.

"Ilee comes from the Palenina, the same Island Mayme was from. Our great, great, great, great grandmothers were sisters or something like that."

"Oh," Elize said closing her eyes again.

Alzo pressed his palm against Elize's. "I used to do this when you were little." He said and smiled at her.

"I remember," Elize mumbled smiling feebly and closing her eyes. Alzo cradled her head in his lap until she was fast asleep.

Ori stood at the edge of the moat looking up at the silver barked Taro Bora tree that covered most of the ground on the tiny island that lay before them. He barely had time to react when Mia raced past him.

"No! No, you won't make it!" Ori shouted grabbing Mia's hind leg and yanking her back. Mia spat in Ori's face. Ori spat back. "It's too wide!"

"I realized that!" Mia fumed yanking her leg free. "I planned on hopping across the brambles."

"Those aren't brambles." Taa mumbled still cradled in Gerawld's arms as the comatose haze started to fade.

"Taa's right." Ori continued refusing to back away from Mia's smoldering stare. "Those extremely poisonous spikes belong to the moat eels. Mia peered down into the moat. It looked like a briar patch to her, but to make sure she picked a large limb off the ground and tossed it into the moat. The briar patch instantly came alive writhing and thrashing turning the limb into splinters in less than a minute. Mia silently stepped away from the edge.

"Put me down!" Taa demanded shoving at Gerawld's chest.
Gerawld growled and dropped Taa. He did not appreciate Taa yelling
at him, she should be thanking him. If he hadn't been holding her, he
might have been able to stop the owls from carrying Elize away.

Taa brushed the loose cat fur off her cloak. "Where's Elize?" She
demanded. Gerawld extended a claw and pointed to the large silver
tree on the opposite side of the moat.

"I demand to be taken to her at once!" Taa huffed stomping over
to the nearest green clad ranger. The ranger, an extremely thin man
dressed in varying shades of green, remained perfectly still his bird-like
eyes frozen in a blank stare.

"Am I invisible!" Taa shouted and tried to push her way past him.
The ranger lowered his spear and pressed it against Taa's chest.

"You shall not pass!" The ranger told her crisply his eyes locked
on hers. Taa flared her nostrils and stomped her hoof firmly. The
ranger stood his ground.

"It appears we are being retained." Taa told the others when she
rejoined them by the moat. Mia growled and went to see for herself.

"I request our party be released at once. Our friend has been taken
against her will and we must go to her aid at once."

"You speak the common tongue!" Yew gulped. He had always
heard that bast were feral savages. He never expected this sleek, black
feline to speak the common tongue.

"Of course," Mia hissed tilting her nose in the air. Yew coughed
and tried to regain his composure.

"I cannot allow you to leave until I receive orders from my
commanding officer." He replied crisply.

"You are right," Mia told Taa. "We are being detained."

"Move!" The green clad ranger shouted at Mukrot poking him
roughly with his saber. Mukrot moaned and remained in his rubbish
pile mode, refusing to budge.

"Oh, for Zot's sake!" Ori fumed shoving his way through the
rangers to stand next to Mukrot.

"Stop sniveling!" The rangers shouted poking Mukrot's thick
green skin with his needle-sharp spear.

"Knock it off," Ori blustered grabbing hold of the spear shaft and
forcing it aside.

"Ori," Mukrot sobbed. Tears rolled down his rubbery cheeks
dripping off his chin to mingle with the greenish pus oozing from the
punctured boils dotting his neck. Ori gagged.

"Look Mukrot," he coughed and tried to sound sincere. "I'm sorry
I left, but I was coming back. I swear." Mukrot refused to look at him.
"Aw come on man. The only reason I left was because I was worried
about my friend."

"Mukrot Ori's friend." Mukrot blubbered wiping his nose across his arrow dotted sleeve.

"Yes, that's true. Mukrot is Ori's friend," Ori emphasized pushing the spear away again, "but you are not my only friend. Elize is my friend too and she was in trouble."

"EEELess?" Mukrot snuffed glancing sideways at Ori with large chocolate drop eyes.

"Yes, Elize," Ori said pointing up at the trees. "The lady you helped rescue."

"Mukrot rescued EEELess?" Mukrot exclaimed hardly able to believe what he was hearing. "Mukrot's a hero?"

"Why yes," Ori said smiling widely. "I guess that does make you a hero."

"Ha!" Spruce, Commander of the Eastern Rangers laughed as he dropped out of the tree to take command of the situation. "I'd hardly call the troll a hero! Look at all the damage he's done."

"He was just trying to save..."

"Doesn't matter what he was trying to do," Spruce cut Ori off curtly. "What matters is what he did. It will take months to clean up the damage he caused."

Mukrot moaned again. He did not like the skinny, stickmen with their pointy spears and arrows. Taa slipped over to have a look at Mukrot. She had only seen pictures of swamp trolls, and this might be her only chance to see one in the flesh.

"He's looks kind of frail for a swamp troll." Taa said slightly disappointed. "I was expecting him to be much wider and taller than he is."

"I don't think he's eaten much since he left the swamp." Ori explained. "You see Mukrot here is the seventh son of a seventh son. His older brothers didn't appreciate him jumping to the front of the heir line and threw the poor fella out of the swamp. It's his first time out on his own and it hasn't been easy for him."

"We need to get Mukrot some proper food immediately." Taa told Spruce placing her hands on her hips to let him know she meant business.

"And what pray tell is proper food for a swamp troll?" Spruce asked sarcastically. He had no intention of going out of his way to cater to a damn troll.

"Something that grows in a swamp or bog." Taa replied not exactly sure what swamp trolls ate. Frogs maybe?

"A bog we can do!" Spruce perked up as the solution to at least one of his problems seemed to be resolved. "Yew, have your men escort the troll to the bogs and while they're at it take the others as well."

"Sir?" Yew sputtered not at all happy.

"Take them all to the bog." Spruce repeated irritably. "This is all of them isn't it."

"All but three."

"All but three!" Spruce shouted throwing his arms over his head. "All but three!"

"Yes sir, the woman was taken by the Neognathae into the Taro Bora tree and the other two, males I believe, were thrown by the explosion and their whereabout is currently unknown."

"Two?" Ori muttered under his breath. Then he hadn't been dazed after the blast. Behr had split into two people. "That can't be good."

"No," Mia agreed. "We must find the demon before he finds Elize."

"How?" Ori asked. "We're surrounded by rangers." Mia winked at Ori and leapt over the ranger's heads and onto the nearest tree.

"Stop her!" Spruce screamed. Several rangers raced up the tree after the sleek bast cat, all but Yew was tossed out of the tree.

"Oh dear," Taa fussed rushing over to help a young ranger who had broken his arm when he landed.

"I'll take care of him." A ranger wearing the brown tunic of a healer nodded at Taa.

Instead of trying to stop Mia, Yew followed Mia up to the top of the tree. Making sure he kept out of striking distance, Yew scanned the canopy for any signs of movement.

"What are we looking for exactly?" He asked Mia. Mia flicked her tail across his cheek to let Yew know he wasn't as clever as he thought, and one false move would send him down with the others.

"The winged demon." Mia replied. Summing Yew up with one quick look, Mia decided he could be trusted. "The one who flew off the man."

"One man was tossed towards the road and the other winged man flew that way." Yew whispered not wanting his commander to hear him. Spruce would not appreciate him sharing information with the enemy, not that he considered Mia an enemy.

"What's over there?" Mia pointed to a flat, dark brown splotch far to the northeast.

"That would be the bogs." Yew answered flatly. "Not a pleasant place to go."

"But we must," Mia told him reluctantly. She had no desire to go to the bogs either, but it seemed like a likely place for the demon to be hiding.

"Yew!" Spruce's voice thundered up the tree.

"We'd better go down." Yew told Mia. Mia nodded and skittered down almost as quickly as she had climbed up.

"Remove the Bast's belt," Spruce, ordered Fir, a sapling ranger still in training. Fir gulped and reached out for Mia's belt. Mia slapped the end of Fir's spear. The hilt flipped upward and struck Fir sharply under the chin.

Pushing Fir out of the way, Spruce leaned his narrow face so close to Mia's that it looked like their eyes were touching. Surely the feral knew the penalty for trespassing on their lands was a painful death. Yet she showed no fear. No fear what-so-ever.

"Your belt!" He shouted thrusting his hand out to rip it off. Something orange flashed to his left and then a sharp claw pressed into the center of his throat. The rangers surrounding them lifted their weapons.

"I wouldn't do that." Ori warned joining Mia and Gerawld. "Not unless you want a war. Scat, Leader of the Grassland Bast would not take you killing his daughter lightly."

"He's right," Taa agreed her head bobbing as if it were on a spring.

"Release me at once!" Spruce sputtered his face red with outraged.

Mia blinked at Gerawld. Gerawld pressed his claw deeper into Spruce's bark-like skin. Spruce lowered his hand. Gerawld growled a warning in the commander's ear before releasing him. Visibly flustered, Spruce brushed off his uniform and cleared his throat several times.

"Sir," Cedar shouted dropping out of a nearby tree and landing lightly in front of Spruce.
We followed the man as you ordered, sir, but he vanished into the crowds on the road. We believe he used magic to disguise himself."

"Bad magic," Mia spat.

"Yes," Cedar confirmed, "bad magic indeed."

"And the winged creature?" Spruce gurgled still rubbing his spindly throat.

"I have asked the birds and isopteria to be on the lookout for it, but so far it has not materialized."

"Mia believes the winged demon is hiding somewhere near the bogs." Yew interrupted. Spruce glared at him.

"And Mia is?"

"I am Mia." Mia answered her yellow-green eyes flashing menacing at Spruce. "We must go to the bogs. We must find the demon before it finds Elize."

"A demon." Ori mumbled rubbing his chin. "So that's where he got his power."

"Who?" Everyone asked at once.

"Behr," Ori answered. "I was wondering what he was doing so far from Astaria."

Behr was also wondering why he was so far from Astaria. When he received word about Roz wanting to sell information about the one who fell, he had her brought to him. Of course, the silly gnat had gotten cold feet by the time he got his hands on her and she refused to speak. Not that it mattered. The demon Scythe easily forced the information out of the stupid bug. Behr had no intention of traveling to Milendor, but Scythe had grown considerably stronger, and he could no longer control him. Behr rued the day his mother had convinced him that hosting the demon was a good idea. The longer he carried the vile demon, the more it took over.

The blast had surprised Behr. More than surprised him. It had shocked him, stunned him, almost stopped his heart, but most of all it had freed him.

Dazed and badly burnt, Behr stumbled onto the road blending into the crowd that had stampeded onto the Forest road. Behr snuck into a wagon full of small apples being pulled by several boys peddling the fruit. The boys didn't notice Behr among the apples until the cart got stuck in a small stream running across the road and chased him out.

"You idiot!" his mother's icy voice bubbled out of the stream. "How could you let Scythe escape!"

"Let had nothing to do with it." Behr replied wearily as the water maiden rose out of the water and changed into a beautiful translucent skinned woman. Being host to Scythe had taken a toll on Behr's psyche. Idiot or not he was glad to be rid of him.

"He'll still be weak," Behr's mother burbled behind him, unaware that he had walked away. "If we're quick we can get him back."

Behr faded back into the mob. His mother could do what she wanted. He was going back to the palace.

* * * * * * * *

The hooded figure in the long black and silver gown glided across the mosaic tiles depicting baby animals playing happily in a flowering garden. Her black forked tongue flickering as she leaned over Alzo fitfully sleeping in his bed.

"Where is the book!" The figure demanded her forked tongue dancing across the ragged gash running down the boy's cheek.

"Alzo!" Elize screamed jerking forward wildly.

"It's okay...It's okay." Alzo shushed taking Elize's hand in his and gently squeezing it. "I'm here." Elize opened her eyes.

"Alzo...Alzo! So, it wasn't just a dream...how did you get here?"

"Not the way you did," Alzo smiled at his little sister. "I had some help," He nodded at the girl standing next to him. "This is Ilee." Elize looked over a Ilee.

"Yeah, I remember her." Elize said smiling at the girl. "Thank you for helping my brother." Elize extended her hand in friendship. Ilee looked at the blue spot on Elize's palm and gasped.

"Where did you get that!" She hissed backing away from Elize. "Only the one chosen by Hohi is worthy of wearing the mark of Monet."

"What?" Elize asked glancing at her palm.

"The mark of Monet. You have no right to wear it!"

"Wear it?" Elize sputtered thrusting her palm in Ilee's face. "You sound like I have a choice! What do you think I did? Shove the damn stone under my skin like a fashion statement? I've had this damn thing as long as I can remember. It's caused me nothing but grief. God knows if I could have gotten of rid it I would have done so years ago!"

"It's true," Alzo said wrapping his arms around Ilee's small frame and holding her tightly. "Elize has had that in her palm since the day she was born."

"But how can that be?" Ilee sobbed letting her body go limp in Alzo's strong arms. She was so confused. How could there be more than one chosen one? It just didn't make sense.

"I don't know," Alzo told her, "but it's true."

"But my older sister Shi was given the mark of Monet," Ilee said slowly leaning her head against Alzo's chest. "Only the one chosen by Hohi can bear the mark of Monet. Shi replaced our mother as high priestess when she came of age. I wasn't allowed to attend the ceremony, but when Shi returned, she bore the Mark of Monet on her palm."

"You said Hohi spoke to you?" Alzo asked staring down at Ilee with his brow furrowed.

Ilee bit her lip and hesitated before answering him. "Hohi speaks to Shi through me." She admitted shyly. Ilee prayed that she hadn't upset Hohi by revealing this truth, but Hohi had spoken to Alzo also, hadn't she?

"Where are we?" Elize asked noticing the rough walls made from sticks, mud and bits of string and vines.

"In a nest," Alzo answered loosening his grip on Ilee.

"An owl nest?" Elize asked still not sure what was going on. She remembered entering the forest, but everything after that was a bit hazy.

"No, not an owl's nest." A soft voice answered as a heart shaped face appeared in the doorway. "A Neognathae nest." Ilee let out a muffled gasp and ducked behind Alzo. Alzo could feel her trembling as the tall, graceful creature hopped into the nest.

"A Neognathae?" Elize asked staring at the beautiful cream colored owl who was as tall or taller than she was. Taa had used that name when she told her about the Oracle of Milendor.

"Don't let her touch you," Ilee whispered harshly from behind Alzo.

"I am Nekita." Nekita said bowing her head at Elize as she spoke. "Grandniece of Su Lei, Oracle of Milendor." Nekita blinked her startling blue eyes and glided towards them. Her silky feathers drifting down her slender frame like a gown, etched with fine golden designs at the tips. She was stunning. Elize couldn't remember ever seeing anyone so elegant as Nekita.

"I'm Alzo," Alzo boomed taking Nekita's tiny hands gently in his. Ilee gasped in horror and pulled at his back. Alzo ignored her. "My name is Alzo, this is my sister Elize and Ilee is behind me."

"One can call themselves whatever they wish," Nekita commented clicking her ivory beak at him, "but it does not change who one is."

Elize gave Nekita a curious look, Nekita winked at her, but didn't elaborate on her comment. Instead, she drifted back to the door and ruffled her feathers.

"The Oracle is resting." Nekita told them as she hopped back out of the nest. "She will send for you after the sun has set. Refreshments will arrive shortly."

"Who was that?" Elize asked glancing out the nest and watching as Nekita gracefully glided down the path and into a vast garden.

"Nekita apparently," Alzo joked.

"A Neognathae," Ilee said creeping up behind Elize and peeking over her shoulder. Her eyes as big as saucers. "I can't believe you touched her." She scolded Alzo. "My Gram told me that the Neognathae can steal your thoughts with a single touch of their tiny hands."

Alzo groaned and held out his arms. "I'm a mindless zombie." He teased rolling his eyes. Elize slapped his arm.

"Knock it off." She hissed. Obviously Ilee believed what her Gram had told her, and it wasn't nice to tease her. After all most lore had a bit of truth hidden in it.

"Hallo, hallo," A voice boomed into the nest as a turkey platter sized plate was shoved into Alzo's outstretched arms. "I brought food." A giant girl announced stepping back to let a smaller, girl with a face like a squirrel climb inside the nest.

"I'm Kara." The large girl announced as she handed the smaller girl a steaming teapot, "and this is Pippy."

"A giant," Elize exclaimed under her breath. She had been fascinated by giants for as long as she could remember. Even though others insisted giants only existed in fairy tales, Elize always believed they were real. She was delighted to finally meet one.

"Oh biscuits!" Kara exclaimed slapping her thick thighs, "we forgot the cups."

The smaller girl wrinkled up her nose and opened her mouth which was full of shiny, pointy teeth. "Screech!" She squealed. Almost instantly a tiny gray owl appeared in front of her. "Cups please." Pippy cooed sweetly. The tiny owl disappeared and reappeared just as quickly with a wooden cup. The little girl held up two fingers. The owl dropped the cup in her hand and in the blink of an eye returned with two more cups.

"Good screechy," Pippy squeaked tossing a crumb into the air. The tiny owl emitted an ear-splitting screech, snatched the crumb in its beak, and disappeared in a puff of smoke.

"I'm Kara," The giant bubbled happily. Too large to fit through the entryway, Kara pressed her face in the hole and smiled widely. "The Oracle said to make you food." Kara nodded at Pippy who was busy filling the wooden cups with tea. "Pippy made tea. I made yellow biscuits." Pippy set down the teapot and pointed at the plate of yellow biscuits. Kara smiled at her. "And meat pies."

"It smells amazing," Alzo exclaimed picking up a piping hot meat pie and taking a big bite. "Mmmm, good." He mumbled raising his eyebrows and taking another bite.

"Oh goody!" Kara beamed clapping her hands joyfully. Not as brave as her brother Elize picked up a yellow biscuit and nibbled at a corner.

"Lemon!" She exclaimed happily. "My favorite!"

Kara smiled wide revealing large tile-like teeth. Kara loved to cook, but seldom had new people to cook for.

Elize studied Kara's face as she munched on the lemon biscuit. She wondered how large Kara would get. Even though Kara was already over seven feet tall she was still a child. A child, Elize sensed, who had experience something very traumatic in her life. Something shut up deep inside of her.

Kara sent Pippy back with the kettle while she waited for Alzo to finish off the last biscuit. Leaving the cups and some fruit, Kara took the tray. She was feeling quite pleased with herself as she carried the now empty tray through the garden. She liked the daytime when Su Lei and the others were asleep. It was her time for doing whatever she pleased. That's why it upset her so when she spotted Nekita in the garden still very much awake. Kara silently pressed her body into a thick crease in the tree trunk so she could see what Nekita was doing without drawing attention to herself. Kara did not like Nekita. Nekita was mean to her and treated her like she was stupid. Nekita was not like Su Lei. The Oracle always treated her kindly and told her secret things.

Luckily for Kara Nekita was too busy focusing on the tiny bones inside the dish by her talons to notice her. If she had, Nekita surely would have told Kara to get lost. Nekita felt Su Lei gave Kara way too much freedom. She did not trust the giant girl. More than once, Nekita had caught her snooping in places she had no reason to be.

Nekita brushed away the small gray owl fluttering about her head. She hated being interrupted when she was reading the bones. The slightest movement could change the message before she had a chance to read it. The little owl continued fluttering above her head until Nekita finally gave up and let it deliver his message.

"Yes, I agree something does need to be done." Nekita told the screecher. Screechers were tiny gray owls who had lived with the Neognathae for as long as anyone could remember. "It's hard to concentrate with all the noise." Nekita fussed scooping up the bones and giving them a good shake before tossing them back into the dish. After several minutes she shrugged and turned back to the screecher.

"Take a message to Spruce." She told the owl slowly continuing to stare into the dish. "Tell him to move the intruders to…wait…yes…tell Spruce to move the intruders down the east road." The screecher squawked. "Of course, I know where the east road goes," Nekita twitched, "but the rebellion will be short lived if they march out the south gate. See?" Nekita pointed at a rib cage impaled with what had once been a rat's forearm. The screecher bobbed his head in agreement. "Have the rangers lead all the intruders down the east road to the bog." The screecher squawked again. "Tell them that the Change will meet them by the old peat houses." The gray owl hooted bobbing his head up and down. "No, I don't know if the Change will be there or not, but his followers will go there if they think he's there."

A darkness brushed past Kara's face, drifting over her cheek and into her bowl sized left ear. Her face screwed up and a deep anger seeped into her heart evaporating the joy, she had felt moments before.

"She has no right," Kara grumbled to herself. "The peat houses belong to my people. Not hers."

The tiny owl spun his head sharply and emitted a glass shattering screech. Kara froze as Nekita's cold gaze crossed over her.

"You should be resting," Nekita called out with a tinge of sternness in her voice as Elize entered the garden. "Didn't you drink the tea?"

Elize smiled slyly and shook her head. "It tasted funny, so I switched cups with Alzo when he wasn't looking." Nekita ruffled her wings and glanced back at the tiny bones.

"What are those?" Elize asked leaning over to get a better look at the dish.

"Bones," Nekita answered giving the dish a firm shake. The mix of mice, rat, and vertebrae from random small rodents she had collected over the years bounced about the surface in response. "They help me to see into the days ahead." Nekita glanced into the dish and frowned, "but not so much today." She clicked her beak in frustration. "Today they do not appear to be saying much."

"Wait," Elize said reaching out to stop Nekita from shaking the bones again. "I think I see something." Elize stared at the tiny bones. The pattern reminded her of binary codes, except instead of ones and zeros these looked like threes and sevens. Placing her right palm over the bones Elize closed her eyes.

"I see...I see you... soaring over a large ocean..."

"Nonsense!" Nekita sputtered shaking the dish so violently several of the bones tumbled over the rim and onto the path. "What you say is impossible!" She snapped flapping her wings. "I am destined to be the next Oracle. A destiny decided for me before I broke free from my egg. I will never leave this tree. I will never leave the Forest of Milendor. When the time arrives, Su Lei will bless me with the memories of all the Oracles who have gone before me and on that day, I will enter the cosmic egg and become one with them. That is my destiny. That is who I am."

"But not who you want to be. Is it?" Elize asked taking Nekita's trembling hands in hers.

Nekita flinched. "Aren't you afraid I'll steal your memories?" She mocked.

"Nah, someone already beat you to that." Elize replied sadly. Nekita stared intently into Elize's eyes.

"No," she hooted softly, "your memories are still there. Hidden behind a fog of misconceptions."

"A fog of misconception." Elize said dropping Nekita's hands. She was not used to being read. It felt eerily intrusive. "That's a nice way of putting it. Lies is more like it. My mother insisted Alzo was a figment of my imagination. An imaginary brother I made up. But all this time, all these years, I knew Alzo was real, and I was right. All these years Alzo lived a half a day drive from where we lived, and she knew it!" Elize choked, her eyes flooding with tears.

"Is that why you are here? To find your brother?" Nekita asked her sharp eyes fixed upon Elize's face.

"No," Elize said looking confused. "I'm here because Taa received a message from the Oracle saying to bring me to her at once."

"Nonsense," Nekita exclaimed flapping her fluffy wings. "The Oracle sent no such message!"

"Well, someone did." Elize said and told Nekita the story Taa told her about the brown owl pecking his way through the roof of her hut.

"That's why Taa left the healing center." Elize told Nekita. "She was so excited about coming to Milendor."

"The Neognathae do not use brown owls to deliver messages. All messages are sent by screechers." Nekita said plucking a large black beetle off a plant and popping it in her beak.

"If you didn't invite us, then who did?" Elize asked trying not to gag.

Nekita finished her snack and snapped her fingers. A fluffy gray owl appeared in front of them. Nekita hooted at the little owl. The owl screeched out an answer. Nekita translated.

"No messages were sent to brown owls or deerlings."

"Are you telling me that the Oracle had no idea we were coming?"

"The bones hinted at unexpected visitors," Nekita replied, "but I must admit I wasn't expecting any to drop from the sky."

"I don't think they were expecting it either." Elize laughed glancing down at a patch of Lily of the Valley. She had always loved Lily of the Valley. They reminded her of tiny church bells. "It's really quite amazing up here. Your gardens are magnificent. I wish Taa could see them."

Nekita clicked her beak. The little gray screecher winked at her and disappeared. "You should rest," she said leading Elize back through the garden to the nest where Alzo and Ilee were still fast asleep. "You'll need your strength for whatever tonight brings."

"I'm worried about my friends," Elize said looking down at her feet. "I hope they're okay."

"They are," Nekita assured her lifting the curtain covering the entrance to the nest.

"Good," Elize said. Stepping inside the nest she was suddenly overcome with sleepiness.

Far below Commander Spruce stood with his hands on his hips surveying the damage caused by the swamp troll. What a disaster this day had turned out to be! If you had asked him yesterday, Spruce would have boasted confidently that the Rangers of Milendor were well prepared to handle any situation. Unfortunately, none of their training scenarios had prepared them for this.

"What?" Spruce snapped at the screecher fluttering about his head. The owl snapped at Spruce's twig-like nose and wiggled his leg. Grumbling Spruce untied the note wrapped from the screecher's long leg and looked at it. "It would have been nice to have had a warning," Spruce complained loudly shaking his knobby fist at the large silver barked tree. "You're an Oracle, right? Supposed to see the future?"

"Sir?" Yew asked leaning over to get a peek at the note.

"None of the trespassers are to be harmed." Spruce announced handing the note to him. Yew quickly scanned the note.

"It says we are to take all the intruders to the bog." Yew read the note aloud. "Not just the five we planned on. They are to make their way from there to the peat houses where the Change will join them in two nights."

"If that's what it says, that's what we'll do," Spruce announced returning to the trees. "The sooner we get this mob out of our forest the better."

"The bog!" Ori exclaimed throwing his hands in the air. "You can't be serious?" Ori had never been to the bog, but he was sure it wasn't a place he wanted to go.

"This is unacceptable!" Taa exclaimed stepping around Ori. "I demand to be taken to the Oracle at once." Taa placed her hands on her hips. Yew coughed and looked at Taa like she'd lost her mind.

"No one goes up the Tara Bora uninvited."

Taa flared her nostrils and pawed the ground. "But I was invited!" She insisted pulling the tattered ribbon from her cloak and shaking it in Yew's face.

"If that's the case," Yew answered grabbing the ribbon out of her hand, "why weren't you carried away with your friend?"

"I don't know," Taa replied tossing her nose up, "but I was invited, and I demand…"

"You are a prisoner," Yew informed her firmly, "you're in no position to demand anything."

"But sir," Fir exclaimed keeping his voice below a whisper. "We've never traveled the east road by foot."

"We will follow you on the ground," Mia offered, tightening her belt. "Gerawld and I are seasoned scouts. If there is a way we will find it. But keep in mind what I told you before." Yew nodded and returned to the trees to brief his team.

"What did you tell him before?" Taa asked still not happy about their situation.

"I told him I sensed the demon hiding near the bog. He is searching for Elize. We need to find the demon before he finds Elize. That is why I did not fight the decision to go there."

"I guess that makes sense." Taa grumbled watching Gerawld feeding Mukrot some dried toads he had picked up along the way. "At least Mukrot should be able to find something familiar to eat there."

A few minutes later Mia and Gerawld took off to mark the way through the badly overgrown east road keeping a keen eye on Yew and a small group of rangers who led the way from the trees above them. The going was not easy. After the peat houses closed no one had any reason to travel the east road. Large parts of it were so overgrown that Mia and Gerawld were forced to hack their way through. When the small group finally reached the bog, the sun had set.

"I suggest you camp out here for the night." Yew told them. Once you step out of the forest the Rangers of Milendor can no longer be of service to you."

"Why?" Taa asked brushing away a cloud of pesky bugs.

"We cannot leave the forest." Yew explained. "If we do the enchantment that gives us life is broken and we return to our natural state."

"And that is?" Ori asked curiously.

"Twigs and sticks." Yew replied sadly. "But if you camp under the safety of the forest, me and my brothers will ensure you are not eaten in the night."

"This is totally unacceptable!" Taa barked, pulling off her cloak and giving it a good shake. "What is that awful smell." She sniffed making a sour face.

"That would be the bog," Ori said raising his eyebrows at Taa's chest. "I never realized you were so...um human." He commented casually.

"Well, I am." Taa huffed tossing her cloak on the ground and lying down on it.

The only one happy about camping next to the bog was Mukrot. The swamp troll inhaled the thick air deeply and sighed. Ignoring Yew's warnings, he ran out of the forest and sloshed into the bog smiling widely as he sunk neck deep into the thick brackish muck.

Exhausted Ori shifted into his fox body and crawled under the nearest bush. Mia left Gerawld curled up next to Taa and joined Yew on the thick branch just above it.

"Taa's right, it stinks." Mia commented stretching her sleek black body along the limb and licking her right paw.

Taa laid awake on her cloak for what seemed like hours listening to Gerawld's snoring.

"There's got to be a way up," she whispered carefully getting to her feet. The dark shape of the Taro Bora tree loomed in the distance like a skyscraper in a blackout. "I was invited." She groused pulling the ribbon off her wrist and giving it a firm shake. To her surprise several gray puffs popped out.

Taa shook the ribbon again. More gray puffs popped out. Before she knew it she was completely engulfed. Frantic Taa tried to brush her way out. Finally, the cloud of gray puffs dissipated and Taa found herself standing in front of Elize.

CHAPTER 9

Kara and Pippy arrived with more food just before sunset.
Flatbread, a slab of brown cheese and tea sweetened with thick golden
honey that sat in the bottom of the cup like a hidden treat. Elize sensed
a change in Kara. Sour, like milk left out in the sun too long.

"Eat," Kara instructed shoving the tray into the nest nearly hitting
poor Pippy in the face. "It's almost time."

"Time for what?" Alzo asked breaking off a bit of cheese to top
his flat bread.

"For the Oracle." Kara replied dryly.

"I won't go," Ilee pouted turning her back on the giant and
refusing to eat.

Kara pulled her head out of the nest and left. She could care a less
what the annoying island girl did or did not do.

"I hate this place." Ilee screamed grabbing a slice of bread off the
plate once Kara had gone. "I can't wait to get my feet back on firm
ground."

"Aren't you curious to see the Oracle?" Alzo asked reaching for
another piece of bread. Ilee shook her head.

"You know what's crazy?" Elize said leaning closer to Alzo and
keeping her voice low. "Nekita said the Oracle hadn't sent for us."

"That's strange." Alzo agreed brushing a crumb out of his beard.
"I wonder who did? I clearly heard a voice yelling Milendor."

"So did I and someone sent Taa a message. By owl." Elize added
snatching the last bit of cheese before Alzo could get his hands on it.

When Kara returned a little while later Ilee still refused to leave
the nest, so they left her there. In the half-light between sunset and
dark the two siblings followed the giant along a plank walkway that
crossed a lush garden which took them under a large arch dripping with
deep blue moon flowers. Moon flowers are like morning glories, but
instead of blooming with the morning sun, their blossoms open at dusk.

"Up," Kara grunted before starting up a staircase woven out of
thick vines. The vines shook and rattled under the giant girl's weight
showering twigs and leaves down on Alzo and Elize. As they followed
Kara up the stairs, Elize was sure the vines were about to snap, but to
her great relief they held fast. Nekita was waiting impatiently at the top
of the stairs. With the soft purple moonlight shining upon her, she
looked like a goddess.

"Good eventide," Nekita cooed bowing her heart shaped face to
her chin before waving her slender hand motioning for them to follow
as she glided gracefully down a well-worn path lined with tiny
luminous flowers. Elize was amazed by the stunning variety of flowers
and other plants growing so high above the forest floor. She had never
seen anything quite like it before. It was truly magical. Nekita stopped

in front of a pair of landscaped branches which had been woven together to form a bowl on which a humongous eggshell sat.

"Where is she," Nekita hissed at Kara clearly unhappy to find the shell empty. Kara brushed the dirty straw-like hair from her eyes and shrugged. Nekita glared at the girl, her sapphire eyes reflecting her displeasure. "Well don't just stand there. Go see what is keeping her!"

Kara flashed Nekita a hard look before sulking off to find Su Lei. She resented Nekita bossing her about, but she knew that disobeying her would upset Su Lei and she didn't want to do that.

"The Oracle refuses to appear until all her guests have arrive," Kara told Nekita sourly when she returned a few minutes later. Nekita looked over at Elize and Alzo and clicked her beak. In her hurry she did not notice Ilee wasn't with them.

"Where's Ilee?" She squawked raising a talon as if she intended to strike the giant girl. Kara pointed back towards the staircase. "Go get her! Now!" Kara's face flared red.

"That girl is getting too big for her feathers," Nekita complained motioning Alzo and Elize over to a row of benches situated in a semi-circle around the base holding the Oracle's egg.

"Sit," Nekita said hopping onto the center bench and grasping the edge tightly with her ivory talons.

Shouts erupted beneath them and a few moments later Kara appeared dragging Ilee kicking and screaming up the staircase. As soon as she saw Alzo, Ilee broke free from Kara's beefy grip and ran to him. Kara let her go and walked over to Nekita.

"Now we can begin," Nekita announced. Kara lifted a large ornate pitcher and began filling one of the seven lamps that hung in a circle under the shell. Each time a lamp was filled, a Neognathae appeared under it holding a mouse skin pouch in her tiny hands.

"Try not to breathe in the smoke." Nekita warned as the seven Neognathae began to chant. One-by-one each owl lady opened her pouch and poured the contents into the lamp in front of them causing the lamp to boil violently. The chanting grew louder, and more hypnotic as rose-colored smoke poured from the lamps and began to fill the shell. The chanting reached a climax when the egg wobbled, and the silhouette of a figure materialize within it.

"Behold the Oracle of Milendor!" Nekita shouted. She hopped off her perch and flapped her wings to part the smoke revealing a plump, almost round, six-foot tall snow white owl. The Oracle turned her snowy head in a half circle and stared at her guests upside down. Her intense blue eyes danced with delight.

"Who, who, whom!" Su Lei hooted playfully. "Can it be Prince Alzotarian and Princess Monetelisadora of Astaria?"

"No!" Elize interrupted getting to her feet. "I'm Elize, just Elize, no princess whatsit."

"And I'm just Alzo," Alzo added getting to his feet to stand next to his sister. "I stopped being Prince Alzotarian the second I stepped on to Earth."

"Wait…What?" Elize exclaimed looking over at her brother.

Su Lei chuckled, her old eyes twinkling with amusement. "There seems to be some mistake," she chortled to Nekita from her perch, "In my vision I saw the prince and princess of Astaria, not a leaping lizard and a little green bird."

Nekita looked up at her grand aunt and hooted several times, her cheeks raised into what could only be described as a smile.

"What are you talking about?" Elize asked, clearly not getting the joke.

Still smiling, Nekita lifted a broad leaf of a nearby plant. A startled a red and brown lizard blinked at them. "Behold an Alzo," she explained. The lizard blinked his lidless eyes at them before gracefully leaping to another leaf well out of Nekita's reach. "And this," Nekita said shaking the tree branch above where a tiny green bird no bigger than a cricket was roosting. The bird opened her sleepy eyes and began singing.

"Is an Elizeadora." Alzo laughed flashing Elize a mischievous smile. "Elizeadora, Elizeadora sitting in a tree," he sang, "Elizeadora, Elizeadora sing a song for me."

Elize curtsied at her goofy brother and sang the next bit, "I will sing, I will sing, I will sing for you Payape. I will sing, I will sing a pretty song for thee."

"Ah memories," Su Lei cooed, her voice dry and worn with age. "Come closer my dear and share your memories with me."

"Memories, or imagination," Elize said remembering what Ilee had said earlier and keeping her distance. "That's the problem really, I'm not sure what I remember is an actual memory or just something I made up."

"Let me help you," Su Lei cooed stretching her neck out and blowing a stream of pink smoke in Elize's face.

Elize coughed and rubbed the smoke from her eyes with the back of her hand. An image of a man appeared dressed in a lime green suit and a canary yellow robe. He had wild hair like Alzo's on a humid day. Elize saw herself as a toddler running to the window he was watching her from with a handful of purple flowers she had picked for him.

"Come play!" Elize heard herself say, but the man shook his head and stayed in the ornate, wheeled chair inside the hall.

"Payape!" A boy screamed from the arms of the guard running into the garden. The boy's face was covered with blood.

"Alzo!" Elize screamed watching as the man pushed himself out of the chair and stumbled to take Alzo in his arms. Elize shivered at the memory of her brother's attack.

"What happened next?" Su Lei prompted rocking back and forth in her shell.

"The snake woman...came to help...Mayme pushed her away. The...the snake woman hissed at Mayme, and her collar rose up behind her...like...like...like a..."

"Cobra," Alzo commented between gritted teeth. "It was Ceen, the Cobrateen. Payape's healer. Mayme hated her. She begged Payape to send her away, but he wouldn't."

"He couldn't." Su Lei answered softly sinking back into her egg.

"Mayme said I had imagined it." Elize told Alzo, "but I knew it was real. Just like I knew you were real. I wonder why she lied to me."

"Must keep the little ones safe!" Su Lei shrieked so loud that Elize jumped. "Keep the little ones safe! Safe from the snake! The snake will nibble their toes and swallow them whole!"

"Is she talking about Ceen?" Alzo whispered to Nekita.

"Perhaps," Nekita replied tilting her head to one side, "but it is not wise to speak that name. The Cobrateen has ears everywhere."

Su Lei clicked her beak sharply and scraped her yellowed talon against the bottom of the shell making a sound like fingernails across a chalkboard.

"Enough of the past!" She squawked loudly slamming her talon against the bottom of the shell. The shell wobbled violently in response. "The past is gone! It is the future that matters!" Su Lei flapped her wings dramatically causing the smoke to swirl about her head like a fiery halo. "The time has come for change! The time has come for YOU!" Su Lei exclaimed leaning out of the egg and pointing a tiny finger at Alzo. "You are the future! You are the Change!"

"No! Alzo shouted shaking his head. "No, I'm not!"

"Nonsense!" Su Lei squawked snapping her beak at him. "I see the Change! He is standing before me, tall and strong with hair like the Shiva tree! It is you! You are the Change! When you speak, they listen. Where you lead, they follow."

"No" Alzo protested. "I'm not...."

"No, no, no!" The Oracle mocked hopping from one talon to the other causing the egg to rock wildly in response. "Know! Know! Know the truth! Accept the truth! You are the Change!"

"I think she's right," Elize whispered squeezing Alzo's calloused hand. "I think you're the one all those people below us are waiting for.

It the prophecy is right and I'm the one who fell then it makes sense that you are the great change I'm supposed to bring."

"What about Ori?" Alzo protested pulling his hand free and waving it in front of him. "He came with us too! Or maybe it's you! After all you're the one with the power. Maybe you're the Change!"

"No!" Su Lei screeched scraping her talon against the bottom of the shell again. "It is not her destiny to be the Change! It is yours!"

"You can't force him to be something he doesn't want to be!" Ilee shouted getting to her feet and standing protectively in front of Alzo.

"Hoo, who, whom," Su Lei demanded staring at Ilee with large piercing blue eyes. "Fish of a feather swim together, but you are neither fish nor fowl."

"I am Ilee, a priestess of Hohi!" Ilee said proudly jutting out her chin and trying not to tremble.

"Not true, not true." Su Lei taunted turning her head back and forth in a half circle. "You are Ilee, High Priestess of Hohi!"

"No!" Ilee replied curtly. "My sister Shi is the High Priestess!

"Not true!" Su Lei told her firmly blinking several times before continuing. "It is you that Hohi speaks to. Not your sister."

"How do you know that?" Ilee gasped embarrassed to hear the truth being spoken out loud. Only Shi and her mother knew that.

Su Lei leaned out of the egg and tilted her snowball shaped head back and forth. "Who whispers to Shi now that you are gone? Who, who, whoo?" She taunted.

"Hohi! Hohi speaks to Shi!" Ilee shrieked leaping at the shell and striking one of the branches holding it up. The egg wobbled erratically.

"Nonsense!" The Oracle squawked fighting to keep her balance. "Hohi speaks to you! Stop fooling yourself and stop wasting our time!"

"Sit down." Nekita told Ilee sharply reaching out for her arm.

"Don't touch me!" Ilee growled slapping Nekita's hand away.

"If Nekita wanted your memories child, they would already be hers," Su Lei spoke in a voice not her own.

"Hohi?" Ilee stopped swatting at Nekita and glanced around searching for her beloved Hohi.

"Since the beginning of time the Neognathae have served as scribes for the nine realms." Su Lei continued in Hohi's voice. "Recording the wisdom of the ages and passing it down to those that followed. The Neognathae were given hands to record memories, not steal them. Knowledge of the past helps us to survive the future. That is the reason it needs to be preserved and shared. If the past is not known, it will surely repeat itself."

"How do you speak in Hohi's voice?" Ilee demanded. When Su Lei didn't answer Ilee looked at Alzo. "How does she speak in Hohi's voice?"

Alzo shook his head. How was he supposed to know?

"Silence!" Su Lei shouted in Hohi's voice. "Your time with the Oracle is short! Stop wasting it!"

"I see a large brown mule," Su Lei said in her own voice. Closing her eyes, Su Lei began to weave her snowy head side to side. "I see the Emperor riding out to greet his son."

"That's not going to happen," Alzo snorted. "Payape never leaves the palace. I wonder if he's even alive. I can't imagine him allowing his people to suffer so."

"Be assured Emperor Tazodorin is alive, but not well." Nekita told him. "It is not he who has allowed the empire to suffer. He only sees what his advisors wish him to see. Happy oblivion. Or so they believe...it was he who saw you...he who believed his children were still alive...he who sent the Vanji to find you. Just as it was Hohi who sent Ilee to rescue you. To help you. Together you are strong. I see you walking side-by-side bravely facing the approaching storm. Behind you Toboria's children stand awaiting your command."

"The tree is on fire!" Su Lei screamed thrusting her head out of the shell and looking up. "Fire is raining down from the sky! Save the books! Save the gardens! Run, run, run for your lives! Fire! Fire!"

Unable to control her fear any longer, Ilee screamed and bolted for the stairs. Alzo started to go after her, but Nekita stopped him. "It's just a vision." She whispered to Alzo. "It will pass." Sure enough a few seconds later Su Lei's eyes cleared, and she settled back into the shell.

"I am old," Su Lei sighed sounding confused. "Older than you can imagine. My time grows short, and I tire easily." Su Lei fixed her gaze on Alzo. "The Oracle of Milendor has provided council to the Emperor of Astaria for over eight generations. We guided the First Emperor on his travels across the planet to bring peace to the Freedlands and beyond. I watched your grandfather's folly and your father's neglect destroy what the First Emperor worked so hard to create. Now I am tired, and the memories jumble in my mind." The old owl stopped talking and looked down at her talons as if she'd forgotten why she was there. Finally, she lifted her head.

"A prince who'd rather be a lizard!" She screamed her eyes rolling back into their sockets. "His father's son no doubt!" She cackled, "boohoo I'm not a leader! Wah! Send my little sister to do my job! Wah, wah, wah."

The Oracle's eyes flew open and locked upon Alzo's. "A wise leader has the heart and eyes to recognize those around him who possess the skills and abilities he does not. A beloved leader is one with faith and trust to allow his followers to use those skills and abilities without hindering them. Look below," she demanded. Alzo looked at his feet. All he saw were leaves.

"The Rangers of Milendor have trained for battle their entire lives. They are among the best archers in the nine realms. They are unrivaled in above ground military tactics, camouflage, and surveillance. The Bast warriors have been in training since the day their eyes opened. Bast are experts in the use of ground weaponry, stealth, tracking, and strategic thinking. Even your timid island girl is a trained warrior. She is at home in the water as well as the land and is well equipped to protect those she loves."

Alzo nodded, what Su Lei said made sense. It didn't matter if he was a skilled fighter. There was a forest of them below him as well as a Vanji. He might not trust Ori, but he'd be a fool not to use him. Vanji's were renown spies. Even if they had no scruples and would sell their information to the highest bidder in a heartbeat it was good to have one on your side.

Su Lei nodded at Nekita satisfied that she had made her point. It was still early, but the weight of this night was already wearing her down.

"Can I see your hand," Nekita whispered softly reaching out to take Elize's hand. Sparks sputtered out from where Askar had bit her.

"Ouch" Elize cried out jerking her hand back. "That really hurt."

Su Lei peered out of the shell. Her blue eyes focused on the tiny bit of blue stone poking out of Elize's torn palm.

"Whoo bit you?" She asked tilting her head completely sideways. "Whoo, who, whom?"

"Askar, the crazy Bast shaman," Elize replied angrily. "He attacked me for no reason and tried to rip my hand apart. Nekita leaned her head closer to Elize's palm and clicked her beak.

"Your hand needs tending to."

"Taa already took care of it," Elize told her frowning at her swollen palm. "She cleaned it and put a bandage on it."

"I don't see a bandage now," Nekita stated clicking her beak as she continued to examined the torn flesh.

"It must have flown off when the power came out."

"Ah," Su Lei tittered, "an unfortunate event. Now your enemies are no longer guessing. Now they know."

"My enemies," Elize repeated shaking her head, "what enemies?"

"Never trust a woman trapped inside her own head!" Su Lei squawked. "The Earth is full of many wonderful things, best not let him get hold of them. A tisket a taskit a red and yellow basket, if you let him close to you he'll put you in a casket."

"Never mind that," Nekita interrupted, her tone gentle, but firm. "Elize needs to have her hand attended to. Where is this Taa you speak of?"

"Down there," Elize replied. Nekita clicked her beak sharply. A puff of gray appeared and disappeared. Moments later a large gray cloud appeared in front of them.

"Shoo!" A familiar voice shouted from within the cloud.

"Taa!" Elize cried when the screechers parted to reveal a startled and quite ruffled Taa.

"Elize!" Taa shouted embracing her.

"Elize's hand needs to be attended to." Nekita said looking Taa over with great interest. She had never seen a deerling before. She wondered what other species might live outside Milendor's boundaries.

Taa looked at Elize's palm and frowned. She was surprised at how infected it had gotten. "I wish I had filled my bags before I left." Taa rifled through the small cloth bags stuffed into her clock pockets and shook her head.

"You will be able to find what you need in the healing gardens." Nekita assured her. "If you don't see what you need ask the isopteria who tend the gardens."

Aggravated at being ignored, Su Lei hobbled to the edge of the shell and spread her wings.

"Oh, nits and gnats!" Nekita exclaimed as Su Lei launched her plump body from the shell frantically flapping her ancient wings. Nekita raced under her fully aware that Su Lei hadn't flew for centuries and her wings were too weak to carry her weight. Propelling herself off the ground, Nekita grabbed Su Lei and safely landed on the ground with minimal bumping.

"Watch out!" Elize yelled shoving Alzo out of the way and catching the huge egg before it crashed to the ground.

"Whoa!" Alzo exclaimed taking the egg from his sister. "I thought it was made of stone." He bounced the shell from hand to hand until Kara stomped over and took it from him.

"Not a toy," the giant scolded and carefully returned the shell where it belonged.

Unharmed by her unscheduled flight Su Lei hopped over to Elize and dropped her head in Elize's palm.

"What do we have here?" The Oracle cooed stabbing her beak downward into the infected wound. A spark like static electricity flared out startling the Oracle. Su Lei squawked and rolled backwards grasping a thin silver whisker in her beak.

Elize clapped her hands over her ears as her mind exploded with sound. Birds chirping, mice and bugs rustling through the labyrinth of tangled roots, peat and the remains of decaying nest that made up the garden floor, and thoughts, so many thoughts. Elize pressed her hands into her ears, but it didn't help.

"Come back here!" Nekita yelled as Su Lei let out an ear-splitting screech and rolled out of her grasp waving the silver whisker like a prize.

"It's mine!" The Oracle squealed manically dancing away from Nekita before she could catch her again.

"It's one of Silver's whiskers!" Elize exclaimed shaking her head to clear it.

"Looks like it," Taa yelped dodging the crazed bird. "The Oracle pulled it out of your wound. Silver must have lost it."

"It wasn't put there by accident," Nekita yelled chasing after her crazed grand aunt. "Whoever put it in there was using you."

"Using me? How?" Elize asked.

"It is an old shaman trick," Taa said in her teaching voice. "Silver must have put a spell on the whisker and slipped it inside your wound so she could see through your eyes."

Su Lei hopped by flapping her wings. "Can't see now! Can't see now!"

"Your aunt really needs to stop inhaling that smoke." Alzo laughed lunging at Su Lei as she ran past. The old bird veered sharply to the left almost plowing into Taa again. Taa made a grab for the whisker but missed. The Oracle snapped at her and spun to her right and straight into Nekita's open arms. Giving her niece a defiant look, Su Lei stuffed the whisker into her beak and swallowed.

"Open your beak!" Nekita yelled giving the old bird a firm shake. Su Lei squawked and hissed at her. Nekita reached into her beak and pulled the whisker free.

"I'll take that," Taa said holding open a small cloth bag. "I'll give it to Mia so she can give it back to Silver when she returns to her family."

"Tell this Silver she'll have to use her own eyes to see from now on." Nekita scoffed dropping the whisker into the bag. Taa started to tell her Silver was blind but decided to leave it.

"Kara!" Nekita yelled gripping her sniveling grand aunt and not letting her go. "Kara!" She screamed louder. Kara appeared next to her. "The Oracle is tired. Take her to her nest and make sure she stays there. I will be in shortly."

Kara picked Su Lei off the ground and carried her squawking out of the moonlit garden. Nekita clicked her beak. A gray ball of fluff appeared in front of her.

"Take our guests to their nest. Then fetch Pippy and tell her to take the Healer to the Isopteria gardens. Tell Pippy to have Green help Taa find whatever she needs to replenish her supplies."

112

"I didn't realize the Oracle was so eccentric." Taa whispered to Elize as they followed the gray puff towards the steps.

"She certainly wasn't what I was expecting." Elize admitted with a laugh.

"She's unique. I'll give her that." Alzo laughed. "I wonder how she knew who we were?"

"Guessed?" Elize shrugged. "Our disappearance must have been common knowledge. So, it wouldn't be too much of a long shot."

"Yeah maybe." Alzo nodded starting down the stairs holding the vine railing just in case it snapped.

As they made their way down the stairs Taa noticed a large snail slithering along the vines and plucked it off.

"Why did you put a snail on my hand?" Elize asked as the large orange snail slithered across her wound leaving a thick, slimy trail across her palm. Taa picked up the snail and turned it back around.

"This particular snail's slime has unique healing properties." Taa assured her lifting the snail from Elize's palm and gently setting it on a leaf. "That should do it. Too much and it'll make you loopy."

"I thought you'd never leave that crazy old bat!" Ilee exclaimed running up to Alzo the second his feet touched the pathway.

"Let them go ahead." Elize said taking Taa by the elbow. "I'm glad you're here, but I'm really sorry I got you into this mess."

"Nonsense!" Taa laughed, her chocolate brown eyes sparkling with excitement. "This is what I've been yearning for! Excitement! Adventure! Roz and I dreamed of leaving the Healing Center for years. When I was young, I lived in a strict environment. Every night I'd sneak into the libraries and devour books until my eyes burned. I dreamed of traveling to places like this. I never imagined I would! Look at these gardens! It's a healer's paradise. Gardens in the treetops! I would have never imagined such a thing was possible! And the Rangers of Milendor! Aren't they fantastic? Did you know they are actually plants? Plants that mimic men, how amazing is that? And then there's Mukrot. Until I met him, I thought swamp trolls were made up to keep kids out of the swamps."

"Who is Mukrot?" Elize asked.

"Mukrot was the large blob that was stomping through the trees screaming Ori's name." Taa explained smiling at her. Elize smiled back. Taa certainly wasn't the same deerling she'd met at the healing center a few days ago.

"So, what else did the Oracle say?" Taa prompted giving Elize a nudge.

"Not much," Elize said with a sigh, "she's a very odd bird. Most of what she said was gibberish, but she did tell Alzo he was the Change and that he needed to lead the people below."

"They definitely need a leader," Taa told her. "The rangers are herding everyone through the bogs to the peat houses. Everyone is waiting for the Change to tell them what to do next. Spruce, the Ranger's commander, received a message from the Oracle. He said that the Change would be at the peat houses in two days. So, tomorrow...I guess."

"I wonder if there will be a war?" Taa said glancing ahead at Alzo. "I hate to think of all those folks down there in battle."

"I don't know, but there's something out there. I felt it..." Elize said closing her eyes, "I don't know what it was, but it felt...well evil. I don't know if there will be a war or not, but if there is you'll be needed more down there than up here."

"Yes, I think your right." Taa said thinking of the Rangers and their lack of medical training, "but first I need to replenish my supplies. If there is a war we'll need more than just a good leader. Healing centers will need to be set up to care for the wounded."

"If they're counting on me to lead them, they're screwed," Alzo groused turning around and running his fingers through his unruly bronze hair. "So, screwed." He continued shaking his head in dismay. "I'm not a leader. I'm not a Prince. I'm..."

"A whiner!" Elize teased. "You've done nothing but whine and complain since Su Lei did her Oracle thing. Like it or not you were born a prince! Deal with it!"

"What about you?" Alzo countered, "if I'm still a prince then you're still a princess. A princess with powers she refuses to use. Maybe if you'd use your powers..."

"All my life I've been told not to use my powers, to keep them hidden. Hell, do you know how many times I was beaten for...oh never mind you wouldn't understand."

"No, I probably wouldn't," Alzo said lowering his voice. "I'm sorry Elize."

"I always wondered what happened to you that day," Elize asked catching up with her brother. "Who attacked you and why?"

"What?"

"The day Payape ran out into the garden. Who attacked you?" Alzo ran his fingers down the long, jagged scar hidden under his thick beard.

"I was a boy who felt trapped behind the walls of the palace. I wanted to travel the world. Like the first emperors did. I knew Ori..."

"Ori? That's right he said you two used to be friends when you were boys."

"Yeah, Ori was an orphan. One of the cook's daughters smuggled him into the palace. I found him hiding in the kitchens one day when I was exploring. We used to pretend we were great warriors of old. I so wanted to be like the first emperors I read about in the history books, but how could I do that when Payape would never allow me to go outside. Ori showed me a secret tunnel in the walls that took us out into the woods. We used to sneak out whenever we could. The day I was attacked we had gone further than we had ever gone before. We were standing near a stream full of little brown fish when I heard voices coming from downstream. Ori snuck up to get a better look. I lagged back. That's when I saw the jacket tucked under a bush. A small leather bound book was poking out of one of the pockets. I pulled it out curious to see what was in the book. The instant I opened it a man shouted and rushed out of the water. I ran, but the man morphed into a... I don't know...a wild thing leapt on top of me. If it hadn't been for Ori, I would have been ripped to shreds."

"Ori told me you found a book in the woods, but this is the first time I've heard the whole story. Do you think the book has something to do with Mayme taking us away?"

"Yeah."

"What was in the book?" Ilee asked.

"Spells and stuff," Alzo shrugged, "at least that's what Ori said. And there were maps too. Maps showing doorways to faraway lands. Of course, we had no way of knowing that these faraway lands weren't on Toboria."

"Ori said Mayme found the book." Elize told him. "He said Mal told him she tried to use one of the doorways in the map to take us to Palenina, but it took us to Earth instead. Mal thought she sang the words wrong."

"And Ori sang the words right." Alzo mused pulling at his beard. "That's why we came out near Palenina."

"Probably," Elize agreed. "Seems like you got an adventure after all, huh?"

"Yeah, and now I'm back." Alzo sighed deeply.

Elize glanced over at her big brother. She could feel his trepidation. It was the same feeling Nekita had when she talked of becoming the next Oracle.

"You know what," she said giving Alzo a firm pat on the back. "You and Nekita are a lot alike. You're both expected to take on responsibilities you're not thrilled about. Nekita fears that when she becomes the next Oracle she will be trapped in this tree and you...you fear that when you become the next Emperor you will be trapped behind the palace walls. But it doesn't have to be that way. Nekita has wings to fly away and you can tear down the walls."

"You make it sound so easy." Alzo huffed.

"I'm not saying it will be easy," Elize assured him, "it won't, but nothing worth doing is. Look at your life so far. You have traveled further than any of the first emperors. When I look into your eyes, I see you outside the walls. I see you working in the fields shoulder to shoulder with the farmers. I see you helping others to rebuild their towns and villages. I see you surrounded by others. Leading by example."

"Yeah?"

"Yeah!"

"Right and years from now they will gather by their fires and sing ballads about me."

"I'm sure I can get Ori to cough out a ballad or two if that'll make you feel better."

"HA!" Alzo laughed, trying not to show Elize how much her words had helped. "I still don't get why all those people think I'm this Change. I mean how do they even know I'm here?"

"Word travels fast in the country-side," Ilee interrupted, "and after the speech you gave to the brownies, it's no wonder. News like that spreads like wildfire in the wind."

"Knot," Alzo fumed. "I should have known he was up to something." He looked over at Elize. "What if I fail?"

"You will only fail if you refuse to act," Elize told him sternly.

"She's right," Ilee agreed. "Toboria needs a hero. Even in Palenina families are desperate. We need someone to be our voice. Toboria needs a strong leader to help them find the strength to stop running and face the enemy that has stolen their lives."

"Then you go," Alzo snapped at her. "You're the Priestess. You lead them! I'll probably end up doing more harm than good."

"We will go together," Ilee told him taking his big hand in her little one and staring deeply into his eyes. "We will go together. We will give each other strength."

They had barely settled back in the nest when Pippy arrived to escort Taa to the Isopteria gardens. After she was gone Elize laid down and stared up at the whitewashed ceiling above her. She wondered if the whitewash was made from owl doo. The thought both amused her and disgusted her. Closing her eyes, Elize thought about everything that had happened since her mother had passed away less than a year ago.

After a while Elize drifted off into an uneasy sleep and her subconscious mind took over. She found herself on the garden path. Thick smoke swirled around her. Several puffy screechers fluttered about disoriented by the thick smoke. Hearing someone in distress, Elize rushed up the vine stairway and into the Oracle's garden, her bare feet crunching on shards of broken shell. Kara was standing in a ring of fire, dark shadows hovered in the early morning sky, like storm clouds, fire rained down from above. Elize woke up with a start.

"What's wrong!" Alzo asked giving her a funny look.

"I need to speak to Nekita." Elize mumbled pushing her way out of the nest.

Pippy left Taa standing alone at the entrance of a lush garden while she went to fetch Green. Unable to control herself Taa tiptoed down the path examining the rare and exotic plants which up till now, she'd only seen in books. She was happily examining a bunch of tall reedy plants with large red flowers when she heard a familiar buzzing.

"Roz?" Taa whispered poking her soft, black nose into one of the flowers. Roz looked up from the pistil she was sitting on and buzzed warily. "Roz! It is you! I've been so worried!"

Roz sobbed and glanced down at the silver thread fastened tightly around one of her ankles. Recognizing the foul thing, Taa muttered angrily and reached down to remove it. Roz let out a high-pitched warning, but it was too late. Taa cursed and licked her burnt fingertips as the air around her erupted with angry buzzing.

Alerted by Roz's cry, the isopteria tending the gardens flew to her rescue and attacked poor Taa tugging at her long ears and yanking out tuffs of fur.

"Stop!" Taa snapped frantically swatting at the isopteria. "Roz is my friend. I'm trying to help her! I'm a healer." The attack continued until Pippy arrived with Green.

"You're Taa?" Green demanded buzzing in front of her face a bit too aggressively for Taa's liking. Fighting off the urge to swat him, Taa nodded. "Well, why didn't you say so."

"I didn't get the chance." Taa grumbled brushing a lingering isopteria from her ear.

"Follow me," Green buzzed without offering any apology.

"Not until I remove that from my friend's leg." Green glanced from Taa to Roz's leg.

"The only way to get it off is to cut her leg above the joint." He told Taa reaching out to pick up a pair of miniature hedge clippers. Roz buzzed miserably. Seeing the look on her face, Green lowered the clippers. "It'll only hurt for a second," he promised, "just a little pinch."

"Why take the limb off so high up?" Taa asked as she extracted her surgical kit from her pocket. "I think it would be better to amputate closer to the affected area."

"The leg won't grow back unless you take it at the joint." Green explained curtly. He didn't appreciate Taa questioning him. Taa considered his reply.

"That makes sense," she agreed removing a pair of specially made scissors from her bag. "I'm sorry Roz," she told her friend, "but it's the only way."

Roz whimpered and begged Taa to leave her there to die. Ignoring Roz's pitiful pleads, Taa waved her hand at Green. "Put those clippers down and hold her while I operate." Green hovered over Roz and placed four hands firmly upon Roz's trembling body.

"Just a pinch," he assured her. Roz whimpered. Taa snipped the affected leg off just below the knee. "Don't touch it!" She warned as a small yellow isopteria reached out to catch the leg. "Whoever put that there used sorcery! Wrap something around the foul thing and seal it in a jar."

While Taa supervised the removal of the leg. Green pulled a blossom off a nearby honeysuckle vine and offered Roz some nectar. Taa watched Roz sipping the nectar, she looked wretched.

Once she was done drinking the nectar Roz told Taa what had happened to her after they got separated. She told Taa that she was very jealous of all the attention Taa was giving Elize. After Taa yelled at Roz, she had flown off in a fit of anger to sell information about Elize to the traders. It was not a well thought out plan. Instead of getting a reward, the traders turned Roz over to Behr. Realizing she had been doubled crossed Roz refused to speak. Behr used the silver thread to bond her to him and read her thoughts. Roz tried to lead Behr away when she spotted Taa and Elize in the crowd. When the cord was cut Roz had flown up into the tree and hid.

"You should have let me die," Roz buzzed miserably.

"I think having your leg amputated is more than enough penance." Taa replied gently. "I'm glad I found you. I've missed you more than words can say."

"I've missed you too." Roz buzzed relieved that her ordeal was finally over. "Tell me all about your adventures."

"I will," Taa assured her friend, "later. Now you need to rest."

Taa left Roz resting in the flower and went with Green to collect the supplies she needed. It took longer than she expected. There were so many plants to choose from. She ended up filling several large bags to take down to the bogs with her. When she returned to the nest, she was disappointed to find Elize gone.

"Where's Elize," Taa asked Alzo who looked like he had just woken up. Alzo stretched out his long arms and yawned widely.

"I don't know," Alzo replied between yawns. "She went to find Nekita."

"Why?"

"I don't know," Alzo said again, "I think she had a bad dream."

"Oh, I was hoping to talk to her before I left," Taa said disappointed.

"Where are you going?" Ilee asked rubbing her delicate hands across her smooth brown skin. She wasn't used to being cooped up like this. She missed the sound of water lapping outside her window. It was so dry in the nest. She felt like all the moisture had been sucked from her skin.

"I'm going back down to the forest floor as soon as it's daylight." Taa told her. "It's fascinating up here, but I'm not comfortable so high off the ground."

Ilee agreed with her completely. "I'm coming with you." She said flipping her long black hair out of her face. "I do hope there's a way down that doesn't involve flying."

"I do too." Taa laughed remembering the funny way she had arrived. "Green, one of the isopteria, told me that there's an old pulley system the giants used to lift peat up from the peat houses. It hasn't been used in years, but Pippy told me she's gone down it with the giantess. So, I figure if it's strong enough to hold a giantess, it's strong enough to hold me."

"And me," Alzo added. "I think we should all go down, but not until Elize gets back. I wonder what's keeping her?" Alzo stuck his head out the nest and looked down the garden path. A stench, like burning rubber filled his nostrils. "Smoke!" He shouted leaping out of the nest.

Elize found Nekita standing at the bottom of the steps leading up to the Oracle's Garden.

"Nekita!" Elize called hurrying towards her. "Nekita!" Elize gasped taking Nekita's hands in hers.

Nekita stared at Elize as if through a fog. "Elize?" She muttered her intense blue eyes fluttering wildly.

"Nekita! Nekita, can you hear me? What's wrong?"

"Elize!" Nekita exclaimed. "I was looking for you. Su Lei wanted me to give you a message. She said to tell you that you possess a great power. A power that is desired by others. She said time passes, love fades, the giver desires back that which was given. Monet's gift is hers no more. It is yours alone to have and hold."

"What does that mean?"

"I don't know," Nekita admitted, "but I feel you are no longer safe here. One who seeks the power is near. He is just a shadow now, but he is growing stronger. Take your brother and the others and leave immediately. And no matter what happens control the energy within you. Do not allow it to control you!"

"Wait!" Elize yelled stopping Nekita before she could fly away. "I had a vision! I saw the tree fill with smoke and a shadow leaning over Su Lei trying to steal her memories."

"I must go to her at once! Su Lei has the knowledge and memories of all Oracles before her back to the beginning of time. If these memories fall into the wrong mind..." Nekita shuddered. "I must go to her at once!"

The shock Su Lei received when she removed the whisker from Elize's palm had opened avenues in her mind that had been closed for centuries. She felt elated, exhilarated, invincible, but as the first shock wore off her mind cleared. It was this clarity that enabled the old bird to see the shadow hovering over Kara. It was this clarity that bought her the time she needed.

Su Lei sent Nekita to find Elize. She knew how her niece felt about Kara and didn't want Nekita interfering. Feigning sleep Su Lei breathed softly. Kara inched closer. Never one for being graceful, Kara stumbled slightly as she leaned forward to place her hefty hand on the Oracle's forehead. Su Lei's eyes flew open. The old owl wrapped her sharp talons around the terrified girl's wrist and pressed her tiny hands against Kara's temples.

Memories poured into Kara's head. Not of the day her people were slaughtered, but afterward. When Su Lei gently treated her burns and took away her fears. How Su Lei taught her words and showed her things, like how to weave and sew her own clothes. Memories of Su Lei having the screecher's bring Kara the things she needed to bake. A safe place, Su Lei had promised her.

Kara's body shivered as the shadow fought for dominance. "My lands," she stuttered, "my people's land, mine not Nekita's. Mine."

"The land and the water will not return until the final sacrifice is made." Su Lei said keeping her voice calm as she stared deeply into Kara's eyes. "The grandmother and grandfather's anger will not be sated until the final sacrifice is made. You, Kara, are the only one left to atone for the sins of your people. Once the final sacrifice is made the river will be freed and the land will be reborn."

"The final sacrifice." Kara mumbled lost in Su Lei's stare.

"What are you doing?" Nekita shouted grabbing Kara and dragging her away from Su Lei. Kara screamed as Su Lei's talons ripped across her skin. Whimpering Kara ran out into the Oracle's garden.

The garden was empty now. The seven had returned to their nests leaving the lamps smoldering beneath the large egg. Kara bellowed and struck at the egg with both her fists. The egg crashed at her feet. Kara kicked it, stomping on the broken pieces of shell, grinding the shards into the garden floor. Kara didn't realize she had knocked over the lamp until the dried twigs and peat floor burst into flames.

Screaming Kara frantically tried to stomp out the fire, but in her panic, she knocked into another lamp spilling more oil onto the floor.

"Kara!" Elize yelled rushing forward and grabbing the giant's hand. "Come on! It's too late! We have to get out of here!"

Kara lowered her head to hide the gleam in her eyes as Elize dragged her towards the vine stairs.

"No! This way!" Kara shouted pulling Elize away before she could start down. Elize hesitated something felt wrong.

"We need to warn the others." Elize protested pulling her hand free and heading back towards the stairs. A gust of wind hit the flames tossing them in her path. Forgetting her premonition, Elize tucked her hair under her collar and darted after Kara.

CHAPTER 10

"Alzo!" Ilee screamed rushing out of the nest with Taa on her heals. A flaming bolt tore through the leaves striking the path in front of Alzo and singeing his beard and eyebrows. Ilee grabbed the back of Alzo's shirt and dragged him backwards away from the flames. With Taa's help they were able to get Alzo to safety.

"Fire! Fire!" Pippy squealed racing up Taa's leg and burying her face in Taa's shoulder.

"I need to find Elize!" Alzo hollered thrashing at Taa and Ilee as he tried to make his way back down the path.

"No!" Taa yelled as another bolt ripped through the branches. "You need to take cover!"

"We're under attack!" A ruffled barred owl hooted as she dumped a bucket of white bird doo on the flames. Alzo pulled free and rushed down the charred path. The damaged path snapped under his weight causing him to fall through the gap up to his knees. It took a joint effort to pull him back onto the path.

"Take cover!" The barred owl hooted as a long rectangular shape appeared above the tree limbs. Alzo recognized it immediately. It was an air barge. Pippy looked up and began to scream hysterically. Desperate to get away from the smoke and fire Pippy leapt off Taa and took off in the opposite direction. Alzo, Taa, and Ilee raced after her.

"We need to take out the raft!" Alzo shouted when they caught up with Pippy anxiously waiting by a sketchy looking pulley system.

"How?" Ilee asked climbing into one of the buckets and plunking the bottom with her heel to make sure it was safe.

Alzo thought a minute trying to recall Captain Bok's supply raft. "The balloons!" He shouted. "We need to pop the balloons."

"I'll do it!" Pippy squealed snapping her fingers. Before anyone could stop her, Pippy was carried off by a flock of tiny screechers. A few moments later there was a loud pop followed by the startled shouts and another pop, pop, pop.

"Is that the only way down?" Alzo asked looking at the ancient pulley system doubtfully.

"I'm not sure it will hold all of our weight." Taa said giving the bucket another kick. "Ilee and I will go down first with the supplies and then you can follow."

"Right," Alzo replied nodding at her. "Ilee, you go first, you're the lightest." Ilee nodded taking a few of the bags of medicinal plants that Taa had collected with her. Once she was ready Alzo released the thick wooden rod blocking the cog. The bucket jerked and started downward.

"I think I heard Taa." Ori told Gerawld as they stood on the far end of the bog inspecting an old pulley system that appeared to be attached to the Tara Bora tree on the other side of the moat.

"No," Gerawld meowed jumping back when a bucket dropped by his feet and a brown skinned girl leapt out.

"You're right, that's not Taa," Ori told him smiling at the pretty brown skinned girl standing less than a foot in front of them.

"Yes, it is!" Taa called out from above.

"Taa!" Ori shouted excitedly running over to help her out of the bucket. "Where's Elize? Is she with you?"

"No," Taa replied pulling more sacks out and handing them to him. "We got separated in the fire. But Alzo's right behind me. Mukrot!" She called to the swamp troll. "Fill the empty bucket with water and send it back up."

"What's going on?" Ori demanded studying the pulley system with great interest.

"The tree is under attack," Ilee told him while Taa explained to Mukrot what she needed him to do. "Bandits are throwing fire bolts from an air barge."

"Where's Elize," Ori asked again growing more concerned by the second.

"We don't know. She ran off to find Nekita before the attack. Alzo went to find her, but when the attack started the path was set on fire and he was forced to retreat."

"You left Elize up there!" Ori exploded.

Ori started up the pulley ropes unaware that Alzo was coming down. The decaying ropes groaned and snapped under their combined weight. Ori, Alzo and the buckets plummeted down into the wet peat showering everyone with thick brown muck. Mia growled and began licking her fur furiously spatting out the foul-tasting liquid between licks. Not as fussy as his little sister, Gerawld gave his body a good shake and sloshed over to help Mukrot lift Ori and Alzo out of the bog.

Another loud pop sounded from above followed by a loud screech. Alzo cast his eyes skyward as the small gray cloud fluttered erratically towards him. The cloud gently laid Pippy on Alzo's outstretched hands. Pippy clutched her chest, watery blood oozed out between her clawed fingers.

"Taa," Alzo called out to the healer.

"Who is she?" Mia asked sniffing the strange creature lying in Taa's arms.

"This is Pippy. She was trying to knock out the barges by popping the balloons." Alzo answered looking curiously at the two cats standing on their hind legs next to Ori. "Who are you?"

Oh, geez," Ori said stepping forward. "Where are my manners?" Ori bowed dramatically before Alzo and waved his hand. "May I introduce..."

"I'm Alzo," Alzo interrupted brushing Ori's fanfare to one side. "Elize's brother."

"And I'm Ilee," Ilee said coming to stand next to him. "Priestess of Hohi."

Ori gave Alzo an exaggerated hurt look and waved his hand towards Mia. "This is Mia, daughter of Scat, Leader of the Grassland Bast and her brother Gerawld. The good fellow who helped you out of the bog is Mukrot, the seventh son of a seventh son. I'm Ori, you've met Taa, and this is Yew." Ori pointed to the Ranger in the tree to their left. "Yew, is one of the many, many Rangers of Milendor."

"Hello," Alzo said nodding up at Yew and his fellow Rangers who dotted the tree branches bordering the bog.

"Hi dee ho down below!" A rough voice shouted as a large blue bird swooped down and landed with a plop in the peat bog scaring poor Mukrot half to death.

"Captain Bok!" Alzo called out as the large man climbed off the birds back and sloshed towards them. "And your pet rat." Alzo chided noticing the pinched faced brownie clinging to the Captain's shoulder.

"Yeah, well I heard the Change had arrived in Milendor," Knot spat back his black eyes sparkling mischievously, "and I figured he'd need my help."

"About that," Alzo said lifting the brownie off the Captain's shoulder.

"No time for chitchat." Knot scolded as he jumped to the ground. A fire bolt broke through the treetops. "Troll, follow me." He shouted at Mukrot thrusting a bucket into the startled swamp troll's hands.

Above them the trees filled with brown and green clad archers, but the barge was too high and most of their arrows fell to the ground without hitting their mark.

"They need to get closer." Alzo told Yew. Turning to Captain Bok who was busy tending to Ming, he asked. "Captain can you help?"

"Sure," Captain Bok yelled back, lifting his fingers to his lips he whistled three times. An instant later three, blue Rocs splashed down in the bog and began filling their long beaks with plump brown tadpoles.

"Shoo!" A large brown blob popped out of the bog and began waving thick, trunk-like arms at the birds.

"Orr-eee," whispered Mukrot staring at the large lump who stopped shooing the birds and winked at the shy swamp troll with large violet eyes.

"Mingy," Pippy squealed with delight breaking away from Taa before she had finished stitching up her wound. Ming squawked and plunged towards her.

"Pippa!" Captain Bok boomed lifting the little girl up into his arms and hugging her to his chest. "We thought we'd lost ya!"

"Paw Paw," Pippy cooed burying her head in his bristly black beard.

"Ah, you got a bad slice there Missy." The Captain said gently placing Pippy on the birds back. "Best you stay here with Ming and rest while I help the Change. Now, now, don't you fret I'll be back. You rest and get your strength back." Pippy nodded and snuggled into the soft blue feathers in the flat space between Ming's wings.

"What are they?" Ori asked Yew eyeing the big birds splashing about in the bog.

"The bogglea or the rocs?" Yew asked.

"The bogglea," Ori replied watching with amusement as another brown blob popped out of the bog and batted her huge eyes at the flustered Mukrot. "I've had the displeasure of meeting a Roc before."

"The bogglea are bog trolls," Yew told him with a twinkle in his eye. "I think they're taken with your big friend."

The bogglea giggled at Mukrot who blushed and stepped back. He didn't have a clue what to do. The only female who had ever been nice to him was his mother.

"Some help here!" Knot yelled at Mukrot throwing another bucket from the now defunct pulley system at him. "Stop fooling around with the ladies and fill that up we have a fire to put out. Mukrot blinked at Knot. He wasn't sure who this bossy little man was, but he didn't want to get him any madder, so he quickly dipped the bucket into the bog.

"Hand it here!" A nut brown bogglea said taking the bucket from Mukrot and passing it to a stout woman standing on the path who Knot had recruited to head the bucket bigrade.

Ori watched the Rocs sloshing out of the water and considered apprehending one to fly over the trees to search for Elize, but he quickly reconsidered. He had tried to apprehend a roc years ago for an entirely different and less noble mission. The scars on his arms were a reminder of that lack of judgement. Still determined to find a way over the moat, Ori was standing on the edge of the moat when he spotted someone moving over the roots of the Taro Bora.

"Elize!" He yelled waving his hands over his head as he raced along the edge of the moat.

"Ori!" Elize yelled back waving frantically at him.

"I'm coming Elize!" Ori shouted back, but to his dismay she was no longer there.

"What's going on?" Alzo yelled as he and Gerawld rushed over.

"I saw Elize!" Ori exclaimed pointing across the moat. "She was right there by the roots of the tree." Alzo and Gerawld scanned the area, but they didn't see anyone. "She was there!" Ori insisted, "She called my name and then she just vanished."

"I heard her too," Taa gasped catching up with them.

"Me too," Mia said scanning the other side of the moat for any sign of movement with her sharp feline eyes. Gerawld lifted his head and sniffed deeply before shaking his fluffy orange striped head. The air was too smokey to make out Elize's scent.

"Hey!" Ilee interrupted. "The Ranger said we need to get across the bogs while there's plenty of daylight." Ilee was irritated at Alzo for running off and leaving her behind. She also felt he should demand more respect. He was a prince after all and therefore, he should act like one. It was time he took command instead of behaving like everyone else.

"Come on," Taa said crisply taking Alzo by the arm. "I love Elize too, but our mission is too important to delay it by going after her. Besides maybe it was meant to be this way. It appears your mother went to great lengths to keep you and Elize apart. Maybe she did it to keep you both safe."

"I guess you're both right," Alzo said sadly. Taking one last look at the Tara Bora tree he allowed Taa to lead him back to the bog. He loved his little sister, but like it or not there were hundreds of people waiting for him on the road. Many of them were sisters or had sisters they loved just as much as he loved Elize.

"I'm going after Elize!" Ori shouted. "She's in trouble! I can feel it in my bones."

To Ori's surprise nobody tried to stop him. Alzo was glad Ori was going after her. He might be a liar and a conman, but Alzo knew how Ori felt about Elize. If she were out there, Ori would find her and do what he could to keep her safe.

"When you find my little sister," Alzo shouted back at Ori, "tell her to meet me in the garden where we used to play."

Ori didn't have the heart to tell Alzo that his mother's marvelous garden had been destroyed.

"Everyone! We need to get through the bogs before sunset." Ori heard Alzo shouting behind him. "There is a path, but it is thin and slippery. Follow me, watch your step, and take care of your fellow traveler."

"Who made you leader!" A red-faced woman with mud on her cheek demanded. Several others joined her demanding to know who gave this newcomer with hair like a Shiva tree the right to order them about.

"He's the Change, you daft cows!" Knot fumed climbing up on Alzo's shoulder and waving his fist at them. "You know, the one you all came here to join forces with."

The jeering stopped and the crowd bunched forward to get a better look at Alzo. Alzo looked at the hope in their grimy faces and froze. Ilee nudged him, but his mind went blank and all he could do was stare back at the faces staring at him.

Ori had been all set on going after Elize until he heard the crowd jeering at Alzo. Who would have guessed Alzo could be so inept at public speaking? Ori decided he'd better do something before the mob got ugly. It wouldn't take long, and he knew it would be what Elize would want. Slipping into the thickening crowd, Ori inched closer to Alzo and began singing. He sang as soft as a breeze, emphasizing Alzo's strength, his resolve, his kindness, and love for all creatures big, small, and in between. Ori's words wove through the crowd like a cool breeze in the summertime making their way to Alzo's ears and back again. The boost worked. Alzo threw back his shoulders and started to speak with confidence and authority. Before long the crowd began to slowly make their way across the sloshy path the bogglea had laid out for them.

Satisfied his job was done, Ori backed out of the crowd and into Taa. If Taa hadn't been paying attention, she would have been caught up in Ori's hypnotic tune, but she had been paying attention and managed to cover her ears before Ori's spell fell upon her. She wondered if Alzo was aware of what Ori had done. If not, she wasn't about to tell him. Alzo needed all the help he could get.

"I need to get to the other side." Ori said moving away from the others. "Any ideas?"

Taa thought a minute. "I bet Mukrot could toss a sly fox across that moat without much effort." She told him with a wink.

"Only one way to find out," Ori laughed and scurried off to find his big friend. He had wasted enough time and was eager to find Elize.

The evil that had hovered over Kara had dissipated when Su Lei touched her skull, but that didn't stop Kara from taking Elize away from her friends. Su Lei's words were still ringing in her head as Kara led the unsuspecting Elize through the hidden doorway and into the hollow center of the Tara Bora tree where the Neognathae stored their libraries.

"Hurry! This way!" Kara urged Elize pulling her down the spiral stairway winding past shelves and nooks filled with books and scrolls. When they reached the bottom of the tree, Kara pushed Elize out onto the twisting roots of the Tara Bora tree.

"Stay here!" Kara told Elize as she looked for the entrance to the tunnel that would take her home. She had just found the right tunnel when she heard Elize shout.

Kara grabbed Elize and wrapped a large spongy hand around Elize's mouth and dragged her to the tunnel. Unable to catch her breath Elize soon passed out. Afraid whoever Elize had called out to would come after them, Kara rushed down into a labyrinth of tunnels running underneath the Tara Bora. The tunnels belonged to the Unders, a tribe of humanoid moles. Usually the Unders were meek, non-violent creatures, but they were known to get extremely agitated when trespassers entered their tunnels.

Once she was sure no one was following, Kara removed her hand from Elize's mouth. The moldy, musty air brought Elize back around. It reminded her of the dirt cellar her stepfather Patrick had locked her in as a child when she misbehaved. Even though it had been a long time ago, Elize remembered it like it was yesterday.

"Where are we?" She yelled at Kara. When Kara didn't answer she pounded on her chest until Kara stopped and put her down.

"It's a safe place," Kara assured Elize taking her hand and pulling her further into the tunnel. "Away from the fire and smoke."

"Why did you drag me down here?" Elize demanded gasping for air.

"Not far now." Kara mumbled over her shoulder refusing to slow or let Elize's hand go. Elize gasped and stumbled after Kara. The fear of being buried alive took her breath away. Unable to go any further, Elize collapsed. Kara shoved a bright red fruit into Elize's mouth.

"Eat! It will help you." Kara assured Elize and popped one of the fruits in her own mouth to show Elize it was safe to eat.

Elize hesitated. Kara popped another fruit into her mouth. "Umm." She said nodding and smiling at Elize.

Elize took a tentative bite. It had the texture of a mushroom, but tasted tart and sweet, like lemonade. Elize continued chewing. It did seem to help her breathe better.

"Come on," Kara urged tugging at Elize's arm. "We need to keep moving. There's fresh air just ahead."

No longer feeling closed in, Elize easily followed Kara through the tunnel which, as promised, led into a larger area where air seeped in from a hidden vent high above them. A small trickle of water dripped down from the top of the tunnel and pooled by Kara's large foot.

"Where's that water coming from?" Elize asked and tried to find the source of the water.

"I don't know." Kara answered cautiously watching as the pool of water expanded and the figure of a woman started to rise out of it.

"Run!" Elize screeched grabbing Kara's arm and pulling Kara away from the puddle and into a new tunnel dotted with strange oval holes.

"Wrong way!" Kara yelled, but it was too late. A long, flat face looked out at them from one of the holes while another leapt out of the wall to block their way. The Unders slapped at Kara with large, flat shovel-like paws. Kara pulled a blue rock from her pocket and shook it violently. Bright light flared out of the rock and temporarily blinded the Unders.

"This way," Kara yelled as several more Unders appeared slamming their flat paws against the walls causing them to collapse.

"Why did you bring me down here?" Elize demanded sharply. The fear of being buried alive returning with a vengeance. "Why didn't you take me to my friends?"

"The Oracle told me to take you away. Keep you hidden." Kara said pushing Elize down a new tunnel.

"I want out of here now!" Elize shouted digging her heels into the ground and refusing to move. Kara started to drag Elize down the tunnel, but before she could a flat leathery paw punched out of the wall and pulled Elize through to the other side. Kara shouted in alarm and shoved her big hands into the loose dirt knocking the wall down.

Eager to get the trespassers out of the tunnels, the short, stocky moleman shoved Elize ahead of him and up a newly dug tunnel. Kara followed crawling on all fours as she forced her way up the tight tunnel. The Under stopped at the bottom of a set of ladder-like dirt steps and waved his leathery paws at Elize.

Elize started up the steps just as Kara emerged from the tunnel. Out of the corner of her eye Elize noticed the water rushing towards them. Kara saw it too and letting out a startled shout shot past Elize.

"It's blocked!" Kara yelled down at Elize. Elize kicked at the watery hand trying to grab her ankle. Terrified Kara slammed her head into the sod and broke through. Elize grabbed hold of Kara's foot as the giant bolted out of the hole pulling Elize behind her.

"Bad magic!" Kara spat slamming the sod door shut.

"We'd better get out of here!" Elize exclaimed grateful to be out of the tunnels.

Kara picked up a large rock and dropped it on the door.

"This way," she told Elize heading towards a rock formation that looked like a sleeping baby.

"Hey!" Elize yelled as she ran after Kara. "Where're you going?"

"Home," Kara yelled back keeping just far enough ahead of Elize to prevent conversation. They did not stop to rest until the late morning sun turned the hills ahead of them a coppery red.

"Where are we," Elize asked looking across what appeared to be a desert, except instead of sand there was miles of cracked ground with huge, oddly shaped rocks scattered across it haphazardly. The large rocks resembled sleeping children of varying ages.

"This was once the mighty Bawe River," Kara replied sadly, "which flowed through the Valley of the Sleeping Children."

Elize found it hard to imagine a river had once flowed in such an arid place. "What happened to the river?"

Kara handed Elize a red berry and began her story. "My people, the river giants, lived in the red hills along the Bawe River for centuries. My family cut the peat from the bogs and dried it in long peat houses. When the peat was dried, the peat was floated down the river to sell in the markets. Before long other folks started using our river to float their goods to market. When the river giants demanded a toll, the other merchants refused to pay it. The river giants dammed the river and forced the other merchants to pay a toll before they would release the water and allow them to pass through their lands. When the Ancients became aware of what the river giants had done, they were angry and punished them for their disregard of the river and all the life which depended on the waters. The Ancients cursed the river giants. They caused the ground to shake apart and swallow up all the water from the river. The Ancients also sent a stampeded of bulimon from the Dimly to slaughter the river giants. My mother hid me under her. I am the only one who survived the massacre. I wandered lost for many days. The Under's found me and brought me to the Oracle. The Oracle tried to take the bad memories away," Kara told Elize handing her another juicy fruit, "but in my sleep the death birds come to feast upon my Maus face and when the plum moon is high in the sky I can hear the ghosts of my people screaming."

"What are they screaming?" Elize asked weaving back and forth on the dry crackling dirt.

"They scream for forgiveness," Kara told her jumping from foot to foot dancing to a song inside her head.

"So why did you bring me here?" Elize asked as she watched Kara dance.

"Su Lei told me to bring you here." Kara sang twirling around in a dizzy circle. "Su Lei is very wise. Su Lei told me the river would return when the final sacrifice was made. You!"

Realizing she was in danger, Elize tried to run, but her muscles turned to jelly, and her mind was flooded with bright, bright light.

"What did you give me?" Elize demanded spitting out what was left of the fruit. Kara laughed and pushed Elize down. Elize tried to get to her feet, but her head spun, and she couldn't quite remember how to make her legs work. Kara began to chant loudly stomping in a wide circle as she started taking off her dress.

"If I were you, I'd run," a rock formation that looked like a boy sitting cross legged on the ground whispered to Elize.

"I'm either really high or you just spoke to me," Elize mumbled using the rock as leverage.

"I did speak to you," the rock boy replied without moving his lips. "I said you should run."

Elize clung to the rock and tried to make her legs move. Kara continued chanting and stomping her feet. Now stark naked, Kara waved her tunic over her head as she stomped her large feet against the dirt. Although her moves seemed random, Elize realized they weren't. Kara's huge feet had created a rough pentagram.

"You really should go," the rock boy whispered as Kara whooped loudly and threw her dress at Elize. Too woozy to walk, Elize began crawling away.

Kara whooped louder and grabbed Elize by the hair dragging her inside the pentagram. Elize kicked Kara hard in the shin and skittered away half walking, half crawling. Laughing Kara smacked Elize hard upside the head knocking her back to the ground. Stars danced around Elize's eyes, and everything started to fade into gray.

"I'd stay awake if I were you," the rock boy's voice shouted urgently inside Elize's head as Kara dragged her back into the pentagram. When Elize's head cleared Kara was standing over her holding a long dagger. Kara shouted and slashed the blade downward slicing her giant thigh and spraying Elize with thick dark brown blood. Elize gagged as the smell of rusty iron filled the air.

"Ya, ya, ya!" Kara shouted manically as she whipped the blade across her other thigh.

"Why are you doing that?" Elize screamed inching further into the pentagram. She had never understood the desire some people had to slash their own flesh.

"The ancients demand a blood sacrifice to atone for the sins of my people." Kara shouted dancing around flinging her blood across the dusty pentagram. She pointed the tip of the dagger at the two massive mountains looming in the distance behind the copper hills before dipping a sausage-sized finger into the blood.

"Ay yay yay yay yay yay," she screamed smearing three bloody lines across each cheek and between her breasts. "Grandmother! Grandfather! You will have your sacrifice and I will have the power of the hand!"

'The power of the hand.' Elize did not like the sound of that. Concentrating on moving her legs, she pushed herself to her knees, but before she could stand Kara pushed her back to the ground. Elize lied sprawled out on her back still very much under the effect of the psychedelic fruit Kara had been feeding her.

Screeching madly, Kara swung the long dagger over her head. Elize watched the blade slice through the air. The rays of sun danced across the flat surface turning it into a dull gold. Elize felt energy moving through her veins as the blade swung towards her wrist, but instead of shooting out of her palm like a bottle rocket, threads of blue-white light flowed over the blade and up into the hilt. Elize watched Kara's face change from manic glee to panic as the giant frantically tried to pull her hands off the hilt. After a minute or two Kara's screams turned into a gurgle. Elize looked through a hallucinogenic fog at Kara lying on the ground. Kara's eyes were rolled back into her head with only the whites showing. Elize soon grew bored watching Kara's body twitch and teetered to her feet. Her mouth felt like it was filled with dirt. Stumbling over to the rock boy, Elize asked him where she could find a drink. The boulder refused to answer.

"Hey!" She shouted kicking at the boy. The motion made her head swim. Feeling a bit woozy, Elize leaned against the boy's knee and closed her eyes. "Wake up." She grumbled patting the boy's rough knee. "I need water!" The rock boy remained silent.

Elize inched her way around to the boy's shoulder and looked across the barren land for any sign of water. The morning sun beamed down warming the cracked dirt. Elize spotted an oblong black spot in the distance. Hoping it was water she started to walk towards it but retreated when the spot started to move. Elize squinted her eyes and watched as the spot morphed into a large scaly lizard. As the sun continued to warm the dried riverbed, more spots appeared. Pulling their heavy bodies onto the surface, the black lizards flicked their long red tongues and blinked in the bright sunlight. They reminded Elize of the Komodo dragons she had seen at the zoo.

"I'd get out of here if I were you," the rock boy's sleepy voice rumbled through her head. Ignoring him, Elize watched the lizards sluggishly moving towards Kara's twitching body. A few stopped to lick the dark splotches of giant blood splattered on the ground. Elize was so engrossed by the sight that she didn't notice the lizard until it was almost upon her.

"Oh shit!" Elize exclaimed kicking at the lizard and climbing up on to the rock boy. Before the lizard could follow her, Elize stripped off her blood stained jeans and swung them at the lizard. The lizard caught Elize's jeans and began ripping them apart with razor sharp teeth.

A large lizard dug his teeth into the bloody gash on Kara's thigh. Kara's body shook one final time before going limp. As another lizard approached Kara's body, the large lizard swished his tail in warning. Instead of fighting, the smaller lizard satisfied herself with Kara's left arm.

More lizards scuttled over towards Kara's body tearing at her flesh. A few of the smaller ones gave up trying to fight for a spot and surrounded the boulder where Elize sat. Their long tongues licked at the blotches of blood covering the rock boy's knee. Elize looked down at the pool of blood by her feet. Until that moment she didn't realize she was bleeding. Pulling off her tee shirt, she clumsily wrapped it around her wrist to stop the bleeding. Sensing her motion, one of the lizards jumped at her. Elize kicked it hard, sending it rolling down the rock and into the other lizards.

Grabbing Kara's tunic off the boy's foot, Elize made her escape by forcing one foot in front of the other. She ran until she couldn't run anymore. By then the lizards were far behind her. Resting she pulled Kara's tunic over her head. It was way too big, but it would help keep the bright sun from burning her skin.

Back in the Unders tunnels, Aturi the water maiden was furious. Furious at the Unders for throwing her down the urine shoot, furious that Elize had escaped, and furious that her son had let the demon go free. Being tied to the water made it impossible for Aturi to go after Elize once the giant took her into the arid riverbed. For now, she would have to let her go and hope Elize was foolish enough to head for Astaria.

Elize had no idea where she was headed as she wandered deliriously down the dried riverbed. The ground cracked and popped under her weight like bubble wrap. Stumbling Elize zigzagged from one rock formation to the next keeping ahead of the imaginary lizards that scurried behind her. Occasionally, Elize saw sad, long faced women standing beside pools of clear water, but the women and the water vanished in the hot rays of the sun when she got close.

Unlike the first rock boy, none of the other rock boys spoke to her. Exhausted, high, and very dehydrated Elize collapsed into the shadow created by a rather large stone boy and began to sob loudly.

"Aw clam up," a grumpy voice shouted. When Elize continued to sob, the stone boy sent a pile of loose pebbles down on her head. "I said knock it!" A boy's voice shouted again. "I'm trying to get some shut eye!"

"I don't care," Elize sobbed even louder brushing the pebbles off her lap. "I'm lost, dying of thirst, and I've got a sunburn!"

"If I give you a drink, will you leave?" The boy asked.

"Yeah," Elize sniffed rubbing a splotch of dried blood off her ankle, "but only if you tell me how to get to Astaria."

"Water, I can do," the boy spat, "but I don't know how to get to Astaria."

"Deal." Elize agreed, letting out a long sigh.

"I'd head west towards the sun." the boy suggested. Elize squinted, she could just make out the outline of what looked like buildings far on the horizon. "You should leave now."

"I won't leave until you give me a drink." Elize told the boy firmly.

"Look under my toes." He mumbled already starting to doze back off.

Elize found a small pool of water forming around five small rocks at the base of the boulder. Cupping her hands, she drank until her thirst was sated and splashed what was left on her face.

Leaving the stone boy, Elize continued across the barren land. The sun seemed to dance in the cloudless sky above as she made her way towards the buildings. Elize followed tiny rivulets of colors rising off the floor of the riverbed marking out her way. The sun was starting to drop in the sky when Elize finally reached the buildings. To her dismay all that was left of the buildings lay in ruins.

Standing amongst the ancient fallen arches and finely engraved columns scattered across the ground, Elize had the feeling she was being watched. Slipping behind one of the standing pillars she peeked out. A cow faced woman stood a few feet away from her. When the woman noticed Elize she waved at her and shouted. Elize stepped closer so she could hear what the woman was saying. She had only taken a few steps when the ground opened underneath her like a huge gaping mouth and swallowed her up.

Elize landed in what could only be described as a Roman bath with marbled walls. The bath was filled with aqua blue water flecked with bits of gold and copper. When her severely burnt skin hit the warm, salty water it stung so badly it took Elize's scream right out of her mouth. After several minutes the sting subsided and Elize was able to breathe again.

Lifting her head out of the water Elize was alarmed to hear merry laughter echoing off the walls. Curious she pulled herself out of the water and began to tiptoe towards an opening in the wall. She was amazed at how much lighter she felt. As she stepped through the opening something tugged at her stomach. Looking down Elize noticed a fine gossamer thread, no thicker than a spider's web coming out her belly button. Following the thread back she discovered her body still soaking in the pool.

Elize gasped sure that she must be dead, but as she watched her body she noticed the water ebbing slightly with each breath that moved in and out of her lungs.

"I'll be back," she promised her body and slipped through the opening and into a fabulous hallway with incredibly high walls and arched ceilings decorated with strange and wonderful images.

CHAPTER 11

The refugees who had come to join the Change trudged out of the Forest of Milendor and onto the peat path the Bogglea had marked out for them. The path was sketchy at best, and it was difficult to stay on the soggy peat without slipping into the bog.

Exhausted from the harrowing trip through the bogs the Followers of the Change, as they had started to refer to themselves, dropped their loads in the decaying peat houses not bothering to set up camp until they had rested. The abandoned peat houses laid hidden under thick blankets of moss and vines. Although they were a bit musty, it was better than living out in the open in the sparce woods outside the Forest of Milendor. Flanked by the bog on one side and the dried riverbed on the others, the peat houses provided the best cover a group of this size could hope for without going underground.

Alzo and his companions went ahead of the others to set up a headquarters in one of the smaller peat houses. Alzo still didn't understand why this hodgepodge group of refugees believed he was their leader. He was sure they would have had second thoughts after his stuttering speech, but he guessed they were just that desperate.

Alzo never realized how many different races lived on Toboria until he watched them flowing out of the bog and into the warehouses. Even though he had been born on Toboria he had spent most of his childhood behind the glassy walls of the Astarian palace. Alzo's father Emperor Taz was attacked during a hunting expedition in the mountainous area outside the palace walls when he was little more than a boy and had been terrified to leave the palace ever since. Not only did his father not go out of the palace, he refused to allow his wife and children to go out also. Perhaps if his father had allowed his mother to take him and Elize to visit her family in Palenina, she wouldn't have run away.

"No! Not like that!" Ilee fussed at two gangly boys who were trying to shore up one of the peat tables that had collapsed in the middle. Ilee had commandeered a group of teenagers to help her get the room together. From the look on their faces the teens were none too happy about being bossed about.

"Let me help," Alzo offered getting on his knees to get a look at the bottom of the table. Ilee frowned obviously not pleased. Alzo got the impression that now that she knew he was a prince, Ilee expected him to act more regal, but that wasn't who he was.

"Here hand me that," Alzo told the closest boy pointing at a thick stump of wood. The boy rolled it over and together he and Alzo shoved it in place. "That should do it!" Alzo exclaimed giving the boy a clap on the back. The boy beamed at him.

Ilee inspected the table. She still wasn't satisfied with it, but it would have to do.

"I found some benches," one of the girls said pulling a long rectangular piece of wood out of the rubble left on the floor where part of the roof had collapsed. "There's more but I'll need help digging them out."

"You'll need to clean them." Ilee scowled running her finger down the dirty wood.

"I'll do it," a mousy girl volunteered brushing at the bench with a broom she had made by tying a bunch of thin twigs together.

"You should have Taa look at that," Alzo said noticing the cut on the back of the girl's hand. "Where's Taa anyway." He asked looking around and not seeing her.

Taa was on the other side of the bog watching Mukrot and two Bogglea females lead the travelers through the bogs. Taa wondered if the shy swamp troll had noticed the way Fern and Moss, looked at him.

Taa had stayed by the east road to help tend the burns and scrapes some of the travelers had suffered when the fire bolts dropped out of the trees and onto the panicking crowds. Taa had been busy most of the afternoon treating the injured, but now that things were settling down she decided to take a well-deserved break. Taa wanted to clear her head before joining Alzo and the others. It had been a long and stressful day. Making her way back to where the pulley system lay in broken bits she stared up at the Tara Bora tree hoping to see Elize or Roz. Instead, Taa spotted Nekita hiding behind the vines not far from where she stood.

"Nekita!" Taa exclaimed pulling back the cover of vines. "What are you doing here?"

"Hiding," Nekita replied looking around her nervously. "No one must know I am here."

"Of course. What can I do to help?" Taa asked calmly noticing right away that Nekita was very shaken. Taa thought it was due to her home being attacked, but she soon learned it was much more than that.

"When I got to her nest Su Lei was almost gone. She was so weak she could barely raise her head, but Su Lei refused to die until she had blessed me with all the wisdom and memories she had gathered throughout her lifetime as well as those of the Oracles who had served before her. With her last breath, Su Lei urged me to leave the Tara Bora tree. She said I must not allow the Oracle's wisdom to fall into the wrong hands. But I didn't know where to go so I tracked you here and hid in the vines. I know it isn't safe to stay here, but it's impossible for me to get away unnoticed with these." Nekita spread her beautiful cream colored wings.

"Maybe we can dye them?" Taa suggested looking over at the bog. Nekita wasn't keen on the idea, but she felt she could trust Taa.

"Good idea," Fern said popping out of the muck and grabbing Nekita. Nekita squawked and spun her head snapping her beak at Fern as the bogglea pulled her into the dark peaty water. Slashing and sputtering Nekita frantically thrashed about.

"It's okay!" Taa yelled wiping bog muck off her face with the edge of her cloak. "Fern's trying to help you." Nekita grabbed at the shore and tried to climb out, but Fern pulled her back.

"Look," Fern shouted at Nekita grabbing her wing and holding it up, "it's working." Nekita looked. Her feathers had turned a rich dark chocolate brown.

"How long will it last?" She asked flapping her wings and looking at her tail feathers.

"At least one moon," Fern assured her, "probably longer."

Nekita liked her new color. It was quite a different look for her. She was glad the gold highlights on the tips of her feathers shone through the dark brown.   As she continued to examine her feathers, Nekita experienced a weird sensation, she suddenly felt free.

"Where will you go?" Taa asked Nekita as she got ready to take off.

"I'm not sure," Nekita answered preening a ruffled wing feather back into place. "Everything happened so fast that I hadn't had a chance to give it much thought."

"Are there other Taro Bora trees on Toboria?" Taa asked nodding at the silver barked tree.

"There used to be." Nekita answered sifting through the memories of past Oracles, "but that was a very long time ago. However, there is a place. Not a Tara Bora tree, but the tree where I was hatched. A large oak in the misty lands which lay between the sea and the dimly. My mother brought me to Su Lei as soon as my wings were strong enough to make the trip, but I'm sure I can find it."

"Why? Why did she bring you here?" Taa asked remembering the day her mother brought her to the healing center and left her there.

"Because I was born with white feathers and sapphire blue eyes," Nekita replied rather sadly, "therefore I was destined to be the next Oracle. My mother brought me to Su Lei so I could be trained to replace her as Oracle when the time came. Su Lei would be expecting me. It would have been foolish for my mother not to obey."

"Do you really remember the way back?" Taa asked amazed. "I doubt if I'd be able to find my herd after all this time."

"Did your mother give you up too?" Nekita asked tilting her head and looking at Taa sideways.

"My mother abandoned me." Taa said with no bitterness or regret. "I was born an impure. My inability to keep up endangered the entire herd. I was too young to understand, no more than a spotted fawn when she left me outside the healing center. The healers took me in and taught me the healing arts. They assured me that my mother had done the best she could for me. If she had left me alone in the wild, I would have died of starvation or been eaten."

"In a way my mother abandoned me too," Nekita said taking Taa's hands and grasping them tenderly. "At least that's how I felt when she left. I hope it will be a happy homecoming. I don't even know if she's still alive."

"Can't you throw the bones?"

Nekita clucked softly and shook her head. "Unfortunately, the bones only reveal the future of others." She thought about Elize looking over her shoulder and reading the bones. What had Elize said? She had been too quick to dismiss her and now she couldn't remember.

"What is it?" Taa asked.

"Nothing," Nekita answered bobbing her head slightly. "I'm glad we met." She said quickly changing the subject. "I'd read about deerlings in the histories, but I never thought I'd get the chance to meet one."

"I'm glad we met too." Taa told Nekita ducking as a large blue bird glided over their heads.

"I'd better go," Nekita whispered leaning close to Taa, "but before I go, I want to give you a gift."

Nekita touched Taa's forehead with her tiny fingertips. Instantly Taa knew more about the healing arts then those who had spent their entire lives studying them and her knowledge wasn't limited to mammals any longer. It included reptiles, fish, amphibians, avian and even plant-based life forms like the Rangers of Milendor with veins filled with sap instead of blood.

"Safe journeys!" Taa called after Nekita. Standing by the bog, Taa watched her new friend fly away before she went to join Alzo and the others.

"Those scallywags won't be causing any more trouble," Captain Bok announced entering the peat house with Pippy perched upon his shoulder like a mutated parrot. Alzo couldn't help smiling. Captain Bok ignored him. "I sent Knot and his crew to gather up what they could of the supplies. I figure we'll need whatever we can get our hands on."

Alzo agreed. He was grateful for Bok's help. He needed all the help he could get. He'd never been in the military and the only arms training he had was sparing with a short sword as a boy. After he landed on Earth, he had been more interested in baseball and football than ROTC or fencing.

"I've sent word for the family heads to come here this evening for a thinking." Captain Bok continued eyeing a bowl of thick brown sauce on the table in front of him. Captain Bok took a bit of bread and dipped it in the sauce. "I figure we don't have long before the bulimon and their cronies are on our doorstep. No way to tell how many there will be, but I figure we'll be outnumbered five to one at least."

"How long do you think we have?" Alzo asked tugging at his beard as he scanned the faces gathered around the table.

"A few days, a week at most," the Captain grunted, "unless they get delayed." He chuckled and winked at those around him.

"We'll never be ready," Ilee moaned shaking her head, There was no way this mob of lame old men, women and children could be trained to take on an army. Gerawld stepped in front of Ilee and meowed loudly.

"My brother's right," Mia translated, her eyes flashing, "we are ducks sitting in a pond."

"Any positive ideas?" Alzo asked gesturing at those gathered around him. "I know you folks have more experience dealing with the bulimon then I do. Surely, you have learned things about them. What are their weaknesses?"

"Knot told us the bulimon are afraid to go underground." Ilee reminded him pushing her way around Gerawld and reclaiming her spot next to Alzo.

"The island girls right," a tall woman with wide hips and thick thighs said as she pushed herself to the table. "The bulimon are superstitious bastards. What about you?" She cooed placing her hands on the table and leaning boldly in front of Alzo tossing a long blond dreadlock over her bare shoulder. "Are you a superstitious bastard too?"

"I try not to be." Alzo replied not flinching as the woman leaned over and studied him with piercing ice-blue eyes. Her face was so close he could have kissed her.

"You have no right to speak to him like that?" Ilee spat glaring up at the brazen woman.

"I have every right!" The woman spat back, baring her teeth as she thrust her long, slender finger into Alzo's chest. "What right does he have? He who claims to be the Change. What proof does he have? None! Only a rumor that he was brought here by the one who fell! Where is this fallen one?"

"Parth! You old hag!" Captain Bok barked slapping his hand on the table. "Here to stir up trouble are you?"

"Captain Bok!" Parth exclaimed reaching over to take Pippy off the big man's shoulder. "Well, now I know this outsider can't be trusted. Anyone who'd hang out with your lot..."

"Aw lay off Parth," the Captain grumbled his cheeks flushing slightly, "you and I both know you wouldn't be here if you didn't have plans to join us."

"We'd be glad to have you," Alzo interrupted holding his hand out to the strange, aggressive woman. Parth looked down at Alzo's hand but didn't take it.

"You look like an Emperor I once served," Parth said looking deeply into Alzo's eyes. "You've got the same silvery eyes."

"And you look like the cook's daughter who used to torment me as a boy." Alzo smiled still holding out his hand. Parth laughed and gave his hand a firm shake.

"So, what's your plan?" She pulled a rough map out of her boot and spread it out on the table. "Where's Ori? I heard he was here."

"Ori went to find my sister." Alzo replied as he studied the map. "Hopefully he's having good luck."

Unfortunately, Alzo was wrong. Ori stood on the back of the sleeping rock boy looking about him at the carnage scattered on the dry, cracked ground below. In his hand he clutched what was left of Elize's jeans.

"Don't get yourself all in a state," a gravelly voice said from behind him. "It's not her." Ori glanced over his shoulder at the swayed backed brown mule grazing on a clump of grass growing out of the sleeping boy's right ear.

"Mal!" Ori shouted sliding off the boulders and throwing his arms about the mule's neck. Although the mule didn't look even vaguely intelligent. Ori knew the old mule was really his mentor, Mal the Magnificent an extremely gifted mage, shrewd conjurer, alchemist, and overall genius. Ori had been under Mal's tutelage off and on for years. Lately it'd been more off than on. This was mostly due to Ori being too big for his britches or so Mal had said very loudly the last time they had talked.

"Oh, will you stop your blubbering and use your senses." Mal grumbled trying to shake free from Ori. "Look at the blood. It's thick and brown and it stinks. Smell it!" Ori sniffed the blood stained piece of denim and coughed. It had a distinct rusty iron and old sock odor. "Doesn't smell like human blood does it?"

Ori shook his head and stuffed the scrap of denim in his pocket. Mal continued to chew on the clump of grass while Ori went to have a closer look at the bits of body parts strewn over what looked like a pentagram stomped into the dirt.

"So, what do you think happened?" Ori asked kicking a sausage sized toe. Mal ambled towards him with his muzzle to the ground. He stopped in front of the large dagger half buried in the dirt.

"It appears that Su Lei's giant girl tried to attack your friend." Mal said rubbing a cracked hoof at the lines Kara had stomped out with her feet. "It appears your friend fought back."

"I wonder where she is now?" Ori asked leaning down to pick up a small, red berry. Mal nipped the berry off Ori's hand with his yellowed teeth and swallowed it.

"She went that way," Mal stated nodding at the trail of broken dirt leading down the dried riverbed. "Depending on how many berries she ate, she'll be hallucinating for hours." Ori and Mal followed Elize's tracks until they vanished in the ruins of an ancient salt temple.

"She couldn't have just disappeared!" Ori exclaimed after they had circled the ruins several times and still not finding any trace of Elize.

CHAPTER 12

"Har, har, har." Deep, rolling laughter bounced off the salt walls making it impossible for Elize to tell where it was coming from. The jovial laughter tickled Elize from head to toe making it almost impossible for her to fight back the temptation to join in.

Elize tiptoed sideways keeping her back against the wall until she reached an arched hall where she hoped to find who was laughing. Instead, she found an empty hallway. Not a hallway like you'd find in a house, but a grand hallway with high, arched ceilings supported by tree trunk-like pillars of salt. The mineral rich water dripping down from the ceilings for eons had formed the stalactites and the stalagmites which had joined creating the thick circular pillars. Elize ran her fingertips across an intricate image painted on the closest pillar. The salt had been dyed with bright colors to make each scene stand out, like pages of a picture book. Elize walked slowly around the pillar. It was covered with heavenly images of winged beings and bright orbs. Marveling at the expert craftmanship, Elize moved from one pillar to the next. Each pillar was unique. One had been carved with hieroglyphs depicting half-animal/half human beings like the ones found on the walls of Egyptian pyramids. Another was covered with a massive army poised and ready to defend their kingdom. She stopped when she came to the pillar depicting the history of Earth. Not the entire history, but major points in time. Some of the scenes she was familiar with, while others she had never seen before. Elize was still examining the Earth pillar when another burst of laughter erupted followed by the sound of hundreds of tiny bells ringing.

Elize slipped across the hall to an adjacent archway and cautiously peeked into the large, dome shaped room. No one was there. 'This is crazy,' Elize thought stepping into the room. The room was covered from floor to ceiling with bright, almost lifelike chalk drawings. Her attention was drawn to a drawing of Ganesha, the elephant-headed Hindu god. He was sitting in a lush hanging garden next to a waterfall where lovely tiny pink naked ladies splashed. The drawing looked so real Elize felt like she could walk right into it. Intrigued she reached out to touch Ganseha's arm. A large gray trunk swung out and knocked her hand away. The pink ladies giggled like hundreds of tiny bells ringing. Elize screamed and stumbled backwards landing in the arms of a handsome, well-built, six-armed, blue skinned man.

"Shiva!" Elize gasped feeling faint.

"Har, har, har," the elephant boomed holding his round belly with all four arms. The tiny pink ladies giggled again. "The silly girl thinks Koh's a god. Har, har, har."

"What's going on?" Elize stammered trying to regain her composure. "Where am I?" She had never liked being laughed at and somehow being laughed at by an elephant and tiny naked ladies made it even more humiliating.

"You are in the Salt Temples." Koh answered reaching out and gently touching the silver thread attached to Elize's belly button. "Now, pray tell who are you? Why are you here and where have you left your body?"

"My name's Elize. I don't know why I'm here and I left my body in the pool. I'm not sure, but I think I might be dead."

"Oh no my dear Princess," RaJa assured her while Koh took her hand and guided her into the drawing. "If you were dead your spirit would not still be attached to your physical body."

"So, what is this an out of body experience?"

"Well, if I have to guess, and I'm very good at guessing," Koh answered smiling at her with bright white, perfect teeth. "I'd say the ancients sent you here to learn something and my friend RaJa and I have been chosen to teach you something."

Elize looked at the two strange men and frowned. "So, you're my spirit guides." RaJa and Koh nodded. Elize frowned again. "I find it hard to believe my spirit guides are Ganesh and…"

"Ganesh!" Koh exclaimed loudly slapping his thigh. "Ha! First you think I'm Shiva and now you think RaJa is Ganesh! Hah!" Koh laughed so hard he almost choked. "What a mess the nine realms would be in if that were true!" He wheezed wiping the tears from his eyes.

"I think I'd make a wonderful god, "Raja huffed bopping Koh on the head with the end of his trunk. "Right princess?"

"I'm not a princess," Elize corrected him. "I'm Elize."

"Oh, little Elize," RaJa chuckled wrapping a thick arm around her shoulders, "don't be silly. Of course, you're a princess. Why else would the ancients send you to us?" Elize blinked her eyes hard. "Har, har, har," RaJa boomed. "I am no illusion. Koh and I are as real as you are."

"Sorry," Elize mumbled still not fully convinced.

"No need to be sorry." Koh cooed putting his muscular arm around Elize's waist and trying to pull her free from RaJa. "You are wise to check. It's good to know if things are real or not. So much time is wasted chasing illusions and too little facing reality."

"Speaking of reality, what about my body," Elize asked glancing over her shoulder. "I left it in the pool. Should I go back and get it?"

"No worries," RaJa assured her waving his trunk at the little pink ladies still playing in the waterfall. "The Debvees will take care your body until it is time for your spirit to return to it."

"Come, you have a lot to learn but not a lot of time to learn it," Koh said leading Elize behind the waterfall and into another drawing.

"It's not good to start on an empty stomach." RaJa commented rubbing his round belly and gleefully leaping into a drawing of young maidens filling baskets with plump red grapes.

"You're sure I'm not hallucinating?" Elize asked as RaJa frolicked after the giggling maidens crushing grapes under his large feet as he chased them through the arbor.

"Yes, I'm sure you are not hallucinating. Your spirit is in the Spirit World. Your body is at rest, but I assure you, you are quite alive." Koh gently lifted the silver cord attached to Elize's belly button. "As I said before this would not be here if you were dead."

"Oh," Elize said looking up at Koh and smiling, "that's a relief, I guess. So, what exactly is the Spirit World."

"The Spirit World has as many names as it does appearances. Some see it as Shangri-La, Eden, heaven, etc., etc. A paradise full of wonder and enlightenment. Others see Hades, Shoal, hell, etc., etc. A place of evil, terror, and suffering. How do you see it Elize?"

Elize shut her eyes and thought about a study she had read where children who had survived near death experiences described the afterlife as being in a beautiful garden. Opening her eyes, Elize smiled at Koh.

"A beautiful garden."

"Wonderful! A beautiful garden it is!" Koh clapped his hands happily. Elize liked Koh. Not only was he good looking, charming and well-manner, but he had an aura which flowed around him like warm water. Almost instantly a lush garden appeared in front of them complete with a gleaming golden table and three matching chairs. Elize stepped forward, but Koh stopped her.

"Oh no! No, no, no! That will never do!" He fussed snapping his fingers three times. Her stained frock vanished and was instantly replaced with a light flowing, intricately embroidered tunic and loose-fitting pants.

"Much better," Koh said raising his eyebrows seductively. Elize rolled her eyes and yanked up the swooping vee-neck before taking the seat Koh held out for her.

"So, if you and RaJa aren't gods, what are you? Gins?" Elize asked removing Koh's hand from her thigh. Sighing extravagantly Koh set all six hands on his lap.

"When you were a little girl," he asked tilting his head sideways and giving her a weird smile, "did you have imaginary friends?" Elize nodded.

"Well, in a way that's what RaJa and I are. Long ago..." Koh stopped as RaJa bounded across the well-manicured lawn carrying a large golden tray loaded with honey cakes and a clear pitcher filled with amber colored nectar.

"I didn't know spirits ate?" Elize commented taking a honey cake. RaJa nodded vigorously as he popped several honey cakes in his mouth. Elize found RaJa genuinely endearing. It was hard not to like him. He was so jovial.

"Of course." RaJa boomed handing Elize a flute filled with nectar. "Haven't you ever heard of food for the spirit?"

"Where was I?" Koh mumbled taking a flute of nectar and waving it at Elize.

"Imaginary friends," Elize reminded him taking a small, polite sip.

"Ah yes," Koh nodded closing his eyes for affect. "A long, long time ago a boy visited this very temple with his parents. Although his parents were very loving and extremely kind, the boy was sad because there were no other children that looked like him. He felt very lonely. While he was here the boy spent hours and hours reading the stories his mother and father brought him. The tales filled his mind with amazing visions. As the boy grew so did his imagination. He began to imagine having adventures with the characters in the stories he read. Two characters quickly became his favorite. One had a large elephant head like him and the other resembled his father as a boy. His imaginary friends were brave, cunning, and loved getting into mischief. At first the boy's parents were puzzled by their son's sudden change in behavior. After keeping an eye on her son for several days, his mother asked him who he was talking to. When the boy told his mother about his new friends, his mother understood and allowed him to continue playing with his imaginary friends. She even used them to help her son with his history lessons. When the boy grew up, he left his imaginary friends behind, but because he believed in us so firmly, we didn't fade away like the others. Whenever the boy, now a man returned to the temple, he was so pleased to find RaJa and I still here. We dined on honey cakes and nectar and talked for days about the goings on in the nine realms." Koh stopped and took a sip of nectar. "Now it seems the boy and time has forgotten us. Occasionally someone stumbles on the temple and tries to steal our salt, but RaJa and I do a good job at scaring the trespassers away. Those that live near the temple believe it to be haunted by angry spirits and usually stay away. A few bring offerings in exchange for bits of salt that have fallen on the steps, but we have little use for such offerings."

"That was until the little bandit showed up," RaJa fussed waving his trunk towards the far hallway where a young ferret was sparing with a line of statues.

"Aww she so cute," Elize said watching the ferret looping, thrusting, and jabbing a pointed stick at the stone statues. The black

145

band of fur across her eyes made the little ferret look like a masked attacker.

"She's a nuisance!" Koh huffed. "We should have left her on the steps to die. But big-hearted RaJa insisted on helping her. Which was fine, until he took things too far and gave her the gift of gab. Once she realized she could speak, the little imp hasn't stopped. But enough of her, what do you need to know?"

"Well, for starters I need to know how to get to Astaria and what I'm supposed to do once I get there."

"Hmmm," Koh thought pursing his lips. "Well, we can head you in the right direction once you return to your body, but we have no clue what you're supposed to do. RaJa and I only see the past, the future is not ours to see."

"Okay," Elize said glancing down at her palm and making a face. "That's strange."

"What's strange?" Koh and RaJa asked looking curiously at Elize's palm.

"The stone's gone."

"What stone?"

"The blue stone. The one I was born with in my palm." Koh and RaJa exchanged confused looks. Koh started scrolling through images that appeared on the tabletop in front of him.

"Ah ha!" He shouted pointing at the image in front of him. Elize peered over his shoulder.

"Is that me?" She asked staring at the tiny baby shaking in the hands of an older woman.

"Yes and look no stone in either hand."

"But there is a blue mark." Elize insisted tapping the table with her index finger. "Ilee called it the mark of Monet or something like that, she said that only the High Priestess of Ohio, no that's not it...Hohi were born with that mark on their hands. When I told Ilee I was born with that mark, she didn't believe me. She said her sister had been born with the mark and that mine was fake."

RaJa tapped the table with his trunk. "Ilee is lying." He told Elize matter-of-factly.

"I don't think she's lying," Elize told them, "I think she's been lied too. But let's leave that for now. What I want to know is what it all means. Why was I born with this gift, not the mark or the stone, but the power in my veins. What is it and why me?"

While she waited for Koh and RaJa to answer, Elize helped herself to another honey cake.

"I think the best place to begin is here," Koh waved his hands in front of him causing the garden to shift into a movie screen. "This is Earth right before the Great Flood."

146

Elize looked at the scene before her. "Aren't you going to start with the Garden of Eden?" She said half teasing.

"No need," Koh said giving her a perturbed look, "obviously you already know it. Now, are you familiar with the reason the Great Flood was sent upon the Earth?"

"I am! I am!" RaJa blurted waving his trunk about sending the table and glasses flying.

"This is Elize's lesson," Koh scolded RaJa and nodded at Elize who was transfixed by the images moving across the screen like a 3-D movie.

"Um," Elize answered not taking her eyes off the screen, "let's see, the Earth was corrupt because the angels left to watch over the fledging humans came down from the heavens and had sex with the human females. The children fathered by the angels were mutated and started to cause a lot of trouble on Earth. People got upset and cried out to God who was so angry at what had happened he set a flood to wipe out all but a select few from the Earth." Koh and RaJa exchanged looks.

"Well, that was a very condensed version of what happened." Koh said getting up and pacing in front of the screen. "You failed to mention that during this time the gateways between the realms were open and Earth being a new and wonderous planet full of rare animals, fruits, vegetables and wonderful spices quickly became a trading mecca. As more and more visitors from the other realms arrived on Earth things began to get out of hand. The watchers who by that time were growing bored."

"So bored." RaJa yawned widely. Koh ignored him.

"The watchers were tired of sitting around and decided to join in the fun. After all the young Earth women were beautiful, bouncy things and they tickled the watchers in ways they had never experienced before."

"What's happening here?" Elize pointed to an image of a tall, alien looking man standing in front of cages full of odd partly human creatures.

"The cages are full of the results of non-human and human experimentation. Almost all the mutants were destroyed in the flood, but a few survived and are found on small, isolated planets like this. Over thousands of years the majority of mutated genes have been bred out, but not all of them."

"Somethings wrong here." Elize said her eyes glued to the screen. "The Bible says only Noah and his family and two of each creature on Earth survived, but obviously there were many others."

"As I said before, the story you've been told is very condensed."

"But I don't even see an ark!" Elize protested.

"That's because Noah and his ark are not relevant to this lesson." Koh remarked flicking off the screen and walking away from the wall.

"Ok, I get that, but what does all this have to do with me?" Elize asked still not sure what Koh was trying to teach her.

"Your story starts with a human female named Monet." Koh stomped the floor under his right foot turning it into a swirling mass of molten lava. Well, not really, but that's what it looked like. "Monet was the oldest daughter of a good man who had no sons. Because he had no sons the man brought his daughter Monet to help bring the offering of first fruits to the temple. Monet caught the eye of a young watcher named Scyathee. Now Scyathee truly loved Monet and took her as his wife. When he saw the other humans growing old, he decided he could not bear for that to happen to his beloved Monet. So, Scyathee put Monet in a deep sleep and gave her a part of his essence as a gift which among other things gave her longevity. Scyathee was captured and condemned to spend eternity in the Ninth Realm, commonly called hell. Monet and her family escaped through a dimensional doorway to Toboria. It is believed that Monet betrayed Scyathee to save her daughters and their families."

"What was the deal?" Elize asked.

"That," Koh said as the images faded and a new set started to form, "appears to have been deleted from the histories."

"Oh look!" Elize exclaimed pointing at the floor. "It's me falling from the sky."

"So it is," RaJa said watching as Elize cannonballed into the muddy water. "Why weren't you killed?"

"The otters saved me," Elize told him as several brown heads appeared bobbing in the water. "See! Oh, look there's Taa and Mia and Gerawld!" Elize's enthusiasm stopped when Kara appeared, her dead body being ripped apart by the blood lizards.

"RaJa's right," Koh said flicking off the scene. "You should have been killed and more than once."

"I fought back," Elize told them thinking they were talking about Kara, "but I didn't mean to kill her. I didn't realize what was happening until it was too late."

A large gray arm wrapped around her shoulders. "Dear Elize, you did not kill the giant girl," Raja assured her gently rubbing her back.

"RaJa's right," Koh said sternly. "Listen to me! You are not responsible for the giant's death."

"But I...," Elize started to protest, but RaJa put his trunk over her lips.

"I know you see yourself killing the girl," Koh told her firmly, "but you were not responsible for her death. It was the girl's own actions that killed her. She was trying to cut off your hand. If she had let go of the knife she would not have died."

148

"But the power."

"The power has no conscious. The giant planned to kill you. She led you away from her friends, drugged you, and then attacked you with a knife. You were in danger. The power sensed the danger and it reacted. If the power hadn't reacted, the giant would be alive and you my dear Elize would be dead. So, RaJa is right you did not kill the giant."

"It doesn't feel that way," Elize sniffed thinking back on RaJa and Koh's original question, "so, why wasn't I killed."

"It wasn't your time." RaJa said pulling a honey cake out of the deep pockets of the purple and gold robe he was wearing and offering it to Elize. Elize shook her head. After seeing the image of Kara, she had lost her appetite. RaJa shrugged and joyfully popped the cake in his large mouth. Koh rolled his eyes and motioned for Elize to follow.

"Come," Koh said linking arms with Elize as they walked out of the gardens and on to a white bridge covered with dangling flowers. "It is time you learned to control this power of yours."

"Finally!" RaJa roared diving into a bed of fragrant flower petals flowing under the bridge and disappearing.

"Isn't RaJa joining us?"

"He'll be along in a while." Koh replied casually as they continued across the bridge arm in arm. "Now, I want you to try to remember the first time you felt the power moving inside you."

"I've always felt it." Elize replied. "It's like my heart beating in my chest. Even though I don't always feel it beating I know it's there. I must have inherited the power but if that's true why didn't my brother Alzo inherit it too?"

"Are you sure he didn't?" Koh asked stopping in front of a bench carved out of a black stone and motioning for Elize to sit.

"Pretty sure, I mean Alzo can pick up languages faster than I can, but no I don't think he inherited the power. Maybe it's passed down the female line."

"Let's take a look and see what we can see?" Koh waved his hand in front of him swiping through the past in rapid succession.

"You're making my head spin." Elize said grabbing his hand.

"Interesting," Koh said pulling his hand away.

"What?"

"None of your ancestors have a blue stone in their palm. The blue mark has been passed down the female line since the time just after the flood beginning with Monet's daughter. The term Gift of Monet isn't used until several generations later."

"So, all these women have the same power I do?"

"To some extent," Koh mumbled not really paying attention to Elize as he continued flicking through images muttering. "Internal, external, external, internal, internal, external, oh dear."

"Oh dear?" Elize asked looking at herself lying on the ground in the Forest of Milendor with a bolt of light shooting out of her hand.

"You definitely need to learn to control your powers." Koh commented shaking his head at Elize. "Although it seems you have more control than you think, when you are upset the power takes over and that is not good. Especially when you have a demon chasing you that needs energy to grow stronger."

"What are you talking about."

Koh flipped back through the images until he found the one he was looking for. It was the image of a little girl, no older than two or three, sitting amongst the mud and rocks with a woman's head on her lap. The little girl is crying with her hands holding the woman's bloody skull together. A whitish blue light is flowing from her right hand.

"That's me," Elize whispered softly reaching out to touch the image, "the night we left Astaria and landed on Earth. I was trying to keep Mayme's brains in her head."

"Yes and even though you were so young you were determined to use the power inside you to save your mother." Koh flipped ahead and stopped at an image of a large, beefy boy holding a girl's head under the water."

"Matty," Elize hissed recognizing the youngest of her older stepbrothers. Matty had tormented her for years until that day. That day Elize had stood up for herself. Not that she had a choice, if she hadn't Matty would have drown her."

"Do you see the difference," Koh asked her as a bolt of white light slammed into Matty's chest and he was thrown out of the water and into a large oak tree. "In the first instance you called the power up inside you and focused it to try to save your mother, in the next you let fear and anger ignite the power shooting it outward in a wild blast."

"Like I did in the Forest of Milendor."

"Exactly."

"Ouch," Elize gasped as the cord attached to her belly yanked her forward.

"Your body is growing stronger." Koh told her looking worried. "Our time is growing short. When your body grows strong enough, it will pull your spirit back inside it."

"Then you need to teach me to control the power before that happens." Elize said eager to learn how to stop the power reacting without her permission. Koh scratched his chin with one of his blue hands and considered Elize's comment.

"I cannot teach what I do not know," he finally told her solemnly, "but I'm willing to try to help you. Let's start with the basics." Koh took Elize's hand as they walked further into the garden. "We will begin with the breath. Controlling the breath seems like a simple task, but even the simplest task can have great benefits. Being aware of your breath, helps you to stay in the now. Taking a second to focus on your breath can be the key to staying in control while amid chaos."

"I've tried meditation in the past." Elize informed Koh. "It helps me most of the time, but if I'm caught off guard or feel threatened, the power just takes over."

"I'm not talking about meditation," Koh clarified, "I'm talking of controlling the breath. They are connected, but not the same. Now let us begin."

Koh began by going over the basics of controlling the breath. Once he was satisfied with Elize's progress, Koh had Elize practice numerous breathing techniques. Each time Elize thought she had mastered a technique, RaJa would explode out of the flowers in disguise and attack her. RaJa took great pride in his disguises. The fire breathing dragon one was especially terrifying. Even after she knew it was RaJa, Elize still reacted. When a killer shark lunged out of the blue bells headed straight for her Elize forgot all about her breath and blasted him back into the flowers.

"Ugh!" Koh scolded throwing all six hands in the air. "Why is this so hard for you!?"

"I'm trying!" Elize protested. "I thought I did better that time."

"Better? Better? The only reason you didn't fry RaJa with that blast of energy is because you're not in your body! How many times do I have to tell you that if you use your power against the demon it will make him stronger? He will continue to provoke you and feed off your power until he is strong enough to use your own power against you. Do you want that?"

"No! I don't want that!" Elize fumed. "I don't want a demon chasing me at all! I don't even want to be on this planet! I want to be home with my friends and my cat and dog. I didn't choose any of this! I don't know why this demon is after me or how he got out of hell or anything!" Elize fumed. "Can't you look into your magic wall and tell me that at least!" Koh let out a long sigh and plopped down into the chair which had materialized underneath him.

"The demon had help getting out of hell," Koh said leaning back in the chair and flexing his biceps. "Help from a woman scorned. Her name is Aturi, a powerful water maiden who isn't afraid to use the dark magics to get what she wants."

"Who scorned her so badly that she'd want to make a deal with a demon?" Elize asked, transfixed by Koh's pulsating biceps.

151

"It was your Grandfather, the former Emperor of Astaria, Grumbul the Grandiose." Koh replied tilting his chiseled chin towards her and smiling so wide most of his perfectly straight, gleaming white teeth showed. Elize blushed slightly and tried to ignore Koh, which wasn't easy because he was so fine-looking.

"Before Grumbul became the fifth emperor, when he was still a young prince, Grumbul's father sent him on a journey, a rite of passage into manhood. His journey took him down the River Bawe all the way to the ocean. It was the same route the first emperor had taken centuries before. During the journey there was a violent storm and Prince Grumbul was thrown overboard and believed drowned. When the young prince was found several days later he told a tale of a beautiful maiden who had lifted him out of the water and nursed him back to life. No maiden was found and Grumbul was returned home and married off to your grandmother."

"Okay, so the maiden thought the prince dumped her and summoned this demon to get back at my grandfather. What does that have to do with me?"

"Aturi didn't just summon any demon. She summoned a demon who once was a watcher. The demon Scythe, is a very powerful demon who bears a grudge against the Astarian bloodline."

"Is he the watcher who gave Monet the gift?"

"Yes."

"And now this demon, Scythe is after me because he wants Monet's gift back?"

"Apparently."

"Ow!" Elize shouted grabbing her stomach.

"Elize!" Elize heard Koh and RaJa calling out in alarm as her spirit slammed back into her body so hard the air was knocked out of her lungs.

CHAPTER 13

It was past mid-night when Mia slipped away from the others and silently made her way to the dilapidated barns behind the peat houses. Gerawld had left earlier, and Mia expected him to be fast asleep by now. Instead, she found him sitting very still by one of the stables his eyes fixed upon the loft. Gerawld flinched when Mia crept up beside him, clapping his large paw over her mouth he shook his head ever so slightly. There was a flicker of movement in the loft above, so slight that Mia wasn't sure if it was real or if her eyes were playing tricks on her.

Mia and Gerawld remained perfectly still, the whisper of their breath the only sound in the otherwise silent barn. After a few moments they watched as four pairs of florescent green eyes dropped soundlessly from the loft. Mia felt Gerawld's soft fur brush against hers as he stepped out of the shadows. Eight eyes narrowed as he stepped forward, followed by a low and threatening growl. Gerawld stopped and lowered his head.

"We are travelers," he meowed keeping his tone soft, "in search of a safe place to rest."

Mia stayed in the corner her fur sticking up like porcupine needles as she hunched forward, muscles tensed and ready to pounce if things got out of hand.

A lean, cream colored bast cat with brown splotches on her fur approached Gerawld. She was larger than the other three who had dropped out of the loft with her and obviously in charge. Growling softly, the female arched her back, gracefully placing one black socked foot in front of the other.   Gerawld lifted his head and fixed his orange eyes upon hers. Slowly he began to match her step for step. The two moved in a slow, tight circle like two lovers alone on a dimly lit dance floor.

Mia was so entranced by their dance she didn't notice the other cats moving until one whispered into her ear.

"Beautiful, isn't it?" A small feline with dust colored fur commented in a thick accent unlike any Mia had heard before. Mia nodded slightly and continued watching the dance. She had never seen Gerawld move so gracefully. He usually tripped over his own tail.

"So, your travelers," the other female said with a slurry purr. "Where are you from?"

"The Grasslands, on the other side of Milendor." Mia answered casually refusing to be intimidated by the strange cats who had boxed her into the corner.

"Hmmm," the third cat, a tall, brown male purred leaning forward and rubbing his head against Mia's shoulder. "Who are the others? Are they from the grasslands as well?"

"No," Mia replied pushing his head away. "The others have come from many different places to join the Followers of the Change and fight to take back their lands and homes."

"Why are you here?" The middle sized female asked eyeing Mia suspiciously.

"My brother and I were tasked to ensure the healer and Elize arrived in Milendor safely." Mia answered plainly. "After we finished that task, we were asked to join the Followers of the Change and have since pledged our allegiance to their leader. When that task is complete my brother and I will return to our family. Why are you here?"

"This is our home. We are River Bast." the large female circling Gerawld answered as she placed her slender front paw on Gerawld's shoulder. Gerawld reached out and placed his paw upon her opposite shoulder.

"Come," the young male whispered in Mia's ear. "Cinn wishes to be alone with your brother."

Mia hesitated until Gerawld winked at her and shooed her with his free paw.

Fee, Fie, and Phoe raced across the barn dragging Mia up the ladder to the loft where they had carved out a cozy nest in the dry hay. While Fee and Fie went to get some warm milk from the pygmy goats they kept penned up outside, Phoe caught a skinny mouse and shared it with Mia. Phoe told Mia how the River Bast population had dwindled since the river dried up. Besides his mother Cinn, and his sisters there were only a few families still living in the barns.

Mia fell asleep in a warm heap of hay with a belly full of mouse and warm milk. When she woke up, Gerawld was lying next to her.

"Did you get any sleep?" Mia teased yanking a tuff of cream-colored fur out of his paw. Gerawld made a face and shook his head.

"I do have news," he whispered.

"Good news?"

"No," he said stifling a yawn, "it's about Tux. Cinn says a black and white cat with one ear sliced was spotted on the cliffs behind us. They thought he was mad. He was thrashing himself against the rocks like he was wrestling with an enemy, but they didn't see anyone else there."

"That's not good," Mia agreed glancing out at the dark gray cliffs in the distance.

* * * * * * * *

"How could Elize just disappear!" Ori shouted kicking a fallen salt pillar. He and Mal had searched the salt temple ruins in the blazing sun for what felt like hours and hadn't found a single clue as to where Elize had gone. It was as if she had stepped out of this world. Which is exactly what Mal thought had happened. It was the only explanation.

"As I was saying," Mal said grumpily swishing his tail across his behind. "It appears Elize has stepped into the spirit world."

"I heard you oh great mage," Ori replied sarcastically waving both hands over his head, "but if that's the case wouldn't her body still be here in the physical world?"

"Not necessarily," Mal said irritably. He did not like being challenged, but the truth was he knew very little about how the spirit world worked. In all his years he'd never actually traveled there, nor had he ever met anyone who had. Except Su Lei, but the Oracle wasn't always a reliable source. She was well known for mixing facts with fiction.

"Not necessarily," Ori snapped, "what is that supposed to mean?"

"Well, Elize had eaten at least a handful of those red berries, so I'm guessing Elize didn't realize she had stepped into the spirit world, let alone that it was impossible to go there in her physical body." Mal smiled widely at Ori quite pleased with his answer.

"That's ridiculous?" Ori huffed kicking the pillar again. "What do we do now? Sit around and wait until she reappears."

"No," Mal told him shaking his dusty mane. "I wait while you go help Alzo."

"What! No!"

Mal set his butt on the ground and yawned widely. All this walking had made his old bones ache. Ori's reaction surprised him. Usually, Ori would want to return to the action. Mal had never known Ori to fall for a female before. Mal flicked a fly off his ear, he'd have to think up a way to convince Ori it was best to leave. The old mule sat on his rump with his front legs braced in front of him. He stretched his neck and moved his long, stiff ears in wide circles. He was quite aware he looked silly, but it helped him think. Ori sat on the pillar and waited. He'd been Mal's student long enough to know the old mule could be as stubborn as he was. After several minutes, Mal clicked his thick, yellowed teeth and looked sharply at Ori.

"You never told me what caused that flash over the trees in Milendor."

"You never asked," Ori grumbled. He was pretty sure Mal already knew the answer.

"I'm asking now."

"It's a long story."

"We have time."

"Elize was determined to meet the Oracle, but the roads leading through Milendor were closed due to the mob gathered outside. Elize and her friends were standing near the forest edge when she ran into the forest. Taa tried to stop her by running after her along with the bast cats who had escorted them to Milendor. I was near the entrance and saw them. I jumped over the ranger's heads and ran towards the Oracle's tree. Behr must have seen me and gave chase. I had just reached Elize when everything went crazy. Behr sprouted wings and flew after me upsetting the swamp troll I had befriended earlier. The troll rushed to my rescue and almost stomped on Elize. Elize freaked out and a lightning bolt shot out of her hand, ricocheted off the trolls blubbery skin, and hit Behr in the chest splitting him in two."

"And after that?"

"After that Elize was carried up into the Tara Bora by the owl ladies and the rest of us were apprehended by the Rangers of Milendor."

"I mean what happened to Behr."

"Oh, well one part of him ran into the crowd that had stormed onto the road and the other shadowy Behr was blasted over the trees."

"You mean the demon." Mal told Ori. "Behr was hosting a demon."

"So that's how he got his power?" Ori nodded. "I knew there was no way Behr could have sprouted wings on his own."

"Yes and now you know as much about Behr and the demon as I do," Mal said figuring a little flattery wouldn't hurt. "As you know Behr has eyes and ears everywhere." Mal got to his feet and began to pace in front of Ori. "As long as Elize is in the Spirit World she is invisible. However, when she reappears she will no longer be invisible. Now, Behr has seen you with Elize so he will have his spies watching you in case you try to meet up with her. I'm sure the last thing you want is for Elize to be taken captive. That is why I suggested you go help Alzo. Alzo could really use your talents in his cause."

Ori wasn't convinced that easily, but after arguing back and forth for several hours, Ori finally agreed with Mal. Ori made Mal swear to send word as soon as Elize reappeared before shifting into his fox form. His red tinged sandy fur blended in with the colors of the riverbed providing a natural camouflage as he jogged towards the peat houses.

Mal was relieved Ori had finally agreed to his plan. Ori could be quite stubborn. Almost as stubborn as he was. That was the reason it was taking Ori so long to learn the ways of the Mage. He had no self-control. No patience. Still Mal was confident Ori had what it took if he'd take his studies seriously.

One night Mal dreamt of tiny pink ladies dangling tasty carrots in front of his nose. The next morning Mal trotted around to the other side of the ruins and found a massive salt stairway where a mound of dirt had been before. The stairway led up to the caved in front entrance of the salt temples. Mal found a pile of carrots waiting for him at the bottom of the steps.

Mal was finishing up his carrots when he noticed something move on the steps above. Lifting his head, Mal brayed out a spell. A few minutes later a cliff swallow swooped down and landed on his head. Mal had promised Ori he'd send word the moment Elize reappeared, and he was a Mage of his word. He would have liked to go himself, but he didn't want to risk losing Elize. Besides he knew cliff swallows to be reliable, trustworthy birds and was confident that his message would be delivered to Ori and only Ori.

As Mal watched the swallow fly away, he wondered about the mighty ones who carved the temples from the massive pillars of salt. The mines had been abandoned long before Mal was born. It was said that the ruins were inhabited by the spirits of the mighty ones who had once lived there. Few who had ventured inside lived to talk about it. Mal had never heard of anyone coming out of the temples. This was another fact that he had chosen not to tell Ori. Was it his fault Ori hadn't paid attention to his history lessons? Well, maybe, but that was beside the point.

Elize laid with her eyes closed taking slow deep breaths and silently said the Our Father over and over again. It was an old habit she had picked up during her years of Catholic school. Like a mantra the prayer always calmed her down and helped her to quell the anxiety welling up in her throat. She was starting to feel calmer when something sharp jab her in the thigh.

"Gitup, gitup, gitup," a high-pitched voice squawked followed by another sharp jab. Elize opened her eyes. A scrawny little ferret stood over her jabbing her thigh with a sharp stick. "Git up," the ferret demanded again, jumping onto Elize's chest and pressing her masked face so close Elize smelled the sour milk on her breath. "Git up!"

"Stop that!" Elize shouted slapping the stick out of the startled ferret's paws. Gingerly pulling herself into a sitting position, Elize watched the skinny creature loop down the steps to fetch her stick. "Great!" She thought, "I'm being taken hostage by a ferret."

Even though she couldn't see them, Elize was sure RaJa and Koh were enjoying the show. The ferret leapt back in front of her waving the stick menacingly.

"You Rixley's prisoner!" The ferret hissed furiously thrusting the sharp point at Elize's nose.

"Nonsense," Elize snapped snatching the stick out of Rixley's paws and holding it high over her head. Rixley gnashed her teeth and tried to crawl up Elize's shoulder. Elize knocked the ferret to the ground and quickly got to her feet. The sudden movement made her head spin. Elize leaned against a broken pillar and flashed Rixley what she hoped was a fierce look.

Rixley bared her teeth and lunged at Elize. Elize had to admit the kid had spunk, but she had had enough of this foolishness. Jutting out her hand, Elize firmly wrapped it around Rixley's boney forehead and held the ferret at arm's length. It was a move she had learned from Matty, her evil stepbrother. As she watched the skinny bandit thrashing about cursing up a blue streak, Elize burst out laughing.

Rixley looked at Elize defiantly. Then her shiny, black eyes filled with tears and the young ferret girl collapsed on the steps sobbing.

"Hey, I'm sorry," Elize said softly, starting to feel like a heartless monster. Rixley peeked at Elize from between her paws. "Are you all alone?" Elize asked noticing Rixley's ribs poking out under her fur. It was hard to tell how old Rixley was, but Elize guessed she was too young to be on her own. "Where's your mama?"

"Gone," Rixley sniffed licking the tears off her paws. "Taken away."

"Taken away," Elize exclaimed, "where?"

Rixley shrugged and wiped her eyes with the back of her arm. "Rixley not know. The bad men took my mama and the others away. They left us pups to die." Rixley lifted her head and threw back her bony shoulders. "But Rixley did not die!"

"I see that." Elize said kindly. "How did you end up here?" Elize asked waving her hand at the massive salt steps.

"Rixley followed mama," Rixley said sniffing her pink nose and creeping up closer to Elize, "but the bad men moved too fast, and Rixley couldn't keep up. I was too weak. I needed mama's milk to stay strong. When Rixley got here I fell asleep on the steps. The Debvee's gave Rixley milk from the bowls. The milk made Rixley strong."

What a rotten trick Elize thought. Koh and RaJa knew she wouldn't be able to leave Rixley behind once she met her. Elize ran her hands over the silky robe she was wearing. It looked similar to the one RaJa was wearing earlier. Reaching into one of the pockets, Elize pulled out a handful of cherry sized berries and held them up in front of her. She was a little leery about eating strange berries after her last experience, but Rixley had no such problems. She snatched them from Elize and shoved them one by one into her mouth until her cheeks puffed out like a gopher.

"So why do you want to take me prisoner?" Elize asked as Rixley munched on the berries.

"Rixley brave!" Rixley mumbled and proudly thrust out her chest, "Rixley strong, but Rixley needs help to get Mama back."

"Do you know where they took her?" Elize asked. Rixley shook her head sadly. "I see," Elize said rubbing her chin. "Well, I…Elize," Elize tapped her chest, "will go with you, but not as a prisoner. We will travel together as companions. Rixley and Elize will be friends."

Rixley looked at Elize and wrinkled her pink nose. "Come pan yons?" She said not sure what that meant, "friends?"

"Yes," Elize said smiling. "Companions are friends who travel together. Friends take care of each other."

Rixley squealed and hugged Elize's leg, "Rixley and Elize be friends! Yes, yes, Rixley be good friend. Rixley strong and brave."

"Rixley strong and Rixley brave, Rixley, Rixley saves the day! Rixley strong and Rixley brave, the bad guy's better stay away!" Elize sang looking out toward the purple mountains in the distance. Koh said that the Astarian Empire lay on the other side of the purple mountains, however he had not known how to get there, or how long it would take.

"Rixley, Rixley saves the day!" Rixley chanted happily hopping down the steps in front of Elize. Elize swore she could hear RaJa roaring with laughter as she made her way down to the fields below. Even though Rixley had stopped singing out loud, Elize could tell by the way the ferret girl pranced about that she was still singing on the inside.

When she reached the bottom step, Elize discovered several paths leading into the weedy fields. Elize asked Rixley if she knew what path they should take. Rixley pointed to a flickering pink light on the path to the right.

"Curious," Elize mumbled walking over to check it out. As soon as she got close the light blinked out and reappeared several yards ahead of her. Rixley squeaked with delight zipping pass Elize to leap on to the pink light and joyfully tumbling head over heels when it disappeared. Chasing the pink lights became a game. Elize and Rixley took turns chasing after the lights until they finally led them up a large brown mound and disappeared for good.

"Bout time." A gravelly voice grumbled below them. Rixley jumped behind Elize holding her pointy stick in front of her and peeked out between Elize's knees.

"Rixley strong and brave," she whispered under her breath.

Elize searched for the mysterious voice but didn't see anyone except an ancient brown mule with a white muzzle. The mule looked up at Elize with dull chocolate-brown eyes and munched on a lump of brown grass with large bucked, yellowed teeth.

"I think the mule spoke," Elize whispered to Rixley. Rixley poked her head out between Elize's knees and shook her head.

"Mules can't talk," she told Elize matter-of-factly. Elize was about to point out the obvious but decided not to. Instead, she addressed the mule.

"Were you talking to us?"

The mule pawed the dry ground with his hoof and looked at Elize like she was disturbing him. "Who else would I be talking to?"

"Were you waiting for us?" Elize asked leaning her head down to get a better look, still not convinced the mule was speaking. She thought perhaps someone was playing a trick on them.

"Why else would I be in this god forsaken place." The mule answered rudely. "We've been searching for you for days."

"We?" Elize asked sliding down the mound. Rixley held onto Elize's robe with one paw and her pointy stick with the other making sure the mule could see it. The mule lifted his muzzle and clicked his teeth at the stick.

"Well, it was we, but now it's just me. I sent Ori..."

"Ori! Ori's here," Elize interrupted scanning the field hoping to see him, "where?"

"Ahem," the mule coughed slapping his rump with his tail, "as I was saying, Ori was with me, but I sent him to help Alzo. Alzo needed his help more than you and we had no way of telling how long you'd be in the Spirit world."

Elize scratched the side of her neck and wondered how this rude mule knew she'd been in the Spirit world. Then she remembered something Ori had told her one night at her house.

"Oh! Oh! I know who you are!" Elize shouted, "You're the Mage! Mal the Magnificent Mage! It's you! Isn't it?" Elize was so excited that she reached out and patted the old mule between his ears. Mal brayed loudly and quickly backed out of Elize's reach.

"Shush!" He scolded Elize, folding his ears back to show his displeasure. "If I wanted the entire planet to know who I was, do you think I'd bother masquerading as an old ass!

Elize tried to look remorseful as she swallowed a snicker. Mal didn't need to masquerade, he was an old ass. It took several minutes for Elize to coax Rixley down off the mound where she had bolted when Mal brayed.

"Rixley brave and strong," Rixley whispered leaping on to Elize's shoulders and looping across her neck like a mink stole.

"We should be going." Mal snorted and moved his thick ears back and forth like a radar. When he didn't hear anything he started to trot towards the purple mountains.

"Wait!" Elize called after him. "Why was Ori here?"

"Why do you think he was here?" Mal huffed without slowing. "He was looking for you. He said he saw you at the bottom of the Tara Bora and was sure you were in trouble. When he found your bloody clothes...well let's just say he became quite upset. Distraught actually, until I discovered your trail."

Elize was surprised at how good it felt to know that Ori had been concerned about her and wondered where he was now.

"Why did you send him to help Alzo? Is Alzo alright?" Elize asked. She had no idea how long she'd been in the Spirit World or what had happened since she had last seen the others. Time passed differently in the Spirit World. There was no day or night, no waking and sleeping.

"Alzo's as well as can be expected," Mal answered a little too nonchalantly. Instead of putting Elize at ease as he intended, she became more anxious.

"What's that supposed to mean? Is Alzo alright or not?"

"As far as I'm aware your brother is fine. He's not thrilled about being leader of the Followers of the Change, but he has good people supporting him."

"Yeah, I know he was upset about becoming a leader, but Su Lei helped him to accept that for the most part. I'm glad you sent Ori to help him. You're right Alzo needs his help more than I do. How long ago did he leave?"

"Just over a day, but he should be there by now."

Of course, Mal had no way of knowing Ori had been delayed on his way to the peat houses. Several times he was forced to detour off his path to avoid being seen. He was almost to the peat houses when his keen sense of smell alerted him to a Wooler camp. The stocky men got their name from the thick, curly, wool-like hair covering their bodies. It had been months since their last sheering and the stench of dirty wool was almost nauseating. Ori guessed the Woolers were here on their own accord and not under any allegiance to the Astarian Empire. Most likely they had seen the posters and had come for the reward. Ducking underneath a broad, leafy bush, Ori focused his attention on the group huddled around a low fire. An old Wooler was telling the others a tale his old gram had told him about the werebeasts who roamed this area. Ori smiled. There was no way he could pass up such a fine opportunity to cause a bit of mischief. Stretching out across the ground, Ori began to sing softly. His song filled the Wooler's heads with images of terrifying werebeasts ready to rip their still beating hearts right out of their chest.

The Woolers shifted uneasily, glancing over their shoulders, they clutched their weapons closer to their chests. The low fire cast dark shadows across the low bushes behind them adding to the spooky atmosphere. When a stick was dragged across the ground behind him, Ori almost jumped out of his skin.

"I figured it was you," Knot chuckled in Ori's ear. "Go on and git. Me and the boys will take it from here." Ori nodded and dashed off into the darkness. He almost felt bad about leaving the poor Woolers at the mercy of the Brownies. Almost.

Melting back into the night Ori was careful to avoid the numerous camps around Milendor's southeastern perimeter. These camps were closer together making them harder to avoid. Ori heard the rough, garbled voices of bulimon close by and quickly skittered into a hole in the roots of a stunted tree. From the snippets of conversation, he learned that most of the bulimon were fed up with doing the emperor's dirty work. They longed to return to their homeland and families. The bulimon were a superstitious lot and every time the breeze rustled the tree limbs they stopped talking and looked nervously at the leaves above their thick skulls. You could almost cut their terror with a knife.

Sensing motion above him, Ori looked up to see several rangers dressed in dark green slipping across the branches. Moments later the night exploded with loud clanging and flashes of light. Within seconds the entire bulimon camp was awake grunting and shouting as fiery arrows rained down from above. Pieces of cloth flew out of the trees screeching across the camp like angry ghosts. Terrified the bulimon ran about in a crazed frenzy slashing their long swords at anything that moved.

When Ori poked his head out of the roots, a stout, broad shouldered bulimon spotted him. The enraged bulimon charged towards him, but to Ori's great relief the bulimon stepped into a rut and tumbled to the ground. The bulimon bellowed in horror as something under the ground grabbed his hoof and began to drag him under.

Ori slipped out of his hole and ducked behind the trees to watch the chaos still unfolding before him. Blinded by fear the bulimon continued to lash out at anything that moved. When it was over all the bulimon in the camp lie dead or wounded. Ori was picking his way through the camp when he noticed a decapitated head watching him. Although the bulimon was mortally wounded, he was not dead. He looked at Ori with deep sadness in his dark brown eyes.

"Take me with you," the head begged. Ori was suddenly overcome with a deep pity for the strange head. Without thought or reason, Ori shifted into his human body, grabbed the cloak off the bulimon's headless body, wrapped the head in it and took off running.

After a while Ori stopped running and set the head on a rock. The bulimon blinked in the morning sun and began to tell Ori about his home. A land covered with fields of clover where he had run free as a calf. Ori asked him why he and the others didn't return to their homes. The bulimon told Ori he couldn't go home or die as long as he was under the demon's control.

"Rip the ring from my nose." The bulimon grunted. "It is the only way I will be free."

Using the cloak to protect his hands, Ori placed one hand on the bulimon's skull while he grabbed the ring with the other. Singing to the bulimon of fields of clover and warm days spent grazing in the field beyond the Bawe River, Ori pulled hard on the ring. When the ring broke free from his nostrils, the bulimon sighed and closed his eyes. Ori threw the bloody ring onto the ground and smashed it under his heel. A bruised mist rose out of the ring and disappeared into the sky. Ori shuttered and scurried through the woods. The vision of the bloodied talking head still clear in his head. When he heard the sound of clashing blades he stopped.

"Die you bovine swine!" A familiar voice grunted.

"Parth?" Ori mouthed poking his head out of the bushes as Parth yanked her long thin blade out of a bulimon's chest.

"And stay dead!" She spat in the bulimon's face as she grabbed the thick brass ring and tore it free from his nostrils. Parth held the ring up into the light and smiled. "Let's see how many lives this will give me." She snarled as she pulled the ring open and lifted it to her ear.

"Don't!" Ori shouted bounding from his hiding place and snatching the ring out of Parth's hand before she could shove it through her earlobe.

"What the..." Parth shouted swinging her bloody blade in a semi-circle, "give that back you furry bastard!"

Ori slapped the blade out of Parth's hand and sent it bouncing across the dirt. Instead of going after it Parth grabbed Ori by the waist and tackled him to the ground. They wrestled back and forth for a minute until Ori kicked himself free and rolled to the left.

"Parth watch out!" Ori shouted as the bloody bulimon picked her blade off the ground. Unable to reach Parth in time to stop the bulimon, Ori spun around and slammed the ring against the rocks smashing it into pieces releasing the bruise colored smoke.

"What the hell?" Parth demanded kicking the bulimon now lying dead at her feet.

"Bad magic." Ori answered picking up her blade and handing it to her. "Didn't you wonder why the bulimon kept getting up even when they were fatally injured?"

"Yeah, that's why I wanted the ring. I thought it'd keep me alive."

"Oh, it would keep you alive alright," Ori scoffed as they walked to the peat houses. "But not in the way you want."

"What do you mean?" Parth demanded cutting her eyes at Ori. She had known Ori most of his life and knew better than to trust him. For all she knew, the shifty vanji wanted all the rings for himself.

Ori told Parth about the talking head begging him to destroy the brass ring so he would be set free from the demon's bond.

"Well shit Ori. You'd better pass that on and quick." Parth said picking up the pace. "Who knows how many rings have been taken as spoils by now. What if the demon can hear what we're saying? If he knows our strategies, that might explain why he hasn't given the order to attack."

They found Alzo sitting outside the main peat house listening to Knot brag about the brownies raid on the Wooler camp. When Alzo saw Ori walking next to Parth he got to his feet and rushed over to him.

"Where's Elize?" Alzo asked urgently. "Did you find her?"

"No," Ori replied shaking his head. "We tracked her as far as the salt ruins and then we lost her trail."

"We?" Taa asked from behind Alzo, also eager to hear news of Elize.

"Yeah we. I ran into Mal shortly after I found the giant or what was left of her. Mal noticed Elize's tracks leading down the riverbed."

"Ah," Taa exclaimed. She had been wondering when the old mage would show up. "So, Elize is still alive."

"Mal thinks Elize has wandered into the Spirit World and will eventually reappear. He's confident she's still alive."

"She is." Alzo stated with conviction. "I feel it in my bones."

"Me too," Ori agreed. Noticing the pained look in Taa's eyes Ori took her hand. "Mal is confident that Elize will materialize once her spirit returns to her body, and he swore he'd send word the second she does."

"Let's hope it's sooner than later." Taa commented and left to tend to the injured. Ori watched her go and then turned back to Alzo.

"Mal sent me back to help you. He thinks the Bawe River will return soon and said we should get across while the riverbed is still dry."

"Why does Mal think the river is returning?" Parth asked.

"I'm not sure," Ori admitted, "I think one of the stone boys told him."

"Well, well, well," Captain Bok chortled strutting over and slapping Ori firmly across the back. "Look what the cat drug in!"

"Don't blame us," Mia mumbled from the roof of the peat house where her and Gerawld were keeping watch. Parth looked up at Mia and laughed.

"Ori says Mal the Mage thinks the river is returning." Alzo told Captain Bok. "What do you think?"

"I thought the old mule was dead." Bok laughed scratching his ear with a gnarled finger, "but seriously, if that's what the mage said we need to pay attention. He's smarter than he looks."

"Tell them about the rings." Parth said nudging Ori roughly in the ribs.

"That's not good." Alzo said after Ori had given his report. "If what you're saying is true then there's a good chance our location is already known. Worst, if the rings are transmitters, whoever is listening knows all our plans and is just waiting for us to move."

"So, what do you propose we do?" Parth asked her eyes locked on Alzo.

"We need to search all the bags and destroy any rings we find."

"Me and the boys will take care of that." Knot volunteered. "We don't want folks thinking you don't trust them. Brownies are renown for sneaking about so they won't suspect nothing if one of us gets caught. Which we won't. I'll tell the boys to destroy the rings and return the bits to the bags that way no one will be the wiser."

"Okay, I'll leave that to you." Alzo said confident that Knot and his boys would take care of that problem. "Now what about the plans? Should we change them?"

"I say we leave them as is," Bok boomed winking at Alzo.

"But..." Ilee interrupted shocked at Captain Bok's suggestion.

"I agree," Alzo cut her off sharply. "But we'll discuss the way forward after we've eaten."

"I agree!" Parth said jumping up and taking Ori by the arm. "You look hungry. Let's get some grub."

"But you might be walking into a trap." Ilee hissed at Alzo as they followed Parth.

"We'll discuss it later," Alzo hissed back.

Later that night when most of the camp had bedded down Mia led Alzo out to one of the empty barns. Most of the others were already there when they arrived.

"As we discussed earlier," Captain Bok told Alzo once he had sat down, "we will keep the plans as they are, but with one minor change. You will already be gone. Parth has found a double for you, as long as it's dark and no one gets too close no one should notice you're a bearded lady."

"Won't that make her a target?" Alzo asked tugging at the end of his beard. "I won't have to shave will I?"

"Yes, it will make her a target and no you can keep the beard." Parth replied for the Captain. "Once the first group gets to the other side of the riverbed Tayla will lose the hair and beard and the group will scatter into the rocks."

"Where will I be?"

"Further up the ridge with an elite team. The first group will keep lower and head for an alternate entrance to the mines making sure they are seen." Parth told him pointing to the crinkled map in front of her.

"How am I supposed to get up onto the ridge without being seen?" Alzo said still not convinced.

"Pippa here has come up with a solution to that," Captain Bok piped proudly, patting Pippy on the head, "but we'll keep that secret until the time comes. In the meantime, we need to build your team. It needs to be a tight group, no more than ten, twelve tops."

"Gerawld and I will go." Mia told Alzo walking over and standing by his side. "My brother and I have pledged our allegiance to you as we did to your sister. Where you go we go."

"Thank you," Alzo said taking Mia's soft paw. He couldn't have asked for better companions and felt honored to have their support.

"You can't take everyone with you." Parth said leaning back into a bale of hay. "Someone needs to stay here and take command. I think Captain Bok and I would be best suited for that."

"I agree." Ilee nodded squeezing in closer to Alzo. She did not like the way Parth looked at Alzo and the sooner the two were separated the better.

"I'm sure Mukrot will be more than happy to stay with the Bogglea in the smelly bog," Ori added, "and of course the Rangers must stay in Milendor. It's their home, and they need to protect it especially since it's already been attacked once."

"I agree," Alzo said looking over at Parth. "Mukrot told me he sent word to his brothers asking them to come help."

"He didn't mention it to me." Parth said flipping a dread lock over her shoulder, but we need all the help we can get.

What Mukrot hadn't told Alzo was that he doubted any of his brothers would come. His younger brothers Zitty and Snuff might come after all they had no aspirations of becoming the Grand Oup and little hope of finding a mate in the swamp. The male swamp trolls outnumbered the females ten to one and their first six brothers already had claimed all the eligible ones. His little brothers would be leery of leaving the swamp to join a fight, but they might leave if there was a chance of finding a mate.

"I don't understand why Alzo doesn't take command." Ilee scoffed after Alzo slipped out of the barn with Gerawld to pee. "Why does he insist on acting like everyone else!"

"Because he is like everyone else." Ori said glancing over at the pretty, brown skinned girl and wondering why he hadn't noticed her before.

"No, he isn't," Ilee said sharply. "You know who he is! I know you do because he told me! Why does he hide who he is?"

"Why do you hide who you are?" Taa asked from behind her.

"That's not the same thing!" Ilee exploded furious at Taa for mentioning what the Oracle had said about her older sister. "I was told that Shi was the High Priestess! Alzo already knew he was the Prince, and he walked away from it!"

"Well, that's not entirely true." Ori said giving Ilee a stern look. "Alzo didn't walk away he was taken away by his mother and if you really knew Alzo you'd know he dreaded being trapped inside the palace walls. When we were boys he dreamed of being out in the world. To be part of the mess and the beauty."

"That's why he likes Parth," Ilee sulked glancing over at Parth who was busy talking strategy with Bok and Knot.

"Exactly." Ori said getting to his feet to see what was keeping Alzo. He found Alzo sitting on the ground with his feet tucked under him like a little boy. Which is how Alzo felt, like the little boy destined to be emperor. Returning to Toboria had awakened the memories he had shoveled out of his mind like the manure he shoveled out of the stables on Emma's farm.

"I needed a minute," Alzo whispered to Ori, "Things are moving so fast, too fast."

Getting to his feet Alzo looked out at the dots of orange-red campfires forming a jagged line separating him from his empire. His empire, he thought with a laugh. It sounded funny now. When he was a boy living in the palace, the thought had made him proud and a bit arrogant. Back then he imagined himself invincible. Then he was woken up in the middle of the night and forced down a hidden passageway under the fountain in his mother's garden.

How had he and Ori missed that? He shook his head. He thought they had explored every nook and cranny, every secret place in the palace. Boy had they been wrong. Neither of them had a clue that underneath the statue of two happy children playing in the spraying water were steps leading deep underneath the palace and up into the jagged peaks of the dark gray granite mountain known as the grandfather.

Alzo stared at the jagged mountainside far in the distance and remembered the night his mother had taken him and Elize away. Even after all this time he still remembered the feeling of dread as he held his mother's hand and stepped through the rock. He could almost hear Elize howling as the sky broke opened above them, slashed apart by the lightening. He had never been out in such a storm before or since. A shiver ran down his spine as he remembered how the wind growled and grabbed at his shoulders like a bone crunching giant trying to rip him away from his mother while the rain pounded down so hard it blinded him. A silent sob escaped from his lips as he remembered how the ground had melted under his feet. Had his mother let go of his hand? Had she? He liked to think she did not, but...Alzo bit down hard on his lip. He hadn't thought about that night for a very long time.

All in all, things had turned out alright for him. He had slid down the mountain with the mud, rocks, and water and into warm arms that told him everything was going to be alright. And everything had been alright. Emma had taken him home with her to her farm in the mountains of West Virginia. Alzo was finally free from the walls that had kept him from the world waiting outside. He had been free to just be a boy. At that moment Alzo wished he could go back in time and be in Emma's cozy kitchen eating warm bread fresh out of the oven. But Emma was gone, and he doubted he'd ever sit in her kitchen again. Something soft moved on the roof. Even though Alzo couldn't see the large, orange cat, he knew Gerawld was there keeping watch over him.

"We'd better get back inside." Ori told Alzo. Alzo nodded and waved at Gerawld who jumped off the roof and walked with them. Ilee was waiting impatiently for Alzo to return. When she saw Alzo with Ori and Gerawld she gave them an icy look. She didn't understand Alzo at all. If he noticed the look Ilee gave him, Alzo didn't show it. He walked right past her to join Parth and Captain Bok who were still studying Parth's map. It was almost dawn when the small group broke up.

It had been agreed that the Followers of the Change should break into several strategic groups. Knot had assured Alzo that allies would be waiting on the ridge to lead him safely through the mines and inside the third wall of Astaria.

Ori would stay with Parth and Knot to help arrange the second wave while Captain Bok supervised the aerial surveillance and counterattacks.

Only the small group that had met in the barns knew about the new plan. Alzo and his team would leave the next night while the moons were still at their weakest. With any luck they would be able to slip off without being notice. Parth was confident that if they didn't let anyone too close to the Alzo impersonator, no one would notice the difference. Ori wasn't as sure and was already working on a weaving song to help with the illusion.

"Don't worry," Parth told Alzo pulling at his hair as she plaited it flat against his head. "It's a good plan." Parth had suggested and Ilee had agreed that Alzo needed a disguise if he wanted to travel to Astaria unrecognized. The highlands were home to a colony of bearded women. With any luck, if Alzo was spotted he would be mistaken for one of them.

"I still say it will take a miracle to pull this off." Alzo grumbled wincing as Ilee forced a flowered blouse over his head. Little did he realize a miracle was stomping their way at that very moment.

With the moons at their dimmest, it was nearly pitch black when Mukrot's little brothers stumbled into one of the larger bulimon camps.

The bulimon had never seen swamp trolls before and mistook the clumsy swamp trolls for werebeasts.

"What's that noise?" Alzo whispered as he and Gerawld joined his team behind the barns.

"I don't know," Captain Bok told him, "But it's just the distraction we need. Everyone here? Good. Pippa?"

"You never told us Pippy's plan." Alzo said looking up at the red haired girl sitting on Captain Bok's shoulder. Pippy smiled widely at Alzo, her piranha-like teeth gleaming through the darkness.

"Better to just do it, then explain." Bok answered with a wink. "Go on Pippa."

Pippy clapped her hands three times and screeched. In the blink of an eye Alzo and his team were engulfed inside a gray cloud of tiny screech owls.

Meanwhile Mukrot's brothers, who had taken a wrong turn in the dark, thrashed their way through the terrified bulimon. By the time they stumbled out of the camp those bulimon that hadn't fled were lying injured and dying. Years later songs would be sung about the brave swamp trolls who had slaughtered a hundred bulimon in one night. Of course, as these stories go, the number of bulimon killed grew with each telling. Still, it was a great victory and did loads to lift morale. Unfortunately, what the Astarian Empire had previously seen as an annoyance had suddenly become a major irritation.

Ori couldn't sleep, so he decided to make his way upriver. He was curious to get a look at the dam Captain Bok had told him about. Even with his night vision, which was as good if not better than the bast cats, he failed to find a way around the huge boulders that blocked the path. Ori marveled at the strength of the river giants who had carried the boulders from the other side of the mountain to block the flow of the water. The plan to hold the water hostage backfired on the river giants when they inadvertently flooded the pastures belonging to the bulimon.

Scraped and exhausted from his unsuccessful attempts at finding a way past the boulders, Ori finally gave up and fell asleep. He was awakened at dawn by an annoying cliff swallow. The cliff swallow brought news from Mal that Elize had returned to the land of the living and was now headed towards Astaria. Ori hurried back to the peat houses to find Parth.

"We don't have much time." Parth shouted over the breakfast chatter. "The sooner we get down to business the better. Now, where do we stand on the nets and pits?"

"The nets are done and strung." A woman with full hips stood and answered proudly.

"And the Unders have finished the pits around the southeastern borders." A short, lumpy man with one leg yelled from behind her. "If the bogs don't stop them the pits will."

"What about the decoys?"

"Looking good," a pale faced boy reported. "Just need to make a few finishing touches."

"Great! Everyone knows the plan." Parth said before dismissing them to get on with their duties.

"A word," Ori whispered to Parth once they were alone.

"Can't be good news from that look on your face." Parth said as they walked towards the bogs to see how Mukrot and his brothers were getting on.

"Elize has reappeared."

"So, you going to ditch us now?"

"Not yet, but soon. I'll go with the first wave as planned and slip off. But that's not the bad news."

"No?"

"Mal believes the demon is nearby and the swallow spotted a group of badger boys headed this way."

"Sounds like it's time to leave." Parth commented glancing over at Captain Bok.

Captain Bok agreed. "We need to speed up our efforts anyhow. I don't think the dams going to hold much longer."

"We'll need eyes in the sky." Parth said looking concerned. She hoped the others were ready to move. "The more warning, the better."

"Got ya." Bok said grabbing two loaves of bread for Ming and Louy.

"We'll take care of the supplies," Knot said with a wink. He and his brownie battalion had been busy keeping the enemy camps on their toes with their late-night hauntings which included reappropriations of the camps supplies. Because of their efforts the Followers of the Change had eaten better than they had in years.

"I overheard you talking about the badger boys." A woman with bony arms wearing a dress that had been mended so many times it looked like a patchwork quilt, told Parth. "I hate to think I might be fighting my own lads."

"Are your sons badger boys?" Parth asked gently.

"Aye, they are if their still alive. I have no way of telling. My poor Lans managed to escape the mines. Lans told us he escaped from a work camp. When we asked him why his brothers hadn't come with him, Lans told us they were too addicted to gyum to bother." Gyum was a sweet, gooey paste made from black and orange poppies. Once you were addicted to the gyum, you'd do just about anything to get more.

"When Lans returned he was in a terrible state. We had to tie him and gag him for several weeks until he was clear of the gyum. It practically killed him, but he's clean now. Although sometimes I see the gleam in his eye, and it worries me. Lans said that he'd spotted some of the boys from our village in the enemy camps. Not the bulimon camps mine you. Lans said the bulimon don't allow the badger boys in their camp."

"I'd hate to have to fight my own boy." Another woman sobbed.

"There may be another way." Taa suggested. "I saw enough cratter weed growing behind the barns to brew ale for several camps."

"How does getting the boys drunk help exactly?" Ori asked raising his eyebrow at Taa.

"Cratter weed helps counteract the effect of gyum." Taa explained. "It may take several doses. I've never treated more than one patient at a time."

"Tell me what I need to do." The women begged Taa.

"You'll have to keep an eye on them for a few days to make sure it works." Taa said scratching out the recipe on a bit of paper and handing it to Lans' mother.

"No worries," Lans' mother assured Taa tucking the paper in her blouse and trotting off to gather the cratter weed.

CHAPTER 14

Elize and Mal walked side by side while Rixley skipped and hopped merrily up the steep incline several yards ahead of them. They had been walking for two days and Mal figured they still had half a day at least before they reached the pass which would take them across the purple mountains.

"Ori said he had jumped through a crack between the realms." Elize said glancing sideways at the old mule. "How was that possible and how did he know where to jump and when? You must have helped him, right? Ori said you were a mage. What is a mage anyway? Is that the same thing as a wizard or sorcerer?"

Mal shook the dust out of his mane and considered each of Elize's questions before deciding to tackle the last one first.

"Wizards, sorcerer's and mages are all practitioners of magic However mages create magic, while wizards and sorcerers use spells already created and tested. Mages draw energy from everything around them. They use the powers in soil, fire, stone, water, atmosphere, plants, flesh, bone, etc., etc. To do this successfully it takes great intellect, ability and control."

"Can anyone learn to be a mage?"

"No," Mal stomped his hoof irritably. "To be a mage, one must be born with the ability."

"And Ori was born with the ability?"

"Yes! Lots of it! I sensed it the moment I first laid eyes on the boy. That's what makes teaching him so frustrating. Ori is blessed with great ability, but he lacks discipline! He'd rather prance about singing songs and playing tricks then do the work! Life is not all fun and games!"

"Rixley likes fun and games and singing songs!" Rixley spouted prancing back down the path to join them. "Rixley strong and Rixley brave. Rixley, Rixley saves the day!" Rixley sang loudly dancing merrily around Mal, swishing his tail each time she passed it.

Elize bit her lip to stop from laughing. She knew if she pissed the old mule off, he wouldn't answer any more questions.

"Ori said he could hear my power," Elize said shooing Rixley away, "he said the power sang to him and that's how he tracked me down on Earth. Is that how he trailed me to the salt temple?"

"Nope," Mal replied kicking at Rixley half-heartedly. "He was too busy boo-hooing over you. I'm the one who spotted the trail you left."

Elize studied the lump in her palm. "I was worried I might be sending out signals."

"Even if you were I doubt anyone would hear it over all the noise that vermin is making." Mal grumbled and stomped his hoof at Rixley.

It was late afternoon when they finally reached the gap in the purple mountains. The purple color came from millions of tiny flowers that covered the ground like moss. The effect was quite magical. Elize could imagine a herd of lambs frolicking about and nibbling their purple lusciousness.

"I think someone's up there," Elize said pointing at the wet, mossy boulders above. Mal sniffed. The smell of stagnant water filled his nostrils. Rixley spotted the thin rivets of water running down the boulders and started towards them. Elize grabbed her by the scruff of the neck.

"No Rixley," she whispered sharply holding the wiggling ferret close to her chest.

"Let Rixley go!" Rixley protested trying to break free. "Rixley want water!"

"You don't want that water. That water will make you wretch." Mal told her pretending to throw up. Rixley broke loose and crawled up on Elize's shoulder.

"Rixley, not want to wretch." She sulked.

"I know another way." Mal said backtracking down the path keeping well away from any water. Finally, he found what he was looking for, a thin trail that went almost straight up the mountain. When they finally reached a place flat enough to rest, they were all gasping for breath.

"Better have a look at that," Mal grumbled nudging Elize's hand. Exhausted Elize held her hand up. Mal sneezed out a stream of yellow snot.

"Oh gross!" Elize gagged shaking her hand violently in front of her.

"Oh gross, gross, grossity, gross," Rixley sang wiggling her pole-like body in a hula motion as she shook her paws. Elize ignored her as she tried to wipe the snot off on the rocks. Instead of coming off, the snot coated her hand completely like a surgical glove. Once the snot dried, Elize had the odd sensation of emerging out of a pool of water. Her eyes and ears popped open, and she could hear and see things that she had been oblivious to before.

"Times a wasting," Mal barked and started back up the trail.

"Are we anywhere close to Astaria?" Elize groaned.

"No, but I know a place where we can stop for the night." Mal assured her. "And hopefully get a hot meal."

"That would be nice." Elize mumbled forcing one foot in front of the other. She swore she had walked more since arriving on this planet then she had walked her entire life. When they stopped Elize's legs felt like rubber bands about to snap.

"Stay here," Mal instructed as he ducked under a cluster of thin, willowy limbs draped over a long flat mesa the size of a football field. Rixley looked at Elize with wide eyes and took her hand.

"Rixley brave." She whispered holding Elize's hand tight.

Elize heard voices coming from under the branches, but they were too soft for her to make out the words. After several minutes Mal reappeared and motioned for them to come in. With Rixley still holding her hand tightly, Elize ducked under the branches. The space under the branches was like a hostel of sorts with tree branches dividing the space into rooms and little apartments. All eyes were locked on Elize as a tall, weathered woman with beautiful silvery white hair stepped forward.

"Is this her?" She asked Mal as she walked up to Elize studying her face carefully.

"Show her your hand," Mal huffed nudging Elize's hand. Elize lifted her snot covered hand and opened it.

"Granddaughter." The older woman exclaimed throwing her arms around Elize.

* * * * * * *

In the west tower Behr had been busy filling any nook where water might pool with garlic. He was in no mood to have his mother come looking for him. Behr knew Empress Ceen was expecting him to give a full report, but he wasn't in the mood to see her either. When the tower door slammed far below, Behr sighed. Apparently the Empress had grown tired of waiting.

"You've looked better." Empress Ceen stated as she slid into the room. Her coils scraping against the rough stone as she moved over to the tower window where Behr stood.

"Do you think it wise to send the badger boys?" He said ignoring her comment as he continued shoving garlic in holes.

"A rebel army is gathering around Milendor," Empress Ceen replied, her voice cold as ice. "What was I supposed to do? Wait until they knocked on our door?"

"Does my brother, the esteemed Emperor Taz know?" Behr sneered at the Cobrateen with cold hard hatred in his eyes. How could he have ever alluded himself into believing she ever cared for him. It was clear to him, so clear, that Ceen would only love one man. His pathetic brother.

"The Emperor is lost in his dreams," Ceen replied her unblinking eyes locked on him, challenging him to cross her.

"Scythe's gone." Behr spat. "The little princess hit me in the chest with a bolt of energy and the demon was dislodged."

"I noticed," Ceen hissed slithering over to one of the holes filled with garlic. "I also noticed you aren't talking to your mother. Are you sure it's the princess?"

"Pretty sure." Behr replied, coming up behind her and wrapping his arms around the long silken gown she wore to hide her reptilian body. "So now what?"

Ceen lifted her head and smiled. "We wait," she hissed seductively.

* * * * * * * *

"Grandmother!" Elize's tongue tripped over the unfamiliar words. "You're my grandmother?"

"Surely you remember me?" Rochelle gasped in mocking surprise. "I taught you about spiders. Remember?"

"Actually, I do," Elize laughed, "but I'm still not convinced spiders are my friends."

The older woman laughed and gave Elize a tight squeeze before letting her go. "Friends join me in welcoming my Granddaughter, Monetelizadora and her friends to the Elderwyld."

"It's Elize," Elize whispered.

"And you can call me Rochelle," Rochelle whispered back. "Grandmother makes me sound ancient."

"Deal," Elize replied looking around for Rixley and not seeing her. She finally spotted the little ferret seated among a group of gray-haired women chatting up a storm. The women watched Rixley with laughing eyes as they snapped beans and dropped them into a large bowl.

"Your little friend makes friends easily," Rochelle said with a twinkle in her eye. "She is so young and full of life."

"A little too full of life." Mal grumbled as Rixley danced about singing happily.

"I'd rather be a little too full of life than a grumpy old ass," laughed Rochelle tapping one of Mal's thick mule ears playfully. "Now old man, will you be gracing us with your presence tonight or joining the other asses in the field?"

Mal gave Rochelle a vile look, shook his head, and let out an ear-splitting bray. Then he walked in a small circle stomping his hoofs hard against the ground until his body was engulfed by a plume of rusty dust. When the dust settled, a naked old man stood in front of them looking confused.

"Oh Lord!" Elize exclaimed covering her eyes and laughing.

"Clothes Mal!" Rochelle shouted before leaning down to whisper in Elize's ear. "He's been hiding out as a mule for so long it takes him a second to come out of it."

"Why is he hiding?" Elize asked as they waited for Mal to snap some clothes on.

Rochelle looped her arm around Elize's arm. "Let's find a quiet place where we can talk. You must be tired from all your travels. Have you eaten?"

Elize shook her head as Rochelle led her into a small alcove. Elize was amazed at how many people were living under the trees. Rochelle explained that after the Emperor had expelled all Astarian's over fifty from the palace many had taken refuge in the mountains. The Elderwyld was one of the larger elder communities.

"We live together and look after each other," Rochelle explained pulling a large loaf of bread off a shelf and setting it on the bench beside Elize. "Some of the others, including your grandfather, prefer living alone in makeshift huts or caves."

Rochelle filled a large clay bowl with steaming soup and handed it to Elize along with a flat wooden spoon. Mal ripped off a chunk of bread and dunked it into his soup. The thin brown gravy dripped down the front of the old man's white beard. Rochelle tossed him a cloth to wipe it off. Mal ignored the rag and kept shoving bits of bread in his mouth.

"I've eaten nothing but grass and carrots for weeks," he explained between bites.

"It's very good," Elize said taking a large spoonful of carrots and meat. "I haven't eaten real food since I left the owl tree. I don't think the food I ate in the Spirit World was real."

"I wouldn't know," Rochelle smiled. "Never been there."

Elize watched the old woman fondly. She reminded her of her mother, except Rochelle seemed younger than her mother. She was definitely more mobile and alert. The head injury her mother had suffered when they came to Earth caused her mother to drift in and out of reality. One day she would be alert and the next not so much. Elize knew it was the injury which caused her mother to grow old before her time.

"I don't understand why you were all forced out into the wilderness." Elize commented between bites. "It's so unbelievably cold hearted. I mean what is the Emperor afraid of. You can't catch old age."

Rochelle's face crinkled up like she had tasted something foul. "My son is afraid of everything." She scoffed with a sad laugh. "Taz was born afraid. Even as a boy. Fear has always been my Taz's greatest enemy. Your father's inability to face his monsters has not only made him a prisoner in his own palace, but in his own mind. Emperor Taz fears the future and the past. We remind him of the life he once had and lost and show him his future and what will happen to him as he ages. Taz spends his days trying to forget the past and hide away from his future."

"He's a fool," Mal snorted looking up from his now empty bowl. "He thinks the snake can keep him young. If there was a portent for staying young, I'd be swimming in it instead of running around with a price on my head."

"Enough," Rochelle exclaimed raising her hands into the air. "This is a joyful day! A day of celebration! My granddaughter has returned to me alive and well! Come let us join the others. Calhoon bring out that wine you made last fall!"

The room filled with happy cheers. Clay cups were lifted and filled with dark red wine. Elize had never liked being in the spotlight and after a few drinks she drifted to the back. Rochelle noticed and walked over to join her.

"I didn't mean to embarrass you," Rochelle said softly sitting down next to her.

Elize looked over at Rochelle and smiled. "Oh, it's not that. I'm just tired and I'm worried I might be putting you and your friends in danger."

"You're safe here." Rochelle assured her kindly, but Elize felt a note of hesitation. "Still, precautions are always the best defense. Come."

As they walked back into the main room Elize told Rochelle about the strange feeling she had gotten when Rixley went to drink from the stream.

"I didn't mean to snatch her away like that. I know it startled poor Rixley, but I had to stop her. I'm not sure what was in the water, but Mal sensed it too. I'm sure of it. That's why he brought us here."

"Mal brought you here because he knows the water maiden will think twice before trying to invade the Elderwyld. The old bitch is not welcome here!" Rochelle voice was so icy Elize felt goosebumps tingling across her arms.

"Madeline!" Rochelle called to a tawny woman wearing an oddly knitted hat. The woman raised her hand enthusiastically and scooted across the room.

"Yes, m'lady?" She said her lavender eyes flashing with excitement.

"Please gather the sisters. We will be erecting the dome."

"The dome!" Madeline squealed and rushed off. Elize spotted the oddly knitted hat bouncing across the room to where a group of women were sitting gossiping and knitting. She couldn't hear what Madeline was saying, but a second later the women got to their feet and followed Madeline out of the room.

"What's going on?" Elize asked unable to contain her curiosity.

"I've asked my coven to erect a shield around the community. It will keep out all unwanted visitors." Rochelle explained before stepping into the center of the room and clapping her hands above her head three times. "Places please!"

Without further explanation the conversation ceased and was replaced with the scuffling of many feet. Noticing Rixley and Mal standing next to each other along the edge of the room, Elize joined them breaking in between her two friends and taking their hands in hers. Once the loop was completed, Madeline, her knitted hat replaced by a sky-blue hood entered chanting. Behind her, dressed in identical robes, were five other knitters. When they reached Rochelle, the group broke into two groups of three taking their places on either side of Rochelle to form a circle of seven. Rochelle raised her knitting needle over her head. With Rochelle as the hub, each knitter threw their knitting needles up in the air. Elize felt rays of energy pulsing down as the needles clicked madly over their heads knitting beams of multi-colored light into a circus tent sized covering. She could almost feel herself bobbing up and down on a painted pony as she stared up at the colorful dome above her head. It wasn't until Mal yanked his hand free that Elize realized the women had stopped chanting and everyone had returned to what they were doing before.

Later Elize sat with Rochelle by the fire sharing a bottle of wine with Rixley stretched out across her lap snoring softly. Mal was slumped in a wicker chair with his eyes closed tight. Elize knew he wasn't really asleep, but she didn't care if he listened to their conversation or not. She looked up at Rochelle and smiled. It felt good to have a grandmother. After her mother died, Elize had been extremely lonely. Even though Ellen, her best friend and her stepbrother Paddy had been a great comfort to her, it wasn't the same as having real family around. Now she had not only reunited with her brother, but she had found her grandmother too.

"After Alzo was born your mother was happy for a time." Rochelle said pouring more wine in her cup. "Euna loved taking Alzo for walks in the green areas between the first and second walls. The people loved to see them. The people loved the Empress Euna, who was so young and beautiful. You remind me much of her."

"Do you know why she left?" Elize asked. Rochelle's face tightened.

"I don't know all her reasons, but the Cobrateen was certainly at the top of the list."

"I only remember the cobra woman from my nightmares." Elize admitted, "but Alzo definitely remembers her. Mayme was the Empress if she disliked the cobra woman so much why didn't she send her away?"

"Taz out ranked her and wouldn't hear of it. He refused to believe Euna. He thought your Mayme was acting out of jealousy. But even if he believed her, my son was too addicted to the cobra venom to ever send Ceen away. I blame myself. I should have never allowed her to get so close to Taz, but she was the only one who could calm him after the attack. I should have been more cautious. Taz is so much like his father...weak." Mal snorted loudly and rolled his eyes. "He is weak!" Rochelle snapped tossing a bit of bread at the old man's head.

"Was my mother ever happy? I mean with my father."

"Oh yes! When she first arrived Euna and Taz were so in love. When Alzo was born they were so happy. The entire empire was thrilled that an heir had been born. And like I said before, Empress Euna was well loved."

"What happened?"

"A few years after Alzo was born, your mother became pregnant again. Your parents were elated, but Ceen was not. No one realized how possessive Ceen had become except your mother. When your mother miscarried that baby and the next and the next she swore Ceen was responsible. I should have paid more attention to her."

"Shortly before she died my mother told me a strange story about Ceen. Like you I wish I had of paid more attention to her, but Mayme was...well she was not always herself...I mean, um...Well you see when we came to Earth Mayme hit her head against the rocks. The wound never healed properly. I tried to help her, but I was too little and...well although I managed to keep her alive, her brain was damaged. Mayme often said things that didn't make sense. Especially when she got older. So, I didn't pay too much attention to her when she told me about a snake woman stealing babies out of her womb."

Rochelle frowned and looked down at her hands. "As I said I wish I'd paid more attention to her. It wasn't until your father built your mother her little cottage in the green space inside the first wall that you were born. Your mother refused to allow Ceen into the cottage and used one of the local mid wives. No one blamed the Empress from keeping Ceen out. Everyone in the palace feared the Cobrateen and with good reason. It was common knowledge that Ceen had made your father an addict. He was addicted to her, so to speak. The withdraw from Cobrateen venom is almost always fatal."

"Is that why you allowed her to stay?"

"Yes, she was the only one with the power to calm Taz when he had one of his fits. Not even your mother could do that."

"Why was I born with a stone in my hand?" Elize asked glancing down at her palm.

"You weren't." Rochelle said picking at the odd sticky substance covering Elize's hand. "I placed the crystal in your palm shortly after you were born."

"Crystal?" Elize asked surprised by her grandmother's answer. It certainly wasn't what she was expecting to hear.

Rochelle sighed and took a long sip off her wine before continuing. "You were so tiny and precious when you were born," she patted Elize's hand affectionately, "I was the first to notice the energy surging inside you. From the moment I laid eyes on you I knew the ancients had marked you for greatness." Rochelle stopped and wiped a tear from the corner of her eye. "As I said you were so tiny and the energy surging within you was so strong. Too strong. Your tiny body trembled and shook so violently I feared it would consume you. The rock was passed to me from my grandmother. My grandmother told me that the crystals in the rock could absorb energy. Your mother and I were desperate to save you. Together we sliced opened your tiny palm and shoved the rock into the cut. Almost at once you stopped shaking and became calm."

"Is that why Askar and Kara tried to take the stone?"

"The crystal soaks up the excess energy like a sponge and contains it." Mal said without opening his eyes.

"So, the stone has energy inside it..."

"Yes," Mal answered, "but when the stone is removed from the source, the energy will start to dissipate."

"But how did you get it in my palm." Elize pondered poking at the center of her palm. "My hand must have been tiny. I can't imagine it fitting inside."

"I used magic to shrink the stone." Rochelle said taking Elize's hand and making a face. "What is this goop?"

"Mule snot." Elize laughed stifling a yawn.

"You're tired." Rochelle said as she wiped the snot off Elize's hand with warm soapy water. "Once I have a proper look at your palm and Mal conjures up a glove more befitting a princess, I'll show you where you can rest."

"I think the crazy bast shaman chipped the stone with his tooth." Elize told Rochelle stifling a yawn. "Ever since he bit my hand, I've been feeling a bit weird."

"It does look like the stone has been chipped. It definitely has grown since I put it in your hand."

"Will the chip affect the way the power works?" Elize asked rubbing her fingers over the lump. Rochelle shrugged and looked at Mal.

Mal pulled his old body out of his seat and poked at the hard lump in Elize's palm. "The chip may affect the stone, but it shouldn't affect your energy. The stone absorbs energy so it makes sense that it would grow. After all it's been soaking up energy since the day Rochelle shoved it in your hand."

"But you don't know how the energy works?"

"Not a clue." Mal said looking over at Rochelle. "You?"

"I know that the Empress was excited when she realized her daughter had been born with the gift of Monet." Rochelle told them, even though Mal had been there and knew how Empress Euna had reacted. "Your mother knew more about the gift then I did. I think that's why she left Palenina to come to Astaria. She said that the Ancient Hohi had spoken to her and told her to come to Astaria and marry Prince Taz. Your Mayme loved your father and Alzo dearly, but you were the one she was hoping for."

"Alzo told me that I was always the special one."

"Alzo? You and Alzo stayed together?" Rochelle asked excitedly, her eyes sparkling with emotion.

"No, we were separated shortly after landing on Earth."

"Then how can you possibly remember anything Alzo said? You were just a toddler." Rochelle asked clearly disappointed.

"Oh, I found him!" Elize said nodding her head vigorously when Rochelle looked up at her. "Ori, the Vanji, helped me track Alzo down at his farm. I brought him back to Astaria with me."

"Alzo's returned?" Rochelle shouted elated by the news. Several heads turned to see what was going on. Rochelle ignored them. "Where is he now?"

"He's leading the Change." Mal informed her.

"The Change?"

"Yeah," Elize told her, "you know the one the Oracle predicted. When I fell out of the sky, I fulfilled the prophecy."

"What prophecy?"

"The one who falls from the sky brings great change." Elize recited with a shrug. "I fell from the sky, Alzo was with me so that makes him the Change."

"Nonsense!" Rochelle laughed waving her hand in front of her as if to sweep the words away. "For one thing, that's not how the prophecy goes."

"And you didn't actually fall from the sky," Mal added warily. "You stumbled out of a tunnel and tripped."

"And fell." Elize insisted stifling a series of yawns. It was very late, and weariness was finally getting the best of her.

"We'll talk more in the morning." Rochelle said ushering Elize past Mal, "but first," she said kicking the old man in the shin. "Mal will conjure up a glove more befitting to a princess."

Mal snapped his fingers and muttered something under his breath. A large, moth-eaten carpet bag materialized by his feet. Mal dug into his bag and pulled out several oddly shaped jars each sealed with a different colored wax. Mal began to unseal the jars sniffing the contents of each one. Some he resealed, others he poured in a clay cup. Stirring the mixture with his finger, he added more ingredients until he was satisfied with the color and consistency. Mal poured the contents of the cup onto Elize's outstretched palm. The warm, pink goop wobbled like gelatin and began to spread over Elize's hand forming a clear glove.

"Much better," Rochelle exclaimed carefully examining Mal's handiwork.

"The glove will absorb the slightest vibrations." Mal assured her, "not even the vanji with his super sensitive ears will be able to detect it now."

"Sleep peacefully child, you are absolutely safe tonight." Rochelle told her before gently kissing Elize's forehead.

Elize laid her head down on the mattress. It was the first time since leaving the healing center that she had slept on an actual bed. Drifting off to sleep, Elize wondered what Alzo, and Ori were doing. Elize's mother had always told her that no news was good news, but Elize had never believed her.

The haunting screech of an animal in distress woke Elize. Thinking it was Rixley, Elize jerked her head up. To her relief Rixley was curled up in a ball next to her. Elize listened for the noise a few more minutes before drifting back to sleep.

When she woke up the next morning Elize found Mal, looking more like a Mage than a mule after a good night's rest. Elize asked him if he had heard anything in the night, but Mal hadn't heard a thing. Rochelle wanted Elize to stay another day or two, but Mal insisted on getting back on the road. When Elize asked him why, he mumbled something unintelligible and stomped away. Elize started to argue with him, but she knew Mal was right. Even though she wasn't eager to leave, Elize realized the longer they stayed the more likely they were to bring danger to the community.

After a couple cups of strong black tea and thick slices of bread slathered with creamy butter Elize went to say goodbye to Rochelle and the others. She walked into the main gathering place just in time to catch the end of Rixley's song. Standing in the doorway next to Mal, Elize watched with amusement as Rixley strutted in front of her adoring fans thrusting out her pointy stick while demonstrating her warrior poses.

"Where in snuff did she learn that?" Mal muttered shaking his head and laughing.

"From the images in the salt temple." Elize whispered back before being shushed by one of the little ferret's fans.

"Rixley brave and Rixley strong," Rixley chirped swinging her pointy stick in front of her like a baton. "Rixley killed the bagobong. Rixley strong and Rixley brave! Rixley, Rixley saved the day!"

"What's a bagobong?" Mal asked Elize. Elize shrugged and clapped along with the others. A few minutes later Rochelle sent them on their way with bags filled with bread, fruit, and water.

"Be sure to tell the old boar I'm expecting ale for the winter festival." Rochelle called after Mal as the three travelers stepped out of the Elderwyld.

"I could have sworn I heard an animal being attacked last night," Elize told Mal as they climbed across a series of large round rocks covered with lavender colored moss, "but I don't feel anything."

"You won't either," Mal told her stopping to sniff the air and listen. "Not with that glove on your hand anyway. It numbs your senses."

"What does that mean exactly?" Elize asked keeping one eye on Rixley as she looped back and forth over the rocks and boulders. It almost looked like she was swimming across a sea of lavender.

"It means just what I said. The glove is muting your extra sensory perception." Mal clapped his hands several times and morphed back into his mule body. "Much better," Elize heard the old mule mumble as he started up the side of the mountain.

"Shouldn't my ordinary senses be enhanced then?" Elize puffed as she followed him up the rough terrain.

"Possibly," Mal agreed, "that may account for your hearing being more acute. Now hush up and tune in. I doubt if were alone up here."

Elize was about to ask him what he meant when Rixley froze. Scrambling to catch up, they found Rixley standing in front of a puddle of clotting blood. Careful not to step in the puddle, Mal sniffed at the blood and frowned. The scent was all too familiar.

* * * * * * * *

Ori would have liked to have left the second he received the message that Elize had appeared out of the spirit world, but he had promised to lead the first wave.

Keeping to the shadows the demon known as Scythe stalked Ori. He had seen Ori with Elize in the Forest of Milendor. Scythe would have attacked Ori and made the fox take him to Elize, but he was still too weak to travel solo and required a new host to carry him.

Taking control of the giant had worn him down. Although Kara's mind was weak, it took a lot of effort to control her, especially where the Oracle was concern. Scythe didn't expect Kara's deep devotion to the old owl. In the end, it was Kara's devotion to Su Lei that caused his plans to evaporate.

Scythe was too weak after climbing out of the moley tunnels to find a new host. Luckily, the water maiden Aturi had found him and helped him search for a likely candidate. Aturi had suggested a bulimon commander named Merlot who was already bond to him. Scythe loathed the foul-smelling mercenaries and would only consider taking on Merlot as a last resort. Scythe watched Ori shift into his fox body. Ori would be a much better fit, but Scythe knew better then to try to take over Ori's body. Even though the Vanji hadn't fully mastered the find art of magic, Ori had covered his aura with a shield powerful enough to prevent any unwanted spirits from entering.

The midday sun made it easier for Scythe to follow Ori without being spotted. The reeds and shrubs cast long shadows giving him plenty of places to hide. Scythe was making his way through a patch of brambles when he first spotted Tux, the large, one-eared black and white bast cat. Scythe watched Tux stealthily move through the brambles, his eyes locked on the fox.

"Damned cat," Scythe fumed, thinking Tux was going to pounce on his prey and eat him for lunch. But when Tux kept his distance, Scythe realized that he and the bast cat were after the same thing. Silently hovering over the cat's two-toned head, Scythe drifted down onto Tux, his shadow seeping through the cats thick fur and settling into the soft skin beneath.

Tux shivered and gave a little shake. Tux was too focused on trailing Ori to realized his body had just been invaded by a demon. Like Scythe, Tux had seen Ori with Elize and Gerawld and he was certain Ori was going to join them. Leaving Tux to chase Ori, Scythe relaxed into the warm body and allowed himself a much-needed break.

The moons had been dipping back down behind the purple mountains when Tux stumbled upon Ori near the Elderwyld. They had fought furiously, and Ori may have bested him if Aturi hadn't intervened. Taking Aturi's advice Tux hadn't tried to enter the Elderwyld. Instead, he had left the badly injured Ori trapped in the rocks and waited for Elize to come to him.

"I knew I heard something last night!" Elize whispered craning her head to get a better look at the path ahead. "That's blood isn't it?"

Mal lowered his head as he carefully made his way up the loose boulders. Rixley went in front of them, stopping to point at a tuff of fur snagged on a weed and part of a bloody footprint.

"It could be a trap," Mal warned Rixley. Rixley circled back and climbed on to Elize's shoulders.

"Over there," she squeaked in Elize's ear and pointed up to a fluffy reddish-brown tail sticking out of the rocks jutting out above them. Not at all used to mountain climbing, Elize slowly maneuvered up the jagged rocks. The more agile Rixley, danced above her, urging Elize on, pulling her fingers into hand holds. Elize knew Rixley was just trying to help, but she was really getting on her nerves.

"Hey," Elize whispered softly when she finally reached the spot. She reached her hand out and gently petted the fox's tail. Ori lifted his head slightly to look at her. Déjà vu swept over Elize when Ori's glassy golden eyes fixed on hers. For a split second she was transported back in time to a starry night when she crawled under her porch to help an injured fox. It was the night Elize discovered her new boyfriend was not what he seemed.

Elize carefully removed the rocks so she could get her hands around Ori's body. Ori yipped and snapped at her.

"Trap!" Mal shouted as the rocks above her began to shake. Rixley squealed and leapt into the pocket of Elize's robe just avoiding the water gushing out of the rock she'd been standing on a second before. The force of the water sent large round stones tumbling down the mountainside.

No time to be gentle, Elize scooped her hands under Ori's body and yanked him free. Holding Ori close to her chest Elize scrambled down the rough, slippery rocks. Water squirted out of the crevices, transforming into transparent hands.

"Elize!" Rixley shrieked poking her upper body out of the pocket to jab the watery hands with her pointy stick. Aturi whipped a water tentacle around Rixley's neck.

"Leave my friends alone, you icy bitch!" Elize shouted as she touched the water and imagined the water freezing into a block of ice. It was a trick RaJa had taught her while in the Spirit world. Something to do with the power of suggestion. RaJa claimed every substance could be influenced by the power of suggestion.

Aturi started to scream, but before the sound could emit from her mouth it was frozen in ice. Knowing the ice wouldn't hold for long, Elize hurried to where Mal and Rixley were anxiously waiting. Before she could reach them, Tux leapt in front of her blocking her path. Elize raised her hand in front of her.

"No!" Mal shouted sensing the demon's shadow around Tux. "That's what he wants you to do!"

Fighting back her fear Rixley used Mal's back as a springboard to launch herself into the air and swat the startled bast cat squarely in the nose. Tux swung and knocked Rixley away. Elize raised her hand. Tux hissed and took off down the rocks.

"What are you doing?" Scythe screamed, "Get the girl you fool!" Tux ignored him and kept running.

"Hurry!" Mal shouted at Elize stomping his hoofs. "Get on!" Rixley jumped onto the mule's back. Elize hesitated.

"I'm too heavy."

"We don't have time for this," Mal snorted. "Get on! And hold on tight!"

Elize laid Ori on Rixley's lap and climbed onto Mal's back. Keeping her elbows close to her sides, she wrapped her arms around Mal's shaggy mane sheltering Rixley and Ori with her body. The old mule stomped his hoofs three times, let out a horrifying bray and shot up the mountain like a supersonic jet. Elize felt Rixley wiggle underneath her and hoped Ori was okay.

Elize wished she were holding Ori, but there was nothing she could do about that now. Mal was moving at an incredible speed winding higher and higher up the mountain. The wind whipped her hair angrily across her face causing her eyes to tear.

When Elize finally braved a look, she gasped. They were on a ledge so thin it was a miracle that Mal's plump body fit on it. Mal was heading directly for the large tree jammed into the sheer rock face. Golden honey dripped from the huge beehive protruding from the large hole near the center of the trunk. Elize was sure Mal could see the beehive, but instead of slowing down the old mule charged straight for it. Elize screamed and flatten her face against his neck.

CHAPTER 15

"You can get off now!" Mal huffed wearily. It wasn't that Elize was excessively heavy, but he was old as dirt and not nearly as spry as he liked to think he was.

Elize slid off Mal's back and looked around. The bees and honey had been replaced by a small, dimly lit room. Elize gently lifted Ori off Rixley's lap and cradled him in her arms. To her relief he was still breathing, but just barely. Freed from her burden Rixley scooted up Mal's long neck, plopped down on his head and poked her face out between his long ears. Elize tried not to laugh at Mal who looked like he was wearing a tiny fur cap.

Mal led them into a larger room with thick red carpet. A tall, well-dressed man with a pointy white beard sat in front of a fireplace with a large gray wolfhound curled up at his feet. The wolfhound opened one eye as Mal approached and growled softly but didn't get up.

"I was expecting you yesterday!" The old man grumbled pushing his body out of the large, ornate chair with little effort. The wolfhound stretched out his forearms and catching a strange scent, twitched his nose like a rabbit. Rixley flatten her chin against Mal's skull hoping to blend in with the mule's mane. The large, scruffy dog sauntered over to Mal, his old gray eyes searching for the source of the musky scent.

"So, you found her," the old man exclaimed walking over to Elize and placing a well-manicured hand against her cheek. "You're the image of my Rochelle when she was still young and pretty."

"And before she got tired of your crap." Mal teased, sidestepping the nosy wolfhound. "By the by Rochelle said not to forget the solace." Mal stomped his hoof at the dog who was getting too close for comfort.

"How do you know Rochelle?" Elize asked stepping between Mal and the dog.

"He's Rochelle's husband," Mal answered nodding at the old man, "and your grandfather, Grumbul former Emperor of Astaria. Grumbul, as you already guessed this is your granddaughter, Princess Monetelisadora who prefers to be called Elize."

"Not Bonie Monie?" Grumbul teased giving Elize a wink.

Elize took Grumbul's hand from her cheek and held it. An image flowed across her mind. "I remember you!" She said smiling at him. "You taught me how to catch the little golden fishes that swam in the fountain."

"Ha," Grumbul laughed shaking his head. "If I remember right, you dropped the net and went after them barehanded."

"Eek!" Rixley squeaked and leapt off Mal's head to Elize's as the wolfhound pounced. Startled Mal brayed so loud he drowned out the wolfhound's barks. Kicking wildly, Mal missed the dog and hit a small table upsetting a large glass of red wine.

"Blast it Blatz!" Grumbul grumbled grabbing the wolfhound by the collar and dragging him away from the irritated mule.

"Rixley not like Blatz," Rixley announced from her perch atop of Elize's head.

"Aw now don't worry about old Blatz," Grumbul laughed forcing Blatz under the large wooden table. "His bark is worse than his bite."

"Rixley not like his bark or his bite." Rixley stated flatly jumping off Elize's head and onto the stone ledge a few feet above the fireplace.

"What's that you're holding?" Grumbul asked nodding at the raggedy heap of sandy fur in Elize's hands.

"It's Ori." Elize replied loosening her grip so he could get a look at Ori's limp body.

"What happened to him?"

"He was attacked."

"Attacked! By whom?"

"Aturi." Mal answered in a shaky voice keeping his eyes on Blatz who was sulking under the table.

"Aturi! What's that damn witch doing in these parts?"

"Attacking Ori apparently." Mal answered shaking his haunches. "She tried to ambush us not far from the Elderwyld and she wasn't alone. I managed to get us away, but I'm sure it won't be long before she tracks us here."

"Well, we'd better get at it then. Set him on the table so I can take a look." Grumbul ordered moving several dirty mugs and bowls out of the way. "Mal change. I need your help. Blatz go to your chair and stay there!"

While Mal morphed into his human body, Grumbul helped Elize lie Ori on the table and began to gently examine him.

"You sure have a strange mix of friends, my dear," he said glancing sideways at Elize, "a bandit, an old ass, and a scoundrel. With friends like that you're sure to go far."

When Elize didn't respond, Grumbul reached over and gently patted the back of her hand. "Don't look so worried. Mal and I have worked on worse. He'll live."

Turning back to Ori, Grumbul leaned his face so close to Ori's stomach his nose brushed the blood clotted fur. "What've you been tangling with, eh kiddo?" He whispered before looked up at Mal. "Any day Mage, and don't forget your clothes." Grumbul glanced at Elize and whispered. "His mind tends to get a bit muddled..."

"There's nothing wrong with my mind." Mal sputtered shuffling over to the table in loose fitting pants and a forest green tunic. "Now where did I put my bag?"

Elize stepped back to give Mal room and tripped over a large brown and green carpet bag which she was sure hadn't been there a second ago.

"You always were a clumsy child," Grumbul teased catching Elize by the arm. His icy blue eyes twinkling. "A nice child, but clumsy. Always stumbling into things."

"He's going to be alright, isn't he?" Elize asked softly. The old men shrugged.

"As Grumbul said, he should live," Mal said dabbing the long gash on Ori's side with a damp cloth, "but who knows what nasty stuff the water maiden put inside him."

"Don't you worry," Grumbul said trying to sound positive and failing. "In a few days, he'll be good as gold."

"Unfortunately, we don't have a few days." Mal grumbled ringing the bloody rag into one of the dirty bowls. "A couple hours at best. It won't take Aturi long to thaw out and come after us. I don't know where that possessed cat got off to. He'd could be outside as we speak."

"I don't think so." Elize told him. "I sent him on a goose chase." Mal looked up sharply. "Don't worry," she assured him, "the only power I used was the power of suggestion. What was I supposed to do? Leave it to Rixley and her pointy stick to save us?"

"No," Mal admitted, "the ferret is recklessly brave, but she's no match for the water maiden."

"The ferret..." Grumbul exclaimed looking around for Blatz who had not gone to his chair as ordered. For such a large dog, Blatz could move like a ninja. To Mal's relief Blatz was lying stretched out in front of the fire.

"Here hold this," Mal said tossing Grumbul a small spool of brown thread. "Do you have any spirits? It'll need to be sterilized."

Grumbul nudged Elize and pointed to the large, brown clay jug next to the ornate chair. Grabbing the jug, she looked up at Rixley curled up like a cream puff on the ledge sound asleep.

Elize watched the two old men standing side by side working on Ori. They were so different from each other. Mal looked like a mad scientist with unkempt gray and white hair swirling around his head like a blizzard. While Grumbul looked like a regal gentleman. His snow-white hair carefully trimmed and combed into a neat little duck tail in the back. His mustache and goatee flowed together so smoothly they could have been painted on. Elize could easily see him in a magnificent palace.

"So, where have you been all these years?" Grumbul asked Elize casually, even though the question had been sitting on the tip of his tongue since the second she entered the room.

"Earth," Elize replied stepping out of Mal's way as he rifled through his carpet bag tossing out random objects until he found a long tube wrapped with gauze.

"Earth?" Grumbul said skeptically. Of course, he was familiar with the old myths about Earth, but he'd never really believed them. "What were you doing there?"

"Living," Elize answered honestly, "or trying to, but I never really fit in. Neither did Alzo apparently. I really don't think Mayme meant to take us there. Alzo thought the same thing."

"Alzo?" Grumbul exclaimed looking up at Elize. "Your brother? He's alive? Here?"

"Yes," Elize nodded.

"He's leading the Change," Mal huffed as he finished stitching up Ori's side. Grumbul sat down on the foot stool looking stunned. "The future Emperor of Astaria is leading the rebellion against his own Empire?"

"Exactly," Elize nodded.

"I wonder how that's going?" Grumbul laughed shaking his head in disbelief. Elize was wondering the same thing. She was sure Ori had an update, but he was in no condition to provide it.

"Are you sure he's going to be alright?" Elize asked leaning over Mal's shoulder.

"Yes," Mal grunted not taking his eyes off Ori as he nimbly stitched up another gash. "It'd be easier to work on him as a human."

"If he were in his human body, he be dead." Grumbul commented bluntly.

"I said easier," Mal griped snipping off the end of the thread, "not better. He's all sewn up now. Let him rest a bit while I mix up an antidote. You should rest too." Mal told Elize before turning to Grumbul. "I need a large pot."

"There's one by the fire." Grumbul said covering Ori's body with a thin blue blanket. "Mal's right you should get some rest too." He motioned to a long, blue velvet daybed, but Elize didn't want to leave Ori's side, so she climbed up on the table and laid next to him. Placing one hand on Ori's paw, Elize closed her eyes.

"Somethings wrong!" Elize exclaimed and tried to rip the film covering off her right hand so she could get a clearer image.

"Hold on, hold on." Mal scolded shuffling over to Elize with a pair of small scissors. Once the glove was off Elize carefully pressed her palm against Ori's chest, Mal put his hand on top of hers. "Damn that's not good." Mal sputtered.

"What? What's not good?" Elize demanded.

"It appears Ori's human body is trapped inside his fox body and is fighting to get out." Mal shouted as a loud rumble shook the room causing bits of ceiling to crack off and rain down upon their heads.

"Damn witch!" Mal shouted lifting his hand off Elize's and rushing over to the pot. "I was hoping we had more time. "Here you'd better put this back on!" Mal tossed the flesh-colored blob at Elize while Grumbul wrapped Ori tightly in the blanket. "Where's the little minx?"

"Rixley not minx." Rixley shouted as she shoved bits of food into a sack she'd found on the floor. Noticing Blatz watching her with hungry eyes, Rixley tossed the dog a chunk of dried meat.

"Here stick this in your bag," Mal said handing Rixley a jar of liquid. "Watch out it's hot! It'll turn bright orange when it's cool enough for Ori to drink. Make sure he drinks all of it. Hold his nose if you have too." Ori opened his eyes slightly and showed his teeth. "Oh, goody your alive." Mal chirped patting Ori gently on his black nose. Ori groaned and closed his eyes again.

"You're not coming?" Elize asked as Grumbul pushed at the side of the fireplace and revealed a secret passage.

"No," Grumbul said shooing them into the passage. "Mal and I will stay here and cause a diversion, so you have time to get away. We'll meet you in Astaria."

"Be on your guard," Mal stressed obviously not pleased at staying behind, "and whatever you do don't use your powers. If the demon senses your powers, he'll be after you in a heartbeat. Now scoot!"

"Wait?" Elize shouted refusing to go. "Why is this demon, this Scythe so bent on attacking me? What threat am I to him?"

"You are not a threat to him," Mal replied taking Elize by the shoulder and guiding her further into the passage. "Scythe needs your energy to survive."

The room shook again causing several rocks to break loose. Blatz yelped and ran into the passage causing Rixley to scurry up Elize's pants legs and onto her shoulder. While she was distracted Mal and Grumbul pulled the fireplace back into place and took their seats in front of the fire.

Elize clutched Ori close to her chest and followed Blatz down the passageway. She hoped the old wolfhound knew where they were going, because she didn't have a clue.

CHAPTER 16

"What's happening?" Alzo asked Pippy who was sitting on his shoulder looking very concerned.

"Too much weight!" Pippy screeched at him frantically. "The screechers are looking for a place to drop us."

"Rowwwl!" Gerawld spat as the bottom fell out from under him and he dropped several feet before landing hard on to the rocky soil beneath him. Alzo was dropped next followed by Ilee and the rest of the team.

"How far from are target are we?" Alzo asked no one in particular as he scanned the ridge line.

"Not far as the crow flies." Phoe meowed stepping out of the brush with his sister Fee. Gerawld confronted the pair and after much hissing and growling returned to Alzo's side.

"What's going on?" Alzo asked Gerawld. Gerawld tilted his head towards Phoe and pointed towards the ridge. Although Gerawld didn't speak the common tongue and Alzo didn't speak bast the two were able to understand each other well enough.

"Do they know the way up the ridge?" Gerawld nodded. "And you trust them?" Gerawld shrugged and put up his paws.

"Yeah, I guess you're right. We don't have much of a choice." Alzo took one last look behind him before giving the signal to move.

"Pippy go back to papa now." Pippy chirped from Alzo's shoulders. "Pippy tell papa what happened." Before Alzo could agree or disagree the little girl clapped her hands and was carried off by a screecher. Alzo wished he could clap his hands and be carried up the ridge, but he was grateful to the screechers for getting them as far as they had.

As night fell over the peat houses, campfires were lit in front of tattered tents and the blue glow of neli lights soon flickered out through the cracks of the peat houses. Parth laid flat down on top of the center house watching and waiting. She'd been lying there since mid-day and was starting to wonder if what the brownies had told her was true. Maybe they had misunderstood. Although that was highly unlikely, brownies rarely got things wrong. They had sharp ears that could hear a pin drop in a hurricane. Hot, tired, and eaten by bugs, Parth was about to move when the red-haired Hari nudged her.

"Here they come," Hari mouthed tilting her head towards the rows of tattered tents. It had been hours since Ori had led the first wave and so far only a handful of pursuers had showed their faces. It looked like Knot was right after all.

A horn blew as row upon row of thick headed bulimon charged into the camp. Swinging war hammers and two-headed axes they slashed the tents to shreds, frustrated when instead of flesh and blood rebels they found clothes filled with straw. Enraged the bulimon let out blood curdling bellows and stampeded towards the peat houses.

Parth waited until the bulimon were almost upon them before giving the signal. Jumping to their feet the rebels let out a unified shout. The air filled with swarms of leathery winged bats that swooped out of the trees to form a living barrier between the bulimon and the second wave of Followers. As the bulimon fought their way through the bats the Followers sprinted towards the riverbed carefully avoiding the surprises left for their pursuers.

Parth smiled as shouts of surprise rang out in the night. Mukrot and his bog army, who the trespasses had been unwarily using as a bridge, had risen out of the bogs tossing the terrified bulimon into the wet peat where Fern and her sister Bogglea were waiting to pull their thrashing bodies under the thick muck.

Upriver, Captain Bok and his birdmen watched the bats taking flight. Knowing timing was everything, Bok waited until the bulimon rushed into the dry riverbed after the Followers. It worried him that so many bulimon had survived the traps.

"Them bastards just don't die." Bok grumbled keeping his eyes on the dark line of heavily armed mercenaries filling the riverbed. He waited until the gap between the pursuers and the pursued had almost disappeared before giving the thick rope he was holding a firm tug. Ming and Louy squawked and unfurled their massive blue wings. The other birdmen followed course tugging at the thick ropes attached to the massive boulders and tree trunks until they gave way with an explosive roar as the force of the water broke through the dam and slammed into the riverbed.

"Keep moving." A mother scolded the group of boys who turned around to see what was happening. "Move!" She ordered, shoving the closest boy. "This is no time for gawking."

Parth shaded her eyes and watched as several large blue birds flew past. She couldn't tell which one was carrying Captain Bok, but she knew he was on one of them. Time was running short and if their plan was going to work the Followers needed to get out of the riverbed now.

"Move, move, move!" Parth's screamed pushing several small children onto the wooden rafts which had been hidden downstream a few days earlier. Parth jumped on the raft and tossed a rope up to the birdmen while Hari threw a handful of neli into the burners to heat up the air for the balloons.

Looking over her shoulder Parth could see the line of brown foamy water splashing towards them as she threw a second rope up to the birdmen. She drew a breath of relief as the raft started to lift out of the riverbed unaware of the huge, leathery hand wrapping around her ankle.

Faster than you could blink, Parth let go of the rope and pulled the short sword strapped across her shoulders out of the sheath. Slashing the blade downward she hit her attacker just below the chin. The bulimon roared and pulled her off the raft. Parth shoved her blade deeper into his neck and yanked the hilt sideways. The bulimon bellowed as the weight of his large body tore free from his neck and tumbled into the raging water.

"Well, that sucks," the bulimon growled, his bloodshot eyes rolling back in his head as Parth slammed his head on top of a jagged stump and pulled herself onto the embankment.

"It gets worse." Parth told him coldly. She had no sympathy for the head. The bulimon had shown no mercy as they terrorized the villagers, burning down their homes, pillaging their stores, and taking their men and boys to sell to the empire as slaves.

"Destroy the ring and let me die," the bulimon pleaded.

"No!" Parth spat at him before running off to catch up with the others. She was in such a hurry she didn't see the bast cat stagger past her.

Tux stumbled forward along the rocks fighting the demon overshadowing him. He was determined to return to the peat houses and confront his brother. It was a hauntingly exhausting trip. He could see the peat houses in front of him, but the riverbed he needed to cross was froth with brown, rushing water.

Using the trunk of a fallen tree to help brace him, Tux waded into the angry water. As with most felines, bast cats were not fond of getting wet, but like tigers they could swim if the need arose. Fighting his way across the river, Tux had almost reached the other side when a brown hand wrapped around his ankle and pulled him down. Tux kicked at the sodden bulimon trying to use his long frame to pull itself out of the water. In his frantic effort to get free, Tux let go of the tree. Taking advantage of the situation, the demon Scythe used the water to drag the bewildered Tux back across the river. Tux thrashed about in the water fighting, both the bulimon and the demon with what little strength he had left. He managed to dislodge the bulimon a second before he passed out.

Scythe left Tux lying face down in a muddy puddle. He no longer had any use for the bast cat. The demon drifted along the riverbank searching for a new host when he came upon Merlot. Well, his head anyway, shoved on top of a jagged stump.

"You've looked better," Scythe said drifting closer to the decapitated head. "What happened?"

"My body was separated from my head." Merlot answered hoarsely. What was left of his throat was dry and caked. He would have liked a strong drink.

"Definitely not your day." Scythe sneered wrapping his wraith-like fingers around the bronze ring wedged into Merlot's bloody nostrils. "Behr!" He shouted staring deeply into Merlot's bloodshot eyes. "I know you can hear me!"

"No one has seen or heard from Behr since he was attacked in the Forest." Merlot mumbled. It was hard for him to talk with the demon's fingers wrapped around the ring. Scythe felt the magical energy flowing through the ring that Behr had used to bond the bulimon to him.

"I know you can hear me Behr!" Scythe hissed.

"What do you want?" Behr answered grumpily definitely not happy to hear from Scythe. He had hoped he was rid of the demon for good.

"I want you! You idiot! Where are you?" Scythe shouted at the image of Behr floating in the bulimon's black eyes.

"I'm in my chambers, in Astaria."

"Good, good! Stay there! The girl is headed your way. Do what you must to keep her there until I get there. But no harm is to come to her. Understand! Hold her there, but do not let that snake Ceen do anything to her!"

"Yes, I understand." Behr answered relieved that he wasn't being summoned back for the demon to repossess.

One more thing," Scythe said feeling the power of the ring reenergizing him.

"What's that?"

"Break the bonds and set the bulimon free."

"Break the bonds?" Behr asked confused at the strange request. "You want me to call off the attack."

"I want you to break the bonds!" Scythe screeched yanking the ring with such force he lifted Merlot's thick head off the stump. The weight of the head snapped the ring in two breaking the connection and sending Merlot's head spinning down into the raging water below. As Mukrot's head hit the water, Scythe swore the bulimon was smiling.

Fie was pissed. First her mother, Cinn, had insisted she stay back while her siblings went on a great adventure, but now Cinn had forced Fie to swim across the rough water to go look for them. They should have been back by now and Cinn was worried that they were not coming back. Fie wouldn't blame them if they didn't. She was tempted not to go back either. Ever since her mother had mated with the ginger Gerawld she had been in a bad mood. Probably because Gerawld had fancied Fee over her.

Fie was taking her sweet time walking along the riverbank. She was in no hurry to return to her mother. Fie had gone further than usual. She knew she should turn back, but something down below had caught her eye. It looked like a black snake, except it was covered with fur instead of scales. Cautiously slipping down the rocky bank, Fie silently approached the strange snake. It wasn't until she was upon it that she realized the snake was actually a tail attached to a large tuxedo cat.

Fie flipped Tux onto his back. He wasn't breathing. Placing her little paw over his triangular nose, Fie blew into his mouth. No reaction. She blew again. Still nothing. On the fifth try Tux shivered and coughed up a lung full of water. As she lifted and turned his head, Fie noticed Tux's right ear had been sliced off. The sign of a traitor. Knowing her mother would not approve, Fie did what most teenage girls would do. She decided not to tell her. It took most of her strength to drag Tux up onto the riverbank and hide him in one of the empty barns.

Tux felt like he'd been to Hell. His head was throbbing and every bone in his body ached. Slowly opening his eyes, Tux looked around him. He didn't have a clue how he'd gotten out of the water, but he had. Besides the freshly killed field mouse laying on the ground in front of him, he didn't see anyone else. Famished he picked up the mouse and stuffed it in his mouth. It wasn't until he'd finished chomping down the mouse that he realized he was locked in a barn.

Fee and Phoe stood by the edge of the river looking anxious. Gerawld joined them.

"Phoe is going back," Fee meowed. "I want to stay with you. If you want me too."

Gerawld purred and rubbed his head against Fee's forehead. Phoe watched Mia keeping pace with Alzo. She did not look back. Phoe rubbed noses with his sister and darted away. Mia had made it clear that Phoe need not linger on her account. Except for Gerawld, Mia had always been a loner and she preferred it that way.

"Do you have any idea what we're walking into?" Alzo asked Knot keeping his voice low and nodding towards the gapping entrance.

"Are you asking if we're walking into a trap?" Knot asked climbing up Alzo's pants leg and shirt sleeve to sit on the big man's shoulder. "Could be, but I don't think so. Even if the blue dwarves are loyal to the Empire, the miners aren't. I'd say the time is ripe for an uprising, but we'll know for sure in a few minutes, won't we?"

Knot's question was answered a few minutes later when Alzo and his followers reached the ridge and discovered six heavily armed bulimon blocking their path. Behind them closer to the mine entrance a line of blue dwarves leaned on their battle axes.

"They must have been tipped off." Knot groused.

Alzo studied the line of bulimon and dwarves blocking their way. Remembering his days playing football in college, he quickly came up with a plan. He was in the middle of explaining his plan to the others when the sound of rushing water drowned his voice. Freed by the broken dam, the water had flowed over the shore and was cresting towards the ridge.

"Run!" Parth yelled from above them as a wall of brown water, tree limbs, rocks, drowned bodies, and other debris too mangled to recognize continued to swell.

"Run!" Alzo bellowed waving his arm towards the bulimon. "Head for the mines!" Gerawld roared and ran next to Alzo while Mia took the other side.

"I'll take out the center," Alzo shouted over the rushing water, "you two knock out the two on either side of him." Gerawld dropped to all fours and lowered his head. The bulimon raised their long lances bracing for impact. Mia pulled the blow tube and several darts off her belt.

"Here," she told Ilee shoving the tube and darts into her hand. Ilee looked down at the darts and knew exactly what to do with them. Slowing she inserted several darts into the tube and blew hard. The first dart struck the center bulimon in the cheek. Thinking it was a bug, the bulimon try to swat it away, but his body grew too heavy for his knees, and he collapsed. The other bulimon quickly followed.

When Alzo and the two bast cats reached the bulimon, the rings in their noses had dissolved into dust. Alzo picked up a lance and leapt over the bulimon's dead bodies, his attention now focused on the stocky, axe bearing dwarves.

One of the dwarves charged towards Alzo swinging his axe in front of him, but before he could reach Alzo several miners rushed from the mines and tackled him. Word that the Change had arrived had reached the miners and they knew the time had come to fight. When they saw the blue dwarves running out with their battle axes the miners began to gather at the entrance. Now the miners took matters into their own hands. Within minutes the other dwarves had been disarmed.

"Hurry!" Alzo shouted standing by the entrance and waving his team inside with the angry water splashing at his ankles.

"Permission to land," Parth yelled letting go of Louy's talons and dropping to the ground near Alzo. Alzo ran out to help her tie the heavy rope around a boulder while a rope ladder was dropped from the hovering raft.

"Hurry everyone get inside!" Alzo yelled lifting the passengers off the ladder and pushing them towards the mines.

"We need to seal the entrance." Parth yelled as she cut the rope free, and the birds flew off to pick up more survivors.

Alzo waited until everyone was safely inside before grabbing the bluish-gray mantel stone holding up the mine entrance. Mustering the strength of Samson, Alzo pulled the mantel piece downward until the huge stone cracked, and the rocks tumbled down around him.

"Impressive!" Parth stated pulling Alzo out of danger as water splashed through the cracks and crevices threatening to tear the rocks apart.

"Something I learned from Emma," Alzo said, "we closed many a rogue mine in our day."

"We're trapped!" Ilee screamed grabbing hold of Alzo's arm. "What have you done! We should have run to higher ground! Once the river calmed down, we could have sailed to Astaria."

"And right into the enemy's waiting arms." Parth mocked.

"Now don't you worry Missy," one of the miners told Ilee kindly. "That isn't the only way out of here. We'll get you to Astaria, but you can forget about sailing there. It's not safe. Better to stay underground where prying eyes can't see you."

"Thank you," Alzo said brushing the rubble off his shirt.

"I'd say this calls for a celebration." Parth called out giving Alzo a wink before relieving two boys of the keg they had commandeered.

On the adjacent mountain, Elize rushed down the passageway keeping one step ahead of the walls which folded behind her as soon as she stepped through them. The passage led into a tight crevice. Elize lifted Rixley up and gently handed Ori to her. The crevice was barely wide enough for Elize to squeeze out. Bruised and bleeding she finally got her butt out of the crevice and collapsed onto the lush violet moss. Rixley plopped down next to her still holding Ori in her paws.

"Where's that bottle Mal gave us?" Elize asked digging into the bag until she found it. Elize gave the bottle a good shake and held it up. The liquid had turned a bright florescent tangerine orange. Elize wondered if it tasted like tangerine, but when she popped the cork instead of tangerine it smelled like fermented urine.

"Get his mouth open!" Elize told Rixley when Ori clamped his mouth shut. Happy to help, Rixley jammed her paws into Ori's nostrils. Unable to breathe, Ori finally opened his mouth just enough to take a breath. Rixley thrust her hind paws in his mouth and forced it open. Elize was ready and quickly poured the foul liquid down her friend's throat. Together they held Ori's mouth shut until he swallowed.

Ori gagged and his eyes shot open wide like a cartoon character.

"He's convulsing!" Elize yelled at Rixley. "Help me hold him down." Rixley stood frozen staring at Ori in horror. Ori yipped and gnashed his teeth. Thrashing wildly as his arms, legs, and torso stretched and his paws flattened into hands and feet.

"You can let go," Ori coughed when the transformation finally stopped. He ran his hands up and down his sides and took several long breaths before raising his head.

"Holy crap!" Elize gasped.

CHAPTER 17

"It's not funny," Ori snarled and smushed down his pointy ears in a feeble attempt to make them smaller.

"Not working," Elize said, trying her hardest to stop laughing.

"Stop laughing!" Ori shouted playfully punching Elize in the arm. Rixley growled and leapt forward, her pointy stick poised and ready to strike. Elize shot her hand forward and grabbed the stick before the little warrior could impale him.

"Rixley!" Elize shouted holding the ferret off the ground by her stick. "Ori's just playing around. It's okay. He's just not himself right now."

"Rixley not like himself right now," Rixley grumbled dropping to the ground and snatching her stick back from Elize. Rixley cut her eyes at Ori.

"We need to move," he said woozily getting to his feet. 'We need to be inside the walls by sunset." Wrapping an arm around Elize's waist for support, the trio slowly made their way down the mountain.

"What's that?" Elize asked nodding towards the ugly brown line snaking across the landscape below.

"That m'lady is the outer wall of the Astarian Empire." Ori quipped in a badly executed British accent. "Within two more walls lays the crystalline palace where you were born."

"It looks like someone shoved a bunch of telephone poles together."

"Yes it does, but they aren't telephone poles. There are no telephones on this planet."

"Is the wall to keep people out or in?" Elize wondered.

"Both," Ori mused. He had never given it much thought until now. "More in than out I suppose."

"So much for freed lands huh?" Elize frowned. Even though the wall was made of poles instead of cement, it reminded Elize of the Berlin wall. The wall grew taller and uglier with every step they took. By the time they reached it, the sun was starting to set.

"We need to get on the other side and find a place to hide," Ori said wearily. He was exhausted and even though he didn't say anything, it was obvious that he was in pain.

"I don't see a way in?" Elize said scanning the wall up one side and down the other and not seeing a break in the poles.

"Rixley not like it here." Rixley grumbled kicking one of the poles.

"Elize not like it either." Elize agreed. "Why don't we take a rest here," she told Ori noticing how worn out he looked.

Ori shook his head. Using the wall for support, he gingerly started heading left. It was a slow boring walk with the ugly wall on one side and stunted, gray trees with thick trunks and short knotty limbs on the other. Spotting a tiny, sunshine yellow frog hopping on one of the tree trunks, Rixley reached out to grab it.

"Sorry kiddo," Ori apologized knocking her hand away, "but those frogs will make you wacky." Startled Rixley hissed and darted behind Elize's legs.

"He was just trying to help you," Elize assured Rixley gently running her fingers over the soft fur on the back of Rixley's head. "I ate some wacky berries in the desert. I don't recommend it at all."

"I meant to ask you about that," Ori said pushing each pole as he passed by. "I thought only the dead could enter the Salt Temples."

"I left my body at the door," Elize replied with a wink. Ori rose his eyebrow and gave Elize a whimsical look. As they continued making their way slowly along the wall, Elize told Ori about her adventures in the desert.

Ori stopped at a pole that looked just like all the other poles and gave it another shove. "Found it." He announced with a smile. "Help me push!"

Elize and Rixley didn't think it would do any good, but they helped him push anyway. The pole gave way and swung inward.

"Hurry scoot through," Ori told Rixley. Rixley looked over at Elize and waited for her to nod before shooting through the gap.

"You go next." Elize said holding the pole up with both hands. Once Ori was through, Elize backed through the opening and lowered the pole back into place. When she turned around she found herself standing in a field of lush green grass. She had the strange sensation of being in Munchkin Land.

"Don't just stand there," Ori urged grabbing her hand. "We need to find cover and for God's sake ditch the robe! You stick out like a sore thumb."

Elize pulled her robe off and shook it. The fabric shifted and darkened into a long, soft leather traveling jacket.

"Better?" Elize asked as she pulled her arms through the sleeves. She had to admit RaJa and Koh had good taste.

"Wow! Where'd you get that?" Ori asked reaching out to examine the jacket.

"The spirits gave it to me. I was wearing it when I returned to my body."

"It has magic pockets." Rixley told him reaching into a pocket and pulling out a green apple.

"Impressive." Ori agreed. "I think you should give it to me." He told Elize half-joking.

"Not a chance." Elize replied looking about her in astonishment as they made their way across a field of knee high grass. "I don't understand, how can the land be so lush on this side and so dead on the other? Doesn't the Emperor know there are families starving outside the walls?"

"I seriously doubt it," Ori replied leaning heavily on Elize. "I'm sure he is happily oblivious of the situation."

"Someone needs to bring the peoples plight to his attention," Elize commented grumpily.

Ori started to tell her that Emperor Taz's advisors were doing just the opposite but held his tongue. Elize hadn't seen her father since she was a small child, and she had no way of knowing how bad off he was. He should have explained the situation to her before, but now he thought it'd be best for her to see it for herself.

"Rixley run ahead and make sure the coast is clear." Ori ordered when they neared a cobbled road. Rixley looked at Ori suspiciously. Knowing Ori wasn't going to get anywhere ordering Rixley about like that, Elize knelt to her level.

"Remember how you went ahead of Mal and I in the mountains to make sure the path ahead was safe." Rixley nodded. "Well, that's called scouting and only the bravest warriors are asked to be scouts."

"Rixley bravest warrior." Rixley told Elize throwing her shoulders back and clutching her pointy stick gallantly in front of her.

"I know you are and so does Ori," Elize replied seriously. "That's why he asked you to go to make sure the path ahead is safe."

"Rixley go." Rixley said giving Elize a sharp nod. "Rixley and Elize are friends. Friends take care of each other."

Rixley dropped to all fours and scurried away. Elize regretted letting her little friend go off alone. After a few anxious moments Rixley returned. She had found a small, abandoned hut just off the road which they could spend the night.

"I guess this is as good a place as any," Ori said following the ferret to the hut. It looked like no one had lived there for a very long time, but in these times looks could be deceiving. When Ori yanked open the door a sharp pain shot through his side. Elize quickly took over, helping Ori inside and lying him on a moldy straw mattress someone had left on the floor. The hut had a slightly unpleasant odor and Elize wanted to keep the door open to let in some fresh air, but Ori insisted she close it.

Rixley curled into a ball on top of a lumpy bit of straw. Within seconds she was snoring softly. Elize sat next to Ori pressing her back against the wall. Ori gingerly moved next to her and laid his head in her lap. Elize smiled. It felt good to have him next to her again.

"Who attacked you?" She whispered. The question had been nagging her ever since she had pulled him from the rocks. "It seemed personal."

"It was," Ori admitted groaning as he lifted his head to look at her. "Aturi, the water maiden, thinks I betrayed her. She, among others, paid me to deliver you to her and her son Behr. I'm not sure what happened to Behr after I left. It was like he was possessed by a demon when he attacked us in the forest."

"Su Lei told me Behr had been possessed by a demon called Scythe." Elize explained sleepily, barely able to keep her eyes open. "Su Lei said Scythe is not strong enough to fully materialize. Which would explain Tux."

"If Tux was possessed by Scythe what made him take off like that?"

"I knew things about Tux that Scythe didn't." Elize said raising her eyebrows at Ori. "I knew Tux hates Gerawld with a passion. I also knew that a family of bast had taken over the old peat barns that used to belong to Kara's family."

"And that's relevant because?"

"It's relevant because I put an image in Tux's mind of Gerawld becoming leader of the bast that took over the peat barns. As I hoped the image infuriated him enough to resist the demon."

"Quite risky."

"Yeah, but it worked. What does Aturi have on you?"

"Believe it or not she saved my life. When I was a pup, my family was attacked by a group of farmers."

"That's terrible!" Elize exclaimed taking his hand in hers. It was very warm. "Why?"

"Well, as your brother once told you, Vanji's are scoundrels and thieves." Ori joked. "At least that's how the folks in the villages thought about us. Vanjis are travelers. They move about from place-to-place telling fortunes, juggling, singing songs, dancing. Unfortunately, Vanjis tend to wear out their welcome and our troupe stayed in a town a day too long. The farmers came just after dawn stuffing the entrance to our den with fiery rags. My mother dug a hole through the back and pushed me out into a small brook. When I landed in the water, I swam under the roots of a tree overhanging the bank and hid. She dropped my sister next. My sister hit the water and panicked, yipping, and thrashing in the icy water. A farmer grabbed her and the rest of my siblings and tossed them into a bag filled with rocks. They would have found me too, but the water maiden drew them away. After the farmers were gone, Aturi and her son, Behr, helped me pull the bag out of the water, but it was too late. All my brothers and sisters had drowned."

"How did you end up living in the palace kitchens?"

"Pure luck," Ori laughed, stifling a yawn. "The cook decided to take his little girl with him when he went to pick fresh greens. Parth found me hiding in a patch of wild garlic and hid me in her basket. She kept me hidden in her room for almost a month until her mother caught her sneaking food out of the kitchen."

"Rixley lost her mama too," Rixley said scooting next to Ori. "The bad man took her away. Rixley tried to follow, but she was too little. RaJa and Koh saved Rixley. They took care of Rixley. They gave me words."

"RaJa and Koh?" Ori asked looking at Elize.

"They are the spirits who live inside the salt temple." Elize clarified stifling a large yawn. "RaJa found Rixley on the steps of the temple and felt sorry for her. He saved her and gave her the gift of speech."

"Is that how you met?"

Elize nodded and closed her eyes. Ori tried to stay awake and keep watch, but soon his eyes grew heavy, and he fell into a restless sleep.

"Where's Ori?" Elize exclaimed when she woke up and discovered Ori missing. Elize nudged Rixley who was stretched out down Elize's thigh. "Where's Ori?" She asked more urgently.

"Rixley not know," Rixley mumbled shoving Elize's hand away.

"Get up and help me find him," Elize demanded nudging the ferret again. Rixley rolled off Elize's thigh and landed with a thud on the dirt floor. When Elize nudged her again Rixley grabbed her arm and wrestled it, kicking at Elize's wrist with her hind paws. Elize lifted the irate ferret off the ground and using her free arm slowly opened the door of the hut and peered out into the dusky dawn.

They found Ori lying face down in a puddle of mud on the back side of the hut. He smelled like pee and was burning up with fever. Elize rolled him over and tried to revive him. Unable to wake him up, Elize lifted his shirt to look at his wound. To her dismay his side was swollen up and the color of an over ripe tomato.

"We need to drain his cut," Elize said to herself. Thinking Elize was talking to her, Rixley poked at one of the stitches with her pointy stick. Dark green pus oozed out.

"Ugh," Elize gasped using the edge of Ori's shirt to wipe the gunk away.

Rixley tugged Elize's jacket urgently pointing in the direction of the sound of many paws moving across the ground.

"Leave me." Ori hissed. Ignoring him Elize reached down to lift him off the ground. "Run you fool!" Ori yipped nipping at Elize's hand, but it was too late. They were already surrounded.

Rixley let out an ear piercing screech and leapt in front of Elize gnashing her teeth and jabbing at their attackers with her pointy stick. Surprised by her furiousness the pack stumbled to a halt. Elize rose to her feet leaving Ori lying in the dirt behind her trying his best to look dead.

"You leave Lee-zee alone!" Rixley snarled slashing at the closest boy with her stick. The boy chattered loudly at Rixley and snaped at her pointy stick with his needle-sharp teeth.

"Baba?" Rixley squealed with surprise looking into the shiny black eyes of a ferret not much bigger than herself. The ferret spat at her. "Baba!" Rixley shouted grabbing her brother by the scruff of his neck and slamming his face into the dirt.

"Rixley?!" Baba squawked arching his back and kicking out, knocking Rixley off her feet.

"Baba!" Rixley exclaimed quickly rolling to one side and kicking him squarely in the ribs.

Distracted by the apparent family reunion, Elize didn't see who belonged to the rough, calloused hands that grabbed her from behind. Elize shouted and tried to wiggle free, but he had too good a grip, so she stomped on his foot. Annoyed her attacker slammed his chin into the center of Elize's skull.

"The notice said to deliver her unharmed, you idiot!" A foul-smelling, hairy man snarled pulling a rope from his pack and winding it around Elize until she looked like a fly caught in a spider's web. The hairy man yanked Elize off the ground and tossed her over his wide shoulder. Before she was carried away, Elize managed to catch a glimpse of Ori still lying in the puddle.

It was impossible for Elize to keep track of where she was being taken because her head was upside down and the bouncing made her nauseous. When Elize was finally tossed to the ground, she heaved up what little was left in her stomach all over the burly man's boots.

"You stupid wench!" The burly man grunted, kicking Elize hard in the ribs before stomping out of the storeroom and bolting the door behind him.

Elize laid on her side hugging her ribs for several minutes. The energy was boiling underneath the glove. Instead of letting it explode out of her, she forced the energy down by focusing on her breath and counting back from one hundred to one. When she got to thirty-three Elize stopped and listened to the conversation seeping under the crack between the floor and the door. Her captors had received orders to keep her locked in the room until the Emperor's guards arrived to fetch her. A hefty reward was expected, and a few of the weasels and ferrets were demanding their cut in advance. Rixley's brother would have liked to be among this group.

Rixley was so surprised to find her brother Baba, that she temporarily forgot about Elize. Overcome with elation, Rixley rolled across the ground for several minutes before letting the startled Baba go. Rixley figured if Baba had survived that her mama must have too.

"Baba, Baba, Baba!" Rixley excitedly squeaked in ferret. "It's me Rixley!"

"Rixley?" Baba squeaked back. Unlike Rixley, Baba had not been blessed with the gift of common speech and spoke to her in ferret. "Rixley dead."

"No, Rixley not dead." Rixley shouted grabbing the stunned ferret by his shoulders and giving him a firm shake. "Rixley live. Rixley come to find Mama. Baba, take Rixley to Mama!"

Baba wove his head back and forth. Rixley thought he was refusing to take her and shook him harder.

"Take me!" Rixley demanded. Baba wove his head back and forth and started chattering incoherently. Rixley was about to give him another shake when Baba broke free and took off running.

Thinking he was running away from her Rixley tore after him, but Baba wasn't running from her. He was running from a large badger named Jetz. Jetz was the self-appointed leader of the badger boys and he had been looking for Baba for several days. He had sent Baba to gather golden frogs, but the ferret had failed to return with the highly sought after hallucinogenic frogs. Jetz knew he'd been foolish to trust Baba, but Baba owed a large debt and had begged Jetz to let him work it off. Jetz agreed even though he knew Baba was a hopeless addict.

"Well, well, well, what do we have here?" Jetz asked grabbing Baba by the scruff of the neck. Baba tried to warn Rixley, but before he could, two scraggly ermines leapt out and knocked Rixley to the ground.

Baba chattered excitedly at Jetz motioning towards Rixley who was doing her best to fight off the larger, pink eyed ermine. Jetz looked over at Rixley and dropped Baba roughly on the ground. Without looking back, Baba scurried away leaving Rixley to fight alone.

Jetz sauntered over to Rixley licking his lips. "You belong to me now." He whispered leaning in close so only Rixley could hear him. Held between the two ermines Rixley stared at the disgusting badger with cold, hard eyes. "You and I are going to be real close friends." Jetz purred ignoring the grimace on Rixley's face. Jetz pulled a yellow frog out of his sack and thrust it at Rixley. "A gift from me to you." He laughed gruffly. Rixley locked her jaw. Jetz was too busy laughing to notice the frog leap off Rixley's lips and disappear behind her shoulder. Jetz stopped laughing and looked up at Rixley. Rixley pretended to choke and swallow the frog. Jetz leaned forward and licked her lips.

"Take that stick and bring the bitch inside the hut!" Jetz ordered kicking open the door. Snickering the ermine dragged Rixley into the hut and held her to the ground. Jetz lowered his heavy body down on top of Rixley.

A fury Rixley had never felt before erupted in her stomach giving her the strength she needed to fight back. Lifting her head Rixley sank her needle-sharp teeth into Jetz squashy black nose and bit down hard. Blood squirted into Jetz eyes causing him to arch back into the ermine who was holding Rixley's pointy stick. When the ermine stumbled and dropped the pointy stick Rixley rolled over and grabbed it. Jumping to her feet, Rixley jabbed her stick deep into the ermine's stomach just under the rib cage. The other ermine rushed at Rixley. Rixley yanked the bloody stick out and swung around impaling the second ermine in the neck. The white ermine stumbled backwards gasping for breath as he grabbed at the stick protruding from his throat.

Jetz cursed and grabbing Rixley by the scruff of the neck began shaking her. Rixley pulled the short blade off Jetz belt and shoved it into his side. Blood splattered across Rixley's cream-colored fur. Jetz howled and grabbed at his side enraged. Rixley snarled and kicked the heavy badger hard in his blood-soaked side with her hind legs. Scrambling across the floor, she yanked her pointy stick out of the dead ermine's throat.

Jetz roared and charged at Rixley. The tip of the pointy stick flared green as Rixley shoved it so far into Jetz' snarling jaws the tip burst out the back of his neck. Jetz' grabbed the pointy stick with both hands before falling backwards on to the floor in a black and white heap. Rixley picked up Jetz knife and slit his throat to make sure he was dead. Then she put her hind paws on his bloody chest and yanked the stick out of Jetz mouth.

Ori had managed to crawl away from the hut only to fall into a dung ditch. Rixley was tempted to leave him there, but she knew Elize wouldn't like that. Not sure if Ori was still alive or not, Rixley dragged him out of the filthy ditch which should have caused Ori's infection to get much worse, but as luck would have it, Ori had landed on a rotting corpse covered with maggots. Leaving the rotting corpse, the maggots covered Ori's infected side and feasted on pus and dead tissue.

With most of the infection devoured, Ori's fever had broken. Dazed and confused, Ori pulled himself up on his elbows and looked at Rixley.

"What happen to you?" Ori asked weakly noticing the splotches of blood covering her fur.

Rixley glanced down at her bloodstained fur, "Jetz." Rixley spat, her black eyes glittering with a feral intensity.

"Jetz?" Ori groaned raising himself up into a sitting position.

"Nasty badger." Rixley fumed brushing at the blood. "Baba tricked Rixley. Instead of taking Rixley to Mama he sold Rixley to Jetz."

Even though Ori had no idea who Baba or Jetz were, he got the gist of what Rixley was saying. He looked at the young ferret and asked gently. "Did he…"

"No," Rixley growled gnashing her teeth. "Rixley strong and brave. Rixley not let Jetz hurt Rixley."

"Where is Jetz now?" Ori asked. His orange eyes fixed upon the glowing tip on Rixley's pointy stick. He was sure the tip wasn't glowing like that before and if he wasn't mistaken, the glowing shard was a chip off a warrior stone. The warrior stone was a stone of lore said to be unbreakable, ever sharp, and it made the one who bore it invincible. It was said that only the truly righteous could wield a warrior stone.

"Jetz dead." Rixley replied tapping the bottom of the stick on the ground until it stopped glowing.

"Where did you get that?" Ori asked not bothering to hide the awe in his voice.

"RaJa gave stick to Rixley. RaJa said only bravest warriors could make work. Rixley make it work" Rixley said proudly. "Rixley bravest."

"Indeed, you are." Ori agreed gingerly getting to his knees. With Rixley's help and much grunting, he finally managed to stand up.

"Foxhead stay here." Rixley said when they reached the hut. "Rixley go find Elize. Elize needs Rixley. Rixley and Elize are friends."

"Ori and Elize are friends too," Ori told her holding on to the hut and slowly making his way sideways, "and I know where they took her."

"Foxhead too weak," Rixley told him. "Foxhead tell Rixley where Elize is. Rixley go."

"Not going to happen." Ori winced letting go of the corner of the hut and clumsily stumbling forward. "Besides, there's too many bodies for even the bravest warrior to tackle. But don't worry, I have a plan."

"Tell Rixley plan."

"I know a song, a magic song that will put all who hear it into a deep sleep."

"Foxhead make bodies sleep. Rixley save Elize."

"Yes." Ori agreed.

The pair moved cautiously across the space between the fourth and third walls. When they reached the round building, that used to be the local tavern, Ori slumped down under one of the open windows. The sound of rough voices and clinking mugs wafted out of the screenless window. Rixley scurried up on top of Ori's head and peeked over the ledge while Ori began to sing softly. Unaffected by his song, Rixley silently slipped through the window and up to the rafters that ran across the ceiling. Lying flat across the main rafter Rixley scanned the room for any sign of Elize.

Sitting alone on the dirt floor of the tavern storeroom, inches from a puddle of her own puke, Elize couldn't recall a time when she'd felt lower. Still wrapped in the sticky web-like rope, Elize had exhausted herself trying to break free. Each time she forced her arms away from her side the ropes tighten. It felt like she was wearing a corset. She was afraid if the rope got any tighter her ribs would crack. Even if she could untangle herself, there was no way out. There were no windows and except for the heavy, barred door, the only opening she could see was the grubby drainpipe in the center of the room.

Elize shut her eyes and tried to clear her mind. She hoped if she concentrated hard enough she could reach Koh or RaJa. After several tries she gave up. It was no use, each time she tried to clear her mind a million questions popped into it. Was Ori dead? Where was Alzo? Was he still alive? Would she ever return to Earth? What did Ellen think when she didn't return? Did Ellen think she was dead? Would she ever see her house again? Was Ellen taking care of Popeye and Olive Oyle? Did her dog and cat even miss her? Was Su Lei dead? What about Nekita? How was Taa and the Bast cats? Was Ori dead?

Her mind kept drifting back to Ori. She remembered her last days on Earth and the good times they had had together. She could almost feel his soft skin next to hers. Sighing deeply Elize allowed the memories to wash over her. She remembered the curve of his jaw. The way his face lit up when he laughed. How he looked so deeply into her eyes she swore he was looking straight into her soul. The memory was so vivid she swore she could hear him singing.

Elize opened her eyes and shook her head. She could hear Ori singing and she heard something else too. A strange hissing noise coming from the pipe, like steam escaping. Her heart skipped a beat, not only was Ori alive he had come to her rescue.

"Hey! What are you doing?" An overly dressed guard shouted rushing towards Ori who ignored the guard and kept singing to give Rixley time to hide. Rixley was halfway across the thick wooden rafters when Ori stopped singing and the tavern door was kicked in by guards.

"They locked her in the storeroom." Ori yelped as the guard dragged him into the tavern. "I was trying to keep them from harming her until you got here. Trust me."

"Ha!" The guard, who had dealt with Ori in the past, laughed and gave Ori a firm shake. "You'd better hope for your sake your little song put them to sleep in time. If any harm has come to the woman you'll be the one to explain it to the Emperor not me."

"Damn weasels," another, more muscular guard who appeared to be in charge, sneered as he stepped around the heaps of badger boys lying across the floor with silly smiles smeared across their faces. Rixley flattened her long body against the beam watching anxiously as the guard slid the wooden beam out of the slot and yanked open the storeroom door.

"What trick is this?" He demanded scowling at Ori angerly. Rixley lifted her head as far as she dared and peaked inside. The storeroom was empty.

* * * * * * * *

The hissing coming from the drainpipe grew louder and more pronounced. What had sounded like steam escaping, now sounded more like shit, shit, shit. When the drainpipe began expanding Elize half wiggled, half rolled into the corner. She was afraid that she had been left as a sacrifice for some horrible sewer creature. Instead of a sewer creature a gray skinned teenager with flat charcoal colored hair climbed out of the hole and shook himself like a wet dog.

"I had no idea that pipe was still being used." The teenager commented looking disdainfully down at the muck dripping off his pants.

"Who are you?" Elize asked unsure if her visitor was friend or foe.

"I'm Selkie." Selkie said brushing at the muck with boney webbed fingers. Selkie's head tilted to one side as he listened to the commotion outside the storeroom door. "Sounds like it's time to go!" Selkie yelped, picked Elize up and dropped her into the drainpipe before jumping in after her practically landing on Elize's head. Helping Elize to her feet Selkie quickly helped Elize out of the sticky rope as the drainpipe above them magically returned to its normal size.

"This way!" Selkie said taking Elize's hand and leading her down the pipe. Elize kept her head down and stumbled after him. She wasn't naïve enough to trust Selkie, but for now she'd take whatever help she could get.

* * * * * * * *

"Where's the girl!" The guard shouted shaking his gloved hand in Ori's face. Ori shook his head. He was as surprised as they were to find the room empty. "Well, at least we won't be returning empty handed." The guard scoffed grabbing Ori's arm and hauling him out of the tavern.

"Wait!" Ori protested acting like he was trying to pull free. "Where are you taking me?"

"To the palace dungeons." The lead guard grumbled. "You won't bring as much as the other two, but at least it'll be enough to buy us a keg or two."

"You're taking me to the palace dungeons!" Ori yelled, hoping it was loud enough for Rixley to hear.

Rixley waited until the guards had left with Ori before silently creeping across the rafters and dropping into the storeroom. Elize had been there. Her scent was strong especially in the corner. Rixley followed Elize's scent which had mixed with another scent, a fishy one, down the drainpipe. When she reached the bottom, she found the discarded sticky rope. She wrapped the rope around her waist like a thick belt before continuing down the foul-smelling pipes.

The stench made it hard for Rixley to follow Elize's scent. When the pipe split into three Rixley took the left pipe and soon lost Elize's scent. She was about to turn around and try one of the other two pipes when her nose detected a familiar musky odor. Snarling Rixley crept forward, her pointy stick out and ready to strike. When she got to the end of the pipe she found her brother crumbled up in a hole, passed out.

Forgetting about Elize, Rixley jumped on top of Baba slamming his face against the wall of the pipe. Rixley pressed her pointy stick into his bony chest hard enough for him to get the point. Terrified, Baba let out a shrill squeak and wet himself.

Rixley's black eyes blazed out of her masked face like two burning coals. "You," Rixley growled, "You Baba will take Rixley to Mama!"

Seeing the dried blood on Rixley's fur Baba gulped and swatted at the stick. When he tried to wiggle free Rixley pinned him to the pipe and snarled.

"No games!" Rixley warned. "Baba take Rixley to Mama now!"

Baba whimpered and wiped his snotty nose across his arm. "Can't, the bad air took Mama's breath away!"

"Take Rixley!" Rixley screamed slamming Baba's face against the pipe busting his lip open.

"Baba take," Baba whined licking at the blood. Rixley tied the sticky rope around his neck like a collar and holding on to the other end pushed him forward.

"No, no," Baba pleaded with Rixley, trying to rip the collar off his neck. Rixley kicked him in the butt. Baba whimpered again and stumbled down the pipe dropping to all fours and pulling Rixley through a series of twists and turns. Soon Rixley had no idea which way she had come.

"Baba, slow down!" Rixley hissed as he pulled her down a dip in the pipe. She tugged at the rope hard to get his attention, but the rope had snapped, and Baba was gone.

Rixley stood in the pipe several minutes unsure what to do. She did not want to go back, but she did not know what lay ahead. "Rixley brave and strong." Rixley told herself firmly. "Rixley needs to get along." Holding out her pointy stick, Rixley took a deep breath and started forward.

"Hey you!" A terrifying voice boomed into the pipe. Thinking she'd been seen, Rixley froze. "I warned you not to come back! You thieving sot!"

Baba wailed and ran past the end of the tunnel. A stubby blue dwarf wielding a long whip chased after him. Rixley crept to the end of the tunnel. When Baba ran by again she held out her stick. The dwarf ran into the stick and cursing tumbled head over heels. Baba turned around and dashed past Rixley and disappeared into the pipe like a puff of smoke. Rixley was about to go after him when a hollowed-eyed ferret waved at her urgently.

"Mama?" Rixley whispered slipping past the whip wielding dwarf and scurrying over to the ragged looking ferret. Rixley studied the new ferret's face. She had so hoped it was her mama. It wasn't.

"Get behind me quick!" The ragged ferret squeaked pushing Rixley out of sight.

"Where is he?" The blue dwarf demanded getting to his feet and picking up his whip. Using her body to block Rixley, the ferret pointed to the pipe. Cursing and flicking his whip in front of him the dwarf charged into the pipe. The diggers who had been busy digging chunks of soft blue rock out of the walls stopped what they were doing and scurried over to block the pipe. They stuffed the pipe full of rocks trapping the dwarf inside. The diggers consisted of various animals renowned for their digging skills, moles, ferrets, badgers, gophers, minks and others.

"What are you doing here?" The older ferret squeaked once the coast was clear. "Where did you come from?"

"Rixley looking for Mama." Rixley replied in rusty ferret. Before coming across Baba, Rixley hadn't spoken ferret since she was a pup. "Rixley come from..." Rixley stopped she wasn't sure where she came from before the salt temples. "Rixley came from outside." Rixley told the curious diggers who had gathered around her eager to hear any news of the outside world. "Rixley follow bad men who took Mama to dig in mines."

"You came from the outside?" A round brown ground hog asked his voice muffled behind long, thick, yellowed teeth. "Is it true? Has the Change really come?"

"I heard he was here too!" Another piped in. "Is it true?"

"Rixley not know." Rixley sputtered, not sure what they were talking about. "Rixley not here with Change. Rixley is here to find Mama! Do you know Rixley's mama?" The diggers looked at Rixley with sad, haggard faces and shook their heads. Rixley sniffed and rubbed her eyes. The funny smelling air was making her eyes burn.

"Why were you with Baba the thief?" The ferret woman asked Rixley gently.

"Baba is Rixley's brother. Baba say he take Rixley to Mama. Baba trick Rixley."

"Baba's mama?" Another ferret squeaked peeking at Rixley over the larger ferret's shoulder. "I knew Baba's mama. She worked in the furnaces, but she...she got sick...bad air took her breath away...Rixley's mama..."

Rixley covered her ears. She didn't want to hear what the ferret was saying. Devastated at finding out her mama was dead, Rixley backed away from the others and sobbing threw herself on a pile of blue rocks. "Rixley lose Elize to find Mama and now Mama's dead."

"Little Warrior, how do you know Elize?" A dark figure asked moving stealthily out from behind the rocks to stand in front of Rixley.

"You're a warrior!" Rixley whispered in awe. Rixley wiped her eyes on her paws to get a better look at the sleek black bast cat. Even though she had never seen a live warrior before, Rixley had no doubt that Mia was the real deal.

"I am." Mia said walking towards the awestricken Rixley. Rixley jerked off the rocks so quickly her pointy stick slipped out of her paws and clattered to the ground. Mia picked up the stick, examined it carefully and handed it back to Rixley. "A warrior never drops her weapon." Mia told Rixley firmly.

Rixley clutched her stick tightly in both her paws and stood at attention. Mia lifted Rixley's chin and pushed her shoulders back. Mia understood all too well how Rixley felt. She too had lost her mother at a very young age, but she refused to feel sorry for the little ferret.

"Now, Little Warrior tell me how you know Elize?"

"Elize and Rixley friends." Rixley replied trying to keep her voice from shaking.

"I see, and where is Elize now?"

"Rixley lost Elize." Rixley sniffed biting her lip.

"Come," Mia told Rixley putting a paw on her shoulder. "You must give a full report to Alzo, the Change. He is worried about his sister, Elize."

Rixley trotted behind Mia. "Rixley tell Alzo, Elize's brother how Rixley lost Elize. Rixley also tell Alzo where bad men took Ori Foxhead."

CHAPTER 18

Ori wasn't worried about being thrown in the dungeons. He had lived in the palace most of his life and knew it inside and out. The downside was that most of the palace guards knew him and his tricks as well. The guards also knew that Ori had a price on his head. He wouldn't be worth as much as Elize or Alzo, but it would be enough to buy a keg or two of ale.

Ori planned to escape from the dungeons as quickly as possible so he could search the palace for Elize. He was sure that whoever had helped Elize escape would bring her to the palace for the reward.

Elize wasn't as sure. She supposed Selkie was taking her to the palace, but after twisting and turning through the pipes, Elize was convinced Selkie was lost.

"Oh fish!" Selkie exclaimed as they backtracked out of one pipe and into another.

"What's wrong?" Elize asked impatiently. They had been squashing through the disgusting pipes for a while now and she was more than ready to get out of them.

"All these stinking pipes look the same." Selkie confessed flustered. Elize put her hands on Selkie's round shoulders and looked into his foggy eyes.

"It's okay. Stop freaking out." Elize told him with authority. "Take a deep breath, hold it, hold it, now exhale. Slowly. Do it again. Now think. You came through the pipes to find me. Did you come with the current or against it?"

Selkie thought a minute. "With the current."

"So, we should head against the current right?"

"Right, but there are three pipes."

"Pick one." Elize said. "The sooner we get to the surface the better. You can figure out where we are once we're above ground."

Selkie picked the left pipe. They hadn't gone ten feet when the pipe dropped off suddenly dumping them into a deep, dark blue pool. Treading water, Selkie carefully studied the walls around them.

"I think I know where we are." He sputtered diving beneath the water and swimming towards the bottom. Elize took a large breath and followed Selkie down into the depths and through a long tunnel. When they surfaced a few minutes later, Elize was gasping.

"This isn't right," Selkie groaned when he saw the crystalline wall of the inner palace gleaming brightly in front of him. "We should be inside the wall not out!"

"Wow!" Elize exclaimed pulling her body out of the pool and looking up at the glassy spires sparkling from behind the walls. They were quite beautiful.

"Wow nothing." Selkie sulked shaking the water off him like a wet dog. "We'll have to walk from here. "Come on."

"Someone's coming." Elize whispered touching Selkie's shoulder. They ducked behind the bright yellow shop they were passing. Luckily the guard had been too busy sneaking into the shop to notice.

"Get out!" A female voice said sharply as the door to the shop reopened and the disgruntled guard slipped out. "I won't have my shop closed down because of your sorry ass." Then in a harsh whisper she added, "wait out back, I'll slip it out the window to you."

Selkie and Elize tiptoed around the corner as the guard came around the other side. The palace guard known as Simeon 112 leaned out the turret window searching the ground below for Simeon 347. Simeon 347 had snuck out of the wall to buy a couple pints of ale. Simeon 112 wasn't worried when Simeon 347 had come out of the yellow shop empty handed. The Alers had to be careful now that the Emperor had appointed Quinn 001 as Commander of the Guard. If the Aler's were caught selling pints to guards while they were on duty, Quinn 001 would shut them down.

Simeon 112 heard a shout and the sound of a scuffle, but the yellow shop blocked his view. He was relieved a few minutes later when Simeon 347 rounded the corner. When Simeon 112 saw the woman marching in front of Simeon 347, he left his post and ran down the wall walk towards the gatehouse.

"Come on!" Simeon 347 snapped at Elize in Selkie's voice. Elize looked at the guard with alarm. Selkie's gray eyes looked back at her from out of the guard's skin. "Get! Let's go." Selkie pushed her in front of him. Elize marched forward obediently.

"What'd you do with the guard?" Elize asked once they were away from the shop.

"I borrowed his skin." Selkie whispered back.

"Is he dead?"

"No, once I'm done with it, I'll slip out and he'll wake up, with a hangover, wondering how he got where he is. He won't remember a thing."

"Do you know where we are?"

"Kind of. The front gate should be right around the corner."

Selkie was right. When they turned the corner the massive gatehouse carved out of smooth, almost clear stone loomed before them. In the center of the gatehouse was a glimmering stairway which had been carved out of the almost clear stone unique to Astaria. The stone had been formed by an ancient lava flow created when two meteors, named the Grandfather and Grandmother, collided together forming the two massive mountain ranges that covered most of the planet Toboria. The heat created by the two meteors colliding sent a river of cloudy lava flowing down between the massive meteors forming what is known as the grandfather's seed.

Flanking each side of the grand staircase were two giant statues. The female statue was carved from the Grandmother's veil, a translucent stone found only on the white mountain behind the palace. The adjacent male statue was carved from the dark gray stone of the Grandfather and had massive wings protruding from his back. Many believed the statues depicted the Grandmother and the Grandfather with hands joined at the top forming an arch over the entrance to the palace, but they were wrong. The first Emperor of Astaria had the statues made in the image of his Grandmother Monet and his Grandfather Scyathee.

"Halt!" A shrill voice commanded from the top of the stairway. Quinn 001, Commander of the Guard, descended two steps at a time. He was followed by a line of Simeon guards eager to be a part of the action. The guards all wore long plum colored dove tailed jackets, gleaming saffron trousers, plum boots, and oversized helmets topped with grapefruit sized saffron puff balls which bounced violently with each step. They looked more like a troupe of showgirls than palace guards.

"Walk in front and let me do the talking." Selkie whispered to Elize as the line of guards rushed towards them.

"Simeon 347 what is the meaning of this?" Quinn 001 demanded in a highly agitated voice that cracked like a boy going through puberty. "Who is this woman that has caused you to abandon your post?"

Selkie stood up straighter and cleared his throat. "I found this woman wandering near the north wall. She claims that the Princess Sabrina sent for her and insisted I bring her to the Princess at once."

"And you believed her?"

"Well..." Selkie stammered pulling at his collar. "You know how the Princess gets. I didn't want to upset her...if the woman is speaking the truth."

Quinn knew exactly how the Princess got and could hardly blame Simeon 347. Still, he could not allow a stranger to enter the palace even if his sister blew her top.

"I'll take it from here, Quinn." An extremely thin teenaged girl sang, her tiny feet barely touching the steps as she gracefully drifted down the stairway.

"Princess Sabrina!" Quinn 001 jerked forward so quickly his helmet slipped over his eyes. Unable to see, Quinn tripped on the last stair and almost impaled himself with his saber. "You...you're not permitted to be out here!"

"True," Sabrina replied glibly lifting Quinn's helmet and smiling at him sugar sweetly. "Tell you what, let's just pretend I'm not here, shall we?"

"But, but…I must inform the Empress," Quinn protested pushing her hand away.

"Of course. Yes, go run and tell Mother." Sabrina cooed in a bittersweet voice, batting her lidless eyes at him. "I'm sure she'll be happy to hear you've been playing tin soldier again."

"I'm not..." Quinn started to protest, but Sabrina cut him off.

"Hello you!" Sabrina cooed at Elize as she tiptoed away from Quinn. "Ugh! What's that smell?" Sabrina wrinkled her almost nonexistent nose and made a face. "Where have you been swimming?" She asked Selkie playfully.

"You know damn well where I've been." Selkie growled under his breath not happy with the little joke Sabrina had played on him. "I've done what you wanted now…"

"No offense, but you look a mess!" Sabrina chirped at Elize, "and you reek! Come we must get you cleaned up at once."

Quinn wrinkled his nose. Sabrina was right the woman did need to get cleaned up, but when Sabrina took Elize by the hand and started up the steps, Quinn raced up and blocked their path.

"You can't take her inside!" He screeched his face turning an odd shade of yellow. "The law strictly forbids strangers from entering the palace."

"Oh, stop being such a ninny." Sabrina stated flatly pushing her delicate, well-manicured fingers in his hollow chest. "Don't you know who this is? No of course you don't, and I don't have time to explain. Come." She told Elize, ignoring any further protests.

Elize followed the odd girl up the steps, marveling at the crystalline statue looming above her. The statue was so incredibly lifelike Elize couldn't resist reaching out and touching the toe as she passed by.

"Don't!" Sabrina shouted slapping Elize's hand away, but it was too late. Elize had already sensed the being living inside. "Our secret," a feminine voice echoed in her mind. Elize shivered.

"I didn't mean to strike you," Sabrina apologized half-heartedly, "but that statue makes my skin crawl. I swear I can feel her eyes watching me. Sometimes, late at night, I can hear her crying. Payape believes me, but Mother says I'm just imagining it."

Sabrina stopped when they reached the top of the stairway where an intricately carved gate without any handles or locks stood. Sabrina placed her hand inside an almost invisible spiral and whispered a chant. A long seam appeared down the center of the gate and the two halves began to slide outward. Outraged, Quinn ran up and threw his reed-like body hard against the gate. Sabrina hissed and kicked him swiftly in the shin. Quinn raised his saber and snarled at her.

"Enough!" A plump, multi-colored macaw screamed flying over Sabrina's head and landing heavily on top of Quinn's helmet. "Bring her to me at once!" The bird screeched hopping around on top of Quinn's helmet eyeing the saffron pompom with glassy green eyes. The macaw tilted her head side-to-side hopping around Quinn's helmet chirping the message several more times before attacking the pompom with her talons.

Quinn shrieked and flailed his arms about frantically trying to knock the bird off. The startled macaw squawked and started to fly off with the pompom. Unfortunately, the pompom was attached to Quinn's helmet by a strap fastened under his chin. When the bird took flight with the pompom grasped tightly in her talons it lifted Quinn's helmet off his head and caused the strap to strangle him. Quinn's face had turned a horrid shade of purple by the time Simeon 112 rushed to his rescue carefully slicing through the strap with his short sword and allowing the macaw to fly away happily with her prize.

"That's the third one this month!" Quinn complained taking off his helmet and tossing it on the ground. Without his helmet, Quinn's thin head and small darting eyes gave him the appearance of a dazed lizard. Elize thought there was something oddly familiar about him, but before she could figure it out Sabrina pulled her through the gates.

"I remember this place." Elize said staring awestruck at the crystal palace.

"Impressive isn't it." Sabrina quipped. "It's carved out of one, massive piece of Astariunite. Extremely rare. Only found here in this very spot. If you believe that rot. The only piece not carved from Astariunite is the cottage. That was made from wood imported from the islands. If it had been made from Astariunite it wouldn't have burnt." Flicking her forked pink tongue between her thread thin lips she faced Selkie who was still in Simeon 347's body. "You stay here and guard the gate till Quinn 001 returns." Before Selkie could protest, the gates closed in his face.

When Elize was little the palace had seemed so huge. It was still impressive. The cloudy walls and domed ceilings reminded her of the pictures she'd seen of the white marbled Taj Mahal. Sabrina led Elize past tangles of overgrown bushes which had once been part of a finely manicured entrance garden. Leaving the garden, they stepped into a magnificent entrance hall lined from floor to ceiling with finely embroidered tapestries. Each depicted a historical scene from Astaria's past. Quinn marched ahead of them. His tall black boots clicked sharply across the well-polished floor. Leaving the main hall, they entered a circular hall dotted with u-shaped doors which had been carved into the Astariunite walls. Although the walls were almost clear, they were too thick to see in or out of the rooms behind them. Although no one came out to greet them, Elize felt unseen eyes watching as they made their way down the hall, and she was sure she could hear the soft shuffling of feet and hushed murmurs behind them.

Sabrina tapped Elize gently on her elbow and motioned for her to slow down. Unaware that he was no longer being followed, Quinn kept walking. He liked the sound of the steady click his boots made across the tiles. The sound comforted him and gave him the illusion of power. Once Quinn was out of sight, Sabrina tiptoed to one of the doors and rubbed her nails against it. A few seconds later a round window slid open and a wrinkled face with huge blue eyes stared out at them.

"Cynder," Sabrina whispered, "quick let us in!" The blue eyes blinked several times as if Cynder hoped Sabrina would disappear. When she didn't Cynder squeaked nervously.

"Princess, I wasn't expecting you."

"Of course, you weren't!" Sabrina snapped. "Now open the door before Quinn figures out were not behind him anymore."

Cynder's head disappeared and a few seconds later the door rolled open.

"Oh," Cynder, a small, potato shaped woman squeaked when she noticed Sabrina wasn't alone. "Empress Ceen won't be pleased."

"Let me deal with Mother." Sabrina snapped. The woman squeaked again and curled up into a loose ball.

"Ceen's your mother?" Elize exclaimed, wondering why she hadn't guessed it sooner. Sabrina had a fork tongue and Quinn and this potato woman had addressed her as Princess. But how could Ceen and her father have children? They weren't the same species.

"Of course, she is." Sabrina laughed, "and you're the lost Princess Monetelizadora. Who do you think sent Ori to track you down?"

Elize shrugged and wondered how many people Ori had tricked into paying him to find her. Looking at the strange girl with new interest, Elize asked.

"So, are you my half-sister or what?"

"Or what." Sabrina giggled dancing around Elize. "Half-sister or cousin or neither. I don't know. I was hatched. You were born. I was made. You were conceived. Who's to say what are relation is, but half-sister will work for now."

"That's crazy!" Elize stammered watching Sabrina dancing on thin legs around her as she tried to get a grasp on the situation.

"Yes, yes it is," Sabrina laughed, quite pleased at the chaos she was causing, "and you stink! Cynder fetch some hot water and pour a bath for my big sister. And don't you go telling anyone we're here. If you do I'll bite your nose off!" Cynder started to roll into a ball again, but Sabrina stopped her. "None of that! Now scoot!"

"I'll need to find you some new clothes." Sabrina told Elize after Cynder had scampered off. "We'll have to throw these stinky ones in the furnace!"

"I'm keeping my jacket," Elize told Sabrina firmly taking off her robe and looking it over sadly. It was covered with grime and one of the elbows had a large hole in it.

"Why?" Sabrina sniffed disdainfully.

"It was a gift."

Sabrina wrinkled her nose, which was much too small for her face and shrugged. "I guess we could wash it, but I hardly think it will dry before we're found out. But if you insist, we'll see what magic Cynder can do."

"If only the Debvees were here." Elize commented rubbing her hands across the filthy jacket. The words had barely left her mouth when the sound of thousands of tiny bells tingling filled the room. Sabrina watched opened mouthed as Elize's jacket cleaned and mended itself and the fabric changed from brown leather to a soft silvery silk.

"Well, I guess we don't need Cynder's magic after all." Sabrina commented staring at the robe enviously. "That's quite a gift." She said rubbing her fingers over the now mended elbow. "Who gave it to you?"

"RaJa and Koh." Elize replied carefully folding the robe over a chair without further explanation before taking off her shirt and pants and throwing them to Sabrina. "Here you can have these. Their made of the same fabric."

"Oh wow!" Sabrina exclaimed catching the clothes and holding them up in front of her. Sabrina flicked her tongue between her thin pink lips and smiled mischievously at Elize. "I have just the thing! You'll look stunning!"

Cynder returned rolling a large wooden tub filled with warm sudsy water and carrying a thick towel over one slouched shoulder. Sabrina took the towel as she leaned over to whisper in Cynder's pointed ear. Cynder blinked several times, took the shirt and pants from Sabrina, and shuffled off.

"Cynder can do magic with a needle and thread." Sabrina bubbled more to herself than Elize. "I bet she can make two pairs of pants and a gown out of those pants and three, maybe four shirts from the top. Sabrina pulled her shirt off revealing rows of soft, skin-colored scales. What Elize had taken for long black hair turned out to be shiny, pine needle shaped scales which flowed from her head down her neck and blended into the deformed cobra hood cowled around her shoulders.

Elize tried not to stare at Sabrina, who was too busy trying on outfits to notice. Humming merrily, Sabrina ran her hands down her thighs examining herself in a long mirror before shedding her clothes

219

and grabbing something else. Watching Sabrina from the tub, Elize figured Sabrina couldn't be more than fifteen.

"You know, I always wanted a little sister," Elize commented as she washed her skin clean with a wash rag. "When I was little, I used to dream about all the fun adventures we'd have."

Sabrina glanced up from the mirror and gave Elize a strange look. "I never dream." She remarked flatly frowning at Elize. "Your hairs a matted mess?" Sabrina pulled her fingers through Elize's tangled hair. Elize yelped and swatted at her. Sabrina didn't stop until Cynder returned with a long silver gown in one arm and several pieces of shimmering cloth in the other.

"I'll take that." Sabrina squealed grabbing the fabric and slipping on the still damp pants Cynder had just stitched together for her. "You fix Elize's hair," Sabrina ordered snatching the gown out of Cynder's hands and laying it on top of Elize's robe. Cynder blinked at Elize's hair several times before pouring the contents of a tiny jar over Elize's head. Elize felt the liquid moving around her head like hundreds of tiny hands untangling each individual strand. Once Elize's hair was fully untangled, Cynder skillfully pleated it into several thick braids before fastening them all together into one large braid down her back.

"Much better," Sabrina chirped helping Elize out of the tub and waiting for her to dry herself off. "Now put this on," Sabrina said tossing Elize the gown. Elize caught the garment and ran her hands over it. She had never felt anything so soft in all her life. Sliding it over her head, Elize let the gown fall over her shoulders and down her hips. The gown felt like it had been specially made for her. Elize slipped on her robe as she stood in front of the mirror. The robe was a few shades lighter than the dress and matched perfectly.

"How do I look?" She asked spinning in a slow circle to face Sabrina.

"Ya, ya, ya!" Sabrina squealed gleefully clapping her hands. "You look just like her! Mother will be furious."

"Just like who?" Elize asked noticing the mischievous glint in Sabrina's eye and wondering what the skinny teenager was up to.

"Empress Euna, of course."

"Of course." Elize repeated as Sabrina continued dancing manically around the room. "I am her daughter after all."

"I knew it! I knew it! Ori said he could do it!" Sabrina sang loudly. "Ori found you! He did! Didn't he?"

"Yeah," Elize said wondering how Sabrina knew Ori. Surely, they weren't lovers? Not that it mattered, she lied to herself forcing down the green-eyed monster.

"So where is he? Why isn't Ori with you?" Sabrina demanded stopping her dance and thrusting her face into Elize's.

"Honestly, I don't know where Ori is." Elize replied stepping back. "The last time I saw him he was lying face down in the dirt."

"No, no, no!" Sabrina shouted shaking her head violently. "He can't be dead! He's not dead! Is he?"

"No, I don't think so." Elize said reassuringly. "I'm pretty sure he was faking it, but he was severely injured during the attack. Still, he seemed to be getting stronger."

"Attack! What attack? Who attacked him and what took you so long to get here? I was expecting you over two moons ago! What happened?"

"Well, I'm pretty sure things didn't go as Ori planned. I don't think he meant to come out where he did and I'm sure he had nothing to do with me falling from the sky."

"You fell from the sky!" Sabrina exclaimed wrapping her arms around her tubular body and hugging herself tightly. "You're the one the prophecy was about? Are you sure? Did you bring a great change? What was it?"

"That's for me to know and you to find out." Elize said growing tired of the twenty questions.

"You must tell me." Sabrina shouted unused to being refused anything. "You must tell me now! You must! I'm the princess and I demand it!"

"No," Elize said defiantly, "I'm the princess too and I out rank you."

Sabrina's eyes narrowed and the small, deformed hood raised around her neck like a vampire's collar.

"Sabrina!" Quinn's voice erupted from the other side of the door, followed by loud rapping. "Sabrina! Open this door at once!"

"Tell him we're not here," Sabrina whispered urgently to Cynder, but Cynder shook her head and disappeared leaving her sewing needle dangling from the thread still attached to Sabrina's pants leg. Sabrina made a frowny face and tucked the needle into the seam.

"Sabrina! I know you are in there! Open this door or I'll knock it down!"

"Don't hurt yourself Quinn," Sabrina sneered unlatching the door and rolling it aside.

Quinn, wearing a new helmet, glared at her from the hallway.

"Sabrina," he growled.

"Princess Sabrina," Sabrina corrected him curtly.

"Princess Sabrina, the Emperor and Empress demand you bring your guest to the throne room immediately."

"You mean her?" Sabrina asked jumping sideways to reveal Elize. Quinn looked at Elize and bit his lip so hard it bled.

"Oh, geez take this," Elize said handing him the damp wash rag. Quinn dabbed his lip unable to take his eyes off Elize.

"She...she's," Quinn stammered.

"The lost Princess Monetelizadora." Sabrina sang dancing merrily into the hallway which was now lined with nosy servants hoping to catch a glimpse of the outsider. "Cynder!" Sabrina cursed under her breath. She should have known the little rolly-poley wouldn't be able to keep her mouth shut.

When Elize saw all the faces gawking at her she hesitated. The memory of being a scared toddler walking beside her mother with hundreds of eyes staring at her flashed across her mind. Shaking the feeling off, Elize squared her shoulders and followed Quinn down the long hallway. By now the Astarian families living in the palace had joined the servants staring at Elize with excited eyes and gapping mouths. As she passed them, Elize couldn't help noticing their clothes. Something was wrong with them. The lacy bodice of one belonged with the skirt of another and the sleeves on that jacket didn't go with the rest of it. It was clear that the original pieces of clothing had been taken apart to create new ones, not always for the better. Elize also noticed that the bottom of some of the tapestry had been cut leaving tattered edges and although the floors were freshly waxed there were spiderwebs in the corners.

Elize noticed the same pair of gray eyes following her from different faces as they moved down the hall. Sometimes the eyes shone out of a woman, a moment later a freckled boy, then a man with a curly mustache, or a young girl with long lashes.

"How does he do that?" Elize whispered to Sabrina motioning towards the girl with long lashes.

"That's what Selkies do silly," Sabrina whispered back.

"Shush!" Quinn warned as they stepped into the main hall. His boots clicked loudly down the tiled floor decorated with detailed mosaics of creatures big and small. More guards joined them, appearing out hidden doorways. They walked ahead of Quinn in pairs towards the twelve-foot high, pearly white doors at the end of the hall. The procession stopped in front of the doors and parted so Quinn could lead Sabrina and Elize inside. Elize felt like a bride walking down the aisle with no one to give her away. As she entered the room her palm began to itch like crazy.

"Stay behind me." Sabrina whispered nervously as they stepped into the throne room. The throne room was the largest room in the palace. Elize marveled at the domed ceiling carved from a bubble of Astariunite the size of three city blocks and supported by seven highly polished smoke gray pillars speckled with flecks of silver, rust, and copper. The pillars had been chiseled from the meteorite known as the Grandfather. The sunlight shone through the clear domed ceiling and reflected off the pillars to form a multicolored prism upon the smooth tiled floor. The effect was quite spectacular.

Closing the fingers of her right hand tightly over her palm, Elize silently counted her steps and tried to remain calm as she approached the raised platform in the center of the room upon which a magnificent throne of deep red garnet had been placed.

"Princess Sabrina!" A horrifyingly, beautiful woman hissed. Empress Ceen's long, black gown rustled as she gracefully slithered across the raised platform to her throne.

"Mothe…I mean Empress," Sabrina snipped smugly.

"Explain yourself, Princess!" The man being wheeled onto the platform in a grandiose, ruby studded throne demanded. His icy tone instantly wiped the grin off the teens face. Sabrina was so shocked to see the man in the Emperor's wheeled throne that she froze in midstride. Realizing Sabrina wasn't moving, Elize stepped around her. Empress Ceen gasped and collapsed into her throne. Seeing her mother's reaction, Sabrina unfroze and began dancing around Elize.

"It's her! It's her!" Sabrina squealed, clapping her hands gleefully. "I found her! I found her!"

"Who exactly did you find?" The man asked, his eyes locked upon Elize. Not that he really needed an explanation. He already knew who the stunning woman in the silver gown was. Elize was the spitting image of her mother.

"The Princess Monetelizadora." Quinn announced clicking his heels together sharply.

Elize looked at the man on the throne and instantly knew it was not her father. Standing with her head up high, Elize looked the man straight in the eyes and without flinching asked.

"And who, pray tell are you?"

Sabrina stopped dancing and looked at Elize with shock. No one dared talk to the Emperor's regent like that. Not if they wanted to live. Sabrina had no way of knowing that Elize had already met Regent Behr in the Forest of Milendor and wasn't the least bit scared of him.

"The Princess Monetelizadora died many years ago." Empress Ceen stated, trying to regain her composure.

"I think we both know that isn't true." Elize replied icily. Elize had few memories of her mother before coming to Earth, but when she saw the Cobrateen sitting in her mother's garnet throne, the memory of her mother and father sitting side by side on their thrones came back as if it were yesterday.

"Get off my mother's throne!" Elize screamed and rushed passed Quinn. Quinn tackled Elize before she could reach the platform.

"Take the imposter to the pink room." Empress Ceen spat. Her hood raised threateningly above her head as she glided down the back of the platform and out a hidden door at the back of the throne room.

"Where is the real Emperor!" Elize screamed, still trying to charge the throne. "I demand to see my father."

"You're in no position to demand anything!" Regent Behr sneered and waved at the guards to take Elize away.

"I am Princess Monetelizadora, daughter of Emperor Tazadorin and Empress Euna of Palenina."

"No, you are an imposter," Behr replied sounding bored, but Elize could feel him shaking in his boots.

"I'm not the imposter," Elize shouted in defiance as several guards grabbed her arms. "You are you bastard! And you know it!"

"You insolent bitch!" Behr swore slamming his fist down on the arm of the ruby throne. "Get her out of my sight!"

Elize heard Sabrina whimpering behind her as the guards dragged her out of the throne room.

"I'm sorry, I'm sorry." Sabrina sobbed as the doors slammed shut behind Elize.

The guards carried Elize up a long flight of spiral steps. She had been expecting to be taken down into a damp dungeon, but it appeared she was going to be locked in a tower, like Anne Boleyn in the Tower of London. Great, she thought miserably as the guards continued up the curving steps. To her surprise the guards stopped about halfway up and deposited Elize inside a small room, slamming the door behind her.

Elize gasped in horror. The room was entirely pink. It would have been horrible enough if everything in the room were the same shade of pink but that wasn't the case. Each wall was a different color pink, cotton candy, bubblegum, pink lemonade, and salmon. The smooth stone floor was a wild rose pink streaked with fuchsia. There was a strawberry ice cream chair in one corner and an electric pink bed so bright it hurt Elize's eyes. Elize felt like she was going to puke.

Elize plopped down on the bed and almost broke her tail bone. The bed wasn't only hard as a rock, it was a rock. Complete with two cherry blossom pink stone pillows. Overcome by immense homesickness and the deep disappointment of not finding her father sitting on his throne, Elize threw herself on the stone bed and sobbed.

CHAPTER 19

Mia had been scouting the caves when she stumbled onto Rixley. Before heading back to the others, Mia had Rixley show her the pipe she had come through. Mia was hoping the pipe would provide a quick way into the palace, but there was no way Gerawld or Alzo would be able to squeeze through it. When Mia finished examining the pipe, she began to retrace her tracks back to the others. Rixley watched with fascination as Mia picked up a single cat hair or paused to examine a faint nail scratch before she moved forward. Seeing the young ferret's interest, Mia took time to explain her methods to Rixley.

Rixley was determined for Mia to see her as a fellow warrior. So, when Gerawld jumped out at them, instead of jumping and hiding behind Mia, Rixley bravely stood by Mia's side clutching her pointy stick so tight it was a miracle it didn't snap in two.

When they reached the throng of Followers of the Change, Mia took Rixley's paw and guided her through. Alzo and Ilee were sitting in a corner having what look like a heated conversation. Mia waited for the snippy Ilee to storm off before approaching Alzo and whispering in his ear. Alzo looked over at Rixley and smiled. Rixley gulped and tried to smile back at the giant man.

"Rixley brave and strong." She mumbled trying not to tremble.

"Pleased to meet you, Rixley Brave and Strong." Alzo boomed holding his hand out. "Mia says you have news about my sister Elize. I am anxious to know if she is all right."

Rixley blinked her beady black eyes. "I don't know if Elize is alright?" She moaned. "Rixley lost Elize."

Seeing Rixley's distress. Alzo picked up the shivering ferret and placed her gently on his knee. "It's okay." He assured her. "Why don't you tell me how you and Elize met. Can you do that?"

Rixley nodded. She already liked Elize's large brother, but the strange faces watching her made Rixley feel extremely anxious.

"Stay strong," Mia said placing a paw on Rixley's shoulder. Rixley gulped back her fears and in a meek voice began telling Alzo how she found Elize on the steps of the salt temple and how Elize agreed to be her friend and help her find her mama.

"Rixley and Elize are friends. Friends take care of each other." Rixley told Alzo starting to feel more confident. By the time Rixley got to the point in the story when they found Ori in the rocks, she had jumped off Alzo's lap and was in full performance mode.

"Why do you call him Foxhead Ori?" Taa interrupted. Taa had arrived just before Alzo had caved in the mine entrance and had been busy attending to the injured when Mia brought Rixley to Alzo.

"Rixley call Ori foxhead because that's what he is." Rixley replied grumpily. She didn't like being interrupted.

"But why?" Taa insisted feeling there must be a reason for Rixley calling him such a strange name.

"Bad water lady hexed Ori," Rixley told Taa acting out the bit where she found Ori stuck in the rocks just before they were attacked by the bad water lady and the one-eared cat. Rixley was so engrossed in her story she did not notice Mia and Gerawld's reaction when she mentioned the one-eared cat. Rixley concluded her tail in the pipe where she sadly admitted losing Elize when she had run off with Baba in the hope of finding her mama.

"Now Rixley lose Mama and my friend, Elize." Rixley sniffed and buried her head in the crook of Alzo's elbow. Alzo gently patted her head while Mia and Gerawld argued. Gerawld wanted to go after Tux, but Mia disagreed.

"Mia's right old man," Alzo interrupted. "It'll do you no good to go after this Tux. Besides I need you with me. Mia, you go with Rixley back in the pipe and see if you can find where Elize ended up. She can't have just disappeared. If the blue dwarf could fit in it, you should be able too. I think Knot and his brownies have managed to get the blue dwarf out. If you do find Elize send word back, but don't leave her."

"I'm going too." Taa said with determination. Alzo started to protest, but Taa continued before he could. "There's a good chance Ori will die an extremely painful and agonizing death if he isn't unhexed. It may be too late already, but I feel it my duty to try."

"Rixley take Mia to find Elize." Rixley said, flipping out of Alzo's arms and landing on her hind legs in front of Mia and Taa.

"Taa will come with us." Mia told Rixley. "With two warriors at Taa's side the healer has nothing to fear."

"Rixley fear deer's butt too big." Rixley said looking at Taa's rear and frowning.

"I can help with that," Knot piped holding up a small brown sack. "I don't have enough for Alzo's big butt, but I think I have enough to get the deer's butt through." With that problem solved Mia and Rixley led the way back to the pipe.

"Don't dally," Knot warned as he sprinkled his magic dust and spoke a simple expanding spell to stretch the pipe wide enough for Taa to fit through. "The spell won't last long."

After pushing and pulling Taa past a couple tight spots, the trio found Baba's hideout. Baba wasn't there, but it was clear Baba had made a quick escape taking what little he had and fleeing. From Baba's hideout Rixley led them to the spot where she lost Elize's scent. Rixley and Taa waited while Mia scouted the other two pipes. After what felt like an awfully long time, Rixley and Taa were starting to grow anxious. Finally, a familiar pair of yellow-green eyes appeared in the pipe to their left.

"I found this," Mia said keeping her voice low. She handed Rixley a long, wavy strand of hair. Taa agreed the hair had come from Elize's head. With Mia in the lead the trio scurried down the pipe. When the pipe ended abruptly at the edge of a deep pool of water, Mia showed Rixley the almost invisible marks in the soft mud. Rixley stood next to Mia and looked at the water. She looked at the partial footprint Elize left by the water's edge, but she didn't see any footprints going back out of the water.

"Elize went this way," Rixley exclaimed, gripping her pointy stick in one paw and diving into the water. Using her hind legs to propel her down to the bottom of the pool it wasn't long before Rixley discovered a way through.

"Rixley find way." Rixley yelled as soon as her masked face broke the surface of the water. "Mia and Taa follow Rixley. Rixley show way."

Taa stood at the edge of the water and shook her head. "I can't bear to have my head under water." She admitted her brown eyes reflecting the terror she felt.

Mia wasn't thrilled about swimming under water either. Although Mia was a strong swimmer it wasn't something she liked doing. Not sure what was wrong, Rixley got out and shook. When Taa and Mia told her what was going on, Rixley looked at them with scorn.

"Isn't there another way?" Taa asked trembling. Taa wasn't afraid of water. She had no problem traveling over it in a canoe and she had no problem wading through a stream, it was full immersion that terrified her.

"No," Rixley replied firmly glancing over at Mia.

"Can't we go back the way you came in through the tavern." Mia asked dipping her toe in the water.

"Mia and Taa can search for other way," Rixley spat angrily shaking her little head at them. "Rixley go this way. Elize is Rixley's friend. Rixley go help Elize."

After tying her blue neli stone to the end of Rixley stick, Mia and Taa followed Rixley into the pool. Using the light as a guide Mia held Taa's arm and dove into the underground tunnel. The tunnel was even longer than Taa had feared and about halfway through she was overcome with panic and froze. Mia wrapped her arms around the panic stricken deer and kicked her hindlegs hard propelling her sleek body through the tunnel with Taa in tow.

Rixley had found the tunnel Selkie should have taken which came out at the bottom of a well a few feet in front of the palace dungeons.

"Now what?" Taa asked as they stepped out onto a pile of broken bones which looked like they'd been there a very long time. Rixley pointed upwards and scurried the well wall using her sharp claws to seek out nooks and crannies invisible to the naked eye. Mia followed and together they pulled Taa up using a wooden bucket and rope they found on the ground next to the well.

Once out of the well Mia, Rixley and Taa stood in the pitch dark. None of them had ever been inside the palace before and therefore they had no idea which way to go. They were busy discussing their next move when Taa's sharp ears picked up the sound of boots approaching.

"Are you sure he's still alive?" A guard's voice broke through the darkness a second before the glow of a neli lantern appeared. The taller guard gave the bundle he was hauling a rough shake. The bundle moaned weakly.

"Ori Foxhead." Rixley whispered excitedly before Mia could get her paw over Rixley's mouth.

"What was that?" The first guard snapped shining his lantern towards the well. Mia tossed a pebble into the darkness behind her.

"Rats," the tall guard grumbled, "I hate rats. The sooner we get out of here the better."

"Let's lock him in with the old guys." The first guard suggested not wanting to go any further into the dungeons then necessary.

"I heard one of the old guys was a Mage. Aren't they supposed to be magical? I wonder why he hasn't escaped. I mean if I had the spells I wouldn't stay in that damn dungeon would you?"

"Nah, but I saw them when they were brought in. They're both old as shat and crazy as bats."

* * * * * * * *

Behr was sitting alone in his rooms in the north tower. He had just lifted the pewter stein filled with a thick amber mead to his lips when Simeon 12 burst into the room.

"Sir," Simeon 12 called out from the doorway. "Sir?"

"What?" Behr demanded annoyed that Simeon 12 had dared to disturb him.

"It's the Vanji, sir."

"What about him?"

"He's been captured, sir."

"Really?"

"Yes, sir. They've taken him to the dungeons."

"It's about time." Behr grumbled emptying his stein in one gulp. Even this news failed to sweeten his foul mood. "Let the Vanji stew for a while and whatever you do, don't tell anyone he's here! Especially not the princess! Understood?"

"Yes, sir." Simeon 12 replied and rushed down the steps three at a time. He needed to tell the other Simeons about Behr's order before word of Ori's capture got out. He feared he might already be too late.

Once Simeon 12 was gone, Behr poured himself another stein of mead and sunk back into his chair. He was still getting over the shock of seeing Elize step out from behind Sabrina. It was hard to believe that this was the same woman he'd seen in a dirty healer's cloak in the Forest of Milendor.

Elize's resemblance to her mother, the Empress Euna, had taken his breath away. After all these years, the image of Euna still made his knees buckle. But unlike Empress Ceen, Behr had held his composure even though it took all his strength to do so.

Scythe had ordered Behr to keep Elize at the palace until he arrived. Behr shuddered at the thought of seeing the demon again. He was not looking forward to Scythe's arrival. He loathed the demon, but he wasn't foolish enough to cross him. He had seen firsthand what Scythe did to those who crossed him. He just wished Elize didn't look so much like her mother. It would be easier to turn Elize over to the demon if she didn't look so much like Euna. He decided he would leave her in the Pink room until Scythe arrived.

Elize had other plans. Elize sobbed until her eyes were dry and then she got off the stone bed determined to find a way out of the dreadful pink room. Unfortunately, the door had melted into the pink once it was shut, and the room didn't have any windows. Elize ran her hands along the walls until her fingertips were raw, but so far, she had not found the door. Giving up, she sat cross legged on the rock bed and closed her eyes blocking out the horrendous pink. Taking several deep breaths, Elize tried to clear her mind. It took several tries, but she was finally able to focus on her breath. With each exhale Elize felt her anxiety drop. After several minutes, voices seeped into her subconscious mind.

"You know the rules." Koh chided RaJa from beyond the mist. "We aren't allowed to interfere. We did our best to teach her to fish..."

"Elize doesn't need a fish." RaJa trumpeted loudly. "Elize needs to get out of that room."

"We can't get her out of the room," Koh said thoughtfully, "but perhaps we could do something about the color."

Elize felt something drop into her hand and opened one eye to peek. Several colored beads were nestled in the palm of her hand.

"Throw them at the wall." RaJa's voice whispered in her head.

"Thanks guys," Elize said and flicked a little blue bead at the wall. The bead burst upon contact and left a navy-blue blotch that bled into the pink forming a lovely tied-dyed circle. Elize dropped the yellow bead on the bed. A tangerine flower with a bright yellow center appeared. Elize continued tossing beads until she hit the spot where the door was. Dark purple seeped into the gap between the door and wall giving it definition. Smiling Elize jumped off the bed and gave the door a push. It didn't budge. She was looking around for something to force the door open when she heard a voice singing in her head.

"Little bird." The voice sang so softly that Elize thought she might have imagined it. "Little bird," the voice sang again. "Little bird, little bird what have you done? You made many colors where there was once only one."

"Payape?" Elize exclaimed aloud. The singing stopped. Elize closed her eyes and sang the words to herself. "Payape, Payape, pink is not for me. Your little bird, your little bird is happier sitting in a flowering tree. Where are you my dear Payape?"

"Day and Night. Night and day. I wait in the room where my children once played."

"Payape, Payape," Elize sang back letting the words dance around in her head, "do you, don't you, won't you play with me."

Their song was interrupted by a muffled shout outside the door followed by a loud thump. A moment later the door was flung open and Selkie appeared in the doorway wearing Simeon 204's body.

"Give me my skin." Selkie growled leaping at Elize.

"What?" Elize gasped shoving him out of the way and slipping out into the stairway.

"My skin." Selkie rushed after her. "Give it back."

"Your skin?" Elize frowned looking down at the gown Sabrina had lent her. Why hadn't she figured it out before, Selkie wasn't his name. It was his species. Selkie was a Selkie. A mythical seal-like creature that can climb out of their seal skin and take on the form of a human. Sabrina must have found his skin and had been using it to control him. Elize ran her hand across the gown and smiled. "You have to do what I say don't you?"

Selkie growled and leapt at her again.

"Ack, ack." Elize said slapping his hand away. "First I need you to take me to my father."

"Fine," Selkie sulked, "who is he and where can I find him?"

"He's in the cottage in the garden by the fountain."

"That burned out heap! No way?"

"Yes way." Elize told him firmly wrapping her robe tightly around the gown and folding her arms in front of her chest. "Take me there."

"Give me my skin first."

"Not going to happen. Take me to the cottage. If my father's there, I'll give you your skin."

"Fine." Selkie barked stomping down the steps.

* * * * * * * *

Once the two guards carrying Ori had left, Mia decided to send Rixley in to check how many guards were left inside guarding the prisoners. Rixley took the job very seriously believing Mia had chosen her to test her bravery. Mia didn't have the heart to tell Rixley it was because she was the most rat-like and had the best chance getting in and out without being noticed.

Rixley dropped to all fours and keeping close to where the floor and wall met crept into the dungeons. As Rixley moved further along the damp floor she was surprised not to find anyone guarding the dungeons. Sensing movement in one of the cells, Rixley crept up and stuck her face through the bars.

"Oh, Blatz ghost!" Mal shouted stumbling back and tripping over Grumbul's foot.

"Rixley!" Grumbul exclaimed recognizing her masked face. Rixley easily slipped through the bars and rushed over to hug the old man.

"Rixley?" Mal sputtered getting to his feet and brushing the dust off his clothes. "Why is Ori's head like that? Didn't he drink the potion?"

"Foxhead drink orange stuff, but Ori not himself."

"Where's Elize?" Mal asked looking behind Rixley hoping to see her. "Isn't she here?"

"No, Elize not here. Rixley lost Elize. Rixley bring new friends to find Elize."

"New friends," Mal huffed turning his attention back to Ori. "Well, I hope ones a healer."

"I am," Taa said stepping into view. Mal looked up at the deerling and nodded.

"Good job Rixley." He said patting Rixley roughly on the head.

"Why aren't there any guards?" Mia asked Mal who had walked over to the door and was busy studying the lock.

"I guess the idiots don't think two old men and a dying fox are worth worrying about." Mal scoffed spitting into the lock. Smoke began to pour out of the lock, followed by the sound of gears grinding and finally the click of the hasp opening. Taa pushed through the door and rushed over to Ori.

"How long has he been like this?" Taa demanded as she lifted one of Ori's eye lids and peered into his bloodshot eye. Rixley put a paw to her chin and tried to think.

"Rixley and Elize give Ori orange stuff when we climbed out of mountain."

"That was two days ago," Mal mumbled and rubbed his chin, "but I don't understand what went wrong. The potion should have reversed the hex she used on him."

"The hex who put on him?" Taa asked pulling a long tube out of her pocket and pressing the flared end against Ori's chest.

"Aturi," Grumbul answered, "she attacked Ori outside the Elderwyld."

"And you have no idea what she hexed him with?" Taa asked lifting Ori's hand and folding each finger one at a time. Mal shook his head. "What did you give him to counteract the hex?"

"A standard reversal potion," Mal said pulling at his beard nervously, "with an antibiotic to help fight the infection."

"I see," Taa said forcing Ori's mouth open and looking inside. "It looks like instead of reversing the hex, the potion caused it to mutate. The mutation is causing Ori's two bodies to fight for dominance causing poor Ori to be stuck between his human and fox form. Unless we find a way to stabilize him, the two bodies will continue to try to dominate one another."

"And if we don't?" Grumbul asked softly.

"If we are unable to find a way to stabilize Ori fast, I doubt if he'll survive much longer. If his heart shifts back to a fox and his body stays human...well...his heart won't be able to support the larger body and if his body reverts to a fox and his heart stays human it will beat too fast for his smaller form."

"What can we do?" Mal asked. Taking the tube from Taa, Mal pressed down hard on Ori's chest. Ori growled and snapped. "Urrr...sorry old man." Mal apologized and released the pressure a tad. He could hear Ori's heart beating, but damn if he could tell if he was listening to a human or fox heart.

Taa scratched her head. "I'm not sure. I'll mix up something that will knock him out until I can shift through the ancient knowledge Nekita gave me and hopefully find a potion to stabilize him, but until we figure out what hex Aturi used, I won't be able to unhex him."

Mia tilted her head and motioned for silence. "I hear someone." She mouthed inching out of the cell and flattening her back against the stone wall. Rixley skittered out next her.

"Go with them." Mal whispered into Grumbul's ear. "You know the grounds. If Elize is here, she'll try to find her father. I'll stay here with the healer." Grumbul nodded and slipped out of the cell. Mia and Rixley were already halfway to the well. They barely had time to hide before a thin, cloaked figure drifted past. Lucky for them, Sabrina was too busy glancing over her shoulder to notice them.

* * * * * * * *

"I remember this place," Elize whispered stepping into what had once been a lush garden. Elize walked over to the figures of two children draped with thick vines. "I remember playing in this fountain with Alzo."

"Touching." Selkie remarked sarcastically thrusting out his hand and wiggling his webbed fingers in Elize's face. "I've kept my part of the bargain, now give me my skin."

"Back off." Elize told him firmly. "You don't get your skin until I find my father."

"Aw come on! You know he's inside." Selkie whined waving his hand at the cottage.

"I'll give you your skin once we get inside." Elize insisted and started for the door.

"That wasn't part of the deal!" Selkie barked.

"It is now." Elize said over her shoulder. "Now stop complaining and help me."

"Go away!" A voice shouted from inside the charred remains of the cottage.

Elize stopped so suddenly Selkie fell into her. Gathering her wits, Elize cautiously approached the cottage. She was sure the voice had come from inside, but the cottage was in such bad condition it was a wonder the building was still standing at all. As they crept closer, Elize thought she saw a face peering out at them from behind the dust coated glass.

"Go away!" The voice bellowed mournfully.

"Help me get the door open." Elize whispered to Selkie. Elize and Selkie pushed at the door until it finally gave way.

"Go away you blasted ghost!" The voice screamed. "Stop tormenting me!"

Elize tiptoed across the threshold and pulled back the edge of a moldy burgundy and gold drape to let in the light. Gold flecks of dust danced in the sunlight as Elize cautiously stepped off the tiled floor and onto an exquisitely woven carpet. The inside of the cottage was in much better shape than the outside. Elize cautiously moved into the main room. The walls were covered with chalk drawings. Elize stopped to examine the cartoonish drawings of large dragonfly flying machines, funny caterpillar trains, and automobiles resembling giant bugs. Scattered about the room she noticed large dioramas made from intricately cut paper. Elize picked up one of the smaller dioramas depicting a house that looked very much like her house on Earth, complete with a miniature bulldog and a skinny cat sleeping on the front porch.

"Euna?" The withered voice whispered from behind a huge stack of colored paper. A frail man in an oversized, ornate burgundy and gold wheeled chair stared at Elize with sunken blue eyes whose color had long ago run out of them. "Euna! You've come back...after so long..."

Elize moved closer careful not to disturb the leaning tower of paper. "Payape?" she asked softly hardly able to speak. "Payape it's me Elize. Eliza Dora, your little bird."

"Little bird," the Emperor repeated staring at her. "No, no it's not so!" He sputtered, the muscles in his face twitching. His eyes flashed first with hurt, then anger, and finally confusion. "My little bird is just a wee girl," he whispered more to himself than to her.

"I grew up and flew back to you," Elize assured him. Giving him a small smile, she reached out to touch his hands. The Emperor yanked his hands back.

"No!" He shouted. "No, it can't be! Where is my Euna?" He looked up at Elize again and his face soften, "Euna," he cooed reaching out for Elize's hands. "You've come back."

"He's quite mad isn't he." Selkie stated from the doorway.

The Emperor's face changed again. "Who are you?" He asked Elize again rubbing the top of her hands.

"I'm Eliza Dora." She told him.

"Impossible," he mumbled running his rough fingers across a lock of her hair which had come loose. "Princess Monetelizadora is a little girl. You are not a little girl."

"I grew up."

"With the crows," he muttered pointing to a paper building that looked amazingly like the Catholic school Elize's stepfather Patrick had sent her to when she was a girl. She had lived with the nuns until she graduated from high school but didn't return home until after Patrick had died.

"Yes, well sort of, but they weren't crows. They were Sisters." Elize explained trying not to laugh. She hadn't thought of Sister Mary Agnes and Sister Marie De Joseph for years. How they would have fussed at being called crows.

"The sister crows taught my little bird to fly." The Emperor sang smiling widely.

"Yes, and now your little bird has flown back home to you."

"Little bird flew home," he sang flapping his bony arms in the air. Selkie sniffed the air behind him. "I smell ferret."

"Ferret?" Elize mumbled as Rixley's masked face appeared in the doorway.

"Elize?" Rixley squeaked excitedly, dashing across the floor and flying into Elize's arms.

"God, I'm glad to see you," Elize exclaimed snuggling Rixley close.

"Rixley not God," Rixley mumbled nuzzling Elize's chin with her cold wet nose. Elize laughed and rubbed Rixley's little head.

"Where's Rixley?" Mia whispered when Grumbul joined her at the edge of the garden. She wrinkled her nose at the smell of burnt, rotting thatch. "What is this place?" The old man brushed back a strand of white hair and cleared his throat.

"This was Empress Euna's garden. Empress Euna was Elize's mother."

"What happened to it?" Mia asked as she carefully stepped across the face of a baby rabbit that peered at her from a broken tile which had once been part of the garden path.

"The cottage was set on fire the night Empress Euna fled with Alzo and Elize. When Emperor Taz saw the flames, he leapt from his chair to rescue his family. It took five guards to hold him back from what would have been a suicide mission. We were sure no one could have survived the fire, but after the fire was extinguished, and the ashes sifted no bones or other bits were found. Everyone except my son was convinced Empress Euna and their two children had been killed. Emperor Taz became obsessed. He was sure his wife and children had escaped and were still alive. He launched a massive search, but as the months wore on into years, even he had to admit the search was futile and with a heavy heart he called it off. It was a time of great sadness."

"I hear Rixley. She's inside," Mia said cutting the old man off before he could drift too far into his memories.

"What's wrong with his face!" Sabrina screeched so loud, Mia and Grumbul heard it in the garden and dove for cover.

"He's been hexed." Mal said stepping out of the way so she could get a better look at him. Like her mother, Sabrina was well trained in the healing arts. Perhaps she knew something that could help Ori.

"Hexed!" Sabrina exclaimed looking scornfully at the fox head on top of Ori's human body. "He looks hideous!" She hissed. "Fix him now!"

"Can't," Mal replied without emotion.

"Can't!" Sabrina screamed in a glass shattering shrill, "Can't? Why can't you!"

"There's a hex on him," Mal explained crossly.

"Well, unhex him!" Sabrina spat in the old Mage's face.

"Can't" Mal repeated defiantly.

"Stop saying that!" Sabrina screeched. The deformed cobra hood flared up around her shoulders like a coat collar caught in a stiff wind.

"Mal's correct," Taa said handing Sabrina the tube so the girl could take a listen to Ori's heart. "Until we can determine what hex the water maiden used, the best we can do is put him in a coma and hope he can hold out until we find a spell to unhex him."

"Are you sure there's a spell?" Sabrina asked leaning down to listen to Ori's heart.

"If we can identify the hex, I'm quite confident we will find a spell to counteract it," Taa explained calmly. "Right now, I require more information on hexes, ancient hexes, most likely forbidden ones."

"I may be able to help you." Sabrina told Taa keeping her voice low so the others couldn't listen in. "I know where there are all sorts of dusty books and parchments. If you want I can take you there."

Empress Ceen was in her chambers when she heard Sabrina's screech. Used to her daughter's melodramatic mood swings she paid it little mind. She had more urgent matters to take care of. Pouring the milky liquid into the onyx bowl, the Cobrateen stared deeply into the bowl waiting for the surface to become clear.

"No!" Empress Ceen screamed smacking the bowl with the back of her hand and sending it flying across the room. The Empresses scream echoed off the palace walls ringing out into the night with such clarity that Mia and Grumbul, who had just come back out after Sabrina's scream, ran for cover again.

"What's wrong?" Behr slurred stumbling into Ceen's chambers unannounced.

"That stupid girl!" Ceen screamed in Behr's face stabbing her nail at a sliver of broken bowl. Behr closed one eye and half-attempted to make out the image dancing across the shard.

"You're going to have to tell me what it is, my dear Empress." Behr slurred. "I'm afraid I left my glasses in the tower." Ceen rolled her lidless eyes at him.

"It's the demon Scythe!" She fumed. "The stupid nit let him follow her here!"

"Well, she didn't exactly let..."

Ignoring the drunken Behr, Empress Ceen stormed out of her chambers and rushed down the steps. She didn't have time for his nonsense. She had to get Emperor Taz to safety before the damned demon arrived.

CHAPTER 20

Elize roamed around the cottage studying the numerous dioramas piled up all around the room. Each diorama was unique and had been created with meticulous care. Elize picked up a diorama which looked a lot like the house she had lived in as a girl with her Stepfather Patrick and his five sons.

"This is incredible!" Elize exclaimed holding the box to the light to get a better look. Elize felt a shiver run down her spine when she noticed the paper image of her mother lying in a bed covered with stiff white sheets,.

"You could see me, couldn't you?" She asked the Emperor who was sitting in his burgundy chair watching her carefully.

Elize hadn't thought about the night her Stepfather and Paddy, his oldest son, came upon Elize and her mother for a very long time, but as she looked in the box the image of her mother lying amongst the mud and rocks with her head busted open was as clear as the night it happened. Paddy told her later that he had seen a strange light flickering in the dark and he and his father had gone out to investigate. They never imagined they would find a young girl holding her mother's head together. Elize's mother had smashed her head against a large rock when the mud slide carried them down the mountain. Elize could still feel the blood gushing through her tiny fingers all these years later. If Patrick hadn't found them, her mother would have died that night. Euna said Patrick finding them was a blessing, but Elize never saw it that way.

Patrick was extremely strict and would lock Elize in the dirt cellar under the house if she didn't do as she was told. Elize had been terrified the first time Patrick threw her in the cellar. She remembered screaming for her father, and in the darkness she heard him singing. Of course, when Elize told her mother about it, her mother had insisted it was all in Elize's head. From then on Elize kept her conversations with Payape secret. The secret talks with her father helped Elize make it through some rough times. Now as she walked about the room looking at the dioramas, Elize smiled. Her Payape had really been talking to her.

"I told them you were alive." Emperor Taz warbled rubbing his hands together nervously. "No one would listen to me, but I told them. I told them."

"And you were right." Elize said, reaching down to pat his hands tenderly. "What's this?" She pointed at a bizarre looking diorama.

Emperor Taz leaned forward and studied the scene carefully. "I don't know." He finally admitted. "Don't you?"

"No," Elize shook her head. "It kind of looks like the Statue of Liberty, but I've never been to New York City. Maybe Alzo knows what it is."

"My son's name is Alzo." Emperor Taz mumbled, his eyes glazing over as he stared dreamily at nothing, "such a brave boy. He'll make a fine Emperor." Elize wished Alzo was there to hear Payape. Alzo was so sure their father had forgotten him. This was proof that he hadn't.

"I always wondered what the black boxes were." Taz twittered pulling out a small pair of scissors and skillfully clipping a cell phone sized rectangle. Elize watched in silence as Emperor Taz chalked in the screen and keyboard. "I think they must be some kind of mind control box."

"It's called a cell phone." Elize told him taking the paper phone from him and holding it up to her cheek. "You can talk to other people on it."

"We don't have any cell phones on Toboria." Emperor Taz sighed. "Unless...you brought one with you." He looked at Elize hopefully.

"No, my phone was dead, so I left it in the car." Elize replied handing him back the paper phone.

"Pity," Taz said pushing at the chalk keys with his fingers. "I would have liked to play with it. I'm sorry it died."

Elize was trying to explain that her phone wasn't actually dead, when Grumbul slipped into the cottage looking spooked. The sound of Empress Ceen's long skirt scraping against the garden path had alerted Mia and Grumbul in time to warn Elize. While Grumbul ran inside, Mia stayed in the shadows outside the door, her body camouflaged by the charred stone.

"Grumbul! Elize exclaimed, relieved to see her grandfather alive and well. "Is Mal with you?"

"No," Grumbul whispered, "Mal stayed in the dungeon with Taa and Sabrina. They're trying to figure out a way to unhex Ori."

Grumbul had no way of knowing that Mal had shifted back into his mule body and as he spoke Mal was making his way out of the dungeons with Ori tied securely to his back.

"We'll walk with you as far as the cottage," Sabrina told Mal checking to make sure the rope was holding Ori in place, "but we won't go in."

"Don't dilly dally," Mal huffed still not pleased with the plan. "The less time you spend in that forsaken place the better!"

"Agreed!" Sabrina whispered kissing the old mage between the ears. Even though he was a grumpy old ass, Sabrina had always had a soft spot for Mal which was one of many reasons why he had evaded capture for so many years.

"Where are you taking me?" Taa asked warily after they had left Mal and Ori outside the cottage. Mal's warning had put her on edge, and she still had no idea where Sabrina was taking her or what to expect.

"It's a secret place," Sabrina replied. As they neared the dark mountainside looming directly behind the palace Sabrina took Taa's hand. It was trembling.

"What kind of a secret place?" Taa asked as they slipped through a hidden entrance and into a cobwebbed filled room littered with rusty equipment and flat tables with thick leather straps dangling from the sides.

"I don't know." Sabrina replied keeping her voice as soft as possible. "A healing center or surgery of some sort."

"This was never a place of healing," Taa stated as she hurriedly tiptoed through the mounds of dust covering the floor. "How did you find it?"

"I followed my mother here one day." Sabrina told Taa nervously glancing from side-to-side before entering another room. "I didn't follow her inside. She would have caught me, but later after she had gone I snuck inside. It's quite ghastly isn't it? I'm pretty sure this is where Quinn and I were created."

"Created?" Taa asked looking at Sabrina with renewed interest. She had been wondering how Empress Ceen had been able to copulate with the Emperor. "Yes, I guess that makes sense."

"There's some books and parchments in the back," Sabrina whispered nervously pointing to the room on their left. Taa took the small neli cube from her pocket and gave it a quick shake. When the blue light flickered on, Taa thought she saw a face watching her from around the corner, but when she shone the light in that direction there was no one there.

"This place gives me the creeps," Taa whispered as she scanned a crumbling parchment laid across one of the tables. "Oh Sabrina," she exclaimed smoothing out the parchment as best she could without cracking it. "Look at this! It looks like...someone was trying to figure out regeneration!"

"You mean raising the dead!" Sabrina hissed and peered over Taa shoulder at the strange drawings. Taa nodded.

Afraid the parchment would crack into dust if she tried to move it, Taa left it and began to pull books off the shelves that she thought might help them. As she handed the books to Sabrina, Taa noticed a thick, skin bound book sitting by itself on the shelf behind her. When she lifted it off the shelf, a creature resembling a demented baby rattle leapt off the book and slithered away.

"Run!" Sabrina yelled and bolted across the room. They didn't stop running until they had reached the fountain.

"Hurry get under here!" Mal sputtered from under the drape of vines surrounding the fountain. "Empress Ceen's in the cottage and she's not pleased."

"You!" Ceen hissed venomously slithering across the cottage floor with her hood raised high behind her petite head. "You should not be here!"

"Now, now," Emperor Taz exclaimed holding his frail hands out in front of him. "Calm down Ceen. There's no need to get your coils in a knot. This isn't who you think it is. It's my little bird all grown up."

Elize slipped behind her father's wheeled chair, her eyes betraying the terror raging inside her. As long as she could remember Elize had had nightmares featuring the fanged snake woman with her silver hood raised over her head about to strike. It took all her nerve not to bolt from the room screaming.

"Even now, the child cringes," Ceen thought flickering her black forked tongue menacingly between her lips. "You should not have returned! Do you have any idea what you've done?" Ceen hissed as she slithered across the floor towards the Emperor.

Empress Ceen was terrifyingly beautiful. From the waist up, she appeared mostly human. The tiny black scales covering her head had been expertly sculptured to frame her face like short, silky hair that highlighted her intense, thickly lined black eyes giving her the impression of an Egyptian queen complete with fine high cheek bones and an almost nonexistent nose, but underneath her billowing skirts, Ceen's body was entirely snake.

"I am no longer a scared little girl," Elize told herself firmly. Taking a deep breath, Elize squared her shoulders and looked her nightmare straight in the eyes. "You no longer frighten me." She lied.

"My little bird has flown home." Emperor Taz cooed flapping his arms. "She's come home to me Ceen. My little bird."

"So, I see." Ceen murmured sweetly and ran a finely filed fingernail under his chin. "Happy day."

"Happy day," Emperor Taz repeated dreamily.

"Rixley not like snake lady." Rixley muttered to herself from her hiding place under the Emperor's chair. Clinging onto the chair with one paw and clutching her pointy stick with the other, Rixley watched warily as Empress Ceen grabbed the front of the Emperor's burgundy chair and pulled him towards her. Elize grabbed the back of the chair and pulled back.

"You silly gnat!" Empress Ceen hissed opening her mouth wide and flashing her fangs. "You have no idea what you've done do you? You have brought a demon to destroy us! I must get the Emperor to safety!"

"I have not!" Elize screamed back at her. "You and that bastard Behr are responsible for the demon!" Ceen yanked the Emperor's chair towards the cottage door.

"My father stays with me!" Elize exclaimed jumping in front of the Cobrateen to block her way.

"Let me pass you foolish twit!" Ceen hissed, her glassy yellow eyes flaring threateningly as she tried to shove her way passed Elize. "The demon Scythe is on his way here. Your father must not be here when he arrives!"

"I'll take care of my father." Elize said blowing a breath of cold air in Ceen's face.

"Let me pass!" Ceen shivered as the temperature in the room began to drop. Elize stood her ground.

"You can pass," Elize stated through blue lips, "but my father stays with me."

Ceen looked down at the crumbled man in the burgundy chair and stroked his head tenderly. "I have dedicated my life to taking care of your father and I will not allow Scythe to torment him. If you insist on keeping him with you, then take the Emperor and flee. But don't delay. Once Scythe gets here it will be too late." Ceen leaned over and kissed Emperor Taz's lips. Emperor Taz smiled up at Ceen, his teeth stained with amber colored venom. "I suggest you go now." Ceen hissed and dashed out of the cottage.

"I don't know about you," Selkie said stepping out from behind one of the stacks of paper, "but that is one frightening woman."

Elize nodded in agreement as she looked down at her father slumped in his chair with his head tilted limply to one side like a rag doll.

"Let's get out of here." Elize said taking hold of the back of the chair and pushing her father out of the cottage.

"What Elize going to do?" Rixley asked crawling out of her hiding place and climbing onto Elize's shoulders.

"I'm not sure." Elize replied as she pushed the chair out the door. "What do you think?"

"I think the sooner we leave this place the better." Mia said slipping around the doorframe to help Elize with the chair.

"Mia!" Elize exclaimed happily. "What are you doing here!"

"Rixley bring Warrior Mia to find Elize." Rixley told Elize proudly.

"Aren't you forgetting something," Selkie asked stepping in front of the chair and putting his foot on one of the wheels. Mia growled and kicked Selkie's webbed foot off the wheel.

"Shut your traps and get over here," Mal huffed sticking his big head out from under the thick carpet of vines.

Mal!" Elize exclaimed pushing the chair under the vines while the others held them up. "And Taa!" She squealed letting go of the chair to give her friend a big hug.

"And Sabrina!" Sabrina added joining in on the hug.

"And Ori," Mal grumbled turning sideways so Elize could see him. When Elize saw Ori tied to Mal's back she stopped hugging Taa and Sabrina and gently placed her hand on Ori's furry forehead.

"And Ori." She whispered tenderly. Ori's eyes fluttered at the sound of Elize's voice, but he didn't wake up.

"Taa put him in a coma until we can find a way to help him." Sabrina explained.

"Ahem!" Selkie coughed and reached for Elize's robe. Mia barred her teeth and leapt at Selkie. If it hadn't been for Taa, Mia would have torn his face wide open.

"It's okay," Elize said stepping between Mia and Selkie. She hated to give up the gown. She had never had a dress fit her as well as this one did, but a promise was a promise. Sensing her hesitation, Selkie thrust out his hand and wiggled his webbed fingers.

"Not...not a good idea," Ori mumbled weakly from Mal's back. "Selkie's can't be trusted."

"Said the Vanji," Selkie smirked as he pulled the long green tunic over his head and tossed it to Elize. Elize took off her robe. "A deal is a deal." She said handing Taa the robe. "Be a curtain."

Taa held the robe up while Elize wiggled out of her dress and let it fall at her feet. Elize barely had time to slip on the green tunic before Selkie reached under the curtain and snatched up his skin.

"How did you get his skin anyway?" Elize asked Sabrina as they watched Selkie melt into his skin and hug himself.

"That's for me to know and you not to find out." Sabrina teased flicking her forked tongue between her teeth at Elize before dancing down the steps hidden inside the now dry fountain.

"Have any of you seen Alzo?" Elize asked as she clumsily tried to maneuver the chair into the fountain and down the steps.

"Last time I saw him, Alzo was in the neli mines headed this way." Mia replied coming over to grab the front of the chair.

"Alzo and big orange cat's butts too big for pipes." Rixley added trying to sound important.

"Well, I hope we'll catch up with him before..." Elize stopped and glanced down at her father's wanning face. Sabrina looked at Emperor Taz and realized the awful trick her mother had played on Elize.

"I need to go fetch something." Sabrina whispered to Taa and slipped back up the steps.

Down in the neli mines Alzo and his followers were busy clearing a blocked passageway leading down to an underground stream which Alzo had been told would lead them to the back entrance of Astaria.

"Why are you doing that!" Ilee complained putting her hands on her hips and looking at Alzo disapprovingly.

"Doing what?" Alzo asked as he hefted a large boulder off the ground and carried it out of the way. "Helping to clear the blocked tunnel? I thought you wanted to get out of here."

"I do," Ilee huffed, "but that's what they're for." She thrusted out her pointy chin towards a group of blue dwarves who were busy moving boulders. "You're a prince. I don't understand why you refuse to act like one!"

"And just how should a prince act?" Alzo countered. Ilee's superior attitude aggravated him. "Do you think I should sit on my ass and order people around while I drink wine and stuff my belly?" Turning his back on Ilee, he lifted another boulder. A shaft of blue light appeared on the other side. "Let there be light!" Alzo exclaimed smiling widely.

Ilee peered through the opening hoping to see the outside world, but instead she found a wide cavern with deep blue stalactites dripping from the lofty ceilings like icicles on a warm day. Ilee had never seen icicles on the islands, but she had heard about them.

"Wow!" Alzo beamed wiping the sweat off his forehead with the back of his hand. Ilee rolled her eyes and stomped off.

"Trouble?" Parth asked stepping out of the way to let the angry Ilee pass. Alzo shrugged.

Ilee didn't mean to be so bitchy, but the lack of sunshine made her more homesick than ever. She longed to feel the warm rays upon her skin and the salty water spraying across her face.

"Oh Hohi!" Ilee sobbed once she was away from the others. "Where are you?"

Ilee hadn't heard from the Ancient Hohi since she visited the Oracle Su Lei in the Forest of Milendor, and it was causing her great worry. Ever since she could remember the Ancient Hohi had spoken to her. Hohi had been like the kindly grandmother Ilee never had. Ilee had a grandmother, two in fact, but they had never treated her kindly.

"Why are you crying, my child?" A soft voice whispered in her head.

"Oh Hohi!" Ilee continued to sob, "is it really you?"

"Yes, my child," Hohi replied. "Now dry your eyes and build me a fire. It's time we had a nice long chat."

Ilee dried her eyes and began to search the area for something to burn. After scraping some dried vegetation off the wall, Ilee pulled out her flint. She was about to strike the flint against the stone when a thick hand with short, stubby fingers grabbed her arm.

"What in Blatz name are you doing!" The blue dwarf gasped with outrage. "Are you trying to blow us all up?"

"No... I wasn't...I... I just wanted to build a fire for Hohi."

"For Hohi? Well, you don't want that shat!" The blue dwarf kicked at the bits of mold Ilee had gathered. "Come on, I'll help you find some wood to build Hohi a decent fire."

"Why are you helping me?" Ilee asked suspiciously.

"You look like you need a friend." The dwarf said kindly yanking at his long beard. "Besides I don't want you blowing up my home." He laughed awkwardly. "Down here we worship the Ancient Gonkuff who carved the original palace out of the gray granite with his bare hands, or so they say, but my family also honors Hohi. The Tearoot's have always been water dwarves and Hohi is the Ancient that watches over the waterways. The way I see it we need all the blessings we can get. Come on! We'd better hurry. Your lot will be leaving soon." Ilee hesitated and looked over her shoulder. Tearoot took her hand. "Don't worry they won't leave you behind. It's my boat."

Alzo was looking for Ilee. It was time to go, but she was nowhere to be found. Finally, hoping she had gone ahead, Alzo started down the sharp incline that led to an underground river. He was supposed to meet a dwarf named Tearoot, who Alzo had been assured, could navigate the river better than anyone and would get them as close to the palace as possible. Tearoot had traveled down the river since he was a boy working on his grandfather's boat and later his father's boat transporting neli stones from the mines to the docks just outside the palace walls.

When he reached the river Alzo spotted Ilee on the shore bent over a small fire made from bits of wood that had washed into the cave and gotten lodged into the rocks.

"I've been talking to Hohi." Ilee informed Alzo when he came over to see what she was up too. "A dwarf named Tearoot helped me find enough sticks to make the fire."

"And what does Hohi say?" Alzo asked and squatted down next to Ilee. Ilee continued to stare into the white puffs of smoke.

"Hohi says it's time for me to return to the islands." Ilee replied without looking up. "She says I'm to travel with you until the one who was sent to escort me home arrives."

"And who might that be?" Alzo asked curiously. He had no doubt that Hohi had spoken to Ilee. He himself had heard Hohi speak.

"I don't know." Ilee said wrinkling her forehead up as the small fire sputtered and went out. "Hohi didn't say."

"Ahem," Tearoot coughed and pulled at his beard. "Hallo, I'm Captain Tearoot and I'm guessing you are the Change everyone's so keyed up about."

"You can call me Alzo," Alzo said reaching out to shake Tearoot's hand. Although Alzo was easily three times taller than the dwarf, Tearoot's hand was almost as big as his.

"Well, we best be getting aboard." Tearoot coughed again and wiped his nose on his sleeve. "Are you planning on taking the cats along?" Tearoot frowned and glanced at Gerawld and Fee. Cats were notoriously bad luck on boats.

"Yes," Alzo replied curtly indicating that there was no room for argument. Tearoot scratched his head and walked over to the fat, round bottomed boat.

"Well, we best be on our way then." He said hopping aboard the ship and tossing a few lumps of neli into the belly of a small black broiler.

By the time Alzo and the Followers of the Change had crowded onto the deck of the boat, there was a steady stream of blue smoke flowing out the top of the funnel. With Tearoot at the helm the barrel boat chugged down the river which flowed deep underneath the neli mines. The steady rhythm of the engine had almost lulled Alzo to sleep when Tearoot suddenly shut the engine off.

"All hands on deck!" Tearoot shouted urgently. Alzo stirred himself and went to see what was going on. The river had turned into a churning mass of whitewater that threatened to toss the heavy-laden barrel boat into the jagged rocks.

"Toss this into the rocks!" Tearoot shouted handing Alzo a thick rope with an anchor stone tied to one end.

Alzo swung the anchor over his head and tossed it between two large rocks where it became lodged. Several more anchor stones were tossed until finally the boat lurched to a stop. Once the boat was as secure as it was going to get Tearoot and Alzo helped everyone climb onto the rocks.

"What about your boat?" Alzo asked as he joined Tearoot on the rocks.

"She's served my family well." Tearoot sighed pulling a rigging ax out of his worn leather sheath. "I'd say it's time to set her free." With his crews help, Tearoot cut the ropes and watched the old tug plunge into the deep chasm ahead of them. As the boat disappeared over the edge the blue dwarves sang an old maritime song of yore.

"I think I know where we are!" Alzo shouted from on top of the rocks.

CHAPTER 21

"What's going on?" Quinn demanded planting himself in front of the crowd rushing down the palace halls wearing makeshift uniforms and carrying candlesticks, peacock feathers and whatever else they could fine that resembled a weapon.

"Haven't you heard," a glassy eyed man dressed in a vest of rusty chain mail three sizes too big for his scrawny frame shrieked joyfully.

"Emperor Taz has been taken and we must rescue him!" Another man shouted from underneath a basket helmet.

"Nonsense!" Quinn shouted firmly tapping his lance sharply against the floor. "Return to your rooms at once!"

"But the Emperor needs us..."

"No, he does not!" Quinn growled thrusting his lance at the crowd to let them know he meant business. "Simeons report!"

Several Simeons ran up to help Quinn. Thinking it was part of the game, the royals raised their weapons and tried to fight their way through.

"What do we do now?" One of the Simeon's whispered to Quinn.

"Lock them up in the dungeon." Quinn ordered loudly. Leaning closer he whispered. "Take them to one of the larger cells so they can all be together and bring them wine, plenty of wine. That'll keep them happy."

"Quinn!" Sabrina squealed. She had hardly been able to contain herself until the Simeons had left with the royals.

"What?" Quinn scowled. He was in no mood to deal with his sister.

"Did I just hear you order the Simeons to lock up the palace goonies?"

"Yes."

"Wow de wow, wow!" Sabrina cooed dancing around him. "I'm impressed! So, you have a backbone after all!"

"Well, I couldn't have them rushing about like lunatics could I?" Quinn snipped and started to walk away. Although Quinn loved his sister, she was a spaz and got on his nerves.

"We'll talk later. Right now, I've got to run!" Sabrina chirped as she skipped past him.

"Where too?" Quinn asked suspiciously.

"To get some venom before Payape wakes back up." Sabrina gave Quinn a wicked smile before pivoting perfectly on her tippy toes and rushing off across the courtyard.

"What! Wait!" Quinn shouted, but it was no good, Sabrina was gone.

Sabrina slipped silently through the hollow space between the walls that the servants used to avoid being seen. She was nearing the tower where Behr had his rooms when she heard voices and stopped to listen.

"I can't believe you let Scythe go!" An icy voice screamed. Sabrina shivered recognizing the voice. It belonged to Aturi, the water maiden.

"As I told you before Mother, let had nothing to do with it!" Behr snarled his voice thick with ale.

"You should have tried to stop him instead of crawling away!"

"How exactly was I supposed to do that mother dear? Reach out and grab him? He's a flipping demon!"

"Where is he now?" Aturi burbled, a puddle was beginning to form under her feet, and she had already shrunk a fraction of an inch. She needed to find water soon. Unfortunately, all the water in the tower had been fouled with garlic.

"How the hell should I know!" Behr shouted. "Scythe doesn't keep me informed of his movements! But be sure of this mother, Scythe needs energy, lots of it. He broke the bulimon's bonds to reserve his power and if you let him get too close, Scythe will drink you up like a tall glass of cold water. I do know Scythe's headed this way, so I suggest you make yourself scarce."

Not wanting to risk being seen by Aturi, Sabrina hurried away. She needed to get in and out of her mother's rooms without being seen and back to warn the others. When she reached her mother's rooms, Sabrina stood outside the door and listened for any sign that Empress Ceen or her maid were inside. Not hearing any movement, Sabrina slipped casually into her mother's chambers just in case her mother was resting.

Luckily, no one was there. Sabrina easily picked the lock on the venom box and wrapped the glass vials carefully in cloth before gently placing them in her pockets. She was on her way out the door when the bits of broken bowl caught her eye. Why had her mother broken her seeing bowl, Sabrina wondered leaning down to pick up one of the broken shards. An image fluttered in one of the beads of milky liquid. Mesmerized by the image, Sabrina watched until it faded and then dropping the shard, she scurried out of her mother's rooms no longer worried about being seen.

"We need to get out of here!" Elize told Grumbul urgently. "But not this way." She started to push her father's chair back up the steps hidden inside the fountain. Grumbul looked at Elize curiously but didn't bother to ask her why. Even as a baby his granddaughter had been able to see things before they happened. When Elize reached the top of the steps, Selkie slipped out of the shadows in front of her.

"I know another way and I assure you it's much safer." Selkie whispered as he helped Elize lift the chair out of the fountain.

"Lead on," Elize told him without consulting the others who raced after her wondering what was going on.

"Now what?" Grumbul grumbled kicking green pebbles into the large stream that blocked their path. Mal trotted over to the stream, dipped his white muzzle into the water, and took a long drink. Ori, who had come out of his coma earlier than expected, gingerly slid off the old mules back and dipped his hand into the water.

"If only we had a boat." Ori said giving Mal a sideways glance as he splashed cold water over his burning face. "You think you can conjure one up old man?"

Mal shook his stiff mane spraying Ori with water before shifting into his human form. This time he remembered his pants. Mal looked older than Ori remembered. He felt older too. All this changing back and forth was wearing him down.

"You feel up to helping an old man?" Mal snorted at Ori and pulled a piece of paper from his tunic pocket and began to fumble with it. His fingers were stiff from being hoofs for so long and refused to work right. Elize took the paper from him and folded it into a small boat.

"How's this?" Elize asked holding the boat by the stern.

"That'll do." He said grabbing the bow and mumbling a spell.

"Don't let go!" Ori shouted as Mal pulled on the bow until the boat was large enough for everyone to fit onboard.

"Won't the chair tear through the bottom of the boat?" Elize asked Grumbul as he pushed the oversized, ornate wheeled chair down to the shoreline. Grumbul scratched his neck. Elize was right, putting the chair on the boat would prove disastrous.

"We'll have to get him out of the chair," Grumbul deduced. Snapping his gnarled fingers at Taa and Mia he yelled. "You two, go into the boat and be ready to grab the Emperor when we pass him over." Mia looked at the water and let out a long, mournful me-ow. Taa understood just how she felt. They had already gotten wet once today, twice was downright unacceptable.

"Careful, Careful." Mal barked at Grumbul and Selkie who were pulling the Emperor up by his armpits. "Wait for Elize to get his feet!"

Taa jumped out of the boat and grabbed the Emperor's rump when they lifted him out of the chair. Working as a team they carried him to the boat. It wasn't pretty, but they managed to get Emperor Taz onto the boat without dropping him. Before climbing aboard Mal sprinkled a handful of silvery powder over the chair. When the chair had shrunk to dollhouse size, Mal picked it up and popped it in his pocket.

After everyone was safely onboard the paper boat, Selkie tied a rope to the bow and swam ahead pulling the boat behind him. As the paper boat floated smoothly across the water Elize sat facing her father. The Emperor's eyes were shut and as far as Elize could tell he was still out cold. Elize closed her eyes. This was definitely not the homecoming she had imagined as a child. No starship tearing open the sky above her school and beaming her up. Or handsome prince appearing out of the mist to take her away to a marvelous wonderland. No, she got a dopey hippy guy who can turn himself into a fox. If Ori had of shown up in a Tardis that would have been cool. But no, Ori slipped through a crack in the dimensions, tried to rip her off and brought them back to the wrong location. On the positive side, Ori had helped her find Alzo. Which was a blessing she supposed. Elize glanced over at Ori. He looked miserable.

"How you doing, kiddo?" Elize asked scooting closer to him.

"I've had better days." He shrugged rubbing his pointed ears. "At least my body stopped freaking out."

"Wasn't Taa able to help?"

"She helped," Ori said raising his eyebrows. "The coma helped a lot. I feel more stable now, but I'm afraid the face is here to stay."

"It's a nice face." Elize told him putting her head on his shoulder.

"Water!" Mia meowed as a spout of water squirted out of a pin sized hole. Taa stomped on the spot, ripping a hoof-sized hole through the bottom of the boat.

"Quick paddle to the right." Selkie shouted from the front of the boat.

Using their arms for oars they managed to get the boat to the shore before it completely fell apart. With the boat turning into pulp, it took all hands to get the Emperor onto the rocks.

"Rixley!" Elize shouted looking about frantically. "Where's Rixley?" In all the excitement no one remembered seeing Rixley on the boat.

"When's the last time you saw her?" Elize shouted at no one in particular as she waded into the water and frantically searched through the bits of pulpy paper.

"Last time I saw her she was sleeping under the Emperor's chair," Mal said wringing the water out of his beard. "You don't suppose…" Mal reached inside his pocket and pulled out the wheeled chair. Setting it on a flat spot, he quickly magicked it back to its normal size. Rixley crawled out from underneath one of the wheels and yawned widely.

"Rixley!" Elize exclaimed splashing out of the water. Rixley rubbed her eyes and looked at Elize confused. She had no idea what had happened or how Elize got in the water.

"We'll have to hike up there," Grumbul announced pointing upward.

"Where am I?" Emperor Taz shrieked thrashing his body about so violently that he fell into the water.

"Mal!" Grumbul shouted and rushed into the water to grab his son before the fool drown himself. Mal waved his hand. A dusty, foul-smelling bubble floated over the Emperor's head and popped. The spell froze the Emperor in full-scream and Grumbul in full grumble. Elize splashed into the water and with Selkie's help they managed to pull both frozen men out of the water before they were swept away.

After dumping the frozen Emperor in his chair. Mal unfroze Grumbul while Taa gave the Emperor something to sedate him. Even sedated, it was agreed that it'd be best to leave the Emperor frozen.

"How are we going to get him up there?" Grumbul asked pointing at the slippery rock face.

After some heated discussion, Mia and Taa helped Mal up the slippery rocks. When they reached the top, Mal shifted back into a mule and Mia tied a rope around his thick neck while Elize attached the other end around the Emperor and the wheeled chair. Rixley and Ori sat on the Emperor's lap and held him in place. Mal pulled on the rope from above, while Selkie and Elize pushed him up the rocky incline. Grumbul took up the rear. They were almost to the top when the left wheel slammed against a jagged rock and cracked.

Elize and Ori were bent over examining the damaged wheel when a dark shadow passed over them. Rixley squeaked and dove under the Emperor's blanket. Emperor Taz opened his eyes and started screeching at the top of his lungs.

"Shut it!" Elize snapped as she huddled behind the chair with her eyes glued to the sky. Her father continued to screech. "Mal! Do something to shut him up!" Elize whispered harshly.

Mal lifted his tail and farted loudly. Emperor Taz gagged and stopped screeching. Well, not exactly, he continued screeching, but no sound came out of his mouth.

"Elizzzz," Rixley whispered tugging at Elize's robe. The ferret's beady black eyes bulged out from her masked face like a cartoon character. Elize watched the figure circling above them.

"Nekita!" Elize exclaimed happily waving her arms over her head. The shadow turned sharply and shot from the sky. Rixley squeaked and bolted up Elize's leg taking cover in the hood of Elize's robe. Elize hadn't realized the hood was there until the ferret landed in it.

"Rixley brave and strong." Elize heard the disgruntled Rixley say as Nekita flew nearer.

"Nekita!" Taa shouted excitedly. "Nekita over here!"

When Nekita flew away from the Forest of Milendor she believed she was being chased by a winged demon. Images of the demon who had attack Su Lei kept her on the move for many days and nights until fatigue made her stop. Taking cover in a large, long needled pine tree,

Nekita searched the sky for her pursuer. No one was there. She had barely shut her eyes when she was approached by an extremely rude barred owl. Although Nekita couldn't make out a word he was saying, she got the message that she was trespassing and wearily flew to an unoccupied tree.

Nekita thought life outside the Taro Bora tree exhilarating. Nekita had never known Su Lei to leave the great tree, but now that Nekita possessed Su Lei's memories she found she could recall times when Su Lei was much, much younger and had traveled across the planet. Tapping into her great aunt's memories, Nekita flew to the faraway places she had only read about.

She flew to the edge of the Dimly where the sun barely shone and across the sea where water splashed against chalky cliffs. She watched the selkie playing among the seal pups and the funny birds that could only fly under the choppy, purple water. She flew over the islands of the Palenina, where Ilee had grown up, and passed the stone pillars of the twin brothers where Elize had fallen out of the sky.

After several weeks of tree hopping Nekita began to long for home and began the long journey back to the Forest of Milendor. Nekita knew the Taro Bora tree wouldn't be the same with Su Lei gone. It pained her to know that centuries of discarded nests piled one on top of the other had been reduced to ashes and rubble. When she neared Milendor Nekita soared high above the trees searching for any signs of danger. The barges which had attacked weeks ago were long gone as well as the tents and encampments that had surrounded most of the forest.

Nekita sat in a tall tree and preened her feathers while she waited for night to fall. The deep walnut bog dye had now faded into soft sandy tones. Nekita considered taking another dip in the bog, but quickly discarded the notion. She liked the darker color but preferred her original color. She stopped preening her feathers when something moved below her.

Nekita watched as several Rangers of Milendor lowered a large limb too damaged to save from the Taro Bora tree and drop it in the moat before crossing the vine bridge which they had strung over the moat. Nekita was shocked at how much damage there was and worried that the rare and exotic plants growing in the gardens might have been destroyed. She hoped the isopteria, who tended the gardens and were botanical wizards, had been able to save them. Nekita closed her eyes and thought of her garden. She missed sitting in her garden at night when the air was filled with sweet aroma of night blooms. Her mouth watered at the thought of the little red bats that circled over the night blooms like a rotating buffet.

"Where's a screecher when you need one?" She wondered aloud. A puff of wind tickled her beak and a small gray screecher magically appeared in front of her dangling a little red bat in his talons. Nekita chirped happily. She never imagined she'd be so glad to see a screecher. Nekita wrapped her tiny arms around the gray puff. The screecher made a sound that can only be described as a purr and tossed the red bat in Nekita's beak before disappearing.

Later when Nekita landed just outside of Su Lei's garden she found the parliament already assembled and waiting for her.

"Screecher," Nekita snapped clicking her beak at the gray puff that appeared in front of her. "For having such a tiny beak, you sure have a big mouth."

The screecher puffed herself up and squawked loudly.

"Well, I guess the news of my return was bound to get out sooner or later." Nekita said flittering her wings to release some stress. "I suppose it's best to get this over with."

Screech squawked again.

When Nekita stepped through the entranceway, the muffled chatter stopped at once and the members of the parliament quickly shuffled to their places under the empty tripod which had held Su Lei's egg. Nekita carefully made her way across the charred floor, careful not to bump into the small brown owl sloshing oil into the hanging bowls.

Nekita knew the parliament expected her to take over as Oracle, but Nekita had other plans. She was not Su Lei and had no intention of staying cooped up in her Great Aunt's garden. The parliament had been taking care of the Taro Bora in her absence. They had also taken care of Su Lei's body, ensuring that her ashes were scattered around the gardens to nourish the roots and promote new growth.

Nekita stood under the tripod where Su Lei's egg had once sat and patiently watched the parliament lighting their respective bowls. No one seemed in the least surprised when Nekita told them she didn't plan on staying. After assuring the parliament that she would return from time to time to visit, Nekita excused the parliament and walked through Su Lei's garden alone. The fire had done so much damage, and although the isopteria had been busy pruning and replanting they still had a long way to go. As Nekita slowly walked around the path, she noticed bits of broken alabaster shell shimmering in the moonlight. Leaning down, Nekita picked up a shard and was startled to see a large blue eye looking out at her.

"Why are you wasting time on dead things," Su Lei's voice crackled. Nekita dropped the shell and spun her head in a circle frantically searching for the source of the voice.

"I'm down here," Su Lei mumbled from another bit of shell by Nekita's left talon. Nekita cautiously turned the shell over. Su Lei's white face appeared on the surface.

"Su Lei," Nekita said staring at the face in the shell. "Is that really you?"

"Were you expecting someone else?" Su Lei cackled and winked, clearly amused at Nekita's reaction.

"What are you doing here?"

"Someone had to get you back on track," Su Lei fussed. "I've only got a little time and none to waste. It's about the prophecy."

"That's why I'm here," Nekita told Elize when she reached the end of her story. "It's about the prophecy."

"Elize!" Mia yelled pointing across the wide chasm in front of them. "There's a man waving at us from the other side!" Elize put her hand over her eyebrows and squinted, but it was impossible to make out who it was. Luckily she didn't need to see him to know who it was.

"It's Alzo." Elize shouted happily. "It's Alzo!"

"And Gerawld!" Mia purred, relieved to see the orange figure standing next to the tall man. She had feared Gerawld might have been foolish and angry enough to go after Tux, but she should have known better. Gerawld had sworn his allegiance to Alzo and even though Gerawld was goofy at times, he was a Bast of his word.

"I'm sorry Nekita," Elize told her. "Can we talk later. Right now, I need to figure out a way to get my brother over on this side of this...this whatever it is."

"But it's important," Nekita protested.

"I know, but I feel Alzo is in grave danger." Elize told Nekita putting a hand on her wing. "Do you think you could carry him across? You know, like how the owls lifted me into your tree?"

Nekita shook her head. "Alzo's too big for me or the screechers to carry. Even if I was accustomed to carrying passengers, I'd be foolish to try flying so far with a load his size. What's going on? Why do you think Alzo is in danger?"

"I'm not sure," Elize answered. Frankly, she hadn't considered that her brother might be in danger until she said it.

A ruckus broke out behind her as the muting spell Mal cast on the Emperor dissipated. Infuriated about being silenced, Emperor Taz bellowed like a banshee and thrashed violently in his chair.

"Isn't there anything you can give him?" Elize asked Taa more sharply than she intended.

"I don't dare give him anymore of the sedative." Taa replied curtly, dodging the small burgundy pillow the emperor tossed at her. "He's had enough to knock out the swamp troll, but his mind and body are craving Cobrateen venom, which I don't have!"

"Well, it's a good thing I brought some." Sabrina announced as she slipped out of the shadows.

Mia hissed and extended her claws. Rixley hopped out of Elize's hood and stood in front of Elize, her pointy stick clutched in front of her like Mia had taught her.

"It's okay," Elize said stepping around Rixley and Mia. "Sabrina's on our side...I think."

"Of course, I am," Sabrina fussed pouring a tiny amount of amber liquid into her father's mouth. "Just a few drops at a time." Sabrina explained pulling several small flasks from her robe and handing them to Taa. "Don't let him talk you into giving him more. What I gave you must last. Give him a few drops every time he starts to realize he's not in the palace. Just a few drops, no more. That's all I could find, so it'll have to last." Sabrina stopped talking and looked around her. "What's going on? I almost didn't find you. I thought you had gone down into the fountain."

Elize didn't answer, instead she turned to Nekita. "Nekita, can you fly over to Alzo..."

"Alzo," Sabrina exclaimed, "Alzo's here? Where?"

"Over there." Selkie told her, pointing to the other side of the chasm.

"Why is he over there?"

"We left him in the mines because he was too big to fit through the pipes." Mia explained, still standing in front of Elize with her claws extended. "Knot had arranged for the blue dwarves to take him and the others down the underground river."

"Blue dwarves!" Sabrina scoffed. "Doesn't Alzo know blue dwarves can't be trusted. Especially if you have a price on your head!"

"No, I'm sure he doesn't." Elize exclaimed, more worried about her brother than she had been a second ago. "Nekita, you must warn Alzo at once!"

"Already taken care of." A high-pitched voice announced from above them. A moment later a flock of starlings landed on the rocks in front of them and several tiny brown men jumped off their backs.

"Brownies!" Sabrina shrieked grabbing the back of the Emperor's ornate burgundy chair and rolling it at them. Emperor Taz looked at the brownies with glassy eyes and cooed at them.

"Knot!" Mia and Taa shouted in unison.

"The one and only!" Knot shouted waltzing over to Mia and Taa.

"Go!" Elize urged Nekita, before addressing Knot. "What did you mean it was already taken care of?" She asked the strange man as Nekita took off across the gorge.

"It's okay," Taa assured Elize. "Knot's on our side. Elize looked down at the pinched faced brownie standing in front of her with his hands on his hips and was glad she had listened to her mother and left bowls of milk on her window ledge for them.

"I meant," Knot growled, "Parth already sent a message to Captain Bok and he's sending Louy to carry the big lug over here."

"Who is he talking about?" Elize asked glancing at Mia.

"Friends," Mia replied distracted. "What about Gerawld and Fee? Didn't you hear the girl? Blue dwarves can't be trusted!"

"You mean that girl?" Knot said leaping at Sabrina. Sabrina squealed and shoved the chair at him. Knot nimbly leapt off the ground and landed upon the Emperor's knee.

"Stop that!" Taa said shooing Knot off the Emperor's knee. Taking Sabrina by the hand she led her away from the mischievous brownie. "What's wrong?" She asked Sabrina when they were out of earshot of the others. "You look like you've seen a ghost."

"I didn't see a ghost, but I did see something I shouldn't have." Sabrina whispered in a shaky voice.

"What?"

"I'll tell you later." Sabrina replied glancing sideways at a group of brownies loitering a few feet away. "Have you found anything to help Ori? I was surprised to see him up and about already."

"I was surprised too." Taa said leaning against one of the rocks and pulling out the skin bound book. "I was expecting him to be out for days."

"Ori's always been a quick healer." Sabrina whispered making sure the brownies had wandered off.

"How did you and Ori meet?" Taa asked flipping through the pages of the book.

"We met in the walls." Sabrina laughed, "he was trying to sneak in the palace while I was trying to sneak out."

"I wonder if Nekita's reached Alzo yet?" Taa said as she scanned the page in front of her.

Nekita was coming in for a landing when a flash of orange leapt from a pile of rocks. Nekita let out a loud hoot as an orange striped paw grabbed her talon. The air around Nekita filled with hundreds of angry gray fluffballs.

"Rrrooarr," Gerawld growled swatting at the screechers who had surrounded him. Fee pounced onto the scene and snatched at several screechers who were busy pulling tuffs of orange fur off Gerawld's long tail.

"Gerawld! Fee! Stop!" Alzo shouted running over and scattering the swarm of screechers. "Drop them! Now!"

Fee scowled at Alzo. She was hungry and these little gray puffs looked tasty. The screecher she was holding let out an ear-splitting screech and was replaced by a startled brown mouse. Fee opened her mouth and tossed the mouse into her watering jaws.

"Nekita!" Alzo boomed reaching down to lift the startled owl off the ground. "It's good to see you again! What are you doing here?"

"It's good to see you too." Nekita told him brushing off her feathers. "Elize sent me."

"Elize! She's here! I thought I felt her nearby. How is she? I haven't seen Elize since Kara took her out of the tree."

"I apologize," Nekita spoke slowly and sincerely. "I did not realize what Kara was up to. I wouldn't have let Elize go with her if I knew what the damned girl had planned. I should have been paying attention, but Su Lei was beyond manic and then the tree was attacked and..."

"No one's blaming you Nekita." Alzo assured her placing a hand on Nekita's wing. "Besides Elize did manage to escape."

"Yes, she did," Nekita agreed, "and now, she is quite anxious about you."

Gerawld growled low in his throat and stepped between Alzo and a starling that had landed on a rock next to Alzo. The starling dropped the square of silvery gray fur it grasped in his talons, and it instantly transformed into a thin, silvery skinned man.

"Selkie!" Ilee exclaimed pushing Gerawld out of her way and throwing her arms around her old friend. "Selkie, Hohi told me a messenger was coming, but I wasn't expecting you."

"Priestess Ilee," Selkie whispered relieved to have finally found her. "You are greatly needed back home."

"Friend of yours?" Alzo asked looking at Selkie and raising an eyebrow at Ilee.

"He is a spirit messenger." Ilee replied curtly taking Selkie by the hand and leading him away from the others. Alzo started to go after them, but Nekita stopped him.

"Alzo, I came to warn you. You must leave this place at once. You are in grave danger." Nekita leaned over so the others couldn't hear her. "The blue dwarves can't be trusted."

"I figured that when Tearoot took the west fork of the river." Alzo told her smiling widely. "My father made sure I learned the lay of the land when I was a boy. I knew my east from my west before I could walk. Mayme said it was like I was born with a compass in my head."

"That's why we had him followed when he left." Parth said walking over to join them. "And sent for alternative transportation."

"Ah here they come now." Alzo said as three large blue birds dropped out of the clouds.

"How can I help?" Nekita asked looking at the group scattered around her. Surely there was no way the three birds could take them over the gulch before the dwarven army Sabrina warned them about arrived with their battle axes. Not that she trusted the girl.

"You can start with those two." Alzo nodded towards Gerawld and Fee who were still busy feasting on mice. Nekita winked at him and clicked her beak three times.

"Those are odd looking clouds," Taa said as two oblong, gray clouds bobbed erratically across the gorge towards them.

"The big one has an orange tail." Grumbul added tilting his head to get a better look as Mia stepped around him, her sharp eyes focused on the tail.

"He's not going to make it." Mia hissed jumping across the jagged stone.

"Mia! No!" Elize yelled as Mia propelled herself upward. Elize managed to catch Mia's hind paws the same moment that Mia grabbed the orange striped tail. Elize was sliding dangerously close to the edge of the gorge when Taa wrapped her arms around Elize's middle and dug her hoofs into the rocky ground. Rixley charged towards Taa and pushed at her ankles causing Taa to stumble backwards dragging Elize, Mia and Gerawld with her.

"Meeer-yowl!" Gerawld howled pulling his tail free as he bounced over the heap of bodies.

"Bravo!" Emperor Taz shouted gleefully clapping his hands and kicking his spindly legs against his chair. "Bravo!"

Taa looked at Mia, Rixley and Elize sprawled across the ground and burst out laughing.

"You've been doing that a lot lately." Elize told her.

"Yes, yes I have." Taa snickered, her brown eyes glittering with amusement. "I never realized how wonderful it felt."

Holding his tail gingerly in his paws, Gerawld stomped over to Fee who the screechers had deposited safely a few feet away. Mia brushed the dust off her fur and went to join them. Gerawld growled mournfully at her.

"I'm sure it's not broken." Mia huffed reaching out for Gerawld's limp tail. Mewing pitifully, Gerawld pushed Mia away refusing to let her touch him.

"Let me have a look," Taa said brushing Mia to one side. "It's okay Gerawld I won't touch it if you don't want me too." Gerawld wailed again and turned away. "Here," Taa reached in her cloak pocket and pulled out a small white ball, "chew on this and see if you can wiggle the end of your tail."

Gerawld took the small white ball and popped it into his mouth. It took several more balls before Taa finally got him to wiggle his tail and two more to get him to move it back and forth. Convinced it was just a bad pull, Taa gave Gerawld a few more balls and walked back to Elize.

"What did you give him?" Elize asked watching Gerawld curiously.

"Goat cheese," Taa replied. "The miners found three pygmy goats roaming about lost in the mines and instead of letting the dwarves slaughter the goats, they hid them away so they could have fresh milk and cheese. The miner's insisted on paying me in cheese for tending to their sick. I didn't have the heart to tell them I didn't eat cheese. I knew it'd come in handy."

Alzo arrived a few minutes later perched on the backs of Louy, followed by Parth aboard Louy's son Tang's back.

"Alzo!" Elize yelled rushing over to hug her brother.

"Hey Elize!" Alzo replied giving Elize a big hug before turning his attention back to the skies which were filled with huge blue birds and tiny gray screechers dropping off passengers.

In all the commotion Elize lost sight of Alzo. She had expected him to come looking for her after things settled down, but when he didn't, she went to find him. Elize found Alzo alone sitting hidden within a niche of boulders looking back over the gorge.

"Hey! I've been looking for you!" Elize exclaimed taking a seat beside him. "What are you doing in here?" Alzo gave his sister a half-hearted smile.

"Hiding," he admitted scooting over to make room. "It's hard to get a second to myself these days."

"I understand," Elize replied looking at the scrap of paper he was holding. "Where's Ilee, I was expecting her to be hanging onto your hip, but I haven't seen her."

Alzo handed Elize the note. "Ilee's gone," he said before Elize had a chance to read it. "She left with a Selkie who Hohi sent to bring her back home to her islands. Apparently her big sister has really screwed things up while Ilee's been away."

Elize studied Alzo's face carefully. "Are you upset she's gone?"

Alzo shrugged, "Nah, not really. Ilee fled the islands because Shi told her she was going to be mated with an older man. I think when she found me, Ilee imagined I was her Prince Charming, but when I didn't live up to her ideas on how a prince should act, she woke up. Selkie just sped up the inevitable. I'm okay with that. Ilee's people need her more than I do."

"So why are you hiding?" Elize asked tilting her head to one side.

Alzo bit his lower lip and raised his eyebrows. "Well...I guess I wasn't expecting to see Payape out here." Elize reached out and took her brother's hand and squeezed it. "How the hell did you get him out of the palace?"

Elize looked at her brother and paused a few seconds before answering. She had learned long ago that sometimes the truth did more harm than good. She felt this was one of those times and chose her words carefully.

"When I told Payape that you had returned he insisted on coming with me to find you."

"Didn't he freak out?" Alzo asked skeptically.

"Yeah, big time." Elize laughed ruffling Alzo's wavy hair. "It took both Mal and Taa to shut him up. But he insisted on coming."

Alzo looked over at Elize. He wasn't sure if he believed her or not, but after several awkward moments his jaw unclenched just a little.

"So, is he still addicted to the snake woman's venom?"

"Yeah, he is, and it's taken a toll on his body. He's not in very good shape. His mind wanders. One second he'll be fine and the next he's a maniac."

"You said Payape used to talk to you? Where was he when I needed him? Why didn't he talk to me too?" Alzo fumed still unable to let go of the hurt. Elize pursed her lips and thought. Why hadn't Payape ever talked to Alzo?

"Did you ever talk to him?" Elize finally asked. Alzo gave her a funny look and shook his head.

"Well, there you have it." Elize said slapping Alzo's arm, "I did. I talked to him all the time when I was a kid, especially during the bad times. When Mayme and I fell to the Earth she was in a coma for a while and then when she woke, she hardly remembered anything at all. That's how Patrick wanted it, I'm sure. I don't know how Patrick's wife and baby girl died, but now that I'm older I'm sure he was terrified that Mayme would remember that she wasn't Anna O'Sullivan. Patrick insisted I speak only English and when I slipped, he would beat me and lock me up in the dirt cellar under the house. It was dark and moldy and covered with spider webs. The first time, I was so scared. I curled up in a ball and cried out for Payape and he answered me. He sang the little bird song and told me that things would get better. After that whenever I was sad or scared or mad, I would call out to Payape, and he'd answer me. Well, most of the time anyway."

"Did you ever call out to me?"

"Kind of. You see Mayme insisted you were just an imaginary friend. When I was little, I insisted you were real, but as I got older and became a teenager, I started to wonder if I'd just made you up."

"So, how bad is he?" Alzo whispered resting his head on Elize's shoulder.

"He's a frail old mad man with drool running down his chin." Elize answered sadly. "Did I tell you he's been living in our old cottage. I guess he moved in there after we left. The outside was all burned up, but the inside looked a lot like it did when we lived there, just more cluttered. Oh yeah, I meant to ask you if you ever went to New York."

"As a matter of fact, I did," Alzo said looking puzzled, "why?"

"Did you go to see the Statue of Liberty?"

Alzo pulled at his beard and made a face. "Well, I went to New York on several occasions, but only visited Liberty Island once…whoa boy that was a bad trip. Literally. My buddy and I got really tore up and my buddy got it in his head that he had to see Lady Liberty. So, we bummed enough cash for the ferry and rode out to the island. Somehow, we missed the last ferry off the island, I don't remember how, but we got stuck there all night. In the middle of the night, I woke up. At least I think I was awake. I looked up at Lady Liberty, but instead of being a statue she had turned into a screaming giant with a fiery torch. Scared the shit out of me. I'll never go back there, that's for sure."

Elize laughed so hard tears formed in her eyes. "You're not going to believe this, but Payape saw you." Elize told Alzo about the paper Liberty with the club in her hand.

"Well, what do you know. I guess it's time I went to see him, huh?" Alzo said getting to his feet. "So, how'd you get Payape away from the snake or is she here too."

"No," Elize told him as they walked towards the dark gray boulders jutting up into the sky for miles behind the translucent palace, "but I'm sure she's not far away. I'm more worried about the water maiden, Aturi than I am about Ceen though. I'm pretty sure she's the one who started all this shit with the demon."

Elize was right to be worried about Aturi.

"What do you mean he's gone!" Aturi demanded wrapping an icy hand around the blue dwarves neck.

"Well…we…we," the dwarf stammered trying to force words out of his mouth and failing.

"Stop stuttering and tell me how you and your brothers allowed my enemy to escape."

"Well…we," the dwarf started again, "we followed your orders…we…we put him on the boat…Tearoot led him down the wrong fork in the river. But he, he…"

"Pray tell," Aturi cooed dangerously, running her nail under the trembling dwarf's neck slicing off several bits of beard which tumbled noiselessly to the floor. The dwarf gulped and looked nervously at his brothers.

"The Change must have been warned by the diggers." One of the brothers blurted out.

"Yes, yes," another brother shouted, "the diggers attacked us before Tearoot could send up a distress signal."

"Bitmore speaks the truth," one of the taller dwarves added, bobbing his head up and down vigorously. "The diggers attacked us with their pickaxes and threw stones at our heads. My brothers and I were lucky to escape with our lives!"

"And yet somehow you did." Aturi sneered rising out of the water until she towered over the sniveling dwarves. "WHERE IS THE CHANGE NOW?"

"We don't know," the brothers cowered shaking in their boots. "They flew away."

"FLEW AWAY!" Aturi screamed splashing the dwarves, she dove into the water and swam towards the palace to find her son. Aturi wasn't the only one looking for Behr.

"Behr!" Ceen hissed sliding into his rooms no longer worried about hiding the coils underneath her long flowing gown. "Behr!"

Behr looked sideways at Ceen. Someone must have gotten under her skin. He hadn't seen her hood up for ages. Behr raised up on one elbow stifling a faked yawn.

"What are you doing lying about? The palace is under attack! Call in your bulimon!"

Behr picked up his mug, frowning when he realized it was empty.

"Did you hear me?"

"Yes, of course I heard you." Behr replied glibly putting down his mug and looking up at the Empress. "The problem is there are no more bulimon to call in. They're all either dead or have run off. You see, Scythe decided he didn't need them anymore and broke the enchantment that bond them to us. It was draining power from him that he'll need to overpower Elize."

"Your mother was right. You should have never let him go."

"As I told my dear mother," Behr said raising his mug to catch the drop of amber liquid dripping from Ceen's fang. "Let had nothing to do with it. The girl, or woman I should say because she is indeed a woman, a beautiful woman, the image of her mother, my dear Euna. You know she's the real deal, don't you? And if she's the real deal, then it's a good bet that the one the Freedlanders are calling the Change is too. You do know Prince Alzo is the Change don't you? No, well it doesn't surprise me. You never could see what was right in front of your face. I'd pack my bags if I were you dear Empress. The real heir has returned, and your time here is about to end abruptly."

CHAPTER 22

"I think they went this way." Elize told Alzo as they hiked up the rocky, nearly vertical incline. Coming around a large boulder, Elize almost tripped over Grumbul who was leaned over examining the cracked rim on the ornate wheeled chair.

"Look who I found!" Elize chirped shoving Alzo in front of her.

Grumbul looked up, the hard edges of his mouth softened, and tears welled up in his ice blue eyes. "Alzo, my boy. Is it really you?"

"Grumpa," Alzo exclaimed rushing over and throwing his arms about the old man's shoulders. Grumbul's face wrinkled up into a smile as he wrapped his arms around Alzo and hugged him tightly.

"Grumpa," Alzo's voice cracked with emotion. "I was sure I'd never see you again."

"Now don't go all misty on me." Grumbul coughed as he wiped the tears off his cheeks with the back of his hand.

"I hate to interrupt," Sabrina told Elize, "but we're not safe out in the open like this. I think we should find cover fast. I don't like the look of that sky."

"She's right," a familiar voice agreed from a thick granite boulder. A moment later Rochelle stepped out with two of her seven sisters. "I don't like the way the sky looks either and if that wind continues to pick up it will blow us all off the mountain."

"It doesn't seem natural." Elize said keeping her eyes on the wave of gray clouds racing towards them like a herd of wild stallions.

"Grandmayme!" Alzo shouted joyfully releasing Grumbul to lift Rochelle off the ground.

"Careful, careful," Rochelle laughed patting Alzo's head. "You don't want to break me."

"Everyone inside!" Mal shouted pushing past Alzo and Rochelle. "Hurry!"

"Grab the Emperor and follow me!" Rochelle told Alzo. Alzo grabbed the back of the chair and pushed.

"Watch that wheel!" Grumbul barked a second too late. The wheel split in two and the chair jerked sharply to one side. Without missing a beat, Alzo swooped the chair off the ground and marched after his grandmother.

"Always were a strong boy," his father mumbled proudly, slouching further down into his chair. Alzo glanced down at the frail man drooped like a wet rag in the ornate burgundy and gold wheeled chair. He looked so weak and pathetic. Instantly Alzo felt all the angry words he'd rehearsed for years melt out of his head.

"Payape," Alzo whispered hardly believing the man in the chair could be his father. Emperor Taz opened his bloodshot eyes.

"My son, my son," he whimpered reaching out a skeletal hand. "Is it really you?"

"It is me, Payape." Alzo's words cracked with emotion. "I was lost until Elize tracked me down and brought me home."

"So much like her mother," the Emperor murmured patting Alzo's arm and giving him a frail smile. Alzo smiled back ignoring the trail of clear drool running down his father's chin.

"This way," Rochelle urged motioning towards a granite boulder jutting upward at least two hundred feet in front of them. Without hesitating Rochelle ran straight into the boulder and disappeared. Alzo closed his eyes and charged after her. When he opened his eyes again he was in a huge room with walls that looked like they had been forged by the hands of giants.

"The Hall of the Ancients." Alzo said under his breath. "Ori and I discovered this place when we were kids, but I never imagined it led out of the Palace."

At the mention of Ori's name, Elize suddenly realized she hadn't seen him come through. Not that she had been paying much attention. Now as she looked around, Elize didn't see Ori or Taa anywhere.

"I'll catch up." She told Alzo and began weaving her way back the way they had come. She had almost reached the exit when she saw Ori collapsed on the ground.

"What's wrong?" Elize asked Taa who was standing next to Ori.

"My legs won't work." Ori replied trying not to sound as freaked out as he felt.

"There's Gerawld!" Elize yelled and ran over to the stocky orange striped bast cat and grabbed him before he disappeared into the crowd. "I need you to carry Ori." Elize told Gerawld urgently.

Gerawld nodded and gently lifted Ori off the ground cradling him in his furry arms like a little baby. Taa and Elize exchanged amused glances.

"What's wrong with him?" Sabrina demanded when she saw Gerawld carrying Ori.

"I'm not sure." Taa told her as she directed Gerawld towards a cave which looked eerily like a burial niche. Gerawld carefully laid Ori on the stone bed and trotted off to find Fee and Alzo. "I think the infection has gone into his blood."

"I have an idea." Sabrina said leaning over so only Taa could hear her. "Quinn and I have to have our blood changed every third moon or so. Otherwise, we get rather loopy. Mother says our bloods not right because we are a cross between warm blooded and cold blooded species."

"I saw something about that in the book we found." Taa whispered back.

"It sounds like a blood transfusion." Elize interrupted. Both Sabrina and Taa looked at Elize with surprise. "Sorry," Elize said when she realized she wasn't supposed to hear what they were saying. "Look if you guys need blood just let me know. I'd better go. Alzo's waving at me."

"How sick is he?" Elize heard Alzo whisper to Rochelle from across the room. She shook her head and wondered what was going on and why her hearing was suddenly amplified much higher than normal.

Elize squeezed between Grumbul and Mal who were standing around the Emperor's chair along with Alzo and Rochelle.

"It's hard to tell," Mal replied swishing his tail impatiently. "It could be days. It could be hours. He's gotten much worse than he was when I saw him a few weeks ago."

"A few weeks ago?" Elize remarked looking at the old mule. "I thought there was a price on your head. How did you get into the palace?"

"I have my ways." Mal huffed, "Emperor Taz had nothing to do with making me an outlaw. That was Ceen and Behr's doing. I didn't visit often, and when I did it was late at night after Empress Ceen had retired for the evening. She refused to stay out in the cottage, so I knew it'd be safe."

"I think he's strong enough now," Rochelle said leaning over to wipe the thread of amber drool from the Emperor's chin, "but the sooner Alzo takes over the better."

"Agreed, but we don't have enough witnesses," Grumbul said glancing about the room. "We need members of both the old and new councils to witness the proceedings. That is if we want to make it official."

"I brought what's left of the old council with me and I've sent word for Quinn to bring whoever he could round up from the new council and bring them here." Rochelle said scanning the crowd for any sign of Quinn.

"Was that wise?" Grumbul barked at his wife. "Are you sure he can be trusted."

"More than you ever could." Rochelle barked back. Grumbul pulled a face and stepped behind Mal. He knew all too well about Rochelle's temper and wanted to ensure he was out of striking distance.

"Is he married?" The silver haired Madeline asked poking her head under Rochelle's arm to get a peek of Alzo. "I hate to be a spoiled sport, but rules are rules, and we need the crown," Madeline said firmly, "it won't be official unless the prince is married, and the crown of the ancients is placed on his head."

"No, he's not married, and you know damn well the crown has been lost as long as he has." Grumbul exploded. Grumbul blamed many of the problems with his and Rochelle's marriage on her sisters.

"Won't be official, not official," Madeline insisted sticking her tongue out at Grumbul.

"Won't be official! Not official." Emperor Taz repeated mimicking his Aunt Madeline like a drunken parrot.

"I have the crown." Alzo announced rolling up his tee shirt sleeve and flexing his bicep.

"What!?" Mal, Rochelle and Grumbul yelled in unison.

"I have the crown. Mayme gave it to me before we left. She said it was to be mine anyway and that Payape would just lose it or let Behr talk him out of it. So, she gave it to me."

Alzo flexed the golden tattoo encircling his bicep. It reminded Elize of the armlets worn by Inca warriors. Unlike the usual blue ink, Alzo's tattoo was gold and blended nicely with his well-tanned skin.

"So, that's how she smuggled it out," Mal mumbled leaning his big head so close to Alzo's arm that the tiny hairs on the old mule's muzzle tickled him. "Your mother was always clever."

Grumbul pushed Mal's head to one side and ran a gnarled finger along the curved lines of the tattoo. "How do you get it off?" He grumbled pinching Alzo's skin.

"Get out of the way." Rochelle fussed pushing both men back and pulling out a small jar from her bodice. "This should do the trick." Rochelle dipped a slender finger into the silvery liquid and carefully applied it to Alzo's tattoo.

Alzo winced as the tattoo pulled away from his skin. It felt like someone was slowly pulling off a bandage from an unhealed wound. Rochelle waited until the crown was fully raised before carefully sliding it off Alzo's arm. It took several minutes more for the crown to dry and solidify. Emperor Taz squinted out of one eye at the shiny crown and before anyone could stop him he picked it up and plopped it upon his head.

"Look at me!" He exclaimed loudly waving his spindly arms about. "Don't I look the silly ass?" No one answered. "I always hated this thing. So plain and unspectacular. I wanted to add rubies..." Taz sneered glancing up at his mother. Rochelle rolled her eyes and taking Alzo by the arm led him away.

"So, who's the lucky bride?" She asked looking about the room.

"As far as I can tell everyone is in that's coming in." Parth announced as she crossed the room to join Alzo. Rochelle and Alzo looked at each other and smiled.

"What?" Parth demanded noticing the strange, animated looks on their faces. "What's going on?" Alzo took Parth's hand.

"It appears I can't be the new Emperor unless I'm married. So, it's either you or the cat." He joked looking over at Mia who was busy cleaning her fur.

"Try the deerling?" Mia replied before coughing up a fur ball and spitting it at his foot.

"I don't think she'll have me." Alzo said faking sadness. "So, what do you say Parth, will you marry me?"

"Marry you?" Parth only half laughed. "Do I have to live in the glass palace."

"Oh hell no." Alzo assured her. "I fully intend to reign like the first Emperor and roam all of Toboria from one end to the next."

"Well, in that case...Yeah why not. Someone needs to keep an eye on you, and it might as well be me. I just hope you're a good kisser." Alzo grabbed Parth and kissed her hard on the mouth. "That'll do." Parth laughed and kissed him back. The chamber burst into applause.

"A wedding!" Emperor Taz squealed clapping his hands. "I love weddings. Do I have time to change? I have the perfect outfit!" Rochelle shook her head firmly.

"It'll have to be a quick wedding." She told the sulking Emperor leaning down to wipe a bit of drool off his chin. "We'll have a proper wedding later and you can dress in your finest."

"Oh goody!" Emperor Taz clapped gleefully. "I put on my crown now, can't I?" Rochelle nodded.

Gerawld growled low as several drunken men stumbled into the hall followed by two giggling women. They smelled heavily of cheap wine and had barely entered the hall when one of them tripped on the rough floor and knocked the others on their butts.

"The new Council," Quinn announced as the guards helped the group get back on their feet, "as requested."

"Emperor!" One of the men slurred as he fell at the emperor's feet. The others screamed with laughter and rushed over to help their fallen council member. In the confusion, Elize slipped away to joined Taa who had been trying to get her attention. Mal trotted after her.

"We're going to need your blood." Taa yelled over the ruckus as she led Elize around the corner where Ori was sprawled out cold on the stone bed. He looked much worse than he had moments ago.

"You can't use Elize's blood." Mal said flatly before stamping his hoof on the hard ground and shifting back into his human form.

"Why not?" Taa and Elize demanded.

"Because your blood is too pure. It'll kill him. That's why!" Mal huffed shoving Sabrina to one side so he could examine Ori for himself. "You'll have to use mine."

"But..." Elize sputtered.

"But, what?" Mal challenged shaking a gnarled finger at her. "You think my bloods too old? Well, it might be, but your bloods too strong, too pure. It'll kill him. Besides, you're going to need all your strength if you're going to stand up to Scythe."

"Which I'm trying my best to avoid." Elize reminded him coolly. "What about Taa or Mia their both mammals?"

"No, their blood is too mammal and before you suggest it, there's no time to go around the hall and test everyone's blood to find a doner. My blood is compatible with the Vanji, so it'll have to do. Besides Ori is my protégé and that makes him my responsibility. Now get! I'm sure you don't want to miss your brother's marriage. These two are more than capable of taking care of things here."

"But..."

"Get!"

"Where have you been?" Mia hissed as Elize rounded the corner.

"Hurry, hurry, hurry," Rixley sang pulling on Elize's hand and dancing through the crowded room to where Alzo and Parth were standing on a large round stone with strange markings on it. Rochelle and the other six sisters stood around them with their arms linked. Behind them were the new and old council. Emperor Taz and Grumbul stood to the left of Alzo.

"It's about time," Grumbul grumbled at Elize.

"Where are the rings?" Emperor Taz chirped. "Need to exchange rings or it won't be official."

"Oh, for Blatz sake!" Rochelle said under her breath pulling at the twisted gold band on her left-hand ring finger. "Where's your ring old man." She barked at Grumbul. Grumbul pulled a chain out from under his shirt.

"Here," he said sheepishly handing it to Rochelle.

"I knew you hadn't tossed it." She said tenderly giving the old man a faint smile. Grumbul lowered his head. He wasn't about to give her the satisfaction of seeing him blush.

Unlike most royal weddings, the wedding of Alzo and Parth was short and sweet. It began with the seven sisters singing a high pitched sonnet about love. Followed by the exchange of rings. After the rings were exchanged Grumbul stepped forward holding a short dagger which he used to slice across Alzo's large callous palm before handing the dagger to Rochelle, who did the same to Parth.

"Blood to blood," Rochelle and Grumbul shouted clapping Alzo and Parth's palms together and holding them tight, "what was two now becomes one!" The room erupted with cheers, which echoed up into the chambers above.

"Lovely," Empress Ceen hissed sarcastically, unconcerned about being overheard as she watched from one of the hundreds of niches carved in the dark rocks. Feeling incredibly tired, Ceen lifted her skirts and headed into the hidden passageway. A loud rumbling stopped her.

"What the hell was that?" Alzo shouted as drops of muddy water sprayed down from high above their heads.

"It's Aturi!" Someone shouted! "She's redirected the river!"

"We're trapped!" Another person shouted as a wave of panic swept through the room.

Slipping out of her cumbersome skirts, Ceen wrapped her coils around the nearest column and slid to the floor, landing with a thud several feet from where the Emperor sat quivering in his broken chair.

"Follow me!" Ceen hissed over her shoulder as she scooped Emperor Taz out of his chair and slithered off the dais.

"Stop!" Alzo demanded blocking the Cobrateen's path.

"Let me pass," Ceen hissed her hood raising up behind her. "Quinn, Sabrina!" Ceen shouted whipping her tail around and knocking Alzo off balance. "Hurry follow me!"

"Why should we follow you?" Alzo demanded refusing to budge.

Ceen faced Alzo, her face flushed with rage. "I wasn't talking to you. You foolish man! Now get out of my way. Quinn, grab your sister and follow me. Make sure you seal the door behind you!"

"No!" Emperor Taz shrieked from Ceen's arms. "Quinn, I forbid you to leave your brother and sister behind. I order you to ensure both Alzo and Elize are safely escorted out of the hall and brought to wherever your mother is taking me."

"Quinn, listen to me I am the Empress!"

"Sorry, my dear but I out rank you." Emperor Taz told Ceen firmly. "Now go Quinn do as I say. Quickly!"

"Madeline gather the sisters!" Rochelle yelled over the panicking crowd, taking control of the situation. "Grumbul have the Simeons lead the Followers into the upper atrium. They should be safe there until my sisters and I can get the shield in place!"

Alzo started after his grandfather, but Rochelle stopped him. "No, Alzo. You and Parth need to stay with your father. Go with Quinn."

"Is Quinn my brother?" Alzo asked Rochelle.

"Half, but there's no time to explain that now." Rochelle replied putting her hand gently on Alzo's bearded cheek. "Once you are safely away, ask your father to explain it to you."

"Everyone, get away from the water!" Mal shouted as he stumbled through the crowd heavily supported by Taa.

"Follow the guards!" Alzo shouted encouragingly to his followers, waving towards the spiral steps curving upward.

"Why should we listen to you?" A burly man in burlap shorts shouted at Alzo. "If it wasn't for you we wouldn't be in this mess. Now we're all going to drown like rats in a well!"

"Not if you follow the guards!" Parth spat, grabbing the man by the collar, she shoved him towards the steps. "Now get moving!"

"Do you really think following the snake is a good idea?" Parth whispered to Alzo as they tripped after Quinn into the hidden hallway Empress Ceen had disappeared through moments before.

"I don't see where we have much choice." Alzo grumbled looking over his shoulder at the skinny girl herding Elize, Taa and the three bast cats towards them. "Besides, my grandmother told me to stay with my father and that's what I intend to do."

"Keep going," Quinn told Alzo crisply, "I need to make sure the doorway is closed to keep any water out."

"Alzo," Mal coughed waving at Alzo urgently from further ahead. "Hurry. Your father is anxious about you. He wants to finish the ceremony before…"

"Before what?" Alzo demanded annoyed at being kept out of the loop. "What's going on?"

"Your father is fading." Grumbul huffed appearing out of the stone wall as if by magic. "The ceremony must be completed before your father...my son..."

"I'm dying." Emperor Taz told Alzo and Elize weakly a few minutes later as they knelt by the bed Ceen had laid him upon. "I've been dying for a long while now. Not that anyone noticed."

"Well, your mother and I would have noticed if you hadn't kicked us out!" Grumbul snapped and motioned for Elize to get up. "Alzo, get closer," Grumbul said and tapped Alzo sharply on the shoulder. "The Emperor needs to be able to reach your head." Alzo scooted closer on his knees. Parth covered her mouth to stop from laughing.

Rochelle slipped into the room just in time to see Emperor Taz lift the crown off his head and hold it in front of himself with trembling hands. Looking up at Alzo, the Emperor smiled at his son weakly.

"Prince Alzotarian, fruit of my loins, my pride and joy… ummm…" The Emperor paused and glance around confused. "My son, my son," he mumbled staring into Alzo's vivid green eyes. Alzo knew his father was struggling, but he neither spoke nor moved, he just waited patiently for his father to continue. "Ah…ah yes, where was I?" Emperor Taz stalled his eyes becoming focused. "Ummm, right. I, Tazadorin, Sixth Emperor of Astaria, hereby relinquish my title as my father Grumbul, the Fifth did before me and declare that from this day forward, my son, Alzotarian, will reign as the Seventh Emperor of Astaria as witnessed by the new and old councils. Long may you rein. Here, this belongs to you now." Taz reached up and plopped the crown on top of Alzo's head. "Now you look like a silly ass!"

"All hail Emperor Alzotarian!" Grumbul shouted.

"All hail Emperor Alzotarian!" The members of the new and old council shouted.

"Congratulations!" Rochelle whispered kissing her grandson on the cheek.

"I need to be with the others!" Alzo said kissing his father on the forehead and grabbing Parth's hand. With the crown still on his head, Alzo pulled the sealed door open and rushed up the steps with Parth at his side. The Followers of the Change greeted the new Emperor and Empress with a mix of applause and astonishment, many wondered what the future would hold. Would the Followers of the Change be lauded as heroes or imprisoned as traitors?

"Aren't you going to join in on the celebrations?" Rochelle asked Elize as they stood below listening to Alzo. With the shield in place the panic which had shaken the hall of the ancients moments before seemed to have been forgotten.

"No," Elize said shaking her head. "I'm so proud of Alzo, but I think I'll wait until things settle down a bit to congratulate him. It's been a long day and my head is pounding." Rochelle looked at Elize with concern. "Also, I want to check on Ori."

"The blood transfusion seems to have worked." Taa assured Elize when she found her a little while later, "but we won't know for sure for a day or two. Ori needs to rest. So does Mal! I don't know who's more stubborn the fox or the mule. I told them both not to move, but do they listen. No!"

"Well, I'm glad Ori's doing better. I was really worried. How's Mal doing? I don't care what he says, at his age something like that is bond to take a toll."

"You're right," Taa whispered giving Mal a sideways glance, "but he insists he's fine."

Elize patted Taa's arm. "Let's hope this is all over soon and we can all go home."

"It's not going to be over soon, you dimwit!" Mal grumbled from the other side of the room where he'd been listening with his radar ears. "Scythe's not going to stop until he gets you! He's been trying to find you since the day you were born and he's not about to stop now!"

"Why?" Elize stormed at the old mage.

"Why! Why!" Mal sputtered, shaking his fist at Elize. "Because Scythe thinks you're Monet reincarnated, and he wants the gift he gave her back! That's why!"

"What?" Elize exclaimed throwing up her hands.

"Mal!" Rochelle growled shooting the old man a hard look. "Let me handle this." Mal flatten his ears, snorted at Rochelle. Rochelle took Elize's hands and gave them a soft squeeze. "Why don't we get Taa to give you something for your headache and find a quiet place where we can talk?"

"Thanks," Elize said taking the clay mug from Taa and following her grandmother away from the others.

Rochelle took Elize up the stairway, but instead of going into the atrium where Alzo and the others were gathered, she stepped off on a lower floor and led Elize into a small niche. Shaking the blue cube she kept in her pocket, Rochelle took a seat on a bench carved out of the stone and motioned for Elize to sit next to her.

"Now," Rochelle said kindly, "why don't you tell me what you know of Monet."

"I know she's an ancestor," Elize answered trying to remember what Koh had told her in the Salt Temples, "and that she came from Earth to avoid drowning in the great flood, but except for inheriting some 'gift' from her I don't know much. What was Mal talking about before? Why would this demon guy think I was Monet? I was under the impression that Monet was immortal? How could I be Monet reincarnated? Don't you need to die before you can be reincarnated?"

"You're right about Monet being your ancestor." Rochelle explained, brushing a silver hair out of her face. "You are a direct descendant of Monet. It is said that Monet was among the group of humans who fled Earth during the great flood before the pathways to the realms were sealed. Prior to the humans arrival, I don't think there were any humans living on the planet Toboria. When the humans arrived, they took refuge in these mountains, carving out the rooms and niches you see now."

"You mean they were hiding?" Elize asked setting down her tea.

"Monet and her family were hiding from the watchers. Do you know who the watchers are?"

"Kind of," Elize answered tilting her head to one side. "If I remember right, the watchers were a group of angels who were left to watch over the young humans."

"Good, and the fallen?" Rochelle asked smiling at Elize encouragingly.

"The fallen were a group of watchers who got bored watching the humans and decided to come down and intermingle with them. Especially with the pretty, young woman who they had sex with and took as wives and concubines. Which got God mad, and he sent the flood to clean up the mess or something like that."

"More or less," Rochelle laughed. "Monet was one of these pretty, young women. She caught the eye of a watcher named Scyathee."

"And now she's encased in the statue." Elize mumbled aloud. "So, is she alive or dead?"

"Somewhere in between, I suppose," Rochelle shrugged, "the point I'm trying to make is Monet may try to contact you. When I was a child my mother and grandmother used to warn my sisters and I never to look at or touch Monet's statue."

"Monet's already tried to contact me." Elize admitted. "I accidently touched her toe, before Sabrina could stop me."

"What happened when you touched it?"

"I heard a voice whisper, 'our secret." Elize replied. "I think the voice has been trying to talk to me again. It might be what's making my head hurt. That and the weird smell."

"So, she's at it again," Rochelle said more to herself then to Elize. "Your mother was wise to take you away."

"What do you mean?" Elize asked curiously. "Are you saying Monet has spoken to me before?" Rochelle nodded.

"When you were, well no older than three maybe younger," Rochelle replied, her forehead creased with worry. "You told your mother about the beautiful lady who lived inside the statue's head and watched you while you played in the garden. At first, we all thought it was a cute game, but then one night your mother woke and discovered you were not in your crib. We finally found you trying to claw out the stairwell leading into Monet's statue that had been filled in centuries before I was born after the horror of the virgins."

"The horror of the virgins?" Elize asked raising her eyebrows.

"It happened long before I was born." Rochelle whispered leaning her sharp chin against her hand. "And as old tales go, it's hard to tell what really happened and what is added spice."

"Added spice?"

"Yes," Rochelle said her eyes twinkling, "bit of spice makes a dull story more flavorful."

"Ah, got it!" Elize said motioning from her grandmother to continue as she took another sip off her now cold tea. Whatever Taa had given her seemed to be helping, but the annoying buzzing in her head was still there.

"Back in the days of the third or was it the fourth emperor. Doesn't matter. Anyway, long ago teenaged girls started to disappear. At first it was thought that perhaps the girl had fallen in love and run off with her unknown lover, but after several girls had disappeared folks started to wonder if something evil was going on. Finally, a girl named Hilya stumbled back to her mother's house, dazed and terrified. Hilya claimed that a witch lived in the statue of Monet's head and had tried to possess her. Hilya also claimed that the statue's head was full of the mummified remains of the missing girls."

"So, you think it was Monet? Why would she want to possess those girls?"

"To escape and find her lover Scyathee who, if I'm right, is now the demon Scythe."

"Scyathee is a fallen angel?"

"Yes."

"I've got to find Nekita!" Elize exclaimed getting off the bench and running out of the room before Rochelle could stop her.

CHAPTER 23

Alzo rushed towards the atrium eager to join his followers. As he topped the steps he became aware of a steady boom, like bass from your neighbor's apartment seeping through the walls until you can feel the noise vibrating through every nerve.

"Do you hear that?" Alzo asked. Gerawld tilted his head and batted at the invisible gnats buzzing about his ears. "What is that?" Alzo asked again looking over at Parth who had been standing next to him a second ago. "Where's Parth?" Alzo searched the crowd for his new bride. He found her bumping and grinding several feet away with two ruby lipped women.

"Parth!" Alzo called over the strong beat that slapped into his body like a rip tide.

"So, the betrayer dares to show his face," a huge man with a long scraggly beard roared angrily jumping in front of Alzo and blocking his way.

"Played us for a bunch of titties," the scrawny woman standing at his side sneered and bared her chipped brown teeth.

"All hail the Emperor of Dung!" A slurred voice shouted as a head of cabbage flew past Alzo's head.

"You fed us on lies!" Yelled one of the ruby lipped women, who had stopped dancing to join the others.

"Did I?" Alzo challenged placing his large hands on his hips and glaring at the crowd. "Did I feed you on lies?" He moved his head from side to side staring hard at the thickening sea of faces. "Was it I that summoned you to Milendor? No! Did I ask you to follow me? No! I wanted nothing to do with it! But you came to Milendor! Why? Because you wanted Change! Isn't that it? You came looking for the Change! Well, here I am! The same man you flocked to see in Milendor. The same man who ate with you, dug pits with you and fought side by side with you. So, what the hell is your problem?"

"You should have told us who you were!" A big bosom woman in a tight green frock shouted from the front of the crowd. "You should have told us you were the Prince! You lied to us?"

"Did I?" Alzo demanded again. "Did I ever lie to any of you? No! I didn't claim to be the lost prince because the day I stepped off this planet as a twelve-year-old boy, I stopped being a prince! On that day I became a lost and lonely child. An orphan without a family. A kind old woman took me in to help with her farm. I shoveled manure, shoed ponies, planted crops and worked until my hands were blistered! I should have told you who I was, but I never lied to you or misled you. As I said all along this is your world, your lands and it is up to you to fight for what is rightfully yours."

A burly man, with curls of red hair covering his body lowered his head and charged at Alzo headbutting him roughly in the chest. Gerawld pounced on the burly man's back knocking him into the crowd. The beat grew louder and more aggressive as the atrium turned into a bar room brawl.

"Enough!" Alzo's voice boomed across the atrium. "We came here to fight for justice, NOT each other. I would not be standing here if it wasn't for your dedication and support. I didn't come in here to fight! I'm here to welcome all of you to a new era! Together we will tear down the walls of Astaria! Hand in hand we will rebuild the Freedlands and beyond. Together we will ensure our families and friends are free to live and grow without fear! Throw open the gates!" Alzo shouted. "No longer will the Emperor of Astaria hide behind these walls."

Elize ran past the atrium with her hands slapped over her ears. The buzzing had become unbearable. Half heard words spun about her skull in haphazard, overlapping repetition.

"Elize!" Rochelle yelled running out of the niche and stopping as the wave of throbbing bass forced her to her knees.

"There you are!" Madeline's bell like voice tingled through the strong bass. Madeline plopped a knitted cap onto Rochelle's head, and helped her sister get to her feet.

"What's happening." Rochelle stammered pulling the cap further down over her ears.

"The demon's arrived and he's playing tricks." Madeline informed Rochelle as she smeared some smelling salts under Rochelle's nose. "Things are getting rowdy in the atrium. I think we'd better go save your grandson before they really get out of hand."

"But Elize…" Rochelle mumbled.

"Hurry," Madeline insisted yanking Rochelle behind her as she danced up the stairs where her sisters were standing in a sea of brightly knitted caps.

"Is Elize with you?" Taa shouted over the noise as she waded through the hats to where Rochelle stood.

"She ran away," Rochelle replied trying not to focus on the long, multi-colored hat Taa was wearing.

"We need more smelling salts?" Madeline said poking her knitting needle into Taa's bag. Brushing Madeline out of the way, Taa searched her bag and pulled out a small bag of salts. Madeline took the bag and passed pieces of salt to her sisters.

"Why isn't the shield working?" Rochelle asked Madeline as Gerawld, and the burly man rolled past her.

"The shield worked on the water," Madeline replied, popping a bright green hat on Gerawld's head before he charged back into the crowd, "but not the sound waves. The only thing that might stop sound waves is white noise."

"White noise!" Rochelle exclaimed as one of the Simeon's flew past, his face a bloody mess. "And just where do you propose we get that?"

"I'll see what Ori and I can do." Mal told her and stomped off to see where Ori had gotten off to.

"How can I help?" Mia asked slipping out of the mosh of sweaty bodies with a bright red scarf wrapped over her ears.

"First we need to get Alzo and Parth out of there." Rochelle shouted stuffing two caps into Mia's paws.

"And Grumbul." Madeline added shoving another hat at Mia.

"You'll need this too." Taa shoved some smelling salts into one of the empty pockets on Mia's belt. Mia fastened the hats to her belt and studied the space between her and Alzo.

"Cup your hands like this," Mia demonstrated. Rochelle cupped her hands and held them tightly together. Using Rochelle's hands as a springboard, Mia bounced over the crowd and pulled an extra-long, green, and yellow, stocking cap over Alzo's ears before gracefully landing next to him. Before Alzo could ask her what she was doing, Mia swiped his mustache with smelling salts.

"Head for the stairs!" Mia shouted at the dazed Alzo before pulling a purple hat with bright pink flowers over Parth's dreadlocks. Taa grabbed hold of Parth's hand before she could slap Mia and shoved some smelling salts under her nose. Leaving Madeline and her sisters to finish hatting and salting the others, Mia and Taa took Alzo and Parth out of the atrium where Rochelle and Mal were anxiously waiting on the steps.

"Is Elize with you?" Alzo asked not seeing her.

"No," Rochelle told him sadly. "I don't know where Elize is."

Elize had no idea where she was either. She had kept running until she was forced to stop and catch her breath.

"Elize!" Sabrina shrieked when she saw Elize.

"Sabrina!" Elize gasped, her head spinning. "Oh, thank God! You've got to help me! I've got to get out of here!"

"It's okay," Sabrina told Elize taking her hand. "I'll take you outside, but first let's get you some fresh air."

"I need to get out of here!" Elize continued to mumble. "I need to find Nekita. Have you seen her?"

"Who?" Sabrina asked, searching along the top of the passageway until she saw what she was looking for. "You should be able to get some fresh air through that hole." Sabrina motioned to a small hole above their heads. Elize stood on her tip toes and lifted her head.

"Nekita, she's an owl." Elize said as she breathed in the cool, fresh air.

"An owl?" Sabrina exclaimed. "You need to find an owl? Now?"

"Yes...well not an owl exactly. I mean she looks like an owl, but Nekita's tall like me and has tiny arms under her wings."

"Nekita's a Neognathae?!" Sabrina sputtered checking Elize's eyes for any signs of a concussion. "A Neognathae? Here in Astaria?"

"Yes! Have you seen her?" Elize asked frantically. "It's really important that I find her. Nekita said she had something to tell me, but I blew her off! I need to know what it is she had to tell me!" Elize lowered her head and began pacing back and forth in front of Sabrina like a caged tiger.

"No, I haven't seen a Neognathae." Sabrina said wondering if Elize had inherited their father's madness. Elize closed her eyes and tried to remember where she had last seen Nekita.

"Can you take me to the statue of Monet?"

"Sure," Sabrina nodded and started back down the corridor. After a few minutes, they reached a space between the walls and Sabrina stopped at one of the now vacant guard posts. "The statues at the bottom of the steps to the right." Sabrina told Elize. "Are you sure you know what you're doing?"

"Not at all." Elize said and leaned over to give Sabrina an awkward hug. "Tell my brother not to worry! Thanks, sis."

Sabrina waited until Elize had run down the steps, before heading for the atrium. She hadn't gotten very far when a furry, cream colored blur rushed past her.

"Take care of my sister." Sabrina whispered after Rixley as she disappeared down the steps after Elize.

"Nekita!" Elize called out as she rushed towards the lone figure standing underneath the statue of Monet. When she reached Nekita, Elize was out of breath again. "You...you said you wanted to talk to me earlier. Sorry...sorry I took so long."

"No matter, you're here now." Nekita said clicking her beak. "That's all that matters."

"What did you want to tell me?" Elize asked.

"I wanted to tell you, that you were right. I was wrong doubt your vision." Nekita admitted shyly, she was not accustomed to making mistakes or apologies. "It is rare for an Oracle to see their own visions. Now I know what caused Su Lei to destroy her shell, my aunt foresaw her own future. Or perhaps she guessed it. Whatever it was, Su Lei acted on her intuition. Su Lei's bizarre actions made it possible for her to transfer her memories and the memories of the Oracles past to me and give me the time I needed to flee before the fallen could find me."

"The fallen," Elize exclaimed putting her hand on Nekita's silky wing. "Oh Nekita, I'm afraid everyone heard the prophecy wrong! I don't think the prophecy is about me!"

"It is about you, but not in the way we thought," Nekita explained bobbing her head excitedly, "The true prophecy reads, 'The one who fell,' not the one who falls."

"The one who fell is the watcher angel Scyathee, which mean Alzo's not the great change, I am!" Elize stopped and glanced up at the statue's hollow eyes. Elize could feel someone watching her from above.

"I think Monet may still be alive." Nekita whispered following Elize's glance. "I believe she's been watching us."

"I think so too, and I think it's about time I see what she wants." Elize said. She hoped she sounded braver than she felt.

"I'm sure it's a trap." Nekita warned, but she didn't try to change Elize's mind.

"Yeah, I know," Elize said biting her lower lip, "but I can't run anymore. I need to face my destiny. If I run away the demon will take his wrath out on you, my family, my friends. I will do whatever it takes to prevent that." Elize looked at Nekita. "Can you get me up there?"

"I can try," Nekita replied and clicked her beak three times. When no screechers appeared, she clicked her beak again. Still no screechers.

"It looks like I will have to carry you myself." Nekita said reluctantly after clicking her beak several more times without any result. "I've never carried a passenger before." Nekita warned Elize. She scanned the statue warily. "I should be able to get you up to her knee. After that we'll just have to see."

"Sounds like a plan." Elize replied following Nekita's gaze up to the knee of the statue.

"Are you sure about this?"

"No," Elize admitted, "but it's something I have to do."

"Step on my talons and wrap your arms around my waist." Nekita instructed nervously. "And hold on tight." Elize put her feet on Nekita's talons and her heels into the crook of skin between Nekita's talons to stabilize herself. "Hold on tight." Nekita repeated as she unfurled her wide wings. As Nekita slowly began to lift off the ground, a masked figure leapt from the ground and grabbed Elize's ankles.

"Damn you, Rixley!" Elize growled trying to shake the small ferret off. Rixley held on tighter and pressed her body against Elize's calves. "Rixley let go!"

"Rixley brave and strong." Rixley squeaked into Elize's legs. "Rixley strong and brave." Rixley continued repeating her mantra as Nekita flew further and further from the ground. Rixley didn't know if she was more afraid of the owl-lady or of flying, but what she did know was that Elize wasn't going without her.

The extra weight made it hard for Nekita to gain altitude and caused her to sway awkwardly. By the time she reached the curved cap

of Monet's knee she was forced to land. The instant Elize stepped off
Nekita's talons, Rixley scurried up into Elize's hood and burrowed
deep inside it. Rixley wasn't worried about Elize being mad at her, she
was more worried about Nekita eating her. Rixley had barely managed
to escape becoming a midnight snack for the large desert owls who
lived outside the Salt Temples and even though Elize assured her that
Nekita would not eat her, Rixley was not convinced.

"We'd better keep going," Nekita said looking at the ban of dark
clouds that encircled the top of the palace.

"Are you sure you're up to it." Elize asked Nekita. Nekita nodded
and told Elize to climb back on. By the time Nekita reached the statues
arm she was spent. Elize stepped onto the statues arm and looked
down. She immediately regretted it, they were at least fifteen stories or
higher.

"I don't think that storms natural." Elize said to Nekita, clinging to
the statues bicep while the wind whipped her hair across her face.
"Take Rixley and go back down while you can."

"No," Nekita refused and flew up to the statue's neck. "I'm not
leaving." Elize flashed Nekita a grateful look.

"Rixley," Elize said, reaching up and giving her hood a good
shake. "Rixley get out here!"

"Rixley not go!" Rixley replied from deep inside the hood.
"Rixley stay with Elize."

"Rixley," Elize repeated sternly. "I need you to get out." Rixley
poked her nose out and peeked at Elize. "Seriously, get out here, I need
you to stand guard."

Rixley refused and dove deeper into Elize's hood. Finally, Elize
pulled off her robe and shook the stubborn ferret out.

"Rixley I'm going to go inside the statue, and I need you to stand
guard and not let anyone follow me?"

"How?"

"How what?"

"How Elize get inside?" Rixley asked curiously.

"I don't know," Elize explained, "but I need to go up there." Elize
pointed at statue's head.

Rixley looked at the statue's head while Elize considered the
question. She remembered the story her Grandmother Rochelle, had
told her about the missing girls. Rochelle had mentioned a spiral
stairway curling up inside the statue. The entrance by the statue's feet
had been filled in, but what if there was a way in higher up. "Nekita,"
she called up to her friend perched on top of a long lock of carved hair.
"Can you fly around and see if you see any way inside?"

Nekita flew around the top of the statue twice before landing on the arm near Elize. "It looks like there may be a door behind the neck," Nekita reported, "but be careful! We are definitely being watched."

"I know." Elize whispered. "I'm pretty sure it's Monet. My grandmother told me old tales about Monet luring young girls to the top."

"Are you sure you really need to do this?" Nekita asked Elize, clicking her beak nervously. "We could just fly away from here."

"This is my destiny," Elize said as she stepped back onto Nekita's talons for the short flight to the statue's shoulders. "I can't run away from it."

When she landed Elize knelt and took Rixley's trembling paws in her hands. "Rixley, my friend, I need you to keep watch over this door and not let anyone in. Understand?"

Rixley nodded and stood with her pointy stick against her right shoulder like Mia had taught her. "Rixley understand. Rixley not let anyone follow Elize."

"Good," Elize said and leaned over and kissed Rixley on the forehead. Elize looked at the darkening sky and shivered. "You're going to have to be very brave and strong."

"Rixley be very brave and strong." Rixley assured Elize clutching her stick tightly.

"I hope this works," Elize said under her breath before taking several deep breaths to center herself. In her mind the numbers 3, 7, 7, 3 appeared. They were the same numbers Nekita used the night she had called forth her visions. Elize focused on the small blue geode embedded under the skin of her right palm until a thin line appeared and blue-white energy seeped out covering Elize's body like an embryonic sack.

"I hope you know what you're doing," Nekita hooted from the statue's shoulder as she watched Elize step inside the rectangular door carved in the back of the statue of Monet's neck.

The second Elize stepped into the statue, the throbbing bass inside the atrium subsided.

"Mal you did it!" Rochelle exclaimed throwing her arms around the old mule's neck. "I didn't think you had it in you!"

"I didn't," Mal huffed scraping his hoof across the floor. "I couldn't find Ori in this crowd.

"Well, if you didn't stop it who did?" Alzo demanded, suddenly very worried about Elize.

Sabrina rushed into the atrium out of breath and fell into Rochelle's arms. "It's Elize! She's gone to face the demon!"

CHAPTER 24

"Elize is what?" Alzo shouted at the strange girl trembling in his grandmother's arms. "Why didn't you stop her!"

"I…I…" Sabrina stammered trying to force the words around the lump in her throat.

"Leave the poor girl alone." Rochelle scolded Alzo handing Sabrina over to Taa. "Can't you see she's had a shock."

"But we need to stop Elize!" Alzo bellowed throwing his arms over his head.

"Then I suggest you follow me." Rochelle told him curtly and started down the stairs without looking back.

"Wait for me," Grumbul called after his wife.

"And me," Ori said gingerly stepping over a heap of unconscious bodies. He was feeling much better after the blood transfusion, but he was still a bit dizzy. Gerawld wrapped his long, striped tail around Ori and walked down the stairs next to him. "Thanks buddy," Ori whispered leaning heavily on Gerawld's tail.

"Yowl awlright?" Gerawld meowed as he studied Ori's face.

"Yeah," Ori winced glad for Gerawld's help. "I hope we reach Elize before she does something reckless."

"They won't be able to stop her." Sabrina whispered into Taa's ear so Alzo couldn't hear her. "Elize was with a Neognathae!"

"Nekita," Taa corrected as she led Sabrina back towards the atrium. "Nekita will help Elize accomplish whatever it is she needs to do. We are healers and it is our responsibility to take care of the injured."

"But you don't understand!" Sabrina exclaimed pushing away from Taa. "I saw…I saw a vision I wasn't supposed to. I saw the Neognathae attacking Elize inside Monet's head! I think Nekita is in league with the demon."

Taa licked her lips and took a step back. She didn't want to offend Sabrina, however she found it hard to believe Nekita would ever betray Elize.

"You don't believe me!" Sabrina shrieked burying her face in her hands. Taa had dealt with hysterical patients before and knew from experience that keeping ones voice calm and steady was the best way to maintain control.

"I do believe you," Taa assured Sabrina calmly, "but perhaps Nekita wasn't attacking Elize. Is it possible that something else may have been going on?"

"Well, maybe," Sabrina admitted reluctantly, "it was only a drop, so the vision wasn't complete."

"Is that why you didn't tell Alzo about Nekita?" Taa asked gently, keeping her eyes on the girl's face.

"Not really," Sabrina replied making a face. "Alzo, I mean Emperor Alzo whatever, freaks me out. I think he hates me! Have you seen the way he looks at me? Like I leave a bad taste in his mouth! For all I know he'll have my head cut off to get rid of me!"

"Well," Taa said slipping her arm around Sabrina's as they continued into the atrium. "I know Alzo, and I can assure you that he will not just cut your head off on a whim. Besides, the last Emperor that acted so barbaric was the third one, and if the histories are right, he was madder than Emperor Taz."

"How do you know this?" Sabrina asked kneeling next to Taa who had leaned over one of the ruby lipped women and was busy examining the long gash on the woman's forearm.

"This will require stitches," Taa told the woman before answering Sabrina. "One of the books we took contained a detailed history of the first three emperors and their predecessors back to the time of Monet. Quite interesting. I'll show it to you when we're done here."

"Aren't we going to join the others?" Sabrina asked as she skillfully glided a needle and thread through the lady's skin like it was a torn piece of cloth.

"No, Sabrina." Taa said. Her voice was so serious Sabrina stopped what she was doing to listen. "When we are done here, we will return to the palace and check on Emperor Taz. I don't think your father has long to live."

"Mother will take care of him," Sabrina told Taa as she finished up the stitching and moved on to the next patient.

"You are very good at that," Taa said examining the gash, Sabrina had just sewn shut. "Someone with your skills should be out in a healing center. They can use all the help they can get out there."

"I don't think I'd be happy in a healing center," Sabrina said tilting her head and smiling at Taa. She had never received such a complement before. Her mother always had a way of finding fault with her work. No matter how good a job she did. "I'd like to travel. Perhaps I could be a traveling healer. Wouldn't it be grand to travel from center to center sharing knowledge!"

"That would be grand," Taa agreed. "Maybe when this business with Elize is over we can set out together."

"I hope it's over soon," Sabrina sighed and gave Taa another smile. She was glad she had met Taa and looked forward to spending more time with her. "I wonder what Elize is doing?"

Elize was halfway up the ladder-like staircase that ran up the back of the statue's neck and ended just above the nape. The stairway resembled a spinal cord, so Elize was protected by a curved wall behind her while she climbed up the disk shaped steps that took her into the base of the skull. The interior of the statue's head was divided into two sections, which looked like the left and right lobe of the human brain minus the gray matter.

In the right lobe, a slender, almost transparent woman was gazing out the statue's hollow pupil. Sensing Elize's presence, she gracefully spun around and faced her. Elize gasped, surprised. Although Monet was thousands of years old, she looked no older than twenty.

"Ḥaṣānu," Monet sang dancing across the floor. Her delicate, translucent dress flowed around her legs like lily pedals. "Ḥaṣānu, ḥaṣānu." Monet sang waving her hands in front of her as she approached Elize. Monet's words unraveled in Elize's mind as she not so gracefully danced backwards to avoid Monet's touch.

"Welcome, welcome!" Monet continued to sing in a thickly accented common tongue. "I, Monet, daughter of the Earth, welcome you Princess Monetelizadora, daughter of the Sixth Emperor of Astaria and granddaughter of the Sixth Priestess of Palenina."

"I am honored, Monet," Elize sang back slightly out of tune as she drifted to one side to prevent Monet from touching her, "but please call me Elize. My name is Elize."

"Elize," Monet said fluttering her hands in front of Elize. "Why do you flitter away. I've been waiting so long for you to arrive."

"For me," Elize challenged, spinning out of Monet's reach once again, "or the gift?"

"Gift?" Monet scoffed, clearly disappointed that Elize wasn't entranced by her beauty like those who had visited in the past. "It has proved to be more of a curse than a gift!"

"Tell me about it."

"It's a long story," Monet replied sweeping her hands up and running her fingers through her gossamer hair.

"Please, I insist." Elize insisted, smiling at Monet sweetly as she could manage.

"Oh, if you insist." Monet pouted and flicked her hand. Two round stools appeared in front of them. Monet sat on one and motioned for Elize to take the other. "It was the year I bloomed." Monet began, a faraway look in her eyes. "It was the Spring I became betrothed to Kronic. Kronic was a shepherd boy. He was very good-looking and very strong. He used to play love songs to me on his lute. My mother and aunts said I was a lucky girl. I was almost a woman, but since I hadn't bloomed yet, our marriage could not take place. That fall my father was blessed with a bountiful harvest. Kronic was pleased because my dowery would be larger than he had expected.

My dearest father had not been blessed with sons. So, it fell upon my sisters and I to help him bring in the harvest. As the eldest, it was my duty to accompany my father when he went to the markets. The markets were a marvelous place full of beautiful ladies dressed in fine silken robes, colorful beads dripped down their necks and shimmering rings glittered from their fingers, earlobes, and noses. I yearned for a life filled with such finery, but I knew that as the wife of Kronic it would never be mine.

That year when our family presented the first fruits of the harvest to the holy ones my father took me with him. It was customary for two holy ones to accept the harvest, but this year a third named Scyathee accompanied them. Scyathee was incredibly beautiful to behold."

"I thought his name was Scythe?" Elize interrupted.

"His name was Scyathee," Monet replied curtly. It was clear from the aggravated look on her face that Monet was not used to being interrupted. "When Scyathee laid eyes on me, he was so overcome by my beauty that he rushed forward to take the offering I carried on my back. My heart stirred inside my breast, the instant his eyes met mine. His skin was the color of honey. His hair fell like ripen wheat across his muscular shoulders. I can still see the way his muscles rippled when he lifted the sheaf off my back. My father saw it too, and shooed me away, but he was too late. The die had been cast.

Scyathee wove the wheat from my sheaf into a basket and filled it with gold dust. My father protested that I was already betrothed. My mother cried and said I was too young. But Scyathee was not swayed. Finally, my father relented. He knew only a fool argued with the holy ones. That very evening, I left with my beloved."

"Were you homesick?" Elize wondered out loud. Even though she had made wonderful friends on Toboria she missed her friends and home back on Earth terribly.

"A little at first," Monet answered, twisting her hair around her finger before letting it go. She rarely thought about her parents and sisters. It had been a long, long time ago. So long it was hard to believe they ever existed. Monet paused and for an instant she looked rather sad, but then she waved her hand in front of her face and smiled at Elize.

"It was hard to be sad when Scyathee was around. Scyathee enjoyed spoiling me with pretty things. No one dressed finer than I. I owned more gold and jewels than the queen herself. We enjoyed the finest foods and drinks and traveled to marvelous places. We were extremely happy."

"When did he give you the gift of immortality?

"Give!" Monet snapped and pushed her hands against the bottom of her seat. "A gift is something given and received. Scyathee never gave me a choice. His actions were prompted by his own ego! Scyathee had seen how the other humans aged, how their beauty was stolen by time, and he could not bear to have that happen to me. At first I thought staying young forever was a blessing but now..."

"What changed?" Elize prompted Monet, sensing that their time was growing short.

"He did," Monet admitted sadly, "or perhaps it was me. After our second daughter was born, Scyathee no longer wanted me to go with him into the towns and villages. He claimed I flirted with the men in the markets who stared at me with hungry eyes. Perhaps I did, but as I told him, it was all in good fun, just harmless flirting. Scyathee became consumed with jealous rage. After he killed an innocent man, I agreed to stop going to the markets with him. But even that didn't quell his jealous rage. When he became violent towards me and my daughters, I ran away. It was during this time that I began to resent what Scyathee had done to me. Can you imagine how horrible it is to watch your children grow old while you remain forever young!"

"Is that when you came to this planet, to Toboria?" Elize asked rubbing her arms to quell the energy pulsing against her skin.

"No," Monet answered getting to her feet. "I fled to the other side of Earth, but Scyathee found me, so I fled again and again. Each time when I thought I'd found a safe place, Scyathee found me. Sometimes it would take months, sometimes years, sometimes a century, but he always tracked me down until..."

"Until what?"

"Until the flood." Monet replied. "In the last days before the great flood, there was a great exodus. Those who had come from different realms were warned to leave before the doorways between the realms were sealed. Once the rains began there would be no escape. I gathered my daughters and their families, and we left with the crowds fleeing Earth."

"None of your family stayed on Earth?"

"No, we all fled, but only my daughters and their families joined me. My only son, was devoted to his father and had stayed with Scyathee."

"And you and your daughters escaped."

"Yes, but just barely. By the time we reached the doorways most of them had already been sealed. Luckily, we were able to slip into this realm and land on Toboria. What a change from Earth! Toboria was a much smaller planet than Earth and very primitive, but I felt safe here and for a while it looked like our escape had gone unnoticed."

"Did Scyathee find you?"

"No, Raphael did."

"Raphael?"

"Yes."

"The angel Raphael?" Elize asked surprised.

"Yes, the angel Raphael." Monet answered looking at Elize like she was a dull child with too many questions. "Raphael had been given the task of tracking down the fallen angels and bringing them to justice."

"And he came here looking for Scyathee?" Elize asked, not clear on why Raphael had come to Toboria.

"No, Raphael had already captured Scyathee. He was looking for me. I must admit I was quite surprised when he appeared on my threshold, but I knew at once what he had come for. I was so afraid. I threw myself at his feet and begged for mercy. Not for myself, but for my daughters and my grandchildren, and great grandchildren."

"Why?"

"Because it was against the law for watchers to have children with humans. I thought Raphael had been sent to annihilate us. Raphael knew what Scyathee had done to me and even though I hadn't asked for the gift, as you call it, Raphael knew that if Scyathee had given me a choice, I would have taken it. The truth is I enjoyed being treated as a holy one.

You see, on the Earth, Scyathee and I had been worshipped. The people believed we held the power to bring them great blessings or great disasters. When I walked in the bazaar the women adored me. They threw flowers at my feet and gave me gems and beautiful beads to wear in my hair and around my neck. I thought they loved me and worshipped me as a goddess. Raphael showed me that it was all an illusion. The women didn't adore me, they feared me. Worse they despised me.

Raphael agreed to spare my family if I agreed to his conditions. Raphael would allow my daughters to live long and fruitful lives, along with their children. Eventually Scyathee's genetic code would be filtered out of their descendants. I also had to agree to give Raphael what Scyathee had given me which was much more than just immortality. Even though I agreed to give Raphael what he wanted, I had no idea how, but Raphael did. Raphael used his divine powers to transfer what Scyathee had given me to the child growing inside my womb. The gift, as you call it, was transferred from my youngest daughter to her daughter, and down through her female descendants to you. Raphael predicted that in the future Scyathee would escape hell, but in order to return to his former self, Scyathee would need to take back the part of himself that he gave to me. The part of himself that you now possess."

Monet stopped talking when a strong gust of wind slammed into the side of the head.

"He's coming!" Monet shrieked.

Outside the storm had intensified. The wind was so fierce that Rixley had to brace herself inside the doorway to keep from being blown off the statue's round shoulders. Somewhere above her, Rixley knew Nekita was perched watching the dark splotch moving erratically up the statue's torso.

Standing with her back against the doorway, Rixley held her pointy stick close to her body. "Rixley brave!" She squeaked, her shiny black eyes searching through the thick clouds for the dark blotch. The bit of green glass on the tip of her stick began to flicker. "Rixley strong!" Rixley squeaked again, her voice shaking. The green glass flared brightly from the tip of her pointy stick illuminating the figure of a man crawling up the statue's left shoulder. Rixley gulped when the man pulled himself up and started walking towards her. He was even taller than Alzo.

"Get away Bagabong!" Rixley shouted bravely, snapping out of her fear trance and thrusting her stick into Scythe's thigh. Scythe yanked the pesky ferret out of the doorway and tossed her off the side of the statue. Rixley shrieked in terror.

"I've got you!" Nekita hooted, wrapping her talons around the terrified ferrets tubular middle.

"Did you see that?" Ori yelled, nudging Mal in the side as he pointed skyward. "Nekita just caught Rixley in mid-air!"

"I see the ferret and the owl," Mal scoffed rubbing his ribs, "but I don't see Elize?"

Inside the statue's head Elize watched the eloquent, well-dressed man step off the top of the statue's neck. She had been expecting a demon, not a handsome man with a finely chiseled face and skin which looked like it had been airbrushed to perfection.

"Scyathee, my beloved." Monet cooed dancing out in front of Elize to face the bronze skinned man. The demon tensed at the sound of Monet's voice. "Oh, my sweet beloved." Monet continued tilting her head to one side. "What have they done to thee? Your eyes which sparkled like sapphires have become as dark as coal. Not even the twinkling stars can penetrate their darkness. Is there no love left inside you for your dear Monet? Have you forgotten your beloved? The one who once drove you mad with passion."

The sound of Monet's voice touched Scythe in a way he had not expected. He had escaped the ninth dimension to retrieve the part of himself he had foolishly given to Monet. A gift that had sent him to hell. He wavered at the sound of her voice for an instant, but only for an instant.

"Ah, my dearest Monet." Scythe said in a tone sweet and sticky like honey. "You proclaim your undying love from one side of your beautiful mouth, while you curse me from the other. You were always quite naïve, weren't you? Do you not see that there is nothing you can give me that I couldn't get from any other mortal woman? Raphael tricked you my dear Monet and as always, you were too dense to realize it."

"I did what I did to save our children." Monet whined fear flickering in her eyes.

"Oh, come on my dear. We both know that is a lie." Scythe smiled dangerously. "You did what you did to save your own skin. Not like this one." Scythe gestured his well-manicured hand at Elize. "This one would die a thousand deaths to save those she loved."

Monet's face grew sour. Scythe ignored her. His eyes were fixed upon Elize. What energy this one has, he thought. Energy that was rightfully his.

"Come to me." Scythe whispered seductively to Elize. "Take my hand. Together we will rule the nine realms. You will be my goddess and I will be your god. Together no one will be able to stop us."

"Noooo!" Monet shouted angrily flinging herself at Elize and trying to possess her. The light sack Elize had woven around her before entering the statue, wrapped around the enraged Monet like a spider's web. The stone in Elize's palm opened and sucked Monet's translucent body into it, trapping her inside like a genie in a bottle.

"Such power!" Scythe moaned closing the distance between him and Elize before Elize could escape.

Elize tried to sidestep Scythe, but he was too quick. Scythe grabbed Elize by the right wrist and forced her hand open. Remembering all the warnings not to use her energy against him, Elize fought to keep the power under control as Scythe's icy fingertips plunged into her palm. Elize screamed and kicked at the demon, but she could not break free.

Ripping the stone out of Elize's palm, Scythe shoved Elize to the ground. As soon as the stone was out of her hand, it cracked open releasing waves of blue-white energy that flowed out and washed over Scythe with euphoric pure energy.

"We have to help her!" Nekita hooted and tighten her grip around Rixley's waist. Folding her wings close to her body, Nekita propelled herself through the statue's left eye like a missile.

Holding her stick tightly in front of her, the florescent green tip flaring like a laser beam, Rixley sliced through Scythe's forearm before he even realized they were there. Surprised by the attack, Scythe roared and lurched sideways. His now detached arm bounced across the floor with the stone still grasped in his hand. Ignoring Nekita and Rixley, Scythe scrambled after his arm.

"Hurry jump on!" Nekita shouted at Elize.

"You and Rixley get to safety." Elize yelled back. "I need to do this bit by myself." Without waiting to hear any arguments, Elize ran out of the eye and leapt into the howling wind.

CHAPTER 25

Seduced by the immense power, Scythe had let his guard down and allowed himself to be attacked.

"Lesson learned." Scythe groused retrieving his arm and shoving it back in place. "Now where did that blasted girl go? Surely she has enough sense to know she can't escape me." After searching the inside of the head, Scythe looked out the right eye and spotted Nekita fluttering around a swirling cloud of light. Smiling widely, the demon shoved the blue stone still containing Monet into his heartless chest and clapped his hands.

Ori was standing outside the gatehouse with Mal and the others when the charcoal gray storm cloud billowed out of the statue's mouth and surrounded Monet's head with tornado forced winds. Caught off guard by the winds, Nekita desperately flapped her wings and tried to stay with the bright sphere holding Elize, but the winds were too strong. Sweeping sharply upward to avoid a blast of wind, Nekita felt Rixley slip out of her talons. Unable to turn fast enough to catch the frantic ferret plummeting helplessly towards the ground, Nekita clicked her beak. Several gray screechers popped out of the air just below Rixley cushioning the flailing ferret and dropping her safely into Ori's outstretched arms.

Elize watched as Monet's head teetered back and forth on the statue's neck. Below she could see a crowd gathering around the gatehouse. Elize realized that if the head broke loose, anyone under it would be crushed. She had to get Scythe away from the statue fast.

Focusing her energy, Elize willed the sphere to spin and form a white cyclone out of the clouds closest to her. Once the sphere was spinning fast enough, the white cyclone shot off across the sky like a comet over the mountain range behind Astaria. As she hoped the darker storm gave chase.

"What's happening?" Alzo demanded when Ori ran into the gatehouse with Rixley cradled in his arms.

"Bagabong!" Rixley muttered clearly in shock.

"Bagabong?" Alzo asked shaking his head.

"A monster that hides in the dark and eats young animals." Mal translated.

"I thought that was a Vagagoon." Ori teased his old friend.

"Same thing." Mal huffed and nuzzled Rixley with his soft muzzle. "You okay, kiddo?"

"Rixley brave and Rixley strong." Ori sang to Rixley as he rocked her in his arms. "Rixley fought the Bagabong."

Mal swatted Ori with his tail. "If you write that imp a ballad, we'll never get any peace."

"Where's Nekita and Elize?" Alzo demanded searching the faces outside the gatehouse. "I don't see Nekita or Elize anywhere!"

"Last time I saw them they were up there," Mal replied pointing at the statue of Monet's head.

"Watch out!" Parth shouted as bits of rubble rained down from the statue's fractured neck.

"We need to get everyone inside!" Quinn shouted and grabbed Alzo by the shoulder.

"I'm not going in without Elize!" Alzo shouted back pulling himself free.

"Alzo, Quinn's right we need to take cover!" Parth pled with him. "It's too dangerous out here. The statue's head could break off at any time. You must think of the others."

"Quinn, get everyone inside!" Alzo commanded, "I'm going to find Elize!"

"Stop this nonsense!" Rochelle roared over the panicking crowd. "You're in danger and need to take cover now!" A thunderous crack erupted over the crowd as a large chunk of neck broke loose. Hundreds of feet scurried around Alzo as they rushed through the gatehouse and into the palace.

Alzo stood, his eyes locked on Rochelle. "I'm not going without Elize."

"Sorry dear," Parth whispered sweetly in Alzo's ear as she pinched the back of his neck rendering him temporarily unconscious, "but I refuse to be a widow on my wedding night."

"Nekita!" Ori yelled, placing Rixley on Mal's back, he pushed his way through the crowd and rushed down the gatehouse steps. "Nekita! Over here!" Ori ran under the teetering owl waving his arms like a mad man. Nekita plopped to the ground a few feet away from him.

"The winds were too strong." Nekita moaned exhausted as she staggered towards Ori. "I couldn't reach Elize. Is Rixley alright? I didn't mean to drop her."

"Rixley's in shock, but she's alright." Ori assured the badly shaken Nekita. "She's in the gatehouse with Mal." Ori wrapped his arm around Nekita's waist and helped her inside the gatehouse where Taa was sitting with Rixley. While Taa examined the ruffled owl, Rixley stared at Ori with feral, shiny black eyes. Ori took Rixley's small, trembling paw and stroked it gently.

"Elize!" Rixley's lip quivered, and her entire body shook. "Elize...Elize," Rixley sobbed burying her head in Ori's lap. "Elize promise Rixley she'd never leave, but she did!"

"I'm sure she didn't mean to..."

"No, no, no, Elize meant to!" Rixley snapped defiantly. "Rixley heard Elize tell Nekita to take Rixley to safety. Rixley told Elize that where Elize goes Rixley goes, but Elize left Rixley!"

"Rixley's right." Nekita confirmed. "Elize said she had to do the next bit alone! I tried to go after her, but the winds were too strong. Now that the winds have settled a bit I'm going to try to find her."

"Rixley go too. Rixley go with Nekita. Elize needs Rixley's help."

"You're right." Nekita agreed. "Rixley and I will go after Elize. I know Elize thinks she has to protect us, but she can't do this alone."

"I'm going too." Ori said, but Nekita shook her head. "I'm too weak to carry you. Besides you'll be more help to Elize here." Nekita explained quickly. She was eager to get back in the air and didn't want to waste time arguing with Ori. "Help Mal study the old histories, hopefully you will find something to help us."

"She's right." Taa insisted putting her hand on Ori's arm. "I know you're feeling better, but it's too soon to tell if the effects of the transfusion will hold."

"You don't even know where they're headed!" Ori protested looking over at Mal for support and not getting any.

"The cyclones were headed east, towards the Dimly." Mal told them pointing his ears to show them the exact direction. "They should be easy to follow, the larger cyclone should have left a trail of debris."

"The Dimly?" Ori exclaimed looking over at the old mule like he had lost his mind.

"Unfortunately."

"Mal's right. I think Elize is headed for the Dimly." Nekita chirped, confirming Mal's suspicions. "Before I took Elize up the statue, I told her about something I saw in the Oracle's memory." Nekita dragged her talon across the ground and etched an image of a strange wheel with many doors hovering under Toboria's two moons. "I think the wheel is located in the Dimly and that Elize is trying to lure Scythe there." Rixley tilted her head and studied Nekita's drawing.

"Is wheel Dimly?"

"The Dimly is the dark side of Toboria," Taa explained, nervously running her hands across the creases in her cloak. "It is called the Dimly because the two moons block out most of the sunlight. It is a land of shadows where nightmare creatures roam."

"Seems like a strange place for the wheel of the realms to be?" Mal remarked, his chocolate eyes revealing his worry. Nekita bobbed her head up and down.

"I agree, but that's where I see the wheel of the realms. It's circling above the Dimly. I don't know the exact location, but even if I did, I've never been inside the Dimly so I wouldn't recognize it until I got there."

Nekita clicked her beak and wrung her little hands nervously under her wings. She didn't want her friends to see how frighten she was. Nekita had seen visions of the Dimly and she had no desire to visit there, but Elize needed her, and she would not let her friend.

"I have something that will help," Ori whispered glancing sheepishly over at Alzo who was just starting to rouse himself from his impromptu nap. Ori reached into a hidden pocket inside his jacket and slipped out a small book no bigger than his hand.

"Hey! That's mine! Where did you find it?!" Alzo exclaimed now fully awake and clearly shocked to see the tattered book.

"It was in a blue jar I found stuck under a floorboard in your kitchen."

"So, in other words you just stumbled upon it?" Parth huffed bopping Ori on the back of the head.

"What is it?" Taa asked curiously peering over Ori's shoulder.

"A very old book," Ori replied as he unlatched the strap and opened the book containing pages of strange symbols etched upon yellowed parchment.

"Last time I saw that book my mother was using it to..."

"Open a forbidden pathway to another realm." Ori finished for Alzo.

"I guess," Alzo said rubbing his neck. "I'm not sure she even knew what she was doing. I think Mayme was trying to open a pathway to Palenina. I guess she stuck the book in my jacket before I was swept away."

"Can you read it?" Taa asked leaning closer so she could get a better look.

"A little," Ori replied, tugging the fur on his chin. It made him uncomfortable to admit he didn't know everything. If he ever became a Mage, others would expect him to know everything, but this book had symbols he'd never seen before.

"Let me have a look," Nekita said snatching the book out of his hands before Ori could stop her. Nekita flipped through the pages. "It is written in a very ancient language." Nekita mumbled. "It contains..." Nekita hesitated as she quickly scanned the pages and realized it would be best to leave most of them unread. The book held knowledge and spells from the time before the Great Flood. Forbidden things, best forgotten. In the back of the book were several old maps. Nekita scanned the maps carefully before ripping one of them out.

"What are you doing?" Ori and Alzo gasped as Nekita folded the map in half and stuffed it under her wing.

"This should be destroyed." Nekita told Ori firmly as she reluctantly handed it back to him.

"Why?" Ori demanded.

"I think you know why." Nekita told him stiffly and turned to Rixley. "Ready?" She asked. Rixley nodded and climbed onto Nekita's sloped back.

"Wait!" Mia called to Rixley.

"Rixley go with Nekita" Rixley protested. "Rixley find Elize."

"You'll need this." Mia said and held up the tiny warrior's belt she had fashioned from a bit of mouse leather.

Rixley could barely contain her joy as Mia looped the strap over her shoulder and fastened the belt tightly around her waist. Rixley looked down at the belt proudly and ran her paws over the loops. The belt was just like Mia's belt, complete with a small dagger, a blow tube, and several fly sized darts. Mia had confiscated the tube and darts from Gerawld a while back after he almost swallowed one.

"You've earned it, Rixley." Mia assured her, giving her a sharp nod.

"All hail Rixley Brave and Strong, Warrior of Astaria." Alzo shouted and raised his right hand high over his head. Rixley saluted Alzo and hugged Mia before climbing onto Nekita's back and burying herself in the soft feathers between the owl's massive wings.

Alzo waited until Nekita and Rixley had become a small dot in the late afternoon sky before returning to the palace.

"Now what?" He asked Parth as they walked side-by-side down the main corridor.

"I know what I'd like to do," Parth said giving Alzo a exaggerated wink, "but I'm afraid that will have to wait. The council will be expecting us, we need to address the masses, and survey the storm damage. After that I'll find us a quiet place. It is our wedding night after all."

* * * * * * * *

"Our new emperor is meeting with the council." Behr scoffed as he limped into the throne room and plopped down into the ruby throne. His body ached all over from the forced possession and drunken flight up the statue of Monet. He prayed he would never have to experience such unpleasantness ever again.

"I see you managed to lose the demon again." The former Empress said with a bored expression on her face. "I imagine your mother will be thrilled to hear that. I hope you've stocked up on garlic."

Behr rolled his eyes. He could care a less what his mother thought anymore. He was through with her and her schemes. Behr watched the former Emperor burbling happily in the ruby studded wheeled chair he used for special occasions. Taz had already forgotten what the special occasion was, but it didn't matter so long as he got to sit in his fancy chair.

"What do we do now?" Behr wondered looking around for something to drink.

"Die?" Ceen suggested casually, a bit too casually, not that Behr noticed. He had always been a weak man, weaker than Taz in many ways. He had never fully pulled away from his mother and stood on his own feet.

"Why don't we leave," Behr murmured half-heartedly as he reached over to take Ceen's delicate hand in his. "Go into the Dimly and just disappear. Start over fresh."

A thin smile crossed Ceen's lips as she slipped her hand from his. The poor sentimental fool, how could he be so blind. Her heart had always and would always belong to Tazadorin. Ceen stood up and gracefully glided across the floor where a small table with three glasses, filled with a thick amber liquid sat.

"Come let us drink to our new life," she murmured lifting a glass towards Behr. Behr glared at her. How dare she taunt him? Without getting to his feet, Behr reached out to take the glass she offered. Smiling defiantly, he lifted it to his lips, but instead of drinking, he dropped it on the floor.

"I'm not that easy," he sneered as the thick liquid dripped through the cracks in the stone. Ceen hissed softly and flicked her fork tongue across her fangs.

"Actually, you are," she hissed and slithered away. Behr listened to the rough, scratchy sound her scales made as they crossed the stone floor.

"Actually, I am," he mimicked Ceen before getting to his feet and picking up the remaining glasses. "To us brother!" He shouted handing one of the glasses to the glassy eyed Taz. Taz looked at the glass in his hand and smiled up at Behr.

"To us!" Taz gurgled happily clinking his glass against Behr's. The two men studied the thick amber liquid a second before lifting the glasses to their lips.

"Mother! Mother!" Quinn gasped as he ran into his mother's rooms breathless. "I've just left the throne room. The Emperor is..."

"Dead."

"Yes, and so is Behr."

"I know." Ceen said without any emotion. "I killed them."

"You killed them!" Quinn exclaimed hardly able to comprehend what his mother said.

"Well, I didn't actually kill them. I gave them a choice." Ceen explained as she slowly moved around the room. "Apparently they chose death. Not that it was really a choice. Even Behr was clever enough to realize it was over. Of course, he could have challenged Alzo for the throne, but I don't think he ever really wanted to be Emperor. That was his mother's obsession, not his. Before I came down here, I left two glasses of venom on a table. I did not force either to drink. Behr knew what it was and what would happen if he drank it and I'm fairly sure Taz did as well. The choice was theirs not mine."

"Why, why did you kill my father?" Quinn demanded. Tears dribbling from his lidless eyes.

"Fathers." Ceen sneered gliding across the floor to her quivering son. "I used a mix of seed to fertilize my eggs. Pity only you and Sabrina turned out right. But to answer your question. My darling Taz had been painfully dying for years. It was my fault. I made him an addict and let him stay an addict way too long."

"Why?"

"Because I was afraid." Ceen replied, keeping her voice even and controlled. "Taz and I shared the same fear. We were both afraid to leave the palace. When I was brought to the palace it was the first time I felt safe. I knew that when my services were no longer needed, I would be taken away. I was not going to let that happen. I genuinely loved Taz. Unfortunately, he did not feel the same way about me. For years I blamed Euna for taking Taz away from me, but I was only fooling myself. Taz never loved me. He loved the venom I fed him. It made the real world seem less real. Like Behr, Taa never really wanted to be Emperor. I truly believe the only reason your father lived so long was because he believed Alzo and Elize were still alive and that one day they would return. He was right all along and now, finally he can rest in peace."

Quinn stood silently taking in all Ceen had just told him. It was the longest conversation he had ever had with his mother. Quinn knew his mother thought he was weak, not deserving of her love and attention. She had told him so often enough, but despite all that Quinn still loved his mother.

"What will we do?" Quinn asked knowing that as chief guard it was his duty to arrest his mother for regicide.

"We - We will do nothing." Ceen told her son firmly. Slithering to the back of the room, Ceen lifted a tapestry and slipped behind it. "I will disappear. You - you will go pledge yourself to the new emperor and become a well trusted member of the new regime."

By the time Quinn realized what his mother was telling him, she had gone. Straightening his uniform, Quinn squared his shoulders and hurried to pledge his allegiance to Emperor Taz and the new regime.

Quinn rushed down the empty halls. How could things have changed so much in one day? Like the majority of Astarians, he had had no idea what went on outside the palace walls. Like the others, Quinn had been perfectly contented living in oblivious bliss. Everyone knew Emperor Taz was mad as a hatter, but for the past twenty years, give or take a few, no one had complained. The Astarians were content to spend their days preparing for the next grand event. Each event had a unique theme which they were expected to dress accordingly for.

After times grew tough, the servants and cooks worked tirelessly to keep the illusion of wealth alive. When new fabric became unavailable, the maids unstitched and re-stitched garments to create new fashions out of old. The cooks were experts in deception as well, molding yams, potatoes, and squash into lavish banquets that resembled fowl, roasts, and legs of lamb. Yes, the servants had done their best to keep the royals happy and satisfied.

That's why, when the Simeons locked them in the dungeons only a few were worried. The majority believed it was all a hoax, expecting Emperor Taz to roll down in his chair any second laughing. Even when that didn't happen and the council members returned with news of a new Emperor, few believed them.

Eager to keep his position as Commander of the Guard, Quinn tracked down Emperor Alzo in the ballroom surrounded by his followers. From the look on Alzo's face Quinn was sure the new Emperor had not yet learned of his father's death. Quinn was relieved. It looked like the Simeons had followed his orders and had not allowed anyone to enter the Throne Room after he had left.

"I've got some ideas." Knot proclaimed pacing across the tabletop in front of Emperor Alzo, "but before I tell you what they are, you need to appoint a new council."

"I'm sure Alzo has some ideas of his own," Rochelle said giving the brownie a sharp look. She had been alive long enough to know it was unwise to allow a brownie to take charge.

"It needs to be a diverse council," Alzo agreed as he got to his feet and stretched his arms over his head. It had been a long, emotional day and he was starting to feel the weight on his shoulders. "I want the council to be comprised of representatives from across the Empire. I have no intention of being an Emperor who hides behind these walls or any walls. I intend to travel across the planet like the First Emperor. Interacting with those living near and far. I intend on becoming a familiar face to all."

"Well said," Parth told Alzo placing her hands on his shoulders.

"A word," Quinn whispered to Alzo from behind his left shoulder.

"Let's take a break." The Emperor suggested sensing the urgency in Quinn's voice. "I need some air anyway."

Flanked by Empress Parth, Gerawld, Mia, and several others, Emperor Alzo followed Quinn into the courtyard. Once they were outside, Quinn told Alzo how he'd found his father and Behr in the Throne Room.

"Where is the Cobrateen now!" Alzo demanded shaken by Quinn's news.

"She disappeared." Quinn replied, trying to keep the quiver out of his voice. "I have ordered the Simeons to be on the lookout for her."

"Has my father's body been moved?"

"No, Emperor," Quinn assured him. "I ordered that no one was to enter the Throne Room until you were notified."

"Take me to him now."

"Alzo!" A syrupy voice called from across the courtyard.

Alzo jerked his head up and was surprised when Ilee appeared from around a corner and ran towards him. He figured she'd be miles away by now.

"Ilee! What's happened?" Alzo sputtered. Grumbul noticed the puddles forming under Ilee's feet as she ran towards Alzo with outstretched hands.

"That's not Ilee! It's Aturi!" Grumbul shouted in alarm.

Knowing her cover had been blown, Ilee's brown skin instantly changed into gray green fish scales that flexed and stretched as the water maiden's eel-like body extended upwards. Alzo watched in a daze as Aturi's shifted Ilee's left arm into a long stingray barb and lunged at him.

A flash of black darted in front of Alzo and shoved the newly crowned Emperor out of harm's way. Gerawld watched in slow motion as the water maiden's barbed arm entered Mia's belly just under the chest and exited out her back. Diving to his sister's side, Gerawld wrapped one paw around Mia cradling her head in the crook of his elbow.

"Finish this." Mia hissed forcing her paw, which still grasped her blade, upward. Carefully lifting Mia's body with one arm, Gerawld grasped Mia's wrist with the other and in one, unified stroke swiped Mia's blade through Aturi's neck. Black water spurted out of Aturi's neck as her head broke free and tumbled towards the floor.

"Catch it!" Mal shouted. Grumbul grabbed a clay pot off the ground and slid it under Aturi's head before it could splatter against the floor. Mal jumped over Aturi's lower body which thrashed against the stone floor like a fish with its head cut off and quickly wove a spell to seal the jar tight.

"Give me a spear." Rochelle yelled. Parth tossed her spear to Rochelle. "Die you wretched creature!" Rochelle spat shoving the spear deep into the putrid heart of the beast.

Gerawld howled in anguish as he cradled his sister gently in his arms. His orange eyes so blinded by tears he didn't notice Mia looking at him.

"Gerawld," Mia said her voice soft as the summer breeze. "Take me home." Gerawld sniffed unsure whether he had heard her or just imagined it. "Gerawld," Mia repeated a bit stronger lifting her paw and placing it on his. "Take me home. I want to lie in the Grasslands next to Mama. Promise."

Unable to speak, Gerawld nodded. Mia had always taken care of him. Taking her role as big sister very seriously. When their father, Scat, Leader of the Grassland Bast sent him to live with the warriors, Mia had disobeyed Scat's orders and went with Gerawld. She had always watched over him, and now...now it was his turn, and he wasn't sure if he was up to it.

"I can't feel my legs," Mia told Taa wincing. Mia tried to touch the barb protruding out of her belly. "Take it out," she gasped.

"I can't," Taa explained gently taking Mia's paw and holding it. "If I pull it out, I'll rip your guts out." Mia winced again and lowered her eyes. "There is something I can do." Taa said and pulled a small bag out of her cloak pocket. "It'll sting a bit." Taa spit in the bag several times to make a thick paste which she rubbed onto the barb just above where it entered and exited Mia's body. The paste fizzed around the barb which withered and snaped off leaving a dark stub where it entered and exited Mia's body. Taa gently wrapped Mia in a blanket.

"I want to go home," Mia said weakly, "to the grasslands."

"Gerawld will take you," Alzo assured her gently petting Mia's head.

"Gerawld and I will take you home." Fee told her soothingly. "Gerawld won't be alone. Together we will take you home. Now rest, you will need all your strength for the journey." Mia blinked at Fee and closed her eyes.

"Mia is strong." Taa told Gerawld. "She will survive the journey back to the Grasslands."

Gerawld sobbed. His heart breaking as he looked down at his sister lying helplessly in his arms.

"We will keep our promise." Fee told him stoking the grief stricken Gerawld's back. "And when our kits are born, we will tell them of Mia the Brave Bast Warrior."

"It's a long, rough journey." Alzo told Gerawld and Fee. "I have asked Captain Bok to take you. I know you don't like flying, but it's the quickest way."

"Thank you." Fee answered for all of them.

The entire camp assembled to see Mia off. Quinn and the Simeon's stood at attention beside Emperor Alzo and Empress Parth. Alzo kissed Mia on her forehead as she was laid on the air barge on a mattress Quinn had taken off his own bed.

After they had left Alzo went back to the ballroom. He wasn't ready to see his father's dead body just yet. Even though he was surrounded by his followers, Alzo felt very lonely. He already missed the big orange striped cat that had stood by his shoulder since the day they first met in Milendor. The room felt empty without Gerawld and Mia faithfully standing watch. Looking into the faces of those gathered around him, Alzo couldn't help noticing those that weren't there. His sister, his father, Ilee, Captain Bok, Nekita and Rixley and all those who had fallen fighting the bulimon and their cohorts on the way here.

"You don't have to do this alone." Parth said leaning down and kissing him hard on the mouth. "Never."

"Yeah, I know." Alzo said, wrapping his arms around Parth's tight frame. "I was just thinking about my friends. It's crazy, but I miss that old furball Gerawld more than I miss anyone I left back on Earth."

"Gerawld promised he'd be back."

"I know," Alzo said, smiling sadly.

"But?"

"That's the last thing I told Susan when I walked out the door."

"And Susan is?"

"A woman I lived with on Earth."

"Do you miss her?"

"Not at all." Alzo replied leaning down to kiss Parth. "Not at all."

CHAPTER 26

Elize had been traveling inside the energy sphere for some time. She was starting to wonder if it would ever land, and if it did where, when the sphere jerked wildly to a stop, and she was thrown forward.

"What did you catch!" Betty snapped excitedly as she tried to pull the net from her sister. Bessie poked a finger into the net and rummaged through the debris.

"Eek!" Bessie squawked yanking her hand out of the net so fast she almost slapped her sister in the face.

"What?" Betty sputtered grabbing the stick from her sister.

"Something bit me," Bessie mumbled sucking on her fingertips.

"I don't know what it is," Betty grumbled peering cautiously into the net, "but whatever it is it's sparking."

Betty and Bessie were co-joined giant twins that lived on the relatively small planet of Beezan. Betty and Bessie were storm catchers and Beezan just happened to be a perfect planet for catching them. Especially every seven years when Beezan aligned with the cosmic wheel. On these years the twins were able to catch storms from Toboria along with other storms blowing through the wheel from other realms. The twins never knew what treasures the winds would bring them from worlds unknown.

This morning there had been two storms one after the other. Bessie had gotten over excited and instead of waiting for both storms to line up, she jumped up and caught the first storm and missed the second.

Their mother had died birthing them and Betty, the older twin by eighteen and a half seconds, had taken on the role of parent after their father left several years before. Sticking her face into the top of the net, Betty was surprised to see a small being staring up at her.

"Who are you?" Betty demanded.

"And how'd you get in the net?" Bessie added trying to push her sister's face away.

"And why did you bite my sister?" Betty asked refusing to move. Both twins waited impatiently for the being to answer. When it didn't Betty gave the net a good shake.

"Great more giants," Elize mumbled under her breath staring up at two sets of hazel, rather lopsided eyes, staring down at her. After her experience with Kara, Elize was about done with giants. When Betty shook the net, Elize grabbed hold of the sides and fought to stay upright.

"Hey! Stop that!" Elize yelped at the huge twins.

"Answer our questions and I'll stop." Betty replied giving the net another, gentler shake to show she meant business.

"I'm Elize and I jumped into the storm to escape a demon."

"Why'd you bite my sister?" Betty demanded jingling the net threateningly.

"I didn't bite your sister. It was a static electric shock." Elize explained holding tightly to the net as she tried to pull herself out of the jumble of debris on the bottom of the net. "Now it's my turn. Who are you?"

"I'm Bessie," Bessie replied cheerfully before Betty could stop her, "and this is my sister Betty. We're storm catchers!"

"Where am I?"

"On Beezan," Betty answered sourly still not sure what to make of the creature in their net, "Beezan is our planet. Since Papa left us, we live here alone."

"Well, not exactly," Bessie interrupted pointing to the bell tower plopped on top of a large, crooked house, "not since Mr. Brown arrived and moved in there."

Rubbing a rather large bump on the side of her head, Elize glanced towards the tower, but didn't see anyone. "Did you catch Mr. Brown in your net too?"

"No," Betty said giving her sister a stern look. "Mr. Brown flew here on his own. He came looking for his true love who he foresaw in a vision. When his true love didn't appear, we told him he could stay in the tower since it hadn't come with a bell"

"Very disappointing." Bessie added shaking her head. Still, even without the bell, the tower had been one of their finest catches until today. "You aren't Mr. Brown's true love are you?"

"Not likely," Elize answered leaning against the side of the net so she could see the twins better. "So, you're storm catchers?" Elize asked casually, even though she had never heard of such an occupation before.

"Yes," Betty said proudly, "we're the best storm catchers in these parts." Bessie was about to add that they were the only storm catchers in these parts but stopped when Betty glared at her.

"Do you know what happened to the storm that was chasing me?"

"It spun off to the left." Betty replied looking up at the sky and frowning. "If we're lucky it'll spin back round, and we'll get another shot at it."

"Why is your hand sparking?" Bessie asked curiously. Elize glanced at the sparks erupting from the gaping hole in her palm.

"It's a long and confusing story."

"Better take you back to the house then." Betty barked. "It's almost teatime."

"I made scones!" Bessie chirped happily into the net.

"Best keep her in the net for now." Betty told her sister when Bessie started to reach into the net. Before Bessie could respond, Betty spun around and headed for the crooked house. Being cojoined Bessie had no choice but to trot along beside her sister. She was careful to keep the net at arm's length, so she didn't get shocked again.

Once they were inside their crooked house Bessie set the net on a lopsided table. While the twins pulled off a pair of mismatched boots, Elize untangled herself from the debris and crawled out of the net to have a look around.

"We weren't expecting visitors," Bessie fussed as Elize walked around the dishes, "that's why the tables only set for two."

"That's okay." Elize told her as she looked at the odd mix-match of furniture and decor that didn't quite go together. "What a unique house you have."

"Yes, it is!" Betty beamed proudly. "Papa built it for us before he left, but Bessie and I have made it a home. We've lived here for as long as we can remember, and every storm brings us new things to add to our collections."

"Your hand is sparking again," Betty noted, nodding at Elize's right hand.

"Damn Scythe," Elize grumbled clapping her left palm on top of the right.

"Looks like that wound was caused by a spike, not a scythe." Betty told Elize with authority. "A scythe would have sliced your hand clear off."

"What? No. Not like a sickle used to cut wheat," Elize explained shaking her head. "Scythe is the name of the demon who was chasing me in the other storm. I had a stone in my hand that helped me controlled the energy until Scythe ripped it out."

"Noirwasp honey should do the trick." Bessie bubbled happily. Before Betty could put in her two cents worth, Bessie lifted a large clay jar off one of the many shelves nailed haphazardly into the wall. "You don't suppose the demon could be Papa?" Bessie wondered aloud as she set the jar on the table.

"No." Betty replied looking worried. The twins papa had left years ago to find them husbands. He'd been gone so long that Betty wasn't sure she wanted him to come back. Bessie and she had gotten along just fine all these years without husbands, and she didn't see any sense in changing things.

"Is your papa a fallen angel?" Elize asked watching Bessie dump the thick goop in a pot.

"No." Betty replied with a snuff. "Papa is certainly no angel by any stretch of the imagination, but he's no demon either."

"Quite right." Bessie agreed clearly relieved. Bessie brought the pot to a boil and stirred it with a large wooden spoon until the thick, walnut colored glop hung suspended between the spoon and the pot. "It's ready."

"Good!" Betty said and reached for Elize's wrist.

"Better use the bladder!" Bessie warned and pulled open a drawer. Betty rummaged through the draw and took out a rubbery, kidney shaped bag. Elize was pretty sure it was an actual bladder.

"We're going to have to work fast." Betty told Elize. "It'll probably sting a bit."

"Once your fist is covered with honey open it up or your fingers will cramp." Bessie instructed as she set the steaming pot on the table next to Elize. "Ready?"

Before Elize could protest, Betty with her hands stuffed inside the bladder, grabbed Elize by the wrist and plunged her hand into the scalding liquid. Elize let out a startled cry and forced her fingers opened. Betty stirred Elize's hand in the thick honey until it had gelled to a wobble.

"Now!" Betty yelled as she yanked Elize's hand out of the pan and plunged it into the bucket of cold water Bessie had waiting.

"That should do the trick." Bessie said pulling Elize's hand out of the bucket and tapping it with her thick yellow fingernail. Elize looked at her hand which now resembled a large, root beer lollypop.

"I thought you said it was honey." Elize said. As she moved her lollypop hand back and forth in front of her Elize realized that the infernal buzzing in her brain had stopped.

"It is honey," Bessie replied, pleased with her work, "but not the kind you eat. Noirwasp feed on the sap of the garl trees. When heated the honey dries hard and clear. We use it to make windowpanes and to seal jars to keep food fresh."

"How do I get it off?" Elize asked, holding her hand up like a scepter.

"Well, if you hit it hard enough it'll shatter," Betty replied, "but I don't recommend that. The shards are sharp, and you're libel to get badly cut. It's best to heat it, I recommend a bath of hot water. The warmer the water the faster it will dissolve."

"How long will it last?"

"Normally it will last for years, but with that energy bubbling underneath it, maybe a month or two." Bessie sounded confident, but in truth was she didn't really know.

"Grab the net Bessie! I think the storm returning," Betty shouted as a blast of wind rattled the house.

"I thought he'd be slowing down by now." Elize said more to herself then to the twins as she followed them out the door. "What's that?" She shouted, using her lollipop hand to point at a cinnamon dot in the sky above them.

CHAPTER 27

Nekita had flown faster and higher than she had ever flown before. At first the damage left under the storms made them easy to track. Than the storms had arched upward, and she had lost site of the land all together. She was wondering if she should give up and turn around when Rixley spotted a patch of land ahead of them.

"Rixley not like this place." Rixley mumbled into Nekita's neck. Nekita did not like this place either. It gave her the creeps. The spindly trees had limbs that reached into the sky with skeleton-like hands and the lumpy ground was an odd color green. Nekita found it hard to imagine that anyone would want to live in such an isolated place, but apparently they did. In the clearing below them was a house. An extremely large, ugly house which looked like it was made from discarded bits of other houses smashed together.

"Rixley do you see which way the storms went?" Nekita exclaimed as she frantically searched for any signs of the dueling cyclones.

Rixley's reply was drowned out by the uproar erupting from one of the spindly trees below them. Rixley ducked beneath Nekita's wings as several red, leather-winged lizards flew out of the trees. Soon the air was filled with the robin sized flying lizards nipping and snapping hungerly at Nekita with razor sharp beaks.

Nekita hooted in alarm as several lizards flew past her and slashed at her legs with long, bullwhip-like tails. Rolling sharply to the right, Nekita attempted to outmaneuver the horde of leather winged demons, but there were too many of them.

Hooting in distress, Nekita dove towards the strange house, while Rixley used her pointy stick to stab at the lizards attacking Nekita's back. "Jump Rixley!" Nekita yelled as she skimmed the roof top, just missing the bell tower.

Rixley kicked the closest lizard swiftly in the chest and rolled off Nekita's back. She landed on the roof with a thump and quickly burrowed into the thick thatch covering the roof. Nekita let out an anguished hoot as a lizard landed on her back and began tearing at her feathers.

"Blood lizards!" Betty hissed as they ran out the door.

"Oh, the poor dear." Bessie gasped when she spotted Nekita fighting for her life above them.

"Those blasted dragons arrived about a fortnight ago." Betty told Elize as she pulled her sling shot out of her apron pocket and loaded it with a round stone. "They've wiped out all of our chickens."

"It's Nekita!" Elize screamed dashing out of the house and waving her hands over her head. "Nekita! Nekita down here!"

"Mr. Brown!" Bessie and Betty shouted as the large brown owl blasted out of the bell tower.

"Mr. Brown!" The twins shouted gleefully, clapping hands. Mr. Brown snatched up a handful of lizards and flung them into the trees. To injured to fly, Nekita's wings gave way and she started to plumet towards the ground. Leaving the lizards, Mr. Brown dove after Nekita and caught her in his arms. The twins cheered and waved at Mr. Brown as he carried the badly injured Nekita to his nest in the bell tower.

"Mr. Brown is a Neognathae!" Elize exclaimed shading her eyes and trying to see where he had taken Nekita.

"Mr. Brown is our friend." Betty told Elize patting her roughly on the back. "Now, don't you worry Mr. Brown will take good care of your friend. That's why he came here. He said he was looking for his true love and by golly it looks like he found her."

"Betty!" Bessie shouted as a lump slid down the roof and scurried into the vegetable garden. "One of those damn lizards is in my garden!"

"Wait!" Elize shouted certain that what Bessie had seen was not a lizard. "Wait! That's not a lizard!"

"I don't care what it is," Bessie bellowed, "I won't have it eating my carrots!"

"Rixley brave and strong," Rixley whimpered running out of the garden and darting up Elize's leg.

"Rixley!" Elize exclaimed when the flustered ferret popped her head out of Elize's robe. "What are you doing here?"

"Rixley go where Elize go." Rixley replied defiantly.

"What is it?" Bessie and Betty demanded in unison, standing in front of Elize with their hands on their hips.

"This is my dear friend Rixley." Elize told them and gently lifted Rixley up so the twins could have a look. "She's a ferret."

"Never met a ferret that could talk." Bessie fussed, still convinced that Rixley was trying to steal her carrots. Spotting several red lizards approaching the garden, Betty loaded her sling and sent a stone flying into the closest one.

"We'd best get inside." Bessie huffed and headed back inside dragging Betty with her. "I don't know about you, but I could use a stiff drink."

"Rixley why did you guys follow me?" Elize asked once they were safely inside. "I left you behind because I wanted you to be safe."

"Rixley not want to be safe." Rixley pouted, staring up at Elize with shiny black, beady eyes. "Rixley want to be with Elize." Elize didn't know whether to hug Rixley or clonk her in the head.

"I think the critter would enjoy an egg yolk instead of brandy." Betty told Bessie reaching over her sister and plucking an egg from a basket.

"Suit yourself," Bessie told Rixley, not unkindly as she pulled a clay jug off one of the top shelves and blew the dust off it, "but I'm having brandy. My nerves are all a rattle."

Rixley watched from Elize's shoulder as Betty cracked a hole in the top of the egg and set it on the table. Curious and hungry, Rixley slowly and cautiously made her way down Elize's arm to the table.

"Nice belt." Elize told Rixley. Rixley ran her paws over the mouse hide warrior belt Mia had given her.

"Mia gave to Rixley. Rixley warrior now." Rixley spouted proudly as she dipped a paw into the thick yellow yolk.

"Wow!" Elize said smiling at Rixley as she licked the yolk off her paw. "Congratulations!"

"Nekita gave Rixley this." Rixley whispered, making sure the twins didn't see her remove the rolled-up paper from her warrior belt and hand it to Elize.

"What is it?" Elize asked unable to make heads or tails of the strange markings.

"Nekita said Elize must go here." Rixley jabbed at a spot on the map that looked like a spoked wheel.

"That doesn't help." Elize said as she spread the strange map out on the table.

"Looks like the wheel of the nine realms." Betty said leaning over Elize's shoulder.

"Mule says Elize must get demon inside wheel before wheel flies away."

"Well, you'd better get a move on!" Bessie commented as she filled Elize's thimble with fermented fruit brandy. "It won't be here much longer."

"You know how to get there?" Elize asked, looking over her shoulder at the twins.

"Well...I guess so," Betty replied, rolling her tongue over her lips before biting down on them. "We know where it is, but we've never gone there. Papa made Bessie and I promise to never go near the wheel. Isn't that right Bessie?"

"Uh huh," Bessie said picking up the map and holding it up to the window. "Look there's something written in the corner." Curious Elize took the map from her to have a look for herself. Bessie was right, there was something written in the corner.

"It's from Mal. Mal's a Mage." Elize explained. She was glad Mal had written the note in English. "It says the wheel has nine doors. Each door leads to a different realm. Toboria is in the sixth realm. Earth is in the third. Once I enter the wheel, I need to find the doorway to the ninth realm and get Scythe to go through it."

"Why?"

"Scythe escaped from the ninth realm and unless I get him back there in time...well there's a good chance we're all screwed."

"What do you mean by all?" Betty asked raising an eyebrow at Elize.

"Scythe bad demon. Scythe will tear your house down and stamp on your carrots!" Rixley squeaked loudly.

"Well, then you'd best be on your way!" Betty boomed clearly alarmed. "No time to waste. I'd say you have three or four days at best."

"You can't just send them off!" Bessie protested, slamming the bottle down on the table with such gusto a spray of brandy hit Betty in the face.

"Well, we can't go with them." Betty fussed as she wiped her face with the back of her arm. "We promised Papa."

"You don't need to come with me." Elize said not wanting to cause a rift between the twins. "Just show me the way and let Rixley stay here until I get back."

"Rixley goes where Elize goes," Rixley told Elize firmly.

"There's no way they can make it in time." Bessie whispered hoarsely into Betty's ear. "Look at their little legs."

"It's not our fight." Betty whispered back.

"It's okay," Elize assured the twins, "You've been very kind to us already and I totally understand you're not wanting to get involved. I wish I had something to give you for your kindness."

"Rixley get," Rixley said and disappeared into Elize's robe pocket. A second later she popped back out with a bag of seeds. Elize took the bag from Rixley and handed it to Bessie.

"Golly!" Bessie exclaimed happily as she ran her fingers through the assortment of seeds. Rixley climbed back out of Elize's pocket and handed Elize a folded piece of paper. Elize unfolded the paper and read the note silently. Forcing back tears, Elize carefully folded the note and stuffed it back in her pocket.

"Elize," Rixley said putting her paw on Elize's hand, "tell Rixley what note say."

"The note is from my father," Elize said sadly. "He wanted me to know that he is in the Spirit world with RaJa and Koh now." Elize stopped to wipe away the tears running down her face. "He also wanted us to know that Mia was badly injured when the water maiden, Aturi attacked Alzo. Mia saved Alzo's life but was stabbed by a barb meant for Alzo. She..."

"Mia gone like mama?" Rixley choked guessing the rest.

"No, not yet, but soon." Elize picked Rixley up and held her close. "Gerawld and Fee are taking Mia home to sleep with her mother in the Bast Grasslands."

"Mia brave warrior," Rixley said, sniffing back the tears. "Rixley be brave like Mia. Rixley make Mia proud."

"I know you will," Elize said hugging Rixley tightly. "I guess we better get going."

"Betty!" Bessie nudged her sister hard in the ribs. "We have to help them!"

"Okay, okay." Betty grumbled, hoping Bessie didn't see her wipe the stray tear out of her eye. "We will take you to the base of the butte, but no closer."

After packing a bag with food and filling a couple skins with water, the twins locked up their house and started off. Even with the twins long stride, it took two days of straight walking to reach the butte of red stone that jutted high into the sky from the otherwise flat landscape. From the ground, the red butte looked more like a redwood tree stump then a landing port.

"This is as far as we go." Betty told Elize as they stood at the base of the butte looking up at the humongous gray wheel hovering high above them.

After thanking the twins, Elize and Rixley waited until Betty and Bessie were no longer in sight before they began searching for a way up. Rixley slowly walked around the base of the large red stone carefully scanning the red rock. Every few feet she stopped to kick the side of the butte. She had almost gone full circle when her paw sank into the rock. Smiling up at Elize, Rixley stepped on to a hidden path.

"The winds are picking up," Betty told Bessie as they watched the dark funnel cloud approach.

"I thought they might," Bessie said with a grin and pulled out her storm catching net. Working as a team the twins held the net high over their heads. The storm was stronger than they expected. It dragged the twins several yards before snapping the net. Not about to let their prize escape, Betty and Bessie stomped after it, but before they could reach it the storm fizzled out and was replaced by a demon that sprouted wings and flew away.

"Definitely not papa." The twins exclaimed as they happily picked through the storm debris.

CHAPTER 28

"He's here," Elize warned Rixley an instant before the demon appeared through a gap in the red rock above them and grabbed Elize's hair. Screaming, Elize swung her hands up so violently that she accidently slammed the noirwasp shell coating her right hand into the hard rock and shattered it.

Intertwining his fingers through Elize's braided hair, Scythe yanked Elize upward unaware of the two dark eyes peering at him from Elize's pocket. Spotting the blue stone pulsing in the demon's chest, Rixley scurried up to Elize's shoulder and leapt on to Scythe's thigh.

"You silly gnat!" Scythe roared. Releasing Elize's hair, he swatted at the irritating ferret scratching her way up his torso. With one mighty reach, Rixley tore the stone out of Scythe's gelatin-like skin. Scythe smashed his hand into his chest, but Rixley was already gone, looping through crevasses in the stone like a snake.

"Run Rixley!" Elize shouted lifting her hands and sending a stream of energy into the rocks directly above Scythe. Scythe winced as the hot rubble rained down burning and bruising his flesh. He had never felt pain before and, if he had his way, he'd never feel it again.

Scythe mouthed a spell and flicked his left hand up. Elize's left hand flew up and smacked her in the face. Scythe laughed as he forced Elize to slap herself repeatedly. With each slap, Elize felt her anger rising. Determined not to give Scythe anymore energy, Elize fought the urge to attack. Scythe was already more powerful than she had expected.

The next time her hand swung up, Elize jerked her head to one side. The sudden jolt of pain from her fist hitting the rock broke the spell. Before Scythe could launch another attack, Elize picked up a piece of the shattered noirwasp shell and slashed at his leathery wings. As the demon cursed and tumbled to the ground, Elize made her escape.

"You okay kiddo?" Elize asked when she found Rixley a few minutes later.

"Rixley okay. Elize okay?" Rixley asked as she jumped onto Elize's shoulders and slid into her hood.

"Yeah, I'm okay. I wasn't expecting Scythe to be so strong." Elize panted as they began to gain altitude. "Look it's going to get worst from here on. You should go back."

"No!" Rixley replied with determination. "Rixley goes where Elize goes. Elize needs Rixley! Rixley got rock back for Elize." Rixley tried to give the dark blue geode back to Elize.

"You keep it safe for now." Elize told Rixley. "Listen, if Scythe tries to possess me again, stab me with something sharp. Okay?"

"Rixley not want to stab Elize."

"I know, but if that's what it takes to break the spell, so be it. Now promise me!"

"Rixley promise." Rixley promised even though she didn't like it one bit.

Knowing that Scythe wasn't far behind, Elize picked up the pace. She wanted to reach the top before he caught up with her, but by the time she neared the top the air was so thin it took more and more effort to keep moving. Elize was steps away from the top when Scythe tackled her to the ground. Above their heads, Elize heard the wheel start to hum, and a stream of florescent, white light beamed down upon them.

The butte shimmered and was replaced by a tall, mud brick ziggurat. Elize found herself standing beside Scythe, watching masses of people weaving up a winding staircase. Each laden with baskets overflowing with gold, silver, precious gemstones, fruits, vegetables, finely woven cloth, animal pelts, and other wonderful things. Elize ran her hands down the gown woven from fine strands of silver and gold. She felt the heaviness of the gemstone necklaces around her neck and the bangles covering her wrists. Her fingers sparkled with magnificent diamond rings. Elize knew she was seeing the world Scythe had promised Monet thousands of years ago.

"You will be my goddess and I will be your god," Scythe whispered seductively into Elize's ear. "Together not even the angels will be able to stop us!"

Elize was dazzled by the vision before her. Such devotion was enticing, but why should she be a goddess when she could be a god. Elize lifted her hands in welcome as her worshipers bowed before her and laid their gifts at her feet. Elize watched curiously as an old toothless man, with a thin stream of drool running down his chin approached holding a tiny green bird in his wrinkled hands.

"Eliza dora, eliza dora, sitting in a tree." The old man sang, slowly making his way towards her. "Eliza dora, eliza dora, open up your eyes and see." The old man opened his hands and released the tiny bird.

"Can't interfere, can't interfere," an old English bulldog barked from the front porch of a paper house. Elize's gaze fell on the paper bulldog.

"Popeye?" She mumbled still in a daze.

"Popeye!" A paper Ellen shouted pushing her swollen belly out the front door. "Popeye stop that barking! Olive Oyle drop that!"

"Hey, hey, hey!" Prof exclaim following Ellen out the paper door and making her sit down on a paper lawn chair. "I'll take care of it, you sit down. I don't want to have to deliver our twins on this rickety front porch!"

"Twins!" Elize shouted happily while the paper Prof rescued the green bird from Olive Oyle's claws. Luckily for the bird, the lanky cats claws were made of paper and therefore entirely harmless.

"What's wrong! Prof gasped noticing the strange look on Ellen's face and thinking his premonition about a porch delivery might be coming true.

"I swear I just heard Elize!" Ellen told him pushing herself out of the chair. Relieved she hadn't gone into labor, Prof put his hands around his mouth and yelled at the clouds.

"Hey Elize! If you're out there in the cosmos listening, you'd better get back soon. You're going to be a godmother any day now!"

"Godmother," Elize repeated beaming. She'd much rather be a godmother than a goddess any day. As the visions of grandeur faded, Elize felt something sharp poking her in the back.

"Wake up, wake up, wake up!" Rixley squeaked jabbing Elize in the back with her pointy stick.

"I'm awake," Elize yelped rubbing the raw spot on her back. "Please stop now." Elize stopped fussing at Rixley when she sensed something moving inside the light. Shading her eyes from the brightness, Elize was surprised to find a shining, winged being leaning on a sword which appeared to be made of liquid mercury, watching her from the top of the butte.

Elize gasped and fell to her knees. "You're an angel!"

"I am." The angel replied slightly amused. "Rise and tell me why you have come." Elize slowly got to her feet. She knew she should keep her eyes averted, but she couldn't take them off the marvelous being.

"I-I-I'm here to return the fallen angel, Scyathee to the ninth realm." Elize stammered nervously.

"I see." The angel replied, "and do you possess the power to complete this task."

Elize lifted her palm. The angel leaned forward and inserted the tip of his sword inside the quarter sized hole in Elize's palm. Sparks flew out of her palm like a volcano erupting, but the angel did not pull his sword free.

"You live between two realms." The angel proclaimed and stared deeply into Elize's eyes.

"Yeah, I guess so." Elize answered so lightheaded it was a wonder she was still standing.

"But which realm do you truly belong in?"

"Earth." Elize told the angel without hesitation. "My home is on Earth."

The angel nodded and removed his sword. Raising his hand towards the humongous wheel hovering above their heads, he motioned Elize forward. "You may enter."

"You may not." The angel said reaching into Elize's hood and pulling out Rixley. Rixley flipped out of the angel's hand and darted through Elize's legs. The angel winked at Elize and vanished.

Oblivious to the presence of the angel, Scythe followed his goddess into the wheel.

"The wheel will depart at first light." The angel's voice reverberated through Elize's brain. "Your task must be completed by then."

"What if it isn't?" Elize asked, but the angel had disappeared. Elize looked around her. She had no idea what to do next. Rixley ran up to Elize and tugged at her pants leg.

"Rixley find door," Rixley whispered pulling Elize down the curved structure. Scythe continued to stare ahead of him, a strange, elated look on his face.

"Do you remember which realm Mal said we were in?" Elize asked. Rixley shook her head and reached into Elize's pocket to get the map.

"The sixth realm," Elize mumbled reading Mal's note as she continued along the gray corridor. "I think we're here," Elize jabbed her finger at a spot on the map. To her dismay the numbers on the map began to move. "Damn, it looks like we're going to have to figure this out on our own." Folding the map, Elize quickly stuffed it back in her pocket.

Rixley led Elize to a round door made from the silvery bark of a tree. Elize placed the flat of her hand on the door. The door opened revealing three full busted, green ladies dancing around a silver tree. When they realized someone was watching, the dryads lifted their angelic faces and began screeching like banshees.

The dryad's screeching woke Scythe from his dream. Realizing he had been tricked, the demon charged down the corridor, cursing and slamming his fist against the wheel trying to escape. Spotting Elize, Scythe shouted a spell. Before she could fight it off, Elize found her hands around her neck.

"Rixley!" She gasped trying to force her hands off her neck. Rixley pulled the little dagger Mia had attached to her belt and jabbed Elize in the back of the hand. The sharp pain activated Elize's defense system.

"The rock!" Elize shouted as she pushed her hands against the side of the wheel and held them there. "Throw the rock Rixley!"

Rixley pulled the rock off her belt and held it over her head to make sure Scythe saw it. It worked. Scythe lunged for Rixley, but instead of throwing the rock, Rixley dashed down the corridor leading him away from Elize.

"Throw the rock!" Elize yelled frantically, but Rixley wasn't listening.

"Elize don't react blindly!" Koh's voice warned from deep inside her pocket.

"Yes, you must remain calm." Her father added in a bubbly distorted voice.

"But Scythe's going to kill Rixley!" Elize protested. Ignoring their advice, Elize raced around the wheel keeping ever vigilant for Scythe. She found Rixley sprawled in a bloody heap on the floor.

"Where the hell is he?" Elize wondered cautiously creeping closer to Rixley. Rixley opened her eyes and tried to put on a brave face. Her pointy stick lay snapped in two by her feet. Seeing her pointy stick broken hurt Rixley more than the long slash running down her side.

"Oh Rixley," Elize said softly, taking Rixley's little paw in her hand. "Are you okay? Why didn't you listen and just throw the stone?"

"Rixley okay." Rixley lied, gritting her teeth, she pressed her torn side against the wall so Elize couldn't see the gash.

"Why didn't you throw the rock?" Elize asked again picking up the top part of Rixley stick.

"Rixley had to stop bad demon from hurting Elize." Rixley answered weakly taking the stick from Elize. "Rixley tried to kill demon, but demon too strong. Demon took stone from Rixley."

Elize grabbed Rixley and rolled out of reach as Scythe dropped from the ceiling.

"Stay here," Elize told Rixley leaving her in a niche beside a tiny rectangular shaped door.

"Hey you stinking bastard!" Elize bellowed racing away from Rixley before she had a chance to protest. Just as she hoped, Scythe raced past Rixley in a blind rage.

"What's happening?" Scythe wondered as his energy began to fade. He stopped chasing Elize and looked at the rock. Had the damn ferret switched stones on him? Why wasn't the rock filling him with energy like before? Scythe was still studying the stone when the geode cracked open and began to suck the energy back out of him.

"She tricked you! She tricked you!" Monet's voice rang out from deep inside the crystals.

"No!" Scythe howled, flinging the wretched rock away from him. The rock bounced off the sides of the wheel and ricocheted like a super ball off one side to the next until it became lodged in the roots of the silver elm tree. Quite shaken by her unexpected trip, Monet laid down among the lavender crystals and fell into a deep, deep sleep.

Scythe stumbled after Elize. His legs felt heavy and sluggish, and his muscles ached. Even in Hell, Scythe had never experience pain. Scythe grimaced and tried to force the pain out of his mind. He had to keep going. He had to catch Elize and feed on her energy.

Elize didn't know how much time had passed, but she had a feeling time was running out. Determined to end this, she flattened herself against the wall. Elize waited until she could hear Scythe's ragged breathing, before she leapt out of her hiding place and rammed his back into the thick, thorny door behind them.

Scythe bellowed as the needle sharp thorns ripped into his back. Yanking himself free, he chased after Elize. Elize scurried down the corridor frantically searching for the doorway to hell. Finally, Elize noticed a red glow coming from around the curve ahead of her. As she ran across the hot floor, Elize was filled with dread. Before her the door to hell stood like a fiery furnace belching hot steam laced with sulfur into the corridor.

Elize staggered backwards and straight into Scythe's arms. Scythe wrapped his long fingers around Elize's neck determined not to let her escape again. The second he touched her, Elize felt a change in Scythe, but she didn't know what it was.

"My secret." Monet's voice sang inside her increasingly foggy mind and an image of a pregnant Monet appeared in front of the stone that would later become her prison. And just like that Elize knew.

"You cannot win!" Scythe hissed in Elize's ear. "You are me. We are we. My essence flows through your veins. We could rule the nine realms together. If you refuse, I shall rule them alone and you shall die."

"I can win!" Elize choked defiantly, ripping at Scythe's fingers with her own. "I am not you! We are not we! Monet's youngest daughter was conceived after she came to Toboria. My ancestors are human and now so are you."

"You lie!" Scythe roared and tightened his grip on Elize's neck.

"You...your...your bleeding." Elize coughed barely conscious. Scythe glanced at the blood pooling at his feet.

Rixley dragged herself down the corridor. She knew she was too weak to fight the demon, but there had to be some way to help Elize. The small ferret ran her paw over the warrior belt Mia had given her searching for anything that would help her save Elize. Rixley's paw ran over a small cylinder and a feathery dart no bigger than a gnat. Rixley pulled the cylinder from her belt, and silently dragged herself forward.

Elize's head spun from lack of air. She knew she only had seconds left. Scythe knew it too. He smiled and absorbed the energy leaving Elize's body. Either he was totally unaware that Rixley was behind him, or he knew and just didn't care.

Rixley put the tube to her lips and blew as hard as she was able. The gnat sized dart hit Scythe in the shoulder. Scythe flinched and took a hand from Elize's neck. Swatting at his shoulder, he unintentionally pushed the tip of the dart further into his skin.

Elize felt Scythe's grip loosen ever so slightly and although she was barely conscious, she knew it was now or never. Pressing her right palm against the wheel, Elize released years of pent-up energy. The force of the blast propelled her body sideways along the corridor. Scythe tried to release his grip on Elize's neck, but the poison from the dart was already in his blood stream and his hand refused to move. When the poison reached his calf muscles, Scythe stumbled and fell on top of Elize.

Elize gasped for breath as she crawled out from under Scythe's body and away from the fiery furnace opening like a horrible mouth. Tongues of fire flared out and wrapped around Scythe's ankles and legs. Unable to move, Scythe could only stare in horror as he was pulled feet first into the gapping mouth. As the demon's head bumped over the threshold, the furnace let out a loud belch and slammed shut, leaving a cloud of sulphury smoke hanging in the corridor.

The thick, yellow smoke stung Elize's eyes and burnt her throat as she crawled on all fours searching for Rixley. Elize found Rixley a few feet away lying motionless on the floor, the small tube still clutched in her paws.

"Rixley, oh Rixley" Elize cried as she gently ran her finger over Rixley's masked cheek. "Why didn't you stay where I left you?"

"Rixley go..." Rixley mumbled weakly without opening her eyes.

"Oh, Rixley!" Elize sobbed burying her face in Rixley's fur. "I thought you were dead! Noticing the clotting blood, Elize untied the sash on her robe and began to rip the sash into strips to wrap around Rixley's body.

"Don't die on me kiddo." Elize sniffed as she lifted the unconscious ferret into her arms and held her close to her chest like one would an infant. "Let's get out of here." Elize continued talking out loud, even though she didn't think Rixley could hear her.

Elize slowly started making her way around the wheel. She needed to find the door to Earth before it was too late. She had just passed a keyhole shaped door when the wheel started humming. A few seconds later she heard a click and then another. Elize hurried towards the next door which looked like the Milky Way, but she was too late. The door snapped shut and the wheel started spinning.

"No!" Elize screamed. "We did what you wanted! We threw the demon back to hell!" When no one answered, Elize started to pound on the wall where the door had been seconds before. "It's not fair! Not fair!"

Elize stopped when Rixley moaned softly. Stooping against the wall, Elize sobbed until she could sob no more. Sitting in a void between space and time, Elize listened to the rhythmic sound of her heart beating. After a while, Elize realized the sound wasn't coming from her heart at all, it was coming from outside her.

Taking off her robe, Elize carefully lifted Rixley into the hood and used the arms as ties to secure Rixley in front of her. Then she started walking along the wheel and tried to find where the beat was coming from. Elize was so intent on listening to the beat that she didn't see the ancient, silver haired man, wrapped in a red woven poncho until she almost stumbled on top of him.

"Are you real?" Elize stammered staring at the old man in disbelief. The old man's wrinkled bronze hand appeared from underneath his finely woven poncho and brushed at the single eagle feather dangling at the side of his silver haired head. The feather danced with the movement but did not fall.

"I am." The old man answered his yellowed eyes twinkling like starlight.

"Are you a ghost?" Elize asked still not convinced he was real.

"No, I am not a ghost. I am a spirit traveler."

"Is there a difference?"

"Yes. A ghost is tied to a past life. I am free to travel where I wish."

"Can you help us?" Elize asked anxiously. "My friend Rixley is badly hurt, and we are trapped in this...this...wheel thing."

"Of course, that's why I am here. Take my hand child." The spirit walker smiled kindly and held out his hand. Elize reached out to take his hand, but the instant she touched it the old man vanished. Startled Elize tripped and fell into the side of the wheel. Hidden fingers grabbed her by the wrist and began pulling her into the wall. Elize braced her feet against the bottom of the wall and tried to break free.

"Stop fighting." The spirit walker's voice floated inside her head. Elize covered Rixley's body with her free arm and let herself be pulled through the wall which scraped her skin like a giant sheet of sandpaper. Just when she was sure she'd never make it out, Elize felt the cool breeze touch the back of her hand and then her arm. A second later her head emerged. This must be how a baby feels when it comes out of the birth canal Elize thought as the rest of her body popped out.

"Thank God!" Elize exclaimed as two brown arms caught her. "Thank you, thank you, thank you God!"

"I'm not God," The woman who caught her said laughing. "I'm Auntie Loo."

CHAPTER 29

Elize pried her eyes open and tried to remember what she'd been drinking the night before. Looking from side to side, she realized she had no idea where she was. Cautiously glancing at the bed, hoping to God no one was sleeping next to her. Elize was greatly relieved to find herself alone.

"Where the hell am I?" Elize groaned closing her eyes again. Outside her window, a young girl screeched joyfully. Elize grabbed one of the lumpy down pillows and shoved it over her ears.

"Rixley!" A woman yelled from the next room. "If you rip open those stitches again Joe will have your hide!"

"Rixley?" Elize mumbled, pulling the pillow off her head. "Rixley!" She repeated as memories exploded in her brain. Leaping up Elize stuck her head out the screenless window. Several little girls wearing shorts and tee shirts were playing with an odd-looking dog.

"Elize!" The dog yelped and flew through the window, landing in Elize's lap. "Rixley didn't think Elize would ever wake up!" Rixley laughed taking Elize's hands as she bounced on the small bed.

"She's been trying to wake you for days." A wiry woman wearing blue jeans and a flannel shirt said as she came into the room holding two mugs of hot coffee. Rixley gave Elize a big hug and jumped back out the window.

"My Elize is awake!" Rixley squeaked joyfully to her friends.

"Please tell me this is Earth," Elize said taking the mug of coffee offered.

"Earth?" The woman replied giving Elize a strange look. "I'm just messing with you." She said bursting out laughing.

"Thank God!" Elize exclaimed.

"I told ya…"

"I know. I know," Elize interrupted. "You're not God. You're Auntie Loo."

The End

Made in the USA
Middletown, DE
07 February 2022

59643923R10176